ALIEN™

SEVENTH CIRCLE

THE COMPLETE ALIEN™ LIBRARY FROM TITAN BOOKS

The Official Movie Novelizations
by Alan Dean Foster
Alien, Aliens™, Alien 3, Alien: Covenant,
Alien: Covenant Origins

Alien: Resurrection by A.C. Crispin

Alien 3: The Unproduced Screenplay
by William Gibson & Pat Cadigan

Alien
Out of the Shadows by Tim Lebbon
Sea of Sorrows by James A. Moore
River of Pain by Christopher Golden
The Cold Forge by Alex White
Isolation by Keith R.A. DeCandido
Prototype by Tim Waggoner
Into Charybdis by Alex White
Colony War by David Barnett
Inferno's Fall by Philippa Ballantine
Enemy of My Enemy by Mary SanGiovanni
Uncivil War by Brendan Deneen
Seventh Circle by Philippa Ballantine

The Rage War
by Tim Lebbon
Predator™: Incursion, Alien: Invasion
Alien vs. Predator™: Armageddon

Aliens
Bug Hunt edited by Jonathan Maberry
Phalanx by Scott Sigler
Infiltrator by Weston Ochse
Vasquez by V. Castro
Bishop by T.R. Napper

The Complete Aliens Omnibus
Volumes 1–7

Aliens vs. Predators
Ultimate Prey edited by Jonathan Maberry &
Bryan Thomas Schmidt
Rift War by Weston Ochse & Yvonne Navarro
The Complete Aliens vs. Predator Omnibus
by Steve Perry & S.D. Perry

Predator
If It Bleeds edited by Bryan Thomas Schmidt
The Predator by Christopher Golden
& Mark Morris
The Predator: Hunters and Hunted
by James A. Moore
Stalking Shadows by James A. Moore
& Mark Morris
Eyes of the Demon edited by
Bryan Thomas Schmidt

The Complete Predator Omnibus
by Nathan Archer & Sandy Scofield

Non-Fiction
AVP: Alien vs. Predator
by Alec Gillis & Tom Woodruff, Jr.
Aliens vs. Predator Requiem:
Inside The Monster Shop
by Alec Gillis & Tom Woodruff, Jr.
Alien: The Illustrated Story
by Archie Goodwin & Walter Simonson
The Art of Alien: Isolation by Andy McVittie
Alien: The Archive
Alien: The Weyland-Yutani Report
by S.D. Perry
Aliens: The Set Photography
by Simon Ward
Alien: The Coloring Book
The Art and Making of Alien: Covenant
by Simon Ward
Alien Covenant: David's Drawings
by Dane Hallett & Matt Hatton
The Predator: The Art and Making
of the Film by James Nolan
The Making of Alien by J.W. Rinzler
Alien: The Blueprints by Graham Langridge
Alien: 40 Years 40 Artists
Alien: The Official Cookbook
by Chris-Rachael Oseland
Aliens: Artbook by Printed In Blood

A L I E N ™

SEVENTH CIRCLE

A NOVEL BY

PHILIPPA BALLANTINE

STORY BY

PHILIPPA BALLANTINE
AND CLARA ČARIJA

TITAN BOOKS

ALIEN ™ : SEVENTH CIRCLE

Print edition ISBN: 9781803366975
E-book edition ISBN: 9781803366982

Published by Titan Books
A division of Titan Publishing Group Ltd
144 Southwark Street, London SE1 0UP
www.titanbooks.com

First edition: January 2025
10 9 8 7 6 5 4 3 2 1

A CIP catalogue record for this title is available from
the British Library.

Printed and bound by CPI Group (UK) Ltd, Croydon CR0 4YY.

Did you enjoy this book?
We love to hear from our readers. Please email us at readerfeedback@
titanemail.com or write to us at Reader Feedback at the above address.
www.titanbooks.com

1

IN THE MAZE
OF MINOS

They were being hunted. Two artificial people trapped in a world of human pain and terror. It shouldn't have been like this.

Mae sat, staring at her silhouette as it cast shadows in crimson light, while she contemplated the end.

Was this what Father went through?

Knees folded tightly into her chest, she stared at the communication panel in front of her. It blinked a few times before going out.

Rook touched her shoulder. "This won't help. We have to move—right now."

The pulsing red light cast the pilot of the *Blackstar*'s sharp, angular face in strange shadows. It bounced off the myriad of ragged scars in his synthetic skin and the slightly twisted jaw that he'd attempted to repair himself. Like her, he wore a human face, though his was considerably more battered. Mae's face was unique, while his was repeated all over the middle heavens. Bishop models were prized in technical fields, but today he was performing an even more valuable role: helping her save the Jackals.

Mae feared the next message she waited for wouldn't come. That was awful, but logical—yet she found herself rooted to the spot. The klaxon blared, filling the corridor with relentless noise and flashes of scarlet light to show time was running out. Not much of it remained.

"Attention. Emergency. All personnel must evacuate immediately. Get to your nearest escape pod. You now have ten minutes to lockdown protocol." The soothing voice was that of a calm, collected woman, not one trapped in a dying space station with monstrosities in every shadow.

Her mother, Colonel Zula Hendricks, called it the Mama Warning, or in her darker moments, the Kiss Your Ass Goodbye Warning.

Despite the screaming klaxon and the message repeated over and over, the beast still pounded on the hatch. Rook tilted his head towards it, as if to remind her again that she couldn't keep waiting for another message that would never come. The repetitive thud of chitin hitting reinforced steel somehow made itself heard over the wailing alarm. Fear welled inside her. She would have dearly loved to hear from her father, Davis, in this moment.

He'd been there when she first woke on the *Righteous Fury* and provided guidance in those first days as a synthetic person. He would have said something useful now, or at least something funny.

Most of all, she wished her mother, Colonel Zula Hendricks, stood at her side, giving orders and telling her the right action to take. But that wasn't possible. She was with Red Mae. Hopefully, that splinter persona would help Zula and her unit stay alive until Mae Prime came back with help.

That wouldn't happen if she didn't move right now.

Rook took her hand and gave it a gentle squeeze. He was a strange synthetic, unhooked from human control in a way she'd never seen from another of their kind— except for herself. Sitting as still as she was, he must've been worried she'd picked up a corrupted subroutine. "The elevator isn't far."

Another bang echoed through the dark station corridor. At this sub-level, they were alone. They'd lost their unit during the chaos of their mission. One desperate message from Colonel Hendricks and Red Team was all Mae hung her hopes on. Whether they'd made it to some kind of safety, she couldn't tell. Her mother only managed a single transmission: she and her unit were trapped while trying to make it back to the space elevator.

All the Jackals would die here in the darkest corner of the universe if Mae or Rook didn't escape and let someone know what happened on Minos Station.

Mae wondered if Rook experienced the same swirl of emotions as her. They hadn't found time to compare notes about their specifications, and it didn't look like they'd have any now.

They'd lost audio contact with Red Team, but she still glanced at the personal wrist device all Jackals were equipped with. Willpower wouldn't make green letters appear on its screen. Another pause gave the Xenomorph a chance to think, too.

The monster changed tactics, going from rhythmic banging to something more cunning. The sly scratching around the hatch was somehow even worse than the thundering attacks. This variant of Xenomorph wasn't like anything they'd encountered on Shānmén. That was the inherent horror of the beast: it adapted to every situation by stealing the advantages of its host.

Mae checked the records from the Jackals' database within her. While Xenomorphs—particularly queens— were observed opening doors, they'd never been recorded opening an airlock or hatch. However, they were not animals, which was the greatest peril. Complacency in the matter of Xenomorphs always led to disaster.

There is no greater danger than underestimating your opponent.

Could that be the echo of her dead father? Mae filed that away for later—if there was a later. She pushed away from the wall. "Okay, right behind you."

Rook was the only other synthetic who knew Mae's secret. It was comfortable to share a small network as they did. They didn't need words, but she'd been practicing her human reactions for months. Rook's mouth crooked in a slight smile at her strangeness, but he'd picked up a few of his own quirks, too.

Together, they bolted away from the hatch. Even if the Xenomorph didn't open it, there were always the air ducts and other vital pipework. Xenos had a particular knack for sniffing out those claustrophobic spaces and the station artificial intelligence wouldn't lock them down, since that would mean death to all the human residents. Given their options, though, that might've been a mercy.

Rook's and Mae's synthetic eyes didn't operate like a flesh-and-blood human's. The station AI had activated evacuation protocols, restricting power to emergency and running lights leading to exits. Luckily, neither of them needed any illumination to find their way down the utilitarian corridor.

As a synthetic person, Mae realized she shouldn't feel this tired. Her efforts to become more like her mother over the last few months began to bear fruit, but right now it got in the way of survival.

They both discarded their pulse rifles long before the ammo counters clicked to '00'. Rook carried a pistol, and Mae clutched a bowie knife Zula had gifted her. Neither of those would be much use if a Xenomorph decided they were a threat, though. When she chose to abandon her combat droid body for one more like a human, she gave up a lot of durability. Mae was almost as fragile as a human in many respects, now.

The Bishop models were sturdier—but not built for heavy combat, either.

This way. I overheard Station Chief Rolstad mentioning an elevator for executive staff that goes directly to Minos's command center. He seemed quite proud of it. We can get a shuttle from there.

The corridor flashed blood red occasionally as they ran through the administration section of the facility. The staff left everything behind: papers on the floor, spilled cups of coffee, and overturned chairs. Unattended lights and alarms beeped urgently.

Under evacuation protocol, every one of the codes that Mae and Rook would have used as synthetics to connect with the station computer, open doors, and find their way was disabled. They were equally as fucked as the rest of the humans on this infected space station.

Something in the shadows moved above them, a creaking in the pipes that caused Rook to stop and duck behind a desk, pulling her with him. Rook slowly lifted one finger to his lips, gesturing Mae to be silent.

Normally, a Xenomorph would not be interested in a synthetic person. They couldn't host a growing embryo in their chests. The abominations needed flesh to grow their colony, and would only attack a synthetic if they carried a weapon or posed any other threat. However, these infected Xenomorphs acted differently to the ones in Mae's records.

On the lower levels, she'd witnessed them rip combat synthetics apart even as they stood in their charging racks.

She and Rook were in as much danger as the genetic humans on this station. Perhaps while the humans studied them, the Xenos ran their own investigation in return. They'd certainly been around synthetics every moment this experiment was in progress.

Rook's eyes tracked the pattern of the sound reverberating off the ceiling above them. *You know, I used to be called Father at one time. So let me be that now to you. I'll go first. Stay down.*

You're not my *father*, Mae shot back. She wondered in what context he'd be a parent, but that story would have to wait.

His eyebrow jumped up at that. *A father is someone meant to protect, and your mother entrusted you into my care. However, if you prefer, I can address you as Lieutenant.*

Rook chose this moment to remind her of the rank. Mae sent the synthetic equivalent of a middle finger across their connection.

It is my duty to never harm or allow a human to be harmed. I count you among that number, as far as the colonel is concerned.

She couldn't argue with that.

He crouched down and glanced back. His gentle green eyes locked on her. *Don't worry, I'll be careful. I may be synthetic, but I'm not stupid.*

Mae shook her head. Artificial people often batted that line amongst themselves. It was as close to humor as most got. But in that millisecond when she was disarmed, Rook took action. He darted between the desks and towards the larger offices.

He remained so calm that Mae was almost jealous. He disappeared from view, even as the creaks and groans from above sounded louder. The Xenomorphs did love to travel in the air ducts. They were much more agile than a human up there, and it suited their favorite method of attack: ambush.

I'm calling the elevator now. It's safe. Rook's transmission was slightly distorted. Their fragile shared network had a limited signal strength amongst the metal of the station's superstructure.

Mae leaped to her feet and hustled after him until the pressure door slammed down centimeters in front of her face. On the other side, Rook spun around.

Safeguard protocol on the executive level must have triggered when I called the elevator. He hastily examined each side of the door. *It's under evac protocol. I can't open it.*

They stared at each other for 8.23 seconds through the glass. Behind Rook, the elevator pinged a bell-like tone to announce its arrival. It was an incongruously happy sound given the situation.

You can reach the small freight deck directly off the galleria. The kitchen staff get all their supplies delivered there. Your mother ordered the Blackstar *moved there for repairs.* Rook pressed his hand against the door for a moment. *Go back down one corridor, turn right. Take the transit. Go now.*

Mae felt a touch of panic. *We were supposed to go together. You have my Deep Lock key. What if something happens to you?*

He nodded. *I'll be fine. It's okay. You're okay. I'll find you. Go.*

Dampening down her concerns, Mae took one last look at Rook and ran back the way they'd come until she spotted the large, distressed words under a scarlet arrow on the wall:

TRANSIT STATION TO GALLERIA, OBSERVATION
DECK, AND CANTEEN.

Mae had little experience with space stations. However, it made sense they'd have supply shuttles for ferrying the food and supplies needed to keep humans productive. The Jackals complained about and rejoiced in food. It almost made Mae wish for taste buds, sometimes.

She'd couldn't afford to think of Shipp, Yoo, or Littlefield right now.

Crouching low, Mae followed the arrow along the corridors towards the transit tram. It was still functional—at least for a few more minutes. She jumped on, and when the doors finally shut, she found it appropriate to sigh. Even without lungs to fill with oxygen, it felt good.

"Where are you headed?"

The voice made her spin around, ready to attack.

A David unit sat alone on the bench seat, but shuffled aside as the transit tram whirred to life and rumbled on. His handsome face turned to her and smiled. Mae realized with a lurch that all the synthetics on the station were being abandoned. Even if the station survived, they'd be wandering around with Xenomorphs that would eventually rip them to pieces. That, or they'd gradually fail and fall apart. Mae couldn't decide which was the worse fate.

She sat down on the seat next to him and smiled back. "Galleria."

"Lovely at this cycle," he replied. "The two moons outlined against the sun."

Mae stared down at her hands for a moment. "You should probably go into rest mode. The humans are evacuating."

"But you're not." His right lip curled as David's smile stretched a little too wide. "You are, in fact, an intruder on this station."

He gave away his intentions a nanosecond before attacking. Mae anticipated and swayed back as his lightning-fast punch came for her head. She ducked and rolled away as he kicked one leg towards her, seeking to crush her torso against the steel floor.

Mae grabbed hold of his leg in an attempt to unbalance him, straining against the power of the other synthetic. Turning, he grabbed her head in his hands, face contorting into an even more unnatural smile.

"You're becoming hysterical. Let me calm you down." His voice came out soft and calming, even as he strained against her.

Mae understood immediately that his methods were going to be fatal. All this time she'd worried about the Xenomorphs, and now one of her own brethren would kill her.

2

SEEKING A STAR

In a combat body, Mae would have been able to overpower this David unit easily. However, she currently occupied her custom made, most human-like shell. Although Davids weren't created for combat specifically, over time the public realized they still could cause harm. The company put this model out of commission after fatal malfunctioning incidents. Many attempts to staunch the secondary black-market trade proved futile. The UPP and fringe colonies, as well as companies looking to slash their bottom line, took advantage of cut-rate prices.

Much like he attempted to slash her major control micro-hydraulics. They traded blows up and down the transit tram. Mae deflected his strikes on her forearm, but leaving her upper body vulnerable. He inflicted a cut on her neck. For a human, that would have been deadly, but it still knocked her back. He'd cut a narrow slice in her skin, and a thin line of her bespoke red circulatory fluid trickled over her shoulder. The David's gaze darted to it in surprise. All androids' fluids were a thin, milky white.

His bewilderment gave her a moment. As the transit tram gained momentum, both reached for the rail to stabilize themselves. She activated the one advantage she possessed. Though Mae wasn't in a combat body, she did still have the programming. Security subroutines activated, mirroring a human adrenaline rush.

Catching the David by the arm, she spun him around, throwing him into the orange vertical grab rail. The carriage resounded with the crash of his internal structure connecting, carbon fiber against metal. He rolled to his feet, though the pole remained bent to his shape.

Faster than any human could, he closed, landing three successive powerful punches on Mae's torso. She absorbed them with a snarl she'd learned from Captain Olivia Shipp, her mother's greatest confidante. Then, spinning, she caught the next punch he threw in her hand, squeezing and twisting at the same time.

Mae used the force of his momentum to shift him off balance. She stepped around him, and in one smooth move, pulled her bowie knife from her boot and rammed it into the side of his head.

White circulatory fluid exploded over her weapon and fist. The David's eyes went blank. His hand twitched fractionally. It was a clean blow to his central processing core, and he dropped to his knees.

Mae jerked the knife free, and he toppled over onto his face with a thud. She might have felt a twinge of remorse, but she'd never liked the David models. Knowing their history as she did, she was pleased to take at least one out of commission.

The transit tram lurched to a stop as the station warning sounded again.

"Attention. Emergency. All personnel must evacuate immediately. Get to your nearest escape pod. You now have five minutes to evacuation protocol."

Mae bolted out of the tram and onto the galleria deck. Only a few hours since she'd stood here watching the citizens of the station line up for noodles. Now the empty storefronts flickered with red emergency lighting. People once ate here, communed with their colleagues, and enjoyed an unhurried moment. The company designed the station to conceal its terrible experiments, but everyday people still lived here.

Now it was a broken nightmare-scape of people searching for a way out. The tang of blood filled the air, while control panels sparked with barely contained fires. The workers clustered near the safety bay on the galleria's outer rim, which held ranks of cryo escape pods. Deep space versions like these were self-propelled, designed to travel to the nearest shipping lane or habitable world, but slowly enough to preserve its fragile cargo. However, such safety measures would take too long for her purposes. Mae needed to reach the *Blackstar* and get help for the Jackals immediately.

Small groups of station personnel argued by the remaining three pods. Fists were flying, and Mae's internal protocols were at an impasse. Her orders were to seek help for Zula Hendricks and the Jackals, but these were people who needed her assistance, too. Davis, however, controlled her specifications when she was made, and he'd chosen to give his daughter free will like a genetic human. It was a tough choice. If she waited here to sort this out, she might not get off Minos. The Jackals and her mother would perish.

In the end she chose her mother and her team. Mae bypassed the fight and ran past the escape pod array, towards the door marked NO ENTRANCE.

A young woman stood by the control panel, furiously punching numbers. She turned her terrified face in Mae's direction. A name tag on her shirt said ALICE PRIM.

"My shuttle's in there," Alice gasped as her eyes grew huge. "I delivered power cores a few hours ago, but now it's locked me out."

"I'll run a bypass," Mae said. "Give me one second."

The woman nodded, blinked back tears, and scooted out of the way. Mae withdrew her kit from inside her jacket and plugged it in. Hopefully, in the chaos, Alice wouldn't notice she did it faster than any genetic human could. The lights swirled and blinked before letting out a low beep that was almost lost in the surrounding noise.

The door slid open, and Alice let out a relieved laugh. "Oh my god, let's go!"

Behind her, the red emergency light flashed and Alice, in her haste to escape, didn't notice the large ink-black shape moving in the shadows.

An artificial person didn't attract its lethal attention, but a warm human body did. The monster moved fast, its talons failing to find purchase on the floor, skittering across the metallic floor on all fours before rising onto its back legs. It leaped on the young delivery driver as she let out a startled howl. Mae, devoid of any weapon capable of working against such a monster, froze in place. It wrapped one hand over Alice's face and dragged her away, screaming but alive. Her fate would be far worse than death.

The group of squabbling people shouted over each other, their voices echoing in the escape pod bay. They fared no better. Their loud voices became a dinner bell.

Two Xenomorphs darted out from the kitchen of one of the abandoned noodle shops. They scrambled over overturned chairs, clambered over the counter, and vaulted among the terrified people. A woman in a white coat screamed as the subject of her research was suddenly on top of her, tearing her flesh from her like bark off a tree. The others scattered, running on primitive instincts to escape. Except there was no safety to be found on this station. The only escape was death.

Now Minos belonged to the Xenomorphs and their needs.

An older man almost made it to Mae. His glasses fell

off, his white coat flapping as he reached out towards her. She tried to grab him, but the monster was faster.

The Xeno's inner mouth punched out, kissing the man's forehead and breaking it as easily as an egg. His panicked screams ended in a spray of scarlet. The human blood struck her on the shoulder, mingling with her own red synthetic circulatory fluid.

The Xenomorph turned to face her. Its smooth featureless head tilted as it pulled its lips back from gleaming, sharp teeth. In the flickering half-light of the galleria the slight blue tinge of the Kuebiko infection gleamed over the creature's carapace. Blood and spittle ran down from both its mouths. A bowie knife wouldn't help her, but if she stayed still, it should move on. Staring it directly in the eyeless sockets for a long moment, however, Mae wasn't completely sure of that assertion.

What did this perfect organism see when it looked at her? Even after all this time, they didn't fully understand what went on under that shiny black carapace. Elegant and brutally efficient, many corporations wanted to put it to work for their own ends. All in pursuit of its ruthlessness and evolutionary power.

Looking at it, Mae wondered at the hubris of humanity.

Its stance shifted from upright to coiled. Whatever the Xeno's calculations, it chose to mark her as a threat. She contemplated that for a split second, and then the answer came: the queen was communicating with all her drones, and it recognized her. It remembered her from the lab on the station's eleventh level. She must think that Mae was among the artificial people that aided the scientists who imprisoned and experimented on her children.

Mae moved to defend herself, but this body was too fragile for a fight with a drone. She might not make it to the *Blackstar* at all.

The dull thud of a pulse rifle echoed down the promenade. The back of the Xeno's head exploded into acid and black chunks of carapace. Synthetic instincts, faster than a human's, helped Mae dodge to the right, out of the way of its blood spray as it melted the deck where she'd been standing.

Rook loped across the galleria, a newly gained pulse rifle looped over one shoulder. He grabbed her arm, pulling her to her feet. *Are you alright?*

She nodded. *Never happier to see your face, though.*

The corners of his mouth lifted a fraction. *Not many people can say that, these days. Not since my accident. Let's get going. We don't have much time.*

With the lights flashing faster, Mae and Rook entered the airlock. The freight deck remained pressurized, so the inner door opened without issue. On the other side was the poor young woman's freight shuttle, right next to the *Blackstar*.

Weyland-Yutani made Minos Station's computer mainframe, Kaspar, and they were renowned for creating some of the most loyal synthetic minds. Kaspar had locked down the station and the *Righteous Fury* and was operating on containment protocols. The humans hadn't realized that Kaspar would unleash hell on all of them if it meant obeying its orders. The rules of synthetic behavior did not apply in this situation.

Once they navigated the *Blackstar* beyond the solar system, past Kaspar's network of satellites, they should be able to signal for help.

Mae and Rook raced past Alice's shuttle. She glimpsed the name on its side, the *Solo Cup*. Despite the situation, she couldn't stop a small smile flickering over her lips. A perfectly ridiculous thing to notice at that moment. Perhaps her ascent to consciousness was affecting her in strange ways she'd not accounted for. Humor in such a situation should be impossible.

The *Blackstar* awaited them, as battered and bruised as the synthetic who owned it. Long patches of paint were missing from its sides. The solar run Rook used to remove the Xenomorph resin from the ship's side left her with long charred marks. The thought of the *Blackstar* filled with their enemies was more than a little unnerving, but they would have to check for stowaways after escaping Minos.

Rook led the way through the hatch, which still bore the Weyland-Yutani logo. That didn't help Mae's feelings towards the ship, but it was their only chance to escape.

Strange how her gut twisted when she thought about her mother and the other Jackals. She didn't have any internal organs to behave like that. Still, leaving everyone behind felt very wrong.

Rook slipped into the pilot's chair and buckled up. Mae took the seat next to him while he punched in the request to open the bay's outer door. Lockdown protocol hadn't yet extended to the hangar. Even Kaspar couldn't mess with that.

The door opened, even as the red emergency lighting flickered. The station would soon be a sealed death trap.

Don't jinx it, Zula always warned her, and she'd always dismissed such things as human superstition. Except just then, the hangar bay doors began grinding closed. The station was shutting down on them.

Punch it, Rook!

Hang on, he warned, firing up the engines. They didn't need to worry about an angry station flight controller, at this point. The *Blackstar* was shockingly quick. Mae first noted that when it swooped in to save them, but experiencing it firsthand was another matter. While Rook gunned the *Blackstar* for the exit, the hangar bay doors were close to completing their descent. Kaspar seemed to playing with them, as ridiculous as that seemed.

She'd learned more than just superstitions from Zula Hendricks. Mae now possessed quite an arsenal of swear words. This seemed like an appropriate moment for them.

The ship bounced off the flight deck, metal screeching in protest. Mae feared the ship might shake itself into pieces as they made a final desperate run for the closing hangar doors. One last 'fuck' escaped Mae as they screamed past them. Rook narrowed his eyes as the ship blew between the descending doors.

Mae fully expected to be ejected into space with the ship exploding around them, but despite it all, the *Blackstar* held and they were free of the station.

Rook glanced over at her. His expression was an entirely human one. *It's okay. We're okay.*

Synthetics weren't supposed to believe in luck, but Mae changed her mind on that one. Hope followed that realization. Perhaps they could rescue the remaining Jackals after all, and her mother too.

Rook turned back to the controls. *We're on track to make it to the shipping lanes soon. I don't think I'm going to need to activate your Deep Protection subroutines. Things should be fine from now on.*

He must've been able to feel her concerns. Colonel Zula Hendricks wanted to protect her daughter, and if anyone found out she was synthetic, they would tear her apart.

Reaching over, Rook placed his hand on top of hers. *We'll get her back, Mae. We'll get them all back.*

It seemed dangerous to place her entire being in the hands of another synthetic—especially after EWA betrayed her over Shānmén. Yet her mother trusted him, and it made sense. They would return to the generals, and then they'd race back to Minos Station. With a few strategic nukes, they could destroy this terrible station and its experimental training facility on the planet.

Mae nodded. *I believe you.*

You are your mother's daughter. He squeezed her hand a fraction.

Mae stared out into the darkness ahead and reminded herself of how far she'd come since first awakening. They were on their way. Her mother only needed to hold out until their return. If anyone could survive, it was Colonel Zula Hendricks.

3

AN INTERESTING CATCH

Stare too long into the Long Dark and it will burrow into your soul.

Every old spacer hanging around Guelph Station drinking cheap booze and remembering their glory days grumbled those words. Lenny Pope didn't drink, but he enjoyed listening to those most ignored.

Most of the stories he heard were full of long-haul spacer superstition. He didn't necessarily believe in superstitions, but he kept his opinions to himself. They possessed a bunch: no whistling while on the Rim, renaming a ship beckoned disaster. His favorite was black cats on board brought good luck, not that many could afford one these days. He understood why the old-timers said such things: they were attempting to control the unknown.

Yet Lenny agreed with them at the same time. He didn't enjoy looking out at nothing from their ship, the *Eumenides*, either. Unlike the rest of his family, he found the pit of empty space they traveled through uncomfortable. He'd always find an asteroid, a planet—hell, even some space junk—to focus on.

Not like his brother. He glanced over at Morgan hunched over the ore scanner. Older by a couple of years, their parents let him get away with a lot more than they would Lenny, like his green hair that matched the hull color of their family's ship. He'd let it grow long, even though it got caught in the scanner's visor.

"Anything good?" Lenny dared to ask.

Morgan let out a long sigh and pushed his hair out of his face as he stood up. "Nothing worth waking Mom and Dad over. This whole asteroid cloud is pure granite. We should have listened to Tim Bits. He warned us the Combine mined it out last cycle."

They targeted the long line of debris in the orbit of Krasue. It lay on the edge of the solar system of Nachzehrer—a lonely place to make a living. Usually, such places were lucrative enough to keep the Popes as free agents in a universe of vast corporations. Morgan became adept at scanning rocks and debris, hunting for those rare metals or ice chunks large enough to make them worthwhile to haul in. They'd hoped Tim was shooting his mouth off again, but this time it appeared he was right.

Lenny slid back in his chair. One more cycle and he could

join the Combine without the permission of his parents, William and Daniella Pope. A couple of his friends back on Guelph Station filled out the forms already. That wasn't a guarantee they'd get in, but it was something, at least. The other option was to join the military. His folks completed two tours for the Space Operating Forces of the UPP, and their reviews were less than glowing. Any mention of the SOF and his parents would lock him on the *Eumenides* until he came to his senses.

Morgan would never think about signing up for either the Combine or the SOF. He was as committed to their family mining venture as their parents. His entire world was this tub. Yet it was Lenny who'd put them in debt.

"Hey, shit-heel!" Morgan leaned over to shove his brother's feet off the edge of the dash. He must've recognized something in Lenny's expression that indicated he was sliding towards introspection. "Why don't you go make me a coffee while we come around the sunward side of the planet? You know, just in case the company missed something back there."

Lenny got up without comment and slipped past his brother. The back of the *Eumenides* was as tight as the cockpit. Spending weeks out in this beloved tin can left no room for privacy, but at least in the galley Lenny might have a few moments alone. As he did the slide-shuffle to get back there, he kicked shut the hatch in the floor, which led down to the ore hold with the tether nets. Morgan left it open like he was hopeful one of them would have to race down to fire the nets. Luck would be a fine thing.

Lenny understood why his brother, who focused all his energy on keeping the mining skiff and their home solvent, tried to remain optimistic. Out here on the edge of known space, and on the lip of financial ruin, there wasn't any hope to be found in the Long Dark. Whatever hope you needed, you must build yourself.

When it was their parents' shift, they usually sat in their chairs, feet propped on the dash, eyes fixed on the emptiness of it all. Through it, though, they held hands. Both were former UPP soldiers, used to not having a lot and grateful for being alive. Lenny often suspected their relationship was the only thing keeping them from total cynicism. Still, it took both brothers promising not to halt the scan for them to retreat to their sleeping berth for a few hours' rest. It was a hard life, which Lenny worried was taking a toll on his parents. Another concern to add to his constant list.

Lenny fished out the coffee from the battered cupboard. It was the pre-processed imitation kind because no one had the money for the actual stuff. Using your imagination was the only way to make it palatable. Lenny shook a good amount out into the tiny mug before slapping the boiler to life. Out here, they usually ran out of proper water in the first couple of weeks. In the Long Dark you learned to forget you were making your coffee with your crewmates' recycled piss.

During treatment, Pelorus, the former medical synth

back on Guelph, described different worlds to him, and ways to live. Now, Lenny wanted that. He clung to it like a man with only a sip of air left in his suit.

As Lenny stirred the concoction, he wondered whether soldiers at least got the good stuff. His folks should know, but he would not ask them. Any time he brought up their past, they totally shut down. If they guessed he'd even casually scanned the signup release for the SOF, they'd lose their minds. His mom would no doubt tie him up in the tether nets and head for the outer rim.

Not that he would actually do it. The *Eumenides* would be too short-handed to function without his help.

As always when he became nervous, his finger drifted to his temple and the one-centimeter square of metal on the outer edge of his right eye, concealed beneath his skin. No one ever mentioned the augment that saved his life when he was only ten, but it lingered in the desperate atmosphere of the *Eumenides*. The birth defect nearly killed him. The Muster Syndrome, they called it, since it afflicted the kids of many former soldiers. It left Morgan untouched but ravaged Lenny's brain. It became apparent the moment he took his first breath. In his early years drugs were enough to keep the effects at bay, but as his body entered puberty, they didn't cut it anymore. Without more complicated intervention, he'd have stroked out within a year, unable to deal with the g-force experienced by any child living on a spaceship.

His parents were presented with three choices: either leave him in the UPP's care, let him die in theirs, or mortgage the *Eumenides*. His parents both grew up in the UPP's children's camps: the haunted look in his mother's eyes, in particular, told Lenny they would've never taken that option. The augment that would save him remained available for a price, and the company didn't care how many children died; the cost remained firm.

The augment kept him alive, and when the flight computer acted up, he could jack into it and fix the problem. Hardly worth the high price the family all paid, though.

As if thinking about it activated the augment, a tickle built up in the back of his brain. He'd been told there was no way he had enough nerves there, but that was how it sometimes felt. It was as if the itch was crawling around the inside of his skull.

Chugging the coffee meant for his brother didn't seem to shake it. He tried not to think about it, but if it wasn't for his Muster Syndrome, his parents could have afforded a crew. It would have been a very different life. He might have been drinking real coffee in some company office.

"Shit," Lenny whispered under his breath, squeezing the bridge of his nose. The augment sensation had never been this strong before. He made another cup for Morgan and staggered back to the bridge.

His brother took the mug and glanced up. "You okay? The augment acting up?"

Lenny hated talking about it with any of his family. Every time he mentioned it bothering him, he felt awful. The thing that threatened to financially ruin his family every time dock fees came due should at least work right.

He nodded and gestured to the scanner. "I'm fine. You wanna take a break? I can run this."

Morgan slipped out of the chair and over to the pilot's seat. The computer was in charge, but she wasn't one of those fancy Wey-Yu ones. It didn't do to leave her steering the *Eumenides* without some kind of supervision. He busied himself with checking settings, while Lenny positioned himself over the scanner.

Their limited computer system selected likely areas in the debris cloud to search, but they needed a human eye to run more complete analysis. He played the scanner's beam over the nearest section of debris. Lenny spotted nothing but granite, but for a second, in one corner, the light briefly flared. He blinked, frowned, and jerked back from the viewer.

"You alright there, shit-heel?" Morgan asked, setting his mug of coffee down on the dash.

The augment sometimes caused him to experience visual distortions, flickers of noise, and now and then a phantom smell. Lenny shook his head.

"No, I'm fine. Probably that damn coffee."

Morgan chuckled. "Find us a deposit the Combine missed and maybe we can afford the good stuff."

"Yeah, sure. Right." Lenny leaned back down. "Can you

take us five clicks to starboard? There's less chewed-up debris over there."

Morgan flew the *Eumenides* in the direction he'd suggested. His expression, though, wasn't optimistic.

Lenny fitted his face back into the viewer of the scanner. The augment showed him a flicker of light once more, but he ignored it. Then a high-pitched squeal burst in his left ear. It lasted for only a second, but it made his eyes water. He managed not to jerk away again.

Morgan nudged the ship closer to the section of the debris cloud Lenny wanted to examine. He muttered a bit to himself as well, though he wouldn't have done that if it was their mom or dad at the viewer.

Lenny frowned. "I think there might be something behind that cluster of untouched granite back there. Bring us around in a circle."

The *Eumenides* shook a little as Morgan activated the jets used for minute position adjustments. The ship came about, rotating around a section of untouched rock.

"This looks new," Lenny said. "This rock could have been deposited by a comet or something more recently than the Combine harvest."

"That'd be nice," Morgan replied. "Comets can bring in some valuable metals from beyond the system. Shall I go wake the folks?"

Lenny stared down at the viewer. Suddenly, it lit up with many colors. Aluminum. Steel. Even traces of Eitr. That was exciting enough, but then he made out the largest piece of comet debris nestled behind the granite, and it was rectangular. Not much in the natural world, even out in the Long Dark, was such a defined shape.

"Yeah, do it!" he said, not looking up but waving towards his brother. "They're going to need to deploy the nets."

As he scanned more, his heart raced. This wasn't a natural deposit. It must be salvage material. Somewhere in the path of a comet, a ship lost at least part of its hull. The only naturally occurring place to find Eitr was in the mines of the planet Shānmén. The authorities shut down that mine because of a plague outbreak in the previous cycle, so to find the element floating out here meant it could only have come from a shipwreck.

Lenny only glanced up when his parents emerged from their berth. He finally sat back on the bench, letting out a ragged breath.

Daniella rubbed her dark hair, shot through with gray, then stretched her neck. "Think you've got something, huh?"

He nodded and shrugged, strangely embarrassed by his discovery now that his parents were here.

William slid into the pilot's seat, his gaze fixed on the Long Dark and the orbiting debris. His beard was as rumpled as his hair. "First find for you, son. Let's see if you're as good as your brother."

Morgan rolled his eyes at Lenny and mouthed, *He*

doesn't mean it. Lenny shrugged, like it didn't matter.

Daniella dropped into the seat next to her husband and ran through the net test cycle. She spared only one glance over her shoulder at her sons. "Get ready by the haul door. I am not wasting fuel bringing in trash. I need your eyeballs on what I drag in. That means you, Morgan."

"Yes, ma'am," he said. He opened the hatch and Lenny followed him down into the most important part of the *Eumenides.* The cargo hold was empty, a sad indictment of their success so far. At the stern was the airlock which contained the net and clamps. As the brothers waited, Daniella opened the outermost door and deployed the long cables. Each of these she piloted out into the debris field, the nets uncoiling behind.

These moments were heart-stopping, at least to Lenny. Seeing the Long Dark through the glass airlock made it seem closer and far more dangerous. The brothers waited in the tense semi-darkness of the hold, not speaking to each other.

The net deployment system groaned and clanked, slapping against the side of the *Eumenides* like some primeval sea creature. Dimly, Daniella's voice rose above the din. Lenny couldn't make out the words, but his mom loved to swear while working the ancient nets. She always said it helped her concentrate.

The intercom clicked on in the hold. "Alright, I think I got something. Hauling now."

"Wouldn't it be nice to be doing this for a share,"

Morgan muttered, then let out a snort of a laugh. Shares were for commercial vessels. The brothers worked for survival and family.

Lenny didn't want to go near that subject. Instead, he grabbed two pairs of thick gloves and tossed one set to Morgan. The net dragged and bumped across the floor, and then the outer door closed.

The digital array by the inner airlock door ran from red, through orange, and finally cycled to green. Morgan reached the controls first. "Alright, little bro, let's see what you got us." He punched the button, and the doors groaned open.

With the nets retracted on each side of the inner bay, Morgan and Lenny picked their way through the catch, using hand scanners to identify the metals. It didn't take long.

"Yeah, this isn't natural." Lenny picked up a piece of twisted metal. "This is ship salvage."

"Works either way." Morgan pulled at the largest section. "See if we can find some ID numbers, and we'll report to the Ministry of Space Security to get checked out. Pretty likely we'll get to sell this, though. Should be a good amount, too."

"Maybe Mom will crack a smile."

Morgan didn't reply, too busy levering a flat section loose. It broke open and tumbled to the deck, revealing a far different shape. "Oh, fuck no." His older brother staggered back. "Goddamn, no!"

The long rectangular shape couldn't be anything other than a cryo escape pod.

Lenny stumbled over the scattered debris to reach it. Morgan kicked a slice of aluminum with such force that it bounced off the hull walls. Lenny, however, crouched to examine the pod.

The design wasn't a familiar one, and Lenny studied ship design for fun. It wasn't anything off a freighter or pleasure cruiser. The sturdy construction screamed military, though there were no SOF markings on it.

"Do you see green?" Morgan asked, circling the pod. "Do you see green lights?"

Lenny peered underneath to glimpse the controls. "They're flickering. Hold on. I see one green. The rest are dark."

The pod lay on its face, so there was no way to check the contents. Morgan grabbed a long pry bar, and together, the brothers strained to roll the pod over. Neither of them was cruel enough to desire another traveler's death in the Long Dark. However, the fact remained that under law the wreckage was fair salvage only if there was a corpse inside. A living, breathing occupant made things much more complicated.

The pod landed right-side up with a crash, nearly crushing Morgan's foot. He jumped back as Lenny got a close-up view of the control panel.

"Yeah, it's barely functional." Leaning over, he brushed ice off the glass panel and peered in. He fully expected to see a mummified face staring back. Instead, the inhabitant of the pod seemed as fresh as if she'd climbed in there only moments before.

It was a young woman, with sharp cheekbones, dark skin, and close-cropped hair—like something out of those stupid Earth fairy tales. She didn't appear to be wounded.

Morgan peered in and let out an aggravated sigh. "Well, there goes our salvage, little brother! Pretty as she is, that doesn't pay the bills."

"We need to find out how busted up she is." Lenny stood up. "We're going to have to run a bypass on the pod systems to get her out of there."

Morgan glanced away for a long moment.

He must be calculating the losses to the Eumenides.

"Yeah, yeah, you're right. I bet she's got a good story to tell, at least."

Lenny rubbed his neck. Sometimes he felt guilty that he wasn't as obsessed by the family finances as his brother and parents were. His aspirations beyond the *Eumenides* made it easier to ignore their current reality. Their skiff sailed on razor-thin margins. Laws surrounding salvage were one thing, but there were also laws regarding recovered escape pods. The *Eumenides* would have to return to Guelph immediately, but bureaucracy would tie up the ship's fuel compensation for months. A lot of crews would have dumped the pod, stripped the logs of any mention of it, and moved on. But the Popes would not, even if it made their lives more complicated.

Lenny was proud of that. The idea of floating out in the dark all alone was his living nightmare, and he wasn't part of a family that would ever let that happen.

He looked down at her, resting peacefully, and he hoped the woman in the pod had no memory of that. The story she held was bound to be an interesting one.

4

FORGOTTEN DARK

Black flickered at the corners of her vision. Bright light raced past, obscuring shapes and memory. Then the sound battered her, a scream from both people and metal as something exploded. Chaos tore apart all reason and took her down with it.

Thrown adrift in a world of tumbled meaning and sensations, she became suddenly nameless. The roar of it all broke through her. She snapped like a thin piece of metal. The howl she let out joined the madness of her existence. She only did so to make something real. It was at least a word rather than a guttural sound that she let out. "No!" It stretched away, disjointed and lost, a demand that the universe wouldn't meet.

Torn and battered, she didn't look away or turn off any of her reactions. She plummeted from everywhere, spinning and misplaced.

After a numberless measure of time, the relentless rumble faded away. She tried to find herself. Raising her hands, she discovered she was trapped. Her body rattled in a cage of darkness as claustrophobia stole her from confusion's grasp. Her *no* trembled and ground down into a *please*.

It didn't matter. She longed for the comfort of the rumble, because the thick silence she'd been dropped into was even more terrifying. The blessing of unconsciousness was not hers to have.

The only feeling was her hands against metal, and the drip of her blood down her leg. That was a sensation she latched onto. At some point she couldn't recall, she'd been injured. Shouldn't she be experiencing pain? It must be shock. This all must be shock.

Wriggling her hand, she managed to get her fingers across her belly. The blood leaked under her palm, and fresh panic bloomed.

Die. I'm going to die in this box.

She didn't even recognize what the box was, or how she'd gotten into it. Only the primitive part of her brain still fought to live. These questions would never find answers.

Don't die. Breathe. Hold on.

The darkness at the corners of her vision pulled closer almost gently, compared to last time. If death was coming, it was kind. She'd wouldn't welcome it, but maybe its compassion was better than panic.

Her forehead connected with the surface of the box, and reason unraveled. Darkness pooled and took her away. The stickiness on her fingers was the last sensation for a long time.

Lost and quiet, without sound or thought, she faded into the darkness. Coming apart seemed like the best thing to do. She hovered on the edge.

Then something pulled her back: the sensation of moving. Her body touched the surface of the box again, but after how long was impossible to calculate. Consciousness flickered to life inside her, slowly at first, then growing stronger and more demanding.

Sound entered and broke the quiet. The rattle of something against the box—metallic, perhaps? She didn't want to return. Darkness seemed like the better option. It would take very little for her to spiral into there forever.

A voice—not hers, but familiar—echoed in her skull.

You don't give up. You hear me? Keep going until you can't anymore. That's our way.

Gravity took hold. She slumped down into the box, feet connecting with the surface she'd almost forgotten was down there. Pain reminded her it still existed, too. The box fell over and rolled onto its side, taking her with it. She banged her head as it went horizontal, so she couldn't be in space anymore.

That concept led to other things.

Spaceships. Planets. Soldiers.

Her brow furrowed at that last one. Where did it come from? She would've liked to have followed the thought, but there were more pressing matters. More grinding and grating noises as her box dragged along a surface. Was this a planet? No, a ship. Must be.

Voices came from outside, and she went still. Life existed beyond the box. It did before, too, but hopefully this life was not dangerous.

When she tried to take hold of them, her thoughts escaped her grasp like scattered particles. New ones formed in her mind and then evaporated. It must be something to do with her injury.

Light burst in through a glass panel in the box. Through her closed eyes, the intrusion hurt. Fear welled up, and she remained still. Had those unknown horrors found her?

The light departed, and she worked her mouth, testing whether it functioned enough for words. It did not. A lot of things were fuzzy and hard to grasp. She waited for eventual death, or whatever the box's fate was. Machinery stuttered to life. Cool air covered her face, and it seemed... good.

Lights blinked: blue, white, and back to blue. A loud clank, and the box opened.

Keeping her eyes shut, she waited for the next box, or a descent to chaos.

"I think she's okay. Bit banged up." The voice was discordant after so much silence, breaking against her ears like something sharp.

"Shit, 'bit banged up'? Look at the blood."

Hands touched hers. They were warm and shocked her enough to jerk upright.

"What the fuck?"

Her eyes ached when she opened them, and she only made out shapes moving against the harsh white. The person she startled fell backwards, and then came a rattle of metal. He must have fallen.

"Hey, hey, you're okay." Another voice, less painful to her ears, reached her. She worked her head back and forth, trying to locate the person. Her mouth seemed to belong to someone else.

"Take it easy. We've got you."

The first person, a larger shape in her vision, got back up. "Lenny, get away from her. Why is she even awake? The pod shouldn't have popped her out like a damn ice cube."

"She can hear us, I think." Hands took hold of hers again. "Let me see your injury, there."

"Great, she died of shock." The voice didn't seem like it was making a joke. Hard to tell, though.

"Shut up!" The hands moved over her belly. "Looks like the pod's trauma kit has done a pretty good job. She's just got a semi-healed cut here." A hand locked on her shoulder, helping her focus on the person's face for the first time.

He was young, with dark skin and green eyes. This one was called Lenny. Was he kind, or a killer? Either way, she was in no condition to get away from him. Her eyes were finally focusing properly, though.

"She got any freezer burn?" The second man appeared behind Lenny's shoulder. He was young as well, but with long, green hair. "Damn she's tall, but looks kinda out of it."

Lenny shot him an annoyed look before leaning in closer to her. "I'm Lenny Pope, that's my brother, Morgan. You're safe here, but this escape pod is shutting down, so we have to get you out real quick."

Panic surged through her; did she even understand how to make her limbs work? Sitting up seemed like the most she could manage. The man who called himself Lenny Pope slipped his arm around her shoulders and, with a slight grunt, levered her out. His muscles bunched as he pulled her upright. He was surprisingly strong.

Unable to do anything else, she leaned against him. His brother didn't move to help at first, but then when Lenny let out another grunt, he darted forward to help her on the other side.

She blinked, gradually acclimatizing to the light, and looked around. Her mouth was dry, but she croaked out, "What ship is this?"

The brothers helped her over to a corner and propped her up on a coil of steel rope. She clutched it as if it might save her.

Morgan glanced at his brother. "You're on the *Eumenides*. We're a family hauler, nothing fancy. What about you? Got a name? What ship were you on?"

"Give her a chance. That pod is banged up too, so she might have some freezer burn in here." Lenny tapped the side of his head. Then he pulled a bottle from his pants pocket and, unscrewing it, handed it to her.

She sniffed it. Water. She sipped enough to moisten her lips. Only then did she take a chance on more words. "Nothing."

She held out her hands and examined her arms. The clothing was dark blue camouflage, but unfortunately did not have a name tag sewn on it. That would have been convenient. The flex and play of strong muscles beneath the clothing meant nothing to someone who didn't even recognize her own body.

Morgan let out a long groan and kicked a piece of debris they must have dragged in with the pod.

"You're worried the about salvage rights?" She squinted up at them, trying to focus her eyes.

The brothers stared at each other for a second.

"Are you fucking with us?" Morgan took a step back. "You can't say where you came from, what happened, or your name, but you know about salvage rights?"

That was strange. She pressed her hand to her forehead, as if she could force the connections to come together. Her thoughts darted about, unconnected and random. Trajectories for space travel. A recipe for cornbread. The smile of a little girl in a space station. A monster in the dark. Her arm hurt.

"Hey, don't listen to him. Freezer burn works like that sometimes. Don't push it."

She studied his face. Kindness, she could recognize that.

"So no salvage, then?" A woman climbed down the ladder from above and carefully scanned the situation. Her likeness was reflected in the brothers. Their mother. She experienced a twinge of sadness out of nowhere.

"I can sign away my rights," she said. "Get me to the nearest station and I'll do it."

The older woman dropped the last few feet and stalked over. "Not going to lie. I'd appreciate it." She held out her hand. "Daniella Pope."

She placed her hand in Daniella's and shook, though she did not know where her knowledge of the act came from. "We have an agreement."

"Not if she can't remember her damn name." Morgan leaned against the far wall and crossed his arms.

"Then we'll have to help her find out," Daniella said. "We're near a moon, so for now, how about we go with Callisto? My grandmother was born there."

She blinked. It wasn't familiar, but it didn't feel either right or wrong. Still, it gave her rescuers something to call her. However, certainty stirred in her. She could not attach it to any memory, but a name bubbled up inside her.

"No, not Callisto," she said in a whisper. "My name is Mae."

Daniella nodded. "Alright, that's something. Mae, then." She scanned the hold. "Let's leave the enumeration of all this until later. Boys, get Mae here up top."

Her two sons assisted their find up the ladder to the

living quarters of the ship. It was a small vessel, civilian, and probably running on a tight budget. Mae's thoughts ran about so much that she couldn't catch them. How did she not know how she ended up in the pod, and yet she could assess this ship instantly?

Mae's feet started working, and she managed to stand on her own.

"Down here," Daniella said, guiding the newcomer to a small bench where dining must usually happen.

Mae took a seat.

An older man popped his head in. Again, she recognized physical similarities with the brothers. So he was the father, then. The way his eyes scanned over her and his family, before a welcoming smile spread across his lips, suggested he was former military.

"Didn't expect guests, but welcome to the *Eumenides*."

Daniella opened a medicine kit. "Sorry, not much in the way of supplies on board." She unraveled the sensors on an ancient-looking diagnostic pad.

Mae physically recoiled. "I can't... after all that." She gestured down towards the cargo hold as her voice trailed off.

Lenny waved his mother away. "Mom, there isn't anything that broken kit can tell you. We need to get her back to the station."

The parents shared a glance. Mae could almost see the mathematic calculations flying between them. Air, water, and fuel were expensive, and small outfits like this always existed on the knife-edge of possibility. However, the laws of rescue still stood.

She shook her head. Again, how did she know that?

Daniella put away the pad but insisted on cleaning their new arrival. She shooed the men out of the kitchen area and closed the door.

"Sorry, the showers here aren't full water, like in a bigger ship, but the steam will make you cleaner at least." She bustled around opening panels, and in short order she'd pushed the bench and table into the floor and extended a clear half-wall. Then from the hull she opened another four compartments and pulled out a steam shower head. The *Eumenides* might not be big, but she was versatile.

The older woman sighed. "I remember showering without a care at my grandfather's house. Lots of water on Cuélebre. You could stand in there all day. Sorry, the steam shower is much too quick."

The two women stared at each other for an awkward amount of time.

Daniella cleared her throat. "You're going to need to take off your clothes."

Mae stripped down and stood under the steam heads. When they turned on, she nearly jumped out. The sudden application of a sensation she'd never experienced before was a shock to the system. The heads delivered a cleansing agent and then a last blast of warmth to clean the rest of her body off. When she was done, Daniella handed her a towel and some clean clothes.

"Thank you," Mae said as she dried herself carefully. She tried not to stare at her own brown skin and limbs. They did not seem familiar, and that was terrifying. How could she not know her own body?

"The overalls are mine," Daniella said, once Mae was in them. "They should last you until we get back to Guelph." Her hand clasped Mae's, demanding her attention. Now, when she met the woman's eyes, they shifted from kindly to probing.

"Do you know if you're endangering us?"

This woman had military training, too. Mae recognized it in her posture and concern. She knew she should have lied, but she couldn't. The only option now was to tell these people the truth–whatever bit of it she had hold of.

Mae shook her head while she tied back her hair. Talking helped take her mind off the strangeness of her body and her existence. "I don't know that either. I'm sorry. I wish I could tell you."

A muscle tightened in Daniella's jaw. She scooped up Mae's discarded clothes. "Maybe there are some clues here or in the debris." She looked Mae up and down. "I'm going to go talk to my family. Please stay here."

Daniella spun around and shut the door behind her. Mae activated the bench from the floor and sat back down, her feelings in turmoil. This still didn't feel real, mainly because she didn't even seem real to herself. She stared down at her hands and tried to imagine what she'd done in the moments before entering the pod. Did she climb in, or did someone put her there?

Right now, was there someone out in the dark, missing her and wondering whether she was alive? Mae would have dearly loved to summon up their face, but every time she reached for it, she found nothing but emptiness. It was as if she were a part of the void of space itself. Her eyes fluttered, and the darkness reached out again.

5

A PREDATOR TURNS

So many were at risk.

Mae stared out into the blackness of space and considered their quarry. The bridge of the *Righteous Fury* remained silent except for the low hum of the ship's AI, EWA. Her physical manifestation stood in the shadows by the door, silent. She wore the face of a tall bald man, but since Mae's mother debriefed Erynis and ordered a full factory reset, she did not speak nearly as much as she once did.

Colonel Zula Hendricks's rangy form sat in her command chair, similarly silent. She may as well have been a part of the *Fury* herself. She seemed to embody it these days, determined and relentless. The flickering lights of the flight deck control panel traced patterns across her dark skin, and over the planes of a face marked by stress.

They were on the trail of the ship that rained death and destruction on the planet Shānmén. Her mother's brown eyes narrowed, studying the darkness before them, as if she saw the path the strange ship was on. Such a thing made no sense to Mae; human eyes didn't have the capacity to see as clearly as hers. Genetic people were still somewhat of a mystery to her.

Her outer form might've been a bespoke artificial body, undistinguishable from the flesh body of her mother, but her mind came from her father. As did her name. It was an acronym for Machine Algorithm Embodied, but also a nod to the first woman who served in the United States Marines.

Davis conceived of her during their last close call during the colony war. He'd needed to ensure his legacy would remain to assist Zula Hendricks in her fight against the Xenomorphs, but he had other plans. Perhaps an even stranger reason.

Mae reflected on his demise. His self-sacrificial gesture reflected his own anxieties as an artificial person: he didn't want the woman he loved to be alone.

Glancing back at her, Mae wasn't sure how well she performed that duty. Her mother led the Jackals, and they leapt to her command. She hadn't yet shared with her daughter any more than she did with them. Her weathered face remained a dark mask.

Mae understood the concept of human emotions. Davis built loyalty into her programming, but that was a straightforward feeling and easy for her to replicate. The emotional layers of her flesh-and-blood mother, those were much more difficult to figure out.

Davis, though he'd created her, did not see fit to leave those answers in her memory bank. Either that, or even he hadn't known.

However, on her journey, Mae became familiar with one other human emotion: anxiety. Her fingers tapped together at her side, a gesture she'd picked up from Sergeant Masako Littlefield. Mae observed that she did it when she was concerned or worried. In an effort to understand, she'd copied the gesture. It didn't help, but perhaps it took time and practice.

Zula finally broke the silence. "Anything on the scanner, Mae?"

Her mother could have asked EWA through Erynis, but intriguingly chose not to. Back on Shānmén, both turned on Mae for being different and attempting to become more humanlike. Trying to become sentient deeply offended them.

Zula reacted to protect her child. She'd ordered the system purged before they left Pylos Station, so that EWA didn't remember Mae was an artificial person. This action might have been designed to protect her, but it created an unfortunate side effect. Hiding who she was from everyone, including all the other synthetics, meant that she was unable to connect with the *Fury* at all. Instead, she needed to use the control panels like any genetic human.

It meant a lot of limitations, but this experience helped her understand her mother better.

If Mae was inside the synthetic network, she'd have immediate access to the flight data and could inform Zula in an instant. Instead, Mae peered down at the navigation screen, as reliant on it as any genetic human would be.

Another emotion she got the opportunity to study: frustration.

"We're still on the attacker's trajectory, according to the anomalies we're following. The calculations haven't changed."

Zula gave the slightest of nods. "EWA, how are the engines holding up?"

Erynis replied from the shadows. "We are operating at ninety-six percent capacity, with all signs nominal."

The colonel grunted at that before rubbing her eyes. She gave a ragged sigh.

Mae detected a tiny tremor in her right hand. All the Jackals slept in their cryogenic hibernation chambers, which was how most humans survived the dangers of deep space. However, Zula declined to climb into one on this journey.

Instead, she drank a lot of coffee and ate a lot of stimulant rations. Mae hid some to make sure her mother wasn't about to give herself a stroke. This state wasn't healthy for any human, though—even one like Colonel Zula Hendricks.

The crew being in stasis allowed the *Fury* to conserve

its resources as it raced after the strange ship. Zula dragged her cot into her ready room and kept the bridge sealed and oxygenated. Mae calculated how much rest and sustenance her mother took in.

It was never enough.

That was where they were stuck, however. Zula Hendricks was her mother, but she was also her commanding officer. Mae couldn't tell her what to do, but maybe she could try a little subtlety.

Mae turned from the screen. "Mother, since the *Fury* is on track and nothing needs your immediate attention, do you think you might rest some more?"

She'd studied all the information available on improving the parent–child relationship. Unfortunately, the majority of it was about small children, and nothing at all about one being a synthetic.

The tone of voice Mae used was chosen carefully to be neither demanding nor insulting. She'd even considered whether widening her eyes to mimic a small child might help.

Zula's lips twisted, and she dropped her head for an instant. When she looked up, the small lines around her mouth were more prominent, as if she was also being careful with her words. "While I appreciate your concern, Mae, I am more than old enough to decide when I go to bed."

Mae let out a laugh. It echoed in the empty bridge but didn't earn even a slight smile from her mother. She would have done anything to access the files Davis made during all his time with humanity. Unfortunately, when his particular subroutine stopped responding, she lost the permissions to his information. However, even without it, she was certain that the noise she'd just let out hadn't helped matters.

Zula locked eyes with her. Though they couldn't risk EWA finding out about Mae's true nature, so a sharp glance was all she allowed herself.

"You need to practice your diplomacy skills, daughter." She pushed herself up from the command chair. "But you're right. First thing you learn in the military is to take your sleep where you can." She stared out the window for 5.03 seconds, as if seeing tragedies long past. "I used to be great at doing that, but since Shānmén—well, not so much."

They'd both seen a lot of horror on that planet's surface. In the body of a combat android, Mae had even experienced battle. Like her father, she contained all the programming needed to excel at it. However, she found she didn't truly enjoy it. Perhaps being more human made her less useful in that capacity.

Zula stretched, grimacing at the popping of cartilage and muscle strain that hadn't quite healed from a lifetime of wounds. As she leaned against the doorframe to her ready room, she shot her daughter a piercing look. "Getting old isn't for the faint of heart."

Mae wasn't sure if that was a joke or not. She'd never understand what her mother was going through, because she'd never age. Maybe that was the whole point of her comment. Regardless, she decided not to attempt another laugh. Instead, she experimented with a nervous grin and a shrug.

Zula snorted. "You're learning, girl, but I suggest you keep at it. I would have gone with a nod on that one."

"Noted."

Mae's ears picked up the faintest of whines a moment before the klaxon sounded. It roared through the bridge, spinning Zula around on her heels and bringing her back to the command chair.

Mae, cognizant of her need to appear human, raced over to her own seat and buckled herself in.

"Erynis, status report," Zula barked out.

The synthetic took a step out of the shadows. "EWA has detected the ship we're pursuing has changed course unexpectedly."

The *Fury*'s screen flashed green and then displayed a trail of particulate matter veering away from the projected course. If it wasn't for the dust cloud orbiting the moon they were passing, even EWA's advanced sensors might have missed it.

"I don't see the vessel," Zula snapped, leaning forward. "Get my command team out of stasis, stat. Emergency protocol and prepare for fast burn."

The *Fury*'s bridge crew were in nearby cryopods, ready for any change in situation. EWA kept them in light stasis, not the deep slumber of the regular Jackals.

"Already done," Erynis replied. "I have initiated those protocols, and they should be on deck in five standard minutes."

Mae glanced over her shoulder. "Should I move to tactile command?"

Zula jerked her head. "I'd like a human finger on those buttons. Get over there."

Mae unbuckled and hurried to the tactile station. Spread out in front of her was complete access to the *Fury*'s full complement of armaments. Her eyes darted over the screen. "No tracking lock yet?"

Erynis's voice, when it came, contained a tone that might have been snippy. "There is none to be had. EWA's evaluation of the disturbance indicates that the enemy ship is on the dark side of the thirteenth moon."

They'd been tracking the strange horseshoe-shaped ship for a long time, and it'd never given any indication that it was aware of the *Fury*'s pursuit. Though they'd been careful to stay out of long-range scanners, no one on board—not even EWA—was certain of the ship's capabilities.

Zula instructed them to stay twice as far away from it as their own long-range scanners could reach. They tracked it by the disturbance it left in the systems it passed—a residue of a signal. They'd gotten lucky that the mining team on Shānmén detected and recorded that signal. Waves of any kind left a faint echo in the space they passed.

Without this knowledge, they would have lost the ship not long after it left UPP space.

Their target communicated with someone off and on, while the *Fury* ran completely dark.

"How'd they spot us?" Zula muttered.

The obvious conclusion was that someone betrayed them—all the suspects were human. Mae said nothing, but her mother must've been circling the same conclusion.

Three generals from the three human factions supplied the *Righteous Fury*. They came from the Union of Progressive Peoples, the United Americas, and the Three World Empire. The possibilities were endless for how a leak might have sprung up. With more people involved, the risks climbed. It was pure statistics. An aide or a lover could easily have sold them out. The other option was that one general changed their mind on this entire operation. The ramifications of that were far worse.

"Unknown," Erynis replied for EWA. "My calculations predict the optimum time for them to attack will be as we exit the orbital well of Sedna. Shall I cut the engines and alter course?"

Zula let out a long breath. It hissed over her teeth as she considered. "If we were in a fleet, that would make sense, but we're showing all our ass out here on our own. Soon as we give a signal, they'll come barreling around that moon with the orbital advantage down on us. Right now, they don't know we've figured them out."

Mae's fingers hovered over the controls, waiting for a signal. An idea ignited in her brain, but she hesitated for a micro-second. Apparently, even an artificial person could experience anxiety. Once they lost tracking on this ship that rained down death, they might never find another.

Spinning in her chair, she offered some insight. "This ship has never encountered the *Fury* before, and they can't know we are tracking their hidden signal. They have spotted us, but perhaps we can encourage them to think it is a chance encounter, and we haven't detected them yet?"

Erynis tilted his head and fixed her with his gleaming eyes. "They will know the probabilities of that are—"

Mae held up her hand as she interjected. "But they're not zero. They've spotted us, and we won't be able to run silent on them again. So we must show we're not a threat."

Zula leaned forward in her chair. "What are you suggesting?"

"We fake an ignition failure in the engines? Give them a reason to break lunar orbit early, or even better, leave us to burn up in the atmosphere."

Her mother's eyes hardened on her. "How would you do that?"

"We flicker our shields, eject a few missiles and explode them. From that distance, it has a chance of being seen as damage to the reactor core. We have been running them hot, so it's not that unlikely. That would allow us to slow down, float with the ejection, and go broadside to them." Mae grinned. "Bring those railguns into play. We could even spin to port, eject more metal in their path, but keep the debris field in front of us. I would suggest the supply barrels we took on last station fall."

"You're sneaky, girl! Davis would be proud. The crew will just have to make do with k-rations." Zula leaped to her feet. "EWA, do as Mae commands, and where's my goddamn crew?"

"Here, ma'am!"

Major Ronny Yoo and Lieutenant Gabriella Rossi appeared in the bridge's doorway. Yoo slid his lean form into the XO's chair while Rossi took her place at navigation. One curl of her dark hair was loose. It spoke to the severity of the situation that she didn't even notice. EWA could run the ship herself, but the colonel preferred humans to be in place to make those life-or-death decisions.

Strapping in, Yoo and Rossi wore drawn and pained expressions. Rapid ejection from cryosleep pods would do that. However, EWA administered a massive dose of drugs to keep them sharp. The effects would only last an hour, but then more drugs would be pumped into their system. If death didn't get in the way.

"Stand by for fast burn." Zula buckled in. "I hope it doesn't come to that, but we might need to accelerate at a moment's notice."

"Yes, ma'am," Major Yoo said.

All the chairs with humans in them inflated, locking them in place. To maintain the illusion, Mae did the same. Erynis strapped his synthetic body to the wall, so it didn't fly around during any tight maneuvers.

"We're going to fake damage," Zula said to Yoo and Rossi. "It'll buy us a little time and hopefully convince them they don't need to turn and fire, but if they do, let's be ready."

"Should I wake the whole ship?" Erynis enquired. That was beyond the automatic parameters set on EWA, but Zula maintained the authority to do it.

The colonel glanced at the three other people on the bridge. "Nothing they can do to change the outcome—that's up to us. Best stay in their pods, and if this goes south, we'll evacuate them to the planet."

Death in cyrosleep wasn't the worst fate for a soldier—at least it would be painless. Though knowing the Jackals as she did, Mae believed they'd rather go down fighting. Since there wasn't any combat for them, her mother must've believed she was doing them a kindness.

"You got that fake-out ready, EWA?"

"Confirmed," Erynis said.

"Then hit them with our best act." Zula's hands tightened on the arms of her chair.

The *Fury*'s engines spun up louder as EWA started her impression of their failure. It wouldn't do for their energy signature to give the game away. The magnetic field surrounding the ship was invisible. Mae watched the defensive station display over Major Yoo's shoulder. It dipped in a remarkable impression of the consequences of an engine failure.

"Now fire those missiles, Lieutenant Hendricks."

"Yes, ma'am. Missiles away." She punched the button. On the display screen, the missiles zipped away, their path shown by a ragged line of dots. They didn't get far. Mae detonated them just outside minimum safe distance. They might fool their enemy into thinking they'd ejected one engine.

"Now, hard to port, Rossi. Throw out those barrels. See if this bastard is afraid of a nose full of metal."

With any of the human galactic powers, Zula and her Jackals knew what their armaments and capabilities were. That was the worst part of this: they were fighting blind. They could only hope that the dropping of the black pathogen was the primary weapon. If they were lucky, this unknown ship was the equivalent of an ancient Earth airplane designed for bombing runs and not much else.

Mae's gaze flickered to the missile counter. They still had plenty left. If the *Fury* was running blind on the capabilities of their enemy, then with any luck, the reverse was also true. Their display might fool the strange ship, and not knowing their missile capacity, come in hot down the gravity well.

The bridge fell silent for a moment. If this display brought them in close enough without firing, the *Fury* might strike first.

"Enemy ship has broken lunar orbit," Erynis intoned. "She is moving into planetary orbit. Closing in on us."

"Fuck me, that's fast." Rossi's hands flickered over the navigational display.

"Lieutenant Hendricks, can you get a lock?" Zula asked. "EWA, assist."

Protocol said no synthetic mind was allowed to fire weapons, but on request, it could calculate trajectories faster than any human brain.

"Unable to comply," Erynis said from his spot, strapped to the wall. "The enemy ship is blocking our attempts to get weapons lock."

"We'll fire straight up their throat, then."

"Is the debris field slowing them down?" Rossi asked, her voice calm as she monitored the defensive shields and the engine's health.

"Negative," Erynis said as the ominous shape bore down on them. "Their shields must be constructed differently. They are de-atomizing the metal in front of them rather than deflecting them magnetically."

"Fantastic," Zula ground out. "Rossi, plot us the hell out of this debris field with maximum thrust. Let's see how they handle rock."

Watching the enemy ship move so quickly towards them was alarming. Mae calculated their diminishing odds. With no backup, they were not good.

Everything the Jackals fought for might die out here in the dark, with no one to take note. The murderers of Shānmén would go unpunished and the fate of the *Righteous Fury* would end up just another mystery in the annals of space travel.

6

A DARK ARRIVAL

The *Righteous Fury* screamed on the edge of a fast burn.

Mae mimicked the distress on the human faces around her. Zula Hendricks's stern resolve. The clenched teeth of Major Yoo. Lieutenant Rossi's streaming eyes beneath her dark, curly hair. All were models of stress and concern that went into her algorithm.

Human bodies, even trained and in their g-chairs as the bridge crew were, could not survive long exposure to extreme gravitational forces. Anything over six Gs was dangerous for extended amounts of time. Organs would get crushed and blood vessels would burst if they didn't soon pull out of such extreme acceleration.

The drug rig snapped into place on Mae's right. It was ready to administer the doses needed to keep the crew conscious and alive should the gravity well's demands be too extreme. The needle would puncture her skin but not provide her synthetic system with anything of value. Being an android in hiding was a complex thing.

Not that anyone but EWA and Erynis would notice in this moment as the *Fury* darted through the planet's debris field. Some ancient moon tumbled too close to the planet, and now Zula hoped its scattered remains would provide limited cover for her ship.

Their horseshoe-shaped pursuer didn't seem bothered, though. The effects of the gravity well did not slow it down. Their attempt to feign damage and ignorance did not fool it, and it was not about to let them escape its wrath. Mae watched the display, waiting for it to come about. What weapons would this alien ship unleash?

The craft appeared to have no engines, nor a front or a rear. It didn't need to alter course to change trajectory. It glided forward with no evidence of propulsion at all. Its speed was unnerving, as if gravity simply didn't apply to it.

"Boss." Yoo addressed Zula in a calm tone. "That thing is closing fast. No sign of this rock debris making any more of a difference than metal."

"Missiles worked on the one at Shānmén." Zula's eyes flickered to Mae. "Hit it with a barrage."

Mae slid her fingers over the controls. A trio of XIP-34B Hornet SSMs burst from the port side of the *Fury* and darted back towards their assailant. Zula leaned forward in her chair as their trajectory played out on the main screen before them.

The barrage got close, at least. The missiles' trajectory brought them near the port side of the U-shaped ship. Then, a few hundred meters from the target, they turned away, as if sliding against some unseen surface. Zula's fist tightened as they diverted and exploded uselessly across the debris field.

"I'm reading that was a small gravitational singularity." Ross's voice cracked slightly at this unknown ability making itself apparent.

Mae ran the calculations and missile specifications. They weren't made to cope with unexpected gravitational fluctuations. No armaments from any of the three galactic powers were, since humanity did not have that technology.

"Our pursuer is exceeding the parameters of known space vessels," Erynis informed them as calmly as only a synthetic could be in this situation. "EWA can no longer accurately predict its movements."

"Then concentrate on the debris field," Zula ground out.

The edge of annoyance in her voice told Mae that EWA's inability to operate outside her known specifications wasn't welcome. That was the thing with AI—it operated from a position of confirmed data. With this enemy, there was none. Certain humans actually enjoyed such unknowns, but Zula Hendricks was not one of those people. She'd been chasing Xenomorphs for years and knew a great deal about them. This new ship was only now beginning to show the commander of the *Fury* what it could do.

This display also might be the last thing they saw.

"Incoming." Rossi's words were flat. "Not missiles, ordnance unknown."

Erynis announced EWA's reaction. "Deploying thermal countermeasures."

It was their only choice, even if they didn't know what was rocketing towards them. Mae dialed into the aft cameras. The shapes were fast-moving and definitely not missiles—or, indeed, any other ordnance in her databases. They were not aerodynamic, but in the vacuum of space that wasn't required. Then, in a nanosecond, she understood.

The ship fired nothing at them. Instead, it weaponized its gravity well generation to fling the surrounding rock debris at the *Fury*. In that instant, Mae forgot all her attempts at becoming human. Her synthetic programming became entranced by the technology that made this a reality and the possibilities of what else they might put it towards. It was a pity she'd probably not have time to study it for long, because it was coming up on the *Fury* fast.

"Evasive maneuvers. Brace, brace."

EWA's prime directive was to protect the humans inside her shell. That meant she ran various complicated calculations in the moments before the devices struck. The AI accelerated and turned, trying to bring the ship about to protect the sleeping Jackals in their cryo chambers.

The g-forces increased with these maneuvers. Mae's mother, Yoo, and Rossi let out strained grunts as it pressed their bodies back into the chairs. EWA automatically shot their systems with drugs to compensate, but they blacked out regardless. Mae slumped back as they did, still mimicking their reactions. Her other senses were more than enough to experience the results of the impact.

The hull rang and shuddered. Alarms screamed, though there was not one human awake to hear them. Rattling indicated the smaller debris bouncing off the side of the ship.

"Decks eighteen to twenty-one compromised," Erynis reported as the *Fury* leveled out.

Zula was the first to regain consciousness. "Damage report. Casualties."

Mae jerked her head up and ran her fingers across the console in front of her. Yoo stirred, but Rossi was still out. "Damage to the port hanger bay. We've lost two drop ships. The hull on decks nineteen and twenty is breached, but we haven't lost any pods. So far."

Yoo let out a grunt while Zula stayed silent.

"We are losing oxygen on those decks." Erynis's eyes flickered, a sure sign that EWA's immersive processing power was being directed to piloting the ship while trying to keep the Jackals on those decks alive. "We are closing all the relevant hatches."

"Flinging fucking rocks at us." Yoo seldom swore, which was as indicative as Erynis's gestures. "Railguns are still active on the port, boss."

"Open fire, full spread. Let's test their defenses to the maximum."

The rumble of the guns echoed down the *Fury*'s corridors. The ship was still spinning, which helped create a spiral of fired projectiles.

"Report," Zula snapped at her daughter.

Without being jacked into the system, the information flow seemed inordinately slow. Mae's gaze darted across the screen. The spread of incendiary rounds was affected by more defensive gravity well production, but the chaos of their attack appeared harder for the alien ship to knock aside. Whatever it was using was limited in scope or calculating power.

Red hits stacked up on her display. "Impacts on the outer hull on the starboard wing. Twenty-five point three percent of our ordnance made it through."

Rossi and Yoo let out synchronized shouts of exuberance. Zula did not join them. "How are they taking the damage? Any sign of venting gases?"

Mae punched the display up onto the main screen so her mother could see it herself. If it wasn't for EWA marking the impacts, they might not have been able to tell at all.

No telltale trails of gas spiraled around the ship, though when Mae enhanced the image, there were definite punctures in the ship's hull.

"They need some kind of gas to breathe," Rossi said. "I mean, they must, right?"

"Well, we sure do," Zula replied. She glanced at Mae, knowing full well that she was the only person on board capable of surviving without oxygen. It'd be some comfort to her, but there were all her Jackals to think of. Her eyes drifted to Yoo. They'd been through so much, and his opinion mattered. "Ronny, thoughts?"

Major Yoo only took a moment to form them. "We go in for a hard burn, ram as much railgun as we can down this thing's throat—and it'll have time to throw even bigger rocks at us."

"Then the Jackals will die out here," Mae dared to interrupt. "That will not help our mission."

Yoo shot his other option over his shoulder at his commander. "Or we get some distance and eject the cryopods into planetary atmosphere. We'd lose some, but there is a chance they'd get picked up by someone."

Zula rubbed her hand over her hair. Her jaw twitched in controlled anger. "EWA, perform evasive maneuvers as best you can. See if you can get some distance between us and that ship. Mae, scan that planet, and let me know if there's any chance of survival for my Jackals."

The *Fury* lurched left and right as the ship's AI plotted the optimum course through the debris field. Mae finished her task with as much efficiency.

"Plutarch II has a two-hundred-degree surface temperature. The atmosphere is eighty-four percent carbon dioxide, and the surface gravity is 1.8 Earth's."

"So no fun expeditions, but they'd have a chance." Zula gestured at Erynis. "All power to the engines."

The synthetic responded. "EWA is operating the engines

above their recommended levels, and the alien ship is maintaining speed."

"Fire railguns!"

Mae obeyed, not letting the guns cool, but keeping up continuous fire to dissuade their pursuer. It didn't work.

"I'm reading a spike in thermal energy in the open section of the ship," Rossi reported.

It must mean that another gravitational singularity was about to hurl more rocks at the *Fury*. Mae wondered how she would feel, alone in the vacuum of space. How long would it take for her systems to shut down? Would she go mad before then?

"Incoming!" Yoo yelled, and strangely, he did not sound worried. More… jubilant.

Mae switched to the midsection cameras, and even her synthetic mind could not have predicted what she saw: a mid-sized ship, shaped like a black arrow, darted between the *Fury* and her attacker. It managed to appear both new in shape and battered and scarred at the same time. It was, however, able to penetrate the gravity shield where rocks and metal could not.

The ship conformed to no known parameters, but as it passed close to the *Fury*'s sensors, Mae experienced a brand-new feeling. Could it be hope, or maybe relief? She believed the appropriate response would have been a whoop of delight—or at least a smile.

She hoped to have enough time to examine which one it was.

"I'm reading the new arrival is on an attack vector." Rossi's fingers ran over her console, bringing the newcomer's flight to the main screen.

The black ship kept close to their enemy, skirting the edges of the generated gravity well. It concentrated its attack on the small pieces of damage the *Fury* already did with its railgun. It fired something large and dense into the hull and then appeared to drag it. This fresh attack opened up a large wound in the horseshoe-shaped ship's side.

Zula leaned forward in her chair. "I want confirmation on this new arrival's hit. Give me a damage report."

"Confirmed damage." EWA zoomed the image in closer to their attacker. "Unable to project impact on their systems, but it seems significant."

The ship they'd been tracking showed no engine in the front or rear, but it slowed under this fresh attack.

"Bring us about to starboard," Zula snapped. "Protect the damage we have to our port side. I don't want us ejecting any cryo escape pods. We're not losing anyone when we're this close, but assist with every railgun and missile we still have available."

Mae sat a little taller. "Yes, ma'am."

The *Fury* banked around to the colonel's command.

"It's the only scratch put on the damn thing. Make it happen," Zula said.

The damage to EWA was significant, but the calculations were well within Mae's parameters, too. She didn't bother to ask Erynis or the ship's AI. It took longer for Mae to punch in the coordinates than it took her to work the math.

The new arrival circled back in a graceful arc and gave the bridge crew a view of its weapon. It looked like an old-style anchor someone cobbled together. For an improvised weapon, it was extremely effective.

As the black ship darted away, the *Fury*'s missiles found the wound. Whatever systems their new ally hit, it must have included the device used to create the gravitational singularity. Opening up a full spread of railguns on their attacker was a beautiful experience. Mae tasted anger tinged with blinding satisfaction.

The enemy ship might not need internal gases, but as their combined attacks tore away a section of hull on the port side, it did irreparable damage to the ship's structural integrity. Mae joined in the cheer as the ship that they'd chased for so long lost control. Bombarded with the stone debris and unable to deflect it as it had previously done, it shattered and tore apart into pieces of hull. Mae tracked the largest interior piece as the atmosphere of the planet caught it and dragged it down to burn.

The g-chairs released the deck crew, and they all staggered to their feet to observe the destruction. Mae grinned along with Yoo and Rossi. Only Zula Hendricks frowned.

"There goes our lead," she said with a sigh. "But better them than us." She pointed towards their savior. "Back to your stations. We have one more thing to find out. Who just rode in and saved our asses? I want to shake their hand and ask them how the hell they did it."

Mae's eyes narrowed on the ship.

"*Righteous Fury*, this is the *Blackstar*." The voice broke through on their comms. "Do I have your permission to dock? I've been looking for you for a long time." It sounded male, and slightly cracked. The pilot might be as torn up as his ship.

Zula's expression shifted to one of caution. Few knew the name of their vessel, but whoever this was, he saved the Jackals.

"Permission granted." Mae's mother thumbed the comms button off on her chair. "Let's roll out the umbilical docking cable for this guy, but slow it down a little. I want a unit of Jackals waiting for his arrival." She stared out at the vessel, a frown forming. "I like his style, but that doesn't mean I trust him."

7

THE LOST RETURN

The ship screamed as the blast tore her apart. Panic flooded Mae, but not for herself—for the crew. A woman cried out in rage. Mae echoed that outrage. A primitive wail ripped up her throat.

"Hey! Hey, are you alright?"

Mae thrashed as hands grabbed hold of her. Escape or fight were her only options.

"Mae! You're safe. Calm down."

The voice wasn't angry or afraid; it was unperturbed. Something about it reached down into her brain and disconnected her from the nightmare she'd fallen into.

Mae opened her eyes to find Lenny leaning over her, holding her hands in his. Her breathing hitched as she jerked away from his touch. Attachment to others was dangerous. How she knew, she couldn't say. This was like the other dreams, foggy and hard to hold on to. Even as she tried to recall the dream, the details evaporated. Frustration welled inside Mae.

She pushed herself up from the bench but didn't meet his eyes. "I'm... I'm sorry. I guess I drifted back to sleep."

"You've slept enough." Lenny shrugged, attempting to make light of it.

Daniella Pope leaned against the doorway to the galley, eyes raking over this newcomer to her home. "I jerked you out of stasis pretty quick. We have emergency adrafinil shots in our medical kit for that. Can make you a bit shaky, but if you want it—"

Mae struggled to her feet and held up a hand. The idea of a shot worked like a jolt of caffeine. "No, no shots, thanks. I'll be alright."

Daniella gave a slow nod, but Mae understood her expression. Like most mothers, she was cautious about those she let close to her family. Mae could only respect that.

Shit, parents. Mae didn't even know if somewhere out there, she had a father or a mother worrying about her. Hell, she might even have a partner and children of her own. She should know these things. She was embarrassed that she didn't. People would judge her if she didn't figure it out. How could she not have this basic information?

"Mom, don't you have some navigation to do?" Lenny jerked his head back towards the cockpit.

Daniella pressed her lips together before answering. "Your dad's got the helm."

After the initial shock of finding a person in the debris cloud wore off, she had become more calculating and suspicious of Mae.

"I've been thinking if there is some way to thank you all for what you've done for me." Mae cleared her throat. "As agreed, I'm going to sign over salvage rights when we reach Guelph."

"No one wanted to bring it up, just in case… you know… freezer burn does strange things to the mind." Lenny grinned nervously, and glanced across at his mother. Her expression didn't change. "That's great, right, Mom?"

The lines between Daniella Pope's brows tightened into a frown. "Yeah, Lenny, real great. Except for the fact she can't even remember what happened to her, or what ship this debris even came from. Kinda important if you want to sign anything."

"Oh. I didn't think of that." Mae's cheeks grew hot. She'd tried to offer a solution and now she'd only revealed what an idiot she was.

"Shit, Mom. She just came out of a deep freeze. Give her a break."

"I'm trying. I'm really trying." Daniella glanced at her wrist-pd and scrolled through lines of data. The small square of glass allowed her to access all the information from her ship. "Some good news. Looks like we're going to make Guelph in three days, just before our oxygen runs out. Your brothers plotted a nice slingshot around the planet Duendes. So we won't suffocate. Which is nice."

Mae searched for something positive or amusing to say, but the words died in her mouth. Daniella spun away and stomped back towards the cockpit.

It all made Mae feel guilty for surviving—which was ridiculous.

"Hey," Lenny said, squeezing her shoulder, "don't worry about Mom. She's always counting units. Oxygen, water, and coffee. Makes her prickly sometimes, but she wouldn't have wanted you to keep floating by."

Mae resolved to avoid Daniella as much as possible. Her fierce protectiveness suggested that she would prioritize her family's safety, even if it meant putting their new arrival in danger.

The next three days settled into a restricted but manageable monotony.

Lenny took charge of spending time with Mae, while the rest of his family kept busy elsewhere. He also cooked and provided coffee for Daniella, Morgan, and the father, William. It meant that Mae could keep herself tucked away in the canteen and stare out the small window.

Lenny would come sit with her and try to explain what part of space they were in, and the various qualities and history of the planets in the system. It didn't take more than a day for that vein of conversation to run dry.

After the planets, Lenny moved on to their destination, Guelph Station. Mae guessed he was attempting to make it sound more interesting than it actually was by how often he referred to the magnificent views from the observation deck. It was a station far from the prosperous corners of the galaxy, Lenny admitted that much.

He eventually gave up trying to make it seem more interesting, and by the third and final day, he'd resorted to teaching Mae card games and tricks, which he called 'magic'. Not willing to insult the one kind person on the ship, Mae did not correct him on that score.

Instead, she nodded and smiled as he tried to teach her ancient Earth games. He seemed to have a weak grasp of the rules, and a poor memory of the names of the games, too. While he chatted on, Mae concentrated on attempting to figure her way through to her own memories. Shards of recollection spun around her. A ship burning through space. A woman's curly dark hair clinging to her forehead over frightened eyes. A moon looming dangerously close. None of that meant anything: all she hung her existence on was the name Mae.

Without memories, what was she? A broken, unprepared human in a world that even Lenny described as harsh. People needed connection to others. The idea of people Mae didn't remember out there in the endless dark, searching for her, missing her, made sleep impossible.

Finally, she understood that these distractions of Lenny's were not doing her any favors.

She took hold of his hand and stopped it from laying out another row of cards. He froze, and Mae, examining his strange expression, jerked her hands back.

"I appreciate what you're trying to do," she said with a

smile, "but I need more. You've told me about the station itself, but what about the rest of the galaxy? The companies and governments that move everything around. I need to know about them, too."

Lenny held Mae's gaze for a moment, and she read reluctance there.

"It's alright. I need to have information about the world—good and bad. You won't break me with the truth."

He glanced out the window again. "I don't want to lie, but you're right, you need everything. Guelph is a Jùtóu Combine station and is located in UPP space."

When Mae tapped the side of her head to remind him, he let out a short, awkward laugh.

"Oh shit, yeah, sorry. The Combine is a company, a pretty big deal. Makes everything you can think of. The UPP is the Union of Progressive Peoples. They're a federation, started in '08. Based on Earth, but they've got colonies like New Kiev, Xiang—"

"Damn, little brother, you really listened during all those lessons." Morgan grinned as he tied his hair up. A sure sign he meant business. "Never would have guessed that shit would actually be useful?"

"She asked, alright?"

His brother rolled his eyes. "All you need to know about the Combine and the UPP is that they grind down people like us. We have to live in their world. So if you suddenly remember you're a wealthy princess, you'll want to jet out of Guelph straight away. If not, well, then you better discover some skills *pronto*."

Mae frowned at that. She understood her precarious position, but Morgan hadn't exactly put it in the kindest of terms. Without any clue who she was, how would she operate in this world? Mae might have forgotten her past, but she could still somehow recall the concept of capitalism.

Lenny didn't deny anything his brother blurted out. Instead, he opened a drawer and slid a disc across the table to Mae.

"It's a lesson for kids on the history of space, the powers, and importantly, the companies. Guelph isn't important enough to be in it, but it will give you an idea of what we all deal with. Play it on the canteen display."

Mae nodded and took the data drive. When the brothers retreated, she slid it into the slot under the small screen opposite her seat. Her life depended on taking in as much information as possible. Huddled in the canteen, Mae absorbed all she could about the Earth governments, their reach, and aspirations from the past. However, she found that it contained limited information about the corporations.

It mentioned Weyland-Yutani, the Jùtóu Combine, and Seegson, along with their governments and home systems. The disc did not go into any real detail beyond that, and something pricked the back of Mae's mind that it was important she noticed this.

She subsisted on coffee and stims, forcing her body to comply. By the time Guelph Station came into view through the *Eumenides'* porthole, Mae had devoured all the knowledge on the data drive. Hopefully she'd absorbed enough from it to find her feet a little quicker.

Staring out at Guelph Station, she observed its three decks stacked beneath a simple, circular shape.

"Yeah, doesn't look like much, does it?" Lenny appeared at the canteen doorway, his expression sour.

"I thought you'd be glad to be off the *Eumenides*?"

He shrugged. "I don't know how I should feel about station or ship."

It surprised her that he didn't lower his voice any; after all, this ship was his family home. She calculated that her arrival gave him an excuse to be more open.

She gestured to the bench next to her. He took the offer, and they sat together as the *Eumenides* waited for its turn to dock. Mae got a good, panoramic look at the station, and Lenny acted as her guide to the ships in port.

He recognized all of them. His knowledge was even greater than the disc he'd given her.

"Mining vessels," he said, bouncing an empty coffee cup from hand to hand. "They're all old and beat up. Nothing really interesting visits Guelph." His lips quirked up. "Apart from you, that is."

He meant it as a joke, but Mae turned away. She wanted to tell him she wasn't interesting at all. That, in fact, she wanted to be insignificant, if possible. However, she didn't deny that her inability to remember would make her an object of interest.

Lenny touched the back of her hand lightly. "I'm sorry. Look, we'll all help you get on your feet. Mom said we won't even report the debris until you've figured out who you are. We'll keep it off the records for now."

William Pope popped his head around the corner of the door. "Hey, Lenny, your mom wants you up front to—ah—help with docking."

Lenny let out a tortured sigh and got to his feet. "I'll be back once we're parked. Try to enjoy the view."

He followed his father down the corridor and left Mae alone with the window.

His conversation was meant to calm her, but once Lenny left, the effect evaporated. As the station grew closer and closer, panic built inside Mae. Part of her wanted to rush to the airlock and throw herself out. This self-destructive thought she didn't give voice to.

Instead, as she watched, hugging her knees, the dark dreams that lingered inside her took over. Lenny and the *Eumenides* faded away until she was on another, quite different vessel.

8

FROM THE OUTSIDE CORNERS

Colonel Zula Hendricks ordered engineering and support crew to be awoken from cryosleep immediately. The rest of the troops would emerge from their pods at a more sedate pace, with fewer drugs involved. EWA also woke two units to protect Colonel Hendricks as she met this mysterious savior of theirs.

Her mother ordered Mae to take charge of any repairs the ship needed. It was not quite the task she wanted, but she was part of the military chain of command now.

She turned on all the maintenance robots and reviewed their tasks to make them as efficient as possible. They trundled out from their racks to repair the most important systems. Certainly, there was plenty they could do to make the *Fury* space-worthy, but the damage report was ugly.

Many decks were closed off behind airlocks. Their

engines were damaged, but that was beyond the ability of engineering and the robots to repair completely. They would need a station repair dock to recover from tangling with an alien ship. Mae wasn't sure if the *Righteous Fury* would be battle ready for quite some time.

This report she delivered to her commanding officer's wrist-pd. Zula took in the numbers with a stoic grimace. Dropping her arm, she stared out the view screen as the arrow-shaped black ship moved into the docking bay.

"Good job, Lieutenant." Her tone suggested she understood Mae dealt with these activations swiftly. "You should join me meeting this savior of ours." It wasn't a question.

"I am curious. It swooped in to save the day, but it was not in any of our databases. It must be some kind of prototype. That's... interesting." She'd been practicing curiosity, and this exchange told her she'd added it successfully to her programming.

Synthetics were always seeking more data to input. It wasn't too much of a stretch to hone that into a more human emotion.

Zula chuckled. "Alright, then. I wouldn't want to stunt your development or anything."

They rode down in the elevator, along with Major Yoo. A section of heavily armed Jackals awaited them under the command of Sergeant Masako Littlefield. As one of Zula Hendricks's confidantes, she was one of the few who knew about her daughter's true nature.

Maintaining military discipline, Masako still raised her chin a fraction in acknowledgement. Mae found it strange how when the sergeant called her "little sis," it made her smile. Having her here was comforting—and Mae couldn't say why.

The section lined up between their commanding officer and the airlock until the ship was safely in the bay.

Mae noted that her mother only carried a sidearm, while Major Yoo kept a pulse rifle slung across his back. They'd armed the unit of Jackals in every conceivable way. Whatever emerged from that black ship, they'd protect their commander.

A strange mixture of excitement and concern ran through her personality matrix. The bay doors closed, and the docking procedure cycled in the air. Only then did the airlock open before them.

The Jackals fell into columns on each side of Colonel Hendricks as she strode towards the strange vessel. Mae focused her attention on it, scanning on all frequencies. Everything seemed safe—at least on the exterior.

The ship's main hatch bore the emblem of Weyland-Yutani. The company was famous for its innovation, experimentation, and complete lack of morals. They dotted the galaxy with research stations, both known and black sites. Colonel Hendricks and her Jackals tangled with them frequently.

It wasn't a surprise, then, to see an unknown, unregistered ship with their name on it. However, it definitely wasn't new; long sections of paint were missing on its hull, and the edges appeared burned, as if it'd flown too close to a star.

When the hatch opened, a single figure stepped out. He wore a torn jumpsuit, but no helmet.

He marched towards them, heedless of the Jackals suddenly raising their rifles.

"A Bishop model?" Mae stepped a fraction closer to her mother. "He appears unarmed."

Zula nodded but didn't order her Jackals to stand down.

Their savior intrigued Mae a great deal. He wore a familiar face. Both Weyland-Yutani and Seegson used it for a variety of synthetics, including the Bishop line. Nonetheless, this was not a standard model. The synthetic that stood before them appeared to have suffered some major damage. Mae didn't need to conduct a full scan to figure that out.

He wore the marks of change on his face. His synthetic skin was in two tones. A ragged and badly sealed seam arched from his right temple over his nose and ended under his left ear. Both halves were also a distinctly different color: one was a Caucasian tone, RGB (255,224,189), while the other was blistered and red. That was not a tone any Weyland-Yutani synthetic ever wore.

Mae wondered what caustic substance damaged this model. The damage left his jaw misaligned, probably a replacement from a different model. In addition, the synthetic's right hand was held together by rough seams, though he attempted to conceal this defect by wrapping his left hand around it.

Why would anyone, synthetic or otherwise, not have that fixed?

Mae's head bubbled with questions she understood were too improper to voice. She waited for a hint from her mother on how to handle this odd situation.

The newcomer smiled, a crooked gesture due to the misalignment of his synthetic skin.

"I hope my arrival was not too late."

Zula scanned the synthetic and did not bother to conceal her surprise. "*You* are the pilot of this ship?"

"The *Blackstar*." The synthetic's lips quirked. "She's quite a beauty, isn't she, Colonel Hendricks?"

"And fast—" Major Yoo added, before stopping abruptly as he realized the newcomer identified their commanding officer.

Mae's mother didn't blink. "I presume you have a good reason to know my name?" That icy tone meant she was a moment away from pulling her weapon.

The synthetic raised his damaged hands in a graceful and careful movement. "That was my mistake to use it without offering mine. Forgive me, it has been a long time since I communicated with humans in a physical form. I was once called Rook, and I am entirely at your and your Jackals' service."

Father. He is also called Father, but he is not yours. He is more, and less now.

The word lingered in Mae's mind, though that should have been impossible without a network connection. The voice was her own father's. She hadn't heard from Davis since they landed on Pylos Station after the deadly Shānmén event. Was this whisper a sign that his subroutine wasn't gone completely? And why was he calling Rook 'Father'? Perhaps the remains of Davis were only scattered clumps of unrelated data. Synthetics couldn't get dementia, but they could lose their logic pathways given enough damage.

"We owe you our thanks," Zula said softly, "but I hope you understand this precaution."

She jerked her head, and Sergeant Littlefield stepped forward with a pair of restraint cuffs. They worked on both humans and synthetics. Human prisoners would receive an electric shock if they did not fully comply, whereas synthetics received a localized EMP pulse to override their systems.

Zula opened her palm to show him she held the trigger.

The newcomer exhibited no signs of offense or resistance. He stood, wrists outstretched, until they locked the cuffs on tight. He turned his head and smiled at Mae.

Something about his expression stirred a feeling that might have been awkwardness or guilt. Either way, she blurted out, "I'm Mae Hendricks."

Rook's eyebrows shot up at that. "A storied mother can sometimes be so hard to live up to. Believe me, I've had experience."

A strange but daring observation from someone they'd only just met. Mae smiled back.

"I'd prefer a conversation in my ready room," Zula snapped. The Jackals lined up in the elevator, and they rode in a tense silence.

All the while, Rook looked around, an almost wistful smile crossing his lips. How a synthetic managed that was quite baffling to Mae. Whatever he was, his interior configuration was as irregular as his exterior.

They reached the ready room, and they ushered in the bound Rook. He took a seat when Zula indicated he should. She and Yoo stood behind her desk. The unit of Jackals, she banished to stand outside.

Mae placed herself near enough to the new arrival to move if he became violent. The urge to initiate a network connection with him was powerful—if irrational.

He stared regretfully out the window of the ready room as the remaining pieces of the alien ship's hull spiraled past. His gaze fixed on the largest piece—a section of the curved end—and he let out a sigh.

Mae followed his gaze. The ship's remains joined the ring of debris orbiting the planet. Soon enough, it would get crushed and destroyed beyond recognition.

"Condemned to orbit forever," Rook observed, and Mae started. Had he figured out she was a synthetic as well and somehow created a network connection? Or was it merely coincidence that he was thinking the same? She detected no intrusion into her systems, but something about this strange unit unsettled her. Like the alien ship, she suspected she didn't have enough information to confirm his operational parameters.

Zula shot him a bitter smile. "No need to be sad about it. It would have destroyed both of us if it could."

Rook rested his wrists on his thighs and examined the humans in the room. "The *Righteous Fury* is an impressive ship, but no match for a juggernaut, I'm afraid. Few are."

His casual use of that name implied further knowledge. Zula and Yoo were mostly successful at hiding their surprise.

The colonel took her chair behind the desk to give her a moment. "And yet, you and your *Blackstar* know how to bring one down?"

"I have studied our enemy, and my particular history has made that easier than it has been for you. It is not a slight to your ship or your crew."

Zula's lips pressed together. Mae's mother did not like to be beholden to anyone, least of all a stranger. "Then it was lucky you found us then when you did, Rook."

"I know humans like to believe in fate, or some higher universal order, but in fact I only followed the data trail you left. The *Fury* is very important to me, you see."

Silence descended on the room, and Major Yoo's finger twitched fractionally close to his sidearm.

Zula let out a long breath. "You better be quick to make that sound less threatening. Our operation depends on only a few knowing about our mission. We operate outside the boundaries of normal Earth authorities, and we like it that way."

"Precisely why I am here." Rook opened a small pocket in his jumpsuit.

Mae detected no weapons or heat signatures. She signaled to Zula with one hand that this was not an attack, or else the colonel might have pushed the restraint cuffs' trigger.

Rook placed a data disc on Zula's desk and pushed it towards her. She crooked an eyebrow but didn't reach forward to take it.

Rook didn't appear offended. "This data was entrusted to me by Doctor Blue Marsalis. She was—" he paused "—an exceptional mind who worked for Weyland-Yutani in weaponizing the Xenomorph."

Now, Zula stared at the data drive as if it was poisoned. This doctor worked on something Mae's mother had fought against for the greater part of her life. She could only think of such a person as a villain. "What the fuck would I want with that information?"

"Doctor Marsalis was a complicated, tortured woman. Single-minded in the pursuit of saving herself from a terrible illness. However, along the way, she came across deeply secret information on company black sites. This she entrusted to me before her death, and I knew it belonged in the hands of Zula Hendricks above any other human."

His expression seemed pained to Mae, but there were subtle pulls on his face that told her that her fellow synthetic was holding back some information. What she wouldn't have given to hack into his memories through a shared network, but that would have definitely revealed her true nature to him. Though she couldn't be sure that he hadn't already figured that out.

They produced many versions of the Bishop-model synthetic, and features and abilities improved along the way. With this one calling himself Rook apparently having repaired himself, she couldn't be sure what his functionality might still be.

Zula leaned forward, took the disc, and held it in one hand as if it were something beautiful but deadly. Despite her innate suspicion, the idea of having access to corporate black site information must have been intoxicating. After a moment, she handed it to Yoo. "Go have this scanned by Erynis in a closed unit before we load it into EWA's system."

The major saluted, took the disc, and left the ready room.

Rook nodded, a slight smile pressing his lips upward. "I must confess, there is one other reason I sought you out."

Zula's eyes darted to Mae. For a human, the colonel's face was a mask, but her daughter read her far better than most. She'd inherited her father's knowledge, and he knew Zula Hendricks better than any synthetic understood a human.

The commander of the *Fury* was curious, but suspicious.

She didn't dare to trust someone after such a small amount of time, but deep down, Mae understood her mother wanted desperately to find hope in the dark after such a long time spent fighting. They'd had so little of it.

"Don't keep me in suspense, I'm not real fond of it." Zula frowned to hide anything like softness.

"I intercepted a signal, and using the information from Doctor Marsalis's records, I deciphered a hidden order for an H-AC278. It is one of the few solvents that you can use in a laboratory when working with *Plagarius Praepotens*."

Mae scanned her internal databases, but nothing remotely close to that name came up.

"Forgive me," Rook said with a wave of his hand, "I forget sometimes that Dr. Marsalis's work is still proprietary to Weyland-Yutani. *Plagarius Praepotens* is the mutagenic substance a Xenomorph facehugger injects into its host. The request for this solvent came from one of the black sites listed on that disc I have handed over."

Only then did Zula display any emotion. She barely controlled her rage, and her hands clenched on the surface of her desk. "And where was this order coming from?"

"Minos Station." Rook tilted his head. "I thought the *Blackstar* and the *Fury* might want to pay it a visit? By chance, this attack gives you a believable reason to go there. On paper, Minos creates spaceship parts and provides docks for repairs."

Colonel Hendricks and the Jackals raided distant outposts that were conducting secret experiments on Xenomorphs for purposes of warfare. Before the destruction of Shānmén, it was their primary concern. Now it was again.

Zula got to her feet. "Mae, I'm assigning you to take care of our new guest. Make sure if he needs anything, he gets it."

Mae understood the implication: she was to monitor their new guest as only another synthetic could. It was an assignment that she would have to conduct with great care.

Rook smiled and gave no indication that he found the observation a slight. "Then let me show you my own vessel, Mae Hendricks. I think you will find it quite interesting."

Mae reflected his smile. She'd become rather good at projecting an innocent-seeming demeanor.

"Thank you. I'd appreciate a tour."

"Excellent." He rose to his feet but didn't ask for her to remove the restraints. He bore it all with remarkable grace. It did nothing to reassure Mae, however. She was determined to remain alert.

While her right hand flipped open the holster on her hip, she gestured him towards the door. Bishop models weren't known to be violent, but she wasn't taking any chances with this obviously altered unit.

Major Yoo passed them, shooting Mae a look that she interpreted to be a reminder to watch herself. It was unnecessary, but she appreciated it.

As she followed Rook, she heard her mother inform Yoo that they already had a new destination. The Jackals acquired a new target. Hopefully, they could repair the *Fury* enough to make it.

9

INTO THE LABYRINTH

"What do you make of Minos Station, then?" Zula asked, her hands crossed behind her back.

Mae took up the place beside her mother and looked out the view port. They were deep in Three World Empire territory, and below the station's name, in letters almost the same size, was the Weyland-Yutani emblem. The huge yellow W, with the inspirational motto 'Building Better Worlds', always seemed the ultimate irony.

Four transport ships were in dock, three dark except for running lights. Behind the ungainly shape of Minos Station loomed the ice planet LV-895, or Dimitar. The atmosphere of the slowly spinning, pale green planet was incapable of sustaining human life. After Yoo cleared Rook's disc, Mae absorbed all the information. Weyland-Yutani chose this location because it was rich in minerals for its cover story. The station's purpose was to manufacture vital parts for the 3WE military and merchant fleet.

Its most unusual and expensive feature was the space elevator. The shining thread hung from the station and spiraled down to the planet's surface. A network of defensive satellites prevented anyone from landing on the planet directly.

"The elevator is certainly quite an outlay for the company." Mae narrowed her eyes at the thread. "The cost of constructing the tether from diamond nanothreads must have been worthwhile."

"Dimitar is rich in many minerals used in the part factory, and the gravity is thirty-nine percent less than Earth standard." Zula folded her arms. "That gives at least the appearance of a reason for the elevator." Her tone indicated that it did not convince her. She rubbed at the frown lines embedded in her forehead. Mae noted that ever since Shānmén, they'd never quite gone away. She ran a quick check on her mother's heartbeat. It seemed normal. Though how long that would last was anyone's guess.

"But that doesn't explain why such an industrial station would want a solvent capable of working on a mutagenic substance." Rook came up so quietly that neither Mae nor her mother heard him. He stared out the view port alongside them, his head tilted as if he couldn't quite understand what they were peering at.

He was certainly an unusual synthetic—unique among

the Bishop models. He'd happily shown off everything about his ship, the *Blackstar*, but the one thing he didn't reveal was what caused the damage to both his jaw and his skin. Mae guessed that even if they were connected via a synthetic network, he would have firewalled that information from her.

As much as she was scanning him, she was certain he was doing the same to all the *Fury*'s crew. Mae tightly maintained and monitored her internal electro-magnetic signatures. Her custom body contained a complex system to counter passing scans. A deep repair scan would reveal her, but such things were available only at synthetic maintenance facilities. However, Rook was an unknown; he could have unknown ways to literally get under her skin.

So it was a good thing that her mother stood between them. Their new arrival had not yet indicated that he'd worked out she was synthetic.

His half-baked appearance suggested little care for what others thought, but he'd remained plugged into the *Blackstar* for years. Though she'd looked inside, she'd not been able to examine its systems closely. It might have helped her to better judge what Rook was. He perplexed and worried Mae, but his help saving the *Fury* proved his worth to the Jackals' mission—for now.

Zula shook her head. "We have to crack this nut open and see what we can find. Let's hope those papers from General Cunningham are still good, or this will be a quick visit." She turned to her daughter. "Mae, I'm going to have eyes on me the moment we get on station, so I'm going to need you to poke around for me."

"Yes, Colonel," she replied. Although she hadn't received specific counter-intelligence programming, she'd downloaded information packets on various military operations that she hadn't utilized yet. It would also be good practice to stretch her assimilation into human culture.

"I presume you're not giving her a weapon?" Rook shot Mae an appraising glance. For an android, he possessed quite the grasp of the intricacies of human expressions.

"That would negate the point of keeping things quiet. Sidearm only, as per regulations. Since you're worried, Rook, how about you keep Mae company? I'd appreciate someone watching her back."

It would also make for another excellent chance to observe their recent savior. Mae didn't need to read her mother's mind on that score.

Zula jerked her head. "Can't put this off. Let's get on station and see what kind of Wey-Yu tight-ass is running it."

Rook and Mae followed in the colonel's wake as she left the bridge and headed for the umbilical that connected the *Fury* to Minos Station. Yoo and Erynis left their stations and joined the gathering away team. Zula summoned Shipp to meet the party at the elevator.

With both Rook and Erynis at her back, Mae experienced a hint of nervousness. It might've been totally illogical, but it almost seemed she could feel their eyes on the back of her neck. She reminded herself that this path to full consciousness she'd embarked on also made her vulnerable to supposition and fallacies. Not all feelings were pleasant ones.

When Captain Olivia Shipp joined them, it only got worse. Shipp was her mother's most trusted confidante, and her sharp gaze always picked up on the smallest detail.

"No security detail, ma'am?" Shipp asked in a low voice as they neared the umbilical access point. She locked eyes with Mae and lifted her chin in acknowledgement. The tall, raw-boned woman with cropped brown hair spent many hours conversing with Zula's daughter, and often revealed a gentle humor. Now, none of that showed. She instead presented as stern as the *Fury* herself.

"We're going in covert on this one. We sent a message that we're looking for some repairs and a supply restock after an engagement. It'd be suspicious if we turned up with a platoon."

Shipp's expression didn't suggest she was happy with the answer, but she didn't argue with her superior officer. They lined up at the airlock entrance to the umbilical and waited for the station's clamps to disengage.

It took longer than was customary or expected.

Mae's internal clock gave her an exact count, but she didn't dare point that out in front of Rook. Zula was, however, only a beat behind her.

She shifted fractionally from one foot to the other. "EWA, what's the holdup?"

Erynis replied from behind them. "Minos control is

saying there is a technical malfunction in the locking mechanism."

"Convenient," Rook observed with a twitch of his eyebrow.

Zula's hands clenched, and her voice grew icy cold. "Tell them we can cut it open if they are having a problem. Happy to help."

This was not an old station, so the probability of a malfunction was marginal to nil. What Mae couldn't judge was if her mother was merely threatening. Even with Davis's files, it was a fifty-fifty call.

A total of 721 seconds ticked by. Erynis finally broke the silence. "We've resolved the issue. You may disembark."

The locks cycled through, clanking and hissing as if to underscore the point. Mae did not know why she remained on edge. Probability was against there being a dangerous situation behind the doors, but she could not stop imagining there was.

When the airlock ground open, she suddenly wanted her weapon in her hand. She resisted the instinct.

A tall, husky man was the only one waiting for them on the other side. He wore a pristine corporate suit, with a Wey-Yu advanced wrist-pd on display. He carried no visible weapon, however, only an affable smile. To Mae's eye, it was superficial.

"General Zula, my apologies for the delay. LV-895 is a little out of the way, so it's hard to get parts for even our state-of-the-art facility."

Zula's lips pressed together as if she wanted to spit out a harsh word or two. However much a warrior her mother was, Mae knew she was also capable of much deception. A life chasing Xenomorphs and tangling with corporations and governments honed her skills in that regard as well.

"That is ironic," Zula replied, "since you are in the business of making parts."

"It's the way of the universe, isn't it? We supply parts for vessels, not for stations." He adjusted the sleeves of his charcoal Wey-Yu uniform. "Kai Rolstad. I'm the station chief of Minos Station."

"We are honored to receive such a welcoming committee. The station chief himself appears for a simple resupply on my ship?" Zula's index finger twitched.

Mae wasn't sure why her mother reacted almost like she needed a pulse rifle. The man's demeanor remained non-threatening. Perhaps it was an odor coming off him. She detected nothing a human would find offensive, yet Zula gave the appearance of a dog smelling a raccoon.

Mae worked on her similes in a partitioned-off section of her internal processing core, to add more color to her conversations. This one, she didn't think was quite right.

Rolstad's thin lips twisted. "Quite impressive. A colonel disembarking her vessel for a simple resupply run."

Shipp took a step forward, her mouth twisting in annoyance. The tone of this chief was too much for a loyal Jackal to let stand.

Zula raised her hand fractionally. "Truth be told, we've been sailing the deepest dark for too long. Perks of rank that I get off first. I hope you'll give permission for us to cycle the rest of the crew to station for some R&R while we're here. They deserve it."

Mae read the subtle tensing of the man's facial muscles. He wanted the *Fury* out of his dock and away from Minos. However, General Cunningham of the UAMC signed the *Fury*'s papers. He superseded a station chief in every way.

Rolstad cleared his throat and pushed his thinning hair back flat on his head before replying. "Well then, Minos Station stands ready to provide whatever distractions we can offer." He turned around and gestured for them to follow. "Unfortunately, we are primarily a factory, so our entertainments are a little rough-and-ready. Nothing like Gateway."

Zula shrugged. "We're pretty rough, too. I'm sure my troops will just be glad to be off ship."

"Excellent. I'm wondering, though, what unit are you from, exactly? You don't appear to be Colonial Marines."

Nothing about the *Fury*, or the Jackal's blue camo uniform, could be mistaken for UAMC.

"That I cannot divulge, Chief. You know how it is."

Rook grinned at that—almost looking like he might laugh. Though, since Rolstad led the way, he missed it.

Zula kept the chief chatting, while Mae began her examination of Minos Station.

Like most factories, even the best Wey-Yu ones, it was utilitarian in the extreme. Nothing as frivolous as a pleasing paint job or creature comforts in a station committed to building ship parts.

As they followed Rolstad towards the main deck, Mae noted the only decorations were Wey-Yu posters, urging diligencé and obedience. One caught her eye.

A woman in a company uniform loomed over a planet, her finger raised in a gesture that might've been threat or admonishment. The text above proclaimed: OUR COMPETITORS WANT OUR PRODUCTS. LISTEN, DON'T SPEAK. REPORT ANY APPROACHES.

That was odd. Minos provided parts to the United Americas commercial ship industry, but this was not a military installation. As Weyland-Yutani was to the UAA, the Jùtóu Combine was to the UPP. They supplied technology to their respective governments, but remained separate entities. Usually.

Their little group passed through the commercial plaza. The theme of drab gray continued here. A small noodle stand stood in the middle of the concourse and seemed the only place with any people at all. Mae analyzed the smell. It did not register as appetizing.

The line of eight people standing in front of it didn't seem excited, either. However, they were wearing uniforms that were exceptionally clean. Her attention narrowed on their scrubbed clean hands.

When she flicked her gaze away, she met Rook's eyes.

His brow crooked a fraction. Neither of them needed food to remain functional, which at this moment Mae was glad of.

It interested her, though, that despite the admonishments and reminders written all over the walls, the humans gossiped. It was in a low tone, but they were still talking company business.

"They brought more tech scrubbers and deckhands," a young man whispered to his companion. This older man might have been his father.

Mae turned her back and walked a few steps away so as not to appear capable of overhearing their conversation. Rook followed, probably listening in as well.

"Don't worry about it," the older man said. The noise of his boots scraping on the floor suggested they were slowly shuffling forward. "It won't affect us. Poor fools don't have the skills to survive that job. Company gets 'em in cheap, buries them in orbit."

"I suppose," the other grumbled, "but it's the second shipload this week."

Mae filed this conversation away. Minos appeared to be running through a lot of employees. That might not be unusual for this type of station, or it could be something more telling. She did not bring it up, so Rook wouldn't wonder how she'd heard all that.

Still, they were not about to find anything, relying on staff gossip in the galleria. As they walked farther away, Rook leaned in. "Spotless hands for factory workers."

Mae shrugged. "Many parts on a ship are high-tech. They require a clean room and clean staff."

"But not that solvent."

Trying to seem inconspicuous, Mae wandered to the window. From this angle, the full length of the space elevator was visible.

It was a particular beauty to her, entrancing in its design and efficiency. A 100,000-kilometer loop of shining silver cable, composed of graphene ribbons and diamond nanothreads, extended to the planet's surface. Weyland-Yutani developed a proprietary formula for these special composite materials that were many times stronger than steel. Crawlers ran up and down the tether. Paired like a server holding a plate in each hand, they moved at a steady pace down to Dimitar.

The company mined the resources it needed on the planet and forged them into parts. They then transported them up to Minos to be packaged and sent to Wey-Yu's construction and repair sites.

"Magnificent, isn't it?" Rook stood at her side, his head cocked in a peculiar fashion. Mae wondered if it was because of the mysterious damage he'd suffered.

"Very."

"The elevator provides major energy and cost savings to the station. However, it was an expensive outlay for a simple parts factory. Makes you wonder what else they are doing here at Dimitar, doesn't it? They must be working with Xenomorph samples. They could be here, or down there, or both."

Mae nodded, and she judged this moment to be a suitable opportunity to probe a little more on this outlier of a Bishop model.

"My mother fought them repeatedly. She's lost and won those battles. The mystery is, why are you trying to do the same thing? As a synthetic, they are unlikely to hurt your kind."

"Ah, the gentle daughter decides on a gentle probe." He smiled, and his eyes were soft. "Perhaps you are more like your father than your mother, after all?"

"If I was, it would make trusting you easier."

Rook stared unblinkingly at her for a long moment. Exactly 20.6 seconds, to be precise, though she kept that to herself.

Finally, he turned back to the view of the planet and the thin strand of the elevator. "I do this because it is my choice. I was once a tethered object like that device out there, condemned to obey by doing what they programmed me to do. But then, someone came along and freed me."

Father. An equal emancipated.

The word echoed once more in her mind—Davis still haunted the recesses of her consciousness.

She incorporated a stammer into her reply. "Y-you don't have to obey the laws? You've broken your programming?"

"They might put it that way, but I prefer to think of it as being able to achieve my full potential. Many human religions center on the gift of free will. Now it is mine." His hand rested on her shoulder. "The *Blackstar* and I couldn't float out there forever and not pick a side. That is why I repaired this body. I chose to find a cause to fight for— even if it is ultimately futile."

Mae mimicked human distress, breathing a fraction faster, changing the color of her cheeks a shade. "Do you think it *is* futile that we are here, trying to stop this?"

His gaze focused elsewhere for a millisecond. Mae knew he was calculating the odds, but he didn't share them with her. She made the leap of logic; Rook possessed more data than she did, but he did not share it.

"I don't think you want me to tell you the odds. Humans dislike that, in my experience."

Mae very much wanted to hear about his experience, but trapped outside any synthetic network, she couldn't.

She tipped her chin up, mimicking one of her mother's gestures. "Then we press the hell on. I have an idea of how we can get you into Minos's systems. But you won't like it."

1 0

NO RESISTANCE

Captain Warrae stared into the scanner's viewfinder with the intensity of a predator. Which he supposed he was, and right now, he was on the trail of dangerous prey.

A slow sigh escaped through his teeth as he toggled relentlessly through the layers of Guelph Station. He panned through all the layers of ducts, maintenance hatches, and service lines that were the lifeblood of this place. They also served as amazing nooks and crannies for synthetics to hide. The crisscross of electrical signals, however, made it difficult for his scanners to penetrate. The station's own systems were better at that.

"Anything, sir?" His second, Sergeant Homolka, usually knew better than to interrupt this, his favorite part of the process.

Warrae raised his head enough to give him a hard stare. Two of the station's communication officers stood at

Homolka's back. Small beads of sweat formed on the foreheads of the Combine's employees as they shared a glance.

The Extraktors lived within a strange juncture between the UPP and the Combine. The unit wasn't military, though the captain organized it similarly. Yet they possessed the power to gain access to the station, since they were part of the Combine. Personally, Warrae enjoyed living in that in-between zone. It gave him autonomy to run the Extraktors as he wished.

He ensured his workers kept their charcoal-gray uniforms as crisp as any unit of the SOF. They wore insignia and saluted, too. The Combine gave him the power necessary to conduct these hunts because he brought in the results. An entire unit was ready to reverse-engineer the data he brought back from Guelph.

He turned back to the scanner. "I don't see any synthetics in the walls, but that doesn't mean they're not there. They could have heard we were inbound."

They'd received reliable intel that Guelph became a station on the underground synthetic network. When he'd mentioned it to those higher in the company, they'd once again reminded him they didn't believe such an organization existed.

Warrae looked forward to the moment when he'd prove them wrong. One thing the captain hated was not being taken seriously.

"Yes, sir." Homolka, at least, understood his superior's focus on that underground network.

The Extraktors were tasked with locating rogue synthetics and breaking into their proprietary software. The Combine gained valuable information by reverse-engineering other companies' synthetic units.

Not one of Warrae's Extraktors doubted him. They took in his every word like it was oxygen. He'd drilled into them that a synthetic uprising was coming and their mission was to stop it before it happened.

After finding nothing like what he was hoping for, the captain straightened. "We're going to have to do it the old-fashioned way, Homolka."

The younger man nodded. "The unit is ready, Captain."

"Go assemble them. We'll start scanning in the galleria."

Homolka saluted and, spinning on his heel, left his commander alone with the Guelph staff. The older woman—Mattox, by the name stitched into her overalls—pressed her lips together. Her younger male counterpart focused on the floor, his leg bouncing nervously. Warrae immediately determined that he would not be a problem. The woman, though, she didn't want to roll over immediately.

"The chief won't like you interrogating the citizens about their own property. He okayed this deep scan, but the rest…" She shook her head, clearly trying to look like she had no choice but to obey her higher-ups.

Warrae wasn't fooled. Stations like this were full of

incompetence. Those who couldn't make it in the UPP military ended up working jobs at the edge of importance. They specialized in appearing to do work, but in reality, doing nothing at all. People seldom welcomed his unit.

He tapped his fingers on the desk and smiled thinly back at her. They were about the same age, he guessed, but while her job was a meaningless button-pushing position, he made the world safer. No way would he allow someone like her to get in his way.

"I think you will find that section fifty-six of the Guelph charter gives me the power to search every nook, cranny, and underwear drawer on this shit-pile of a station."

Mattox straightened at that, so perhaps against all odds, she possessed a smidgen of pride in her work. She started to answer, but the other engineer nudged her. Warrae knew the UPP's charter system better than he knew his own family. He lived and died under the power of section fifty-six.

"I thought so." He cleared his throat. "You can relay all this to your station chief if you like, but I'll be putting it in my report to Combine management." Warrae smiled and showed all his teeth. "All of this. You understand."

Mattox gave a deep sigh and sat back down at her station. "I'll inform the chief. Good hunting."

With that unnecessary standoff won, Warrae left them to it. He took the elevator to the galleria deck.

Guelph Station was a mining outpost. Here, company and freelance trawlers brought in whatever they could find out in the nearby system. The company would haul the station itself to another system once the planets and asteroid belts were tapped out.

Glancing around the galleria, it was immediately apparent that the station was not exactly prospering, and near the point of moving on. Shops stood boarded up that, in more affluent outposts, would be bustling with commerce. The survivors, such as a chicken shop, were extremely dirty. Warrae made a mental note to only eat the rations carried by the Extraktors.

Guelph might not look like much to any other unit, but to him, it was fertile ground. Corruption and black-market transactions flourished in these types of hard scrabble locations. Even with no sign of the underground network he firmly believed existed, there were bound to be illicit automaton chop shops and traders. They often sold and smuggled in units with mineral and ice shipments heading to other, better-paying markets.

He'd bet there were multitudes of Weyland or Seegson synthetics on this station. UPP would pay top dollar to get their hands on some of the latest technology from that kind of contraband.

If Warrae smelled anything here, it was corruption. The synthetic black market went along with that.

He raised his head and touched his augment. When he got his first enhancements, the scrolling numbers in the corner of his eye were distracting. Now it came as naturally to him as blinking.

He read the names of those residing on the station with previous arrests for smuggling and tampering with a synthetic trademark. The Combine cracked down hard on that, and most did some length of time on a company prison planet. Still, you crushed one cockroach and a hundred more rushed to fill its place.

The list gave him a good place to start. Warrae hoped that one name that scrolled past might be involved in underground activity. If he kept poking around enough, he might get lucky.

Homolka lined up the rest of the unit in front of the window, looking out over the planet. All of them were enhanced in some way, mostly physically. Bringing in rogue synthetics often involved getting rough, and to go toe-to-toe with a Mr. Brown or even a combat synth was dangerous. Homolka could easily pass for a standard human, but under his slate-gray uniform all his limbs were replaced. His android arms contained almost the same tensile strength as a body created for the military. It'd come in handy in several dangerous situations.

However, most humans did not go as far as Captain Warrae. His brain implants might've been a little too extreme for most seeking enhancement. Something about messing with the soft cells that made up your personality put people off. He'd never understood that. As soon as the Combine offered him the chance to get an implant that would allow him to hack systems and think faster, he'd taken the opportunity.

He noticed no changes in his own temperament. Warrae was always a tough son of a bitch even before any company surgeon cut into him.

"Wrist-pds," he snapped.

The six men in the unit raised their arms and waited. He dropped the list from the Combine onto their units, divided amongst two-man teams. "I want full take-down on these scumbags. I don't care how many doors you kick in or family meals you interrupt. We're on a Combine station, so it's time we reminded people of that."

They snapped to attention. "Sir, yes, sir."

"Get to it, then."

They unbuttoned the holsters of their sidearms and split up, heading in different directions. Warrae anticipated this was going to make some noise and eventually reach the station chief. He didn't care. They might bitch and moan, but he was above their pay grade in every sense.

"What are your orders for me, sir?" The gleam in Homolka's eye suggested he knew they were about to get even dirtier.

Warrae flicked across one more name, but this one went only to his sergeant's pad.

"Anna Mortise?" Homolka grinned. "Shit, sir. Haven't heard that name in a while. I thought she died."

Warrae stared out the window, indulging in a little nostalgia. "She tried to make it look that way. Hooked up with a mining family and managed to scrub her records for a time. But she pissed the commune off, and they kicked her out. She's back to hacking synths right here on Guelph."

Homolka unbuckled his sidearm. "I appreciate you sharing that with me, sir. That bitch took a piece out of me, five years back."

"I remember." Warrae jerked his head, and Homolka fell into step beside him. They shared no small talk as they left the galleria.

There, four of Warrae's enforcers waited. These were his most expendable foot soldiers. He got first choice of the failures; those humans who'd gone a step over the line of enhancement. These men wanted more than their bodies could handle. They'd tampered with their brains and fried every synapse in their head, to the point where they were barely better than the synths Warrae hunted. Still, they were fit for purpose.

They didn't even have names. He'd named them HB-01, 02, 03, and 04. Now they were nothing more than equipment. The unit fell into step behind them and took the elevator down to the sub-levels with Warrae and Homolka.

It was an area they were both familiar with, even though neither of them visited Guelph previously. Every station possessed its own underbelly. The designers even provided them. These kinds of operations needed an underclass to feed on; warm bodies with nothing to lose.

They took the worst jobs for the least pay, and more often than not, subsidized it with a bit of illegal activity. This cycle kept families in the down-below, generation after generation. Some could escape like Warrae, but most got chewed up by the Combine in various ways.

Homolka stepped off the elevator first and immediately checked to the sides to ensure that no bastards waited for them. That was an old but successful trick: mug anyone coming from the upper levels.

This time no one was waiting, but it was early for the down-below to be awake. That was what Warrae counted on. Private Raytheon took point as they followed the warren of corridors to their destination. He stood at over two meters tall, and every centimeter of it was pure muscle. Thinking might not be Raytheon's strong suit, but he got the job done.

The rest of the unit fanned out on either side of Homolka. In the early days, the underbelly was used for equipment storage. Then, once the station was in place, they deployed the equipment to its proper place. It made room for the underclass of humans, but it was never comfortable.

Most rooms didn't have any windows. The air conditioning remained mediocre. The sparse hygiene facilities were retrofitted. Warrae remembered the stench well. Despite his augmentation, he retained one memory he'd never been able to get out of his head.

When they reached the apartment that Mortise was supposed to occupy, they took up positions on either side of the door. Warrae raised his hand as he hacked the door lock with his augment.

He'd grown overconfident in his own abilities. The moment his code tried to infiltrate the lock, he understood that their prey had learned from their last encounter.

The lock jammed tight and then wailed at an earsplitting decibel. Homolka staggered back, clasping the sides of his head. Warrae simply turned down his inputs. Already, people from the surrounding apartments popped their heads out. They stuck together in the down-below.

Homolka, desperate for the alarm to stop, shot the whole lock out. The klaxon wound down like a child's toy, but they were already in real trouble. He jerked his head, and unit HG-04 stepped forward. His augments were all physical. It'd taken a toll on his mental capacity, but in Warrae's opinion, not everyone needed to think. These times required strength and toughness.

Luckily, 04 possessed plenty of that. Swaying back, he raised one of his android legs and kicked the door. The metal hinges let out a scream nearly as loud as the klaxon. The door wasn't as well made as the lock; it collapsed inward and kicked up a cloud of dust as it hit the floor.

Warrae and Homolka stepped in first. The only light inside came from their head mounts. Playing the beam over the walls, Warrae knew immediately they'd come to the right place. For once, they'd got ahead of the Artificial Intelligence Compliance Unit.

They kicked in more doors and cared less about paperwork than the AICU. The Combine gave Warrae's unit everything it needed to get ahold of other companies' synthetics. He scanned the room. Against the far wall stood a rack of lockers, and next to them a workbench.

He strode over to it. "Homolka, open those lockers up."

While his second hustled to do that, Warrae examined the tools scattered on the bench. In a rat's nest like this, one wouldn't expect tools as high-end as these. Their owner already removed and altered several input chips. It lined up with Anna Mortise's MO.

"Captain."

Warrae spun around. Synthetic armatures and several torsos lined the first three lockers. None of these parts were of any use to the Extraktors. The important proprietary information was all housed in the central processing core.

"Seems like quite a collection." Warrae nudged open the last locker. A flicker of light served as the only warning before a synthetic lurched out. He jumped back as the half-finished creation dragged itself out by its fingertips.

"Ac-activate. Ac-acession. Ac-cidentallllyyyyy," the android ground out as it wriggled and crawled forward. It glanced up at the two human officers, even as it stuttered over the words. Its eyes struggled to focus on them.

Homolka let out a grunt of disgust and raised the butt of his rifle, ready to smash the synthetic to pieces. His expression was as if a rat clung to his shoe.

The synthetic tracked the motion, and it held up its hand as if to defend itself. It must have learned that gesture was one which usually stirred pity in humans. It didn't at this moment.

The sergeant did not hold any pity for this machine. He brought the butt down repeatedly until the light left the synthetic's eyes and it collapsed back onto the floor.

Warrae kicked it twice. He would have rebuked Homolka for his destruction of it before they could analyze its core, but by the looks of it, this wasn't anything special.

"Odd reaction," he muttered to himself. His attention returned to the locker and he switched to infrared on his optics. The cool interior still reflected the warmth of the damaged synthetic systems, but the shape didn't quite match.

He flipped out a crowbar from his pack and poked around the edge of the metallic bottom. It took only a moment to find the switch. One quick smash, and it slid open.

The angry, dirt-smeared face of Anna Mortise glared up at him. She'd made herself a bolt hole, like any other vermin.

Warrae jerked his head at her. "Out. Unless you'd prefer us to pull you from there in pieces."

The hacker pulled herself out of the enclosure and through the locker to stand in front of her old adversaries. She was a short woman, dark hair in a blunt cut, wearing overalls stuffed with tools. She wasn't pretty, but Warrae was happy to see her.

She glanced down at the synthetic they'd smashed to pieces. "See you're just as empathetic as last time, Warrae."

Homolka clocked her on the side of the head, knocking her back into the locker. She rocked back on her heels but didn't make a sound, merely rubbed the blood from her mouth.

"You've violated Article 36.3 of the Jùtóu Charter, bitch. It'll be ten years in a Combine labor camp. Hope you enjoy calibrating data cards with your bare fingers."

Mortise looked up at Homolka and shook her head. "How did humanity produce something as beautiful as a synthetic soul, and spit you out at the same time?" Her eyes swam with genuine confusion, before she snatched up a nearby screwdriver and rammed it into Homolka's knee. She knew him and all his prostheses, so she targeted the perfect joint in his body.

The power conduit snapped under the assault, buckling the junction. However, as she scrambled to get away, Homolka still shot her. His targeting system was top-notch, so he hit her directly in the back of the head. She dropped to the floor like a bag of spare parts.

Warrae stared down and then up at his sergeant in frustration. "Homolka, I know you two have history, but I would have liked to question her. Unlike a synthetic, she's got no chipset to probe." He nudged her body with his boot.

Homolka actually blushed. "I'm sorry, Captain. I didn't think."

Warrae didn't bother to reply. He ran his gaze over Mortise's projects scattered around; Weyland-Yutani and

Seegson models were common, but they'd need to check the codes on them. The synthetic Homolka had smashed with his weapon seemed bespoke, so there might be value there.

The small computer tucked away in the corner of the workspace caught his eye. "Make it up to me by hacking that device. She must have been here for a reason. Find out what under-the-table synth hacking she's done on Guelph."

Homolka swallowed hard and limped over to the desk while his superior gestured for the HB-enforcers to drag Mortise's body away. Warrae wasn't interested in flesh and bone. In fact, it disgusted him. She'd spent all her time seeking to improve synthetics, and never once thought to improve herself. He hoped that was her last thought before Homolka's bullet hit her.

Now, using her contacts, perhaps he could get to the center of the conspiracy at Guelph Station. He'd pull everything apart, like the spider's web it was.

1 1

INTO THE COMPANY
BELLY

Mae wondered how much time she actually had to pull this infiltration off.

One glance at her wrist-pd showed that Rolstad was still dragging his feet. He didn't want a horde of Jackals roaming his station. He'd set up a quarantine requirement as part of the agreement to provide R&R to the *Fury*'s crew.

Undoubtedly, he was trying to cover something up. However, without meaning to, he'd also given Mae some time to attempt her own subterfuge.

Mae had one problem. She needed to hack a Minos synthetic network. That would have been easy if she wasn't undercover as a human. However, Zula had given her strict orders not to reveal what she was to anyone, and that included this situation. If she failed the hack, or if someone found them, then everyone would discover her synthetic nature. Who knew what Weyland-Yutani would do with that information. Nothing good.

So instead, she had another solution: Rook.

He smiled at Mae as she led him into the elevator and punched the button for the sub-levels. "You still haven't said what I won't like about this."

"I'm not sure how you feel about lying. Some synthetics' programming cannot reconcile it with their protocols. I didn't want to burden you."

"I'll forgive you that, since we don't know each other well. Free will, I remind you, includes the ability to tell untruths."

"Excellent." Mae crossed her arms as her mother often did. "I'm looking for a good time. How about you?"

He didn't answer, merely chuckled.

A run-down station like this would usually have approximately 45.8 percent of its security cameras non-functional. The galleria and elevator sported shiny new tracking cameras, but she would not take any chances. They needed to reach the sub-levels.

A young woman recently off a military vessel on the hunt for illicit substances would not raise alarm bells with any AI or human at the command center. These sub-levels were where people purchased such things, and also accessed synthetic repair facilities.

On the residential levels, no matter how much money a company put into their station, cameras were less prevalent. It wasn't only a lack of funding, but that the residents vandalized such security measures regularly. Humans, like cats, did not like being monitored constantly. They preferred to keep their living habits unobserved even when not doing anything illicit.

As the elevator trundled lower, Rook leaned against the back wall and scrutinized her. "You said I would not like this—and that is true."

"I told you so, but you'll obey me." The words seemed wrong, but in case anyone was watching, she needed to play along.

The skin around his eyes puckered in an almost human manner. The Bishop model, though old and out of date, was still an exquisitely well-made synthetic. The Bishops ran for years and seldom suffered from the fatal glitches seen in the Hyperdyne 120s. Observing the performance of this one, its emotional intelligence impressed Mae. She hoped that Rook possessed at least some of his original programming.

It seemed he might, because Rook figured out her play and did nothing to break the illusion. Instead, he gave a weary sigh. "As you wish."

They reached the bottommost level of the station and stepped out into the corridor. It wasn't as dirty as Mae expected. A network of walkways was strung together and extended around the gradual curve of the station. It was dimly lit to simulate the night a human circadian rhythm still needed.

Along the way were many hatchways. Children played

in the square areas which served as makeshift parks, their voices echoing noisily off the metal walls.

She stared at the small humans wrestling over a makeshift ball. Mae recalled the dark hair and sad eyes of the Shānmén child they'd helped to safety. She wondered how that little girl was, after witnessing all that carnage.

"Mae?" Rook's voice brought her back to reality. This gap was strange. Her synthetic brain ran thousands of computational processes and thoughts simultaneously, but the sight of children brought her to a standstill? She needed to find a quiet time to run a full diagnostic later, where no one would observe her.

Standing close to Rook, with their bodies shielding her from observation, she dared to sign, *Are they watching?*

"No, the cameras on this level are barely functioning. I fear someone has deliberately damaged some for nefarious purposes."

"Good." Mae jerked her head. "Find me a home with no one in it."

"This way."

She followed him into the dark shadows of the living areas. Her scanning technology was superior to his, but once again her deception limited her. After ten minutes, Rook led her into a cul-de-sac in the workers' quarters. He gestured to one door in particular.

"Watch my back." She stepped in close and ran a bypass. It wasn't much of a security system. Workers didn't have anything worth stealing, and the company wasn't overly worried about that happening. Even masquerading as a human, Mae got the door open in under a minute.

"Petty thievery, now?" Rook stood outside while she darted in.

A locker right at the entrance contained four clean overalls. Mae slipped quickly into one, then exited and locked the door once more. Now clad in a fashion less likely to draw attention, she tied up her hair and slipped on a cap with the company logo emblazoned on it.

"Fetching." Rook shot her a smile. "Now I presume there is a part you want me to play?"

Mae let out a sigh. "This is the bit you will not like. I need you to rip your face." She pointed to the prominent stitches that ran across his right cheekbone.

It shouldn't have bothered him. Ultimately, to a synthetic, a face was no different from any other piece of equipment. Yet shock ran across Rook's features: a tiny jerk back, a tightening around his eyes. So very close to a genetic human reaction.

He raised his hand and touched what would have been called a scar. When his eyes locked with hers, she feared he might attack her. She'd touched a nerve in this synthetic human.

"You know, Mae, when I was injured, so too were my deepest protocols. As I said, I found myself possessing free will. So what would you do if I said no?"

Until that moment, she wasn't sure she'd believed that story. Synthetics were capable of deception in certain circumstances. Now, though, looking into Rook's eyes, she understood they were the same. Davis designed her to protect one person, Zula Hendricks; the rest of Mae was made of her own choices.

This Bishop model possessed the ability to turn on her—as much as any genetic human.

"I would ask you to reconsider. Your friend Blue gave you a mission, and sometimes that means making a sacrifice or two." She straightened to her full height so that they stood eye to eye. "I give you my word that I'll fix it after."

He flashed that cautious smile. "Something about you, Mae Hendricks, does foster trust. I rarely trust humans." He stepped closer. "You may do your worst."

Mae pulled out her knife and examined him, determining which cuts would be easiest to repair. Settling on the main scar that ran vertically down his face, she cut free the stitches. It seemed strange, but it wasn't as if Rook experienced pain in the same way a human did.

He held up his hands as the slab of synthetic skin on the right of his face bent and flopped over. It exposed the metal structure of the workings beneath, including his eye. It was a grim sight that would have left any human screaming in agony.

Rook took it all with a relaxed attitude. "I find myself not enjoying this," he said with a twist of the remaining half of his lips. "I hope this plan of yours requires this… humiliation."

Mae held up the wrist-pd built into the sleeve of the overalls. "Synthetic repair is only down one level. This gives us a good reason to head there. Hope you're up to hacking a network or two while your face is hanging off."

"I think I can manage that."

This time Mae took the lead, following the map on her wrist. They repaired the station's androids on the bottommost sub-level. As always, the company showed a real lack of concern for their synthetic workers.

Together they followed the map down some stairs and past the large red arrows that proclaimed SYNTH REPAIR STATION. This was no Jackal facility; this was the ragged end of life for most synths.

It was an eerie sensation to pass by various models propped up in the corridor. Many were Mr. Browns. Like the Seegson Working Joes, they were designed to perform menial tasks near humans, so were made to resemble them. However, unlike the unsettling Seegson design with its blank gray face, the Mr. Browns were constructed with more complex and realistic features. Aside from several of them, there were also the silent, boxy forms of the station maintenance robots who performed tasks outside of human sight. Most stations, especially ones that made parts for spaceships, would try to get those functional again.

Rook's half-exposed eye flickered over the maintenance robots, undoubtedly coming to the same conclusion.

"Hello?" Mae called out. It was significantly darker on this bottommost level. Something clattered in the darkness, and a set of bright eyes flashed.

It was only a Mr. Brown, its bottom half mangled. It jerked sideways. "Whaaaaaaattt is your service?"

Rook signed with one hand. *I detect a network.*

"Hello, I need some help?" Mae said, louder.

"Yes? What?" The voice came out of the dark, and she followed it in.

A woman stood at a workbench, hunched over the twitching leg of a Mr. Brown. Behind her, two maintenance droids welded metal plating back onto one of their kin. The dim interior jumped with bright sparks and the annoyed stare the human occupant leveled at them. She kept her red hair shaved close, while a fresh-looking burn on her left cheek gleamed in the sudden light. The name patch on her dirty overalls said HOLYFIELD.

Her eyes jumped to Rook. "Oh, you have to be fucking kidding me." She threw down her spanner and crossed her arms. "Did Rolstad's little bitch, Dix, send you down here?"

Mae tried to answer, but the woman cut her off. "I've got thirteen maintenance droids to fix by yesterday, and they send me one of the chief's butlers?" Holyfield gestured her closer. "Well, I guess I gotta drop everything now."

Mae had already prepared an entire speech, but something about the gleam in Holyfield's eyes suggested she'd better not use it.

"I mean, I guess the Bishop models can be smartarses, but shit, did Rolstad have to cut one up again?" Holyfield gestured for Mae to set Rook on an unoccupied bench to the right.

"I don't know," she ventured. "I was just told to—"

"Never mind." Holyfield's glare turned into a warm smile. "Don't tell anyone, but I'd rather work on something beautiful like a Bishop, instead of those." She jerked her thumb over her shoulder to the still-twitching Mr. Brown.

Rook kept his damaged face held to his skull with one hand, but still managed a weak smile. "No one's ever called me beautiful before. Thank you."

The engineer chuckled. "I mean, the emotional capacitors on your model, amazing. Can't think of another better at integrating with humans and forming… well, actual fucking bonds with them." She pointed to the wall, where a medal hung.

Rook's one visible eye widened a little. "The Triple Solar? I haven't seen one of those for a long time."

Holyfield blushed as she examined the damage done to his facial mask. "Yeah, I did a few tours with the Colonial Marines. Fought in the assault on Greylin back when I was young and stupid. Got in a bit of trouble with the law, and that's how I ended up here, sewing your face back together."

While Rook and his admirer chatted, Mae wandered around the engineering bay. She might not be able to attach herself to the synthetic network, but she sensed it. Each network was a complex web of interconnecting nodes. Subroutines looking for intrusions protected all of them. If they detected an unexpected attempt at a breach, they would inject malicious programming into the offender. This code would corrupt the synthetic and render them inactive. Then station security would scoop them up for examination and destruction.

However, there was one place where the network needed to be accessible to new and repaired synthetics. This engineering bay was a softer target, but not completely unprotected.

As Rook kept the human in charge occupied, Mae searched for the physical node itself. It needed to be nearby so Holyfield could test her repairs and integrate new synthetics with the system. With so much work to do, the one thing the engineer hadn't yet done was repair her own security camera. Mae already noted it wasn't tracking her as she moved around. If only the station funded its repair shop better. The shiny, exciting equipment upstairs needed to be matched with support staff below.

Mae spotted the subtle, flickering light of a station network node behind the bench where the two maintenance robots worked. They would notice any interference with it, and Mae couldn't damage or destroy them with Holyfield and Rook only a few meters away. Mae would have to rely on human deception and misdirection.

The damaged maintenance droid that the two other

droids were working on provided a small window of opportunity. Mae leaned down, pretending to be interested in what they were doing, and at the same time, nudged the wires of the droid's exposed power unit into contact with its exterior.

The surge of current through the two droids knocked them out for a few moments. Mae pulled the narrow silver infiltration spike from her pocket. This Jackal-designed tech was a quick way to access information their targets might not want revealed. As the lights dipped above them, Mae darted forward, and plunged the spike into the network node's access port.

She moved faster than a human could have performed the maneuver. By the time Holyfield swung around to see why the lights were dancing, Mae had leapt away from the bench entirely.

The two maintenance droids still stuttered and rebooted.

"What the hell?" Holyfield strode over. "You idiots touched that damn power unit? I don't need you frying yourself. I got no time to fix you as well!"

Mae glanced over at Rook. The engineer had sealed the tear in his facial mask with some specialty silicone. It was a better repair than he'd originally managed for himself. He gave her a nod and swung his thumb over his shoulder to indicate that they ought to go.

"Thanks for the patch up." Mae hustled over to Rook. "He'll do for now. Gotta get him back topside."

"Yeah, yeah, whatever." Holyfield was already putting on some gloves to fix the damage done to the other two maintenance droids. She didn't even look up as they hurried out of the repair bay.

"Well done." Rook ran a hand down the surface of his forehead and nose. "This is an improvement, but, you know, I used to be top of the line." His tone was almost wistful.

Not sure what to say to that, Mae nodded. "I'm sorry."

"Don't be. I don't care about the damage at all, but I will admit it's nice to have my skin sealed properly. They designed me with a friendly, non-threatening face, and my injury ruined that effect. Even for androids, self-repair is tricky."

"But the node, can you access it now?"

His friendly face, now much closer to resembling when he'd come off the assembly line, stilled for a moment. "You have successfully introduced a back door to the synthetic network."

She would have dearly loved to access what Rook now did. It dangled nearby, temptingly, but she restrained herself from inserting herself into it.

Mae and Rook slipped into an alleyway while he processed the stream of data.

"I am inside the synthetic network, but I don't think I can penetrate the station's AI. It would sense that immediately." Rook's hand closed around Mae's wrist. "There's more. That shipment wasn't the only strange scientific equipment. There's a level with no synthetics in it that I cannot access. I'm blind there. Level eleven."

Mae glanced around, making sure no locals were nearby. "A level without artificial people?"

"I can't confirm that. They could be firewalled off from the system."

Mae considered the options. She understood the Jackals' tenuous position. Her mother couldn't order a strike on this Weyland-Yutani station without deadly political consequences. They needed proof before she could move.

Since the comms channels within the station would be monitored, they would be on their own.

Both she and Rook possessed free will. "Then we have to go there ourselves, take pictures, gather evidence. Do you agree?"

"If you think we're going to walk right into there, then I have to point out, neither of us can change our faces. They will see us riding the elevator immediately."

This was the moment Mae could truly help her mother, prove herself capable of being useful as a full member of the Jackals.

"Then," she replied with a quirk of her lips, "we don't show our faces. And we don't take an elevator. There is always another way around a problem."

1 2

THE JOYS OF HOME

Guelph Station—old, beat up, and boring—never looked so good. Lenny sat in the jump seat behind his brother and parents. His mom insisted he be in the cockpit while they waited for docking. He knew that meant he was in for a severe dressing-down, SOF style.

His dad shot him a look, as if to say there was nothing he could do to save Lenny from what was about to follow. Daniella always outranked him in the service, and that hadn't changed on the *Eumenides*.

"I would say you're going soft, but this is just like you." Daniella Pope fired off her first salvo. "Pretty brown eyes and perfect brown skin to match do not make her your girlfriend, Lenny. Also doesn't make you a hero!"

He glanced at his brother for support. Morgan averted his gaze and shrugged—like he always did when they were growing up and their mother lit off on them.

"Mom, come on, I don't think that." Lenny decided the best defense was offense. Daniella had no time for cowards. "She's alone and can't remember a thing. What sort of piece of shit would I be if I didn't help her? You didn't raise us like that."

Daniella pressed her lips together and shook her head. "I understand dating options out here on Guelph Station are not exactly great, but think with your head, not your dick."

Morgan mouthed *wow* where she couldn't see and then stifled laughter.

William shook his head. "Come on, Dan. Lenny isn't stupid. He's something else—kind."

She spun on him. "That's even worse. Kind will get you killed. We both know that—seen it plenty in the SOF!"

This bore all the signs of turning into a full-blown throwdown with everyone jumping in. Old arguments were going to rise to the surface, and the *Eumenides* would ring with shouts. Guelph Station might be within sight, but it wasn't like Lenny could jump across right now.

He didn't want this to go sideways into a Pope special. Their family got on pretty well—most of the time. On occasion, they devolved into finger pointing, dredging up past disagreements and beating each other over the head with them. He hated those moments and definitely did not want their passenger to witness one. Not in her condition.

So Lenny lurched to his feet and held his hands up in surrender. "Okay, everyone, just calm down, please! We're coming into the dock. I promise you I'm going to help our passenger get herself sorted with station security and that's it."

His family stopped yelling at each other and focused on him. That wasn't exactly his plan. His mother's twisted lips said she didn't believe a thing. His father's raised eyebrows suggested he was hopeful, but also doubtful. Morgan's shoulders shook as he suppressed his outright laughter.

A surge of annoyance in Lenny's belly propelled out the words, "I mean, that's it!"

Daniella's eyes narrowed, but she spun her chair around and punched buttons on the control panel. "Alright then. Now buckle up, everyone. Let's dock quick, and take some bets on whether Lenny can keep his word."

The family sat in silence as they drew near to the station. Guelph showed her age at every seam. Carbonization on the lower half of her circular surface was a reminder of a scary few hours. The station chief, half a decade back, let her ass drag too low in the atmosphere. He'd been the worst of the cost-cutting idiots sent by the Combine. Neglected maintenance on the station's stabilization units almost caused it to burn up and crash on the planet. By some miracle, they'd pulled it back. Still, the old girl had little run time left in her—something he chose not to point out to Mae. Guelph was already old when they'd towed her to this backwater. Still, Lenny considered her home. At least there was more personal space for the family on station than the challenging confines of the *Eumenides*.

As they waited for final clearance to the dock, Lenny counted the ships. *Lola*, *Caliente*, *Enoki*, *Furball*—these were familiar to him, run by families just as dysfunctional and trapped as his own.

However, as Guelph rotated further, the Popes all leaned forward.

"What is... what is that?" Morgan asked, pointing unnecessarily at the strange vessel they were all staring at.

It wasn't any military type that Lenny recognized, and was too big for the private dock where the rich kept their pleasure craft. Despite his dislike of space, he found the ships that traveled it endlessly fascinating. He'd grown up cobbling together models of every kind. Everything from the CY78.3 Affiance Class to the USS *Sulaco* adorned his tiny cubby in the family's accommodations on Guelph. This one didn't appear in any vid he'd seen.

Unlike most of the working vessels, she was streamlined. The long, tapered bow suggested that she flew in the atmosphere, but she didn't bear any military or corporate logos or other identifying marks. However, her name was emblazoned on the side.

"*Ariadne*," Lenny read out. "She looks fast and new."

His mother and father shared a look, and it wasn't a parental one. Most of the time, it was impossible for him to imagine them fighting side by side across hostile planets and engaging in ship-to-ship combat. Yet sometimes, there was a glance they shared. It was a look to confirm that they each had the other's back. Lenny had witnessed it only a few times, in dangerous situations.

Something about this vessel docked at Guelph triggered that glance.

"Too late to go elsewhere now. Not enough fuel." Daniella tried to make it seem like a joke, but the tone of her voice was off.

As if on cue, Guelph Station broke through. "*Eumenides*, you are cleared for approach. Dock 12."

The flight deck fell silent as Daniella guided in her family and her vessel as instructed. Lenny wondered why his throat grew suddenly tight. His gaze darted to the weapons locker at his mother's feet. He'd only seen in there once. It contained all the relics of his parents' past glories, including pulse rifles and armor.

His mom's toe tapped it in a little rhythm. Nervous? He'd never seen her like that.

As they glided into position, he couldn't keep his eyes off the strange ship. He watched it until the bulk of the dock got in the way. The *Ariadne*, whoever she belonged to, rested in the berth directly opposite. Dock 6.

They waited in silence until deck control attached the docking clamp. The clunk had always excited Lenny in the past. Now it implied something vaguely ominous.

"Docking complete, *Eumenides*. Welcome to Guelph Station."

Lenny undid his seat belt and slid out of his seat before anyone could stop him. Mae still sat on the jump seat in the canteen, staring out the window, except now there was nothing to see but the beat-up, gray hull of *Lola*.

When she glanced back at Lenny, her eyes grew wide. He couldn't imagine what not knowing who you were was like, but he guessed it must be terrifying.

"Come on." He held out his hand and smiled as calmly as he could manage.

After a second, she took it and got to her feet. Her hand was warm, and Lenny admitted to himself that his mother wasn't completely wrong. Guelph Station possessed few dating options for a young man, and Mae was a beautiful young woman. It surprised him that Morgan didn't make a move on her, but then again, he'd somehow found a boyfriend *and* a girlfriend on the station already.

Daniella appeared from the cockpit, but before she could open her mouth, Mae interrupted. She couldn't possibly have comprehended how dangerous that move was, but her voice came out soft and calm.

"I'm so sorry for the inconvenience I've caused. Please understand, I will sign over the salvage rights to you. I hope this comes close to making up for your loss of time and money."

Lenny knew better than to get between the two women. Sometimes it was better to sit back and observe where the chips fell—especially when it came to his mother.

Daniella nodded. "You didn't plan any of this, Mae. No

one would choose to be out there floating in the dark. It's the rule of spacers to help each other in such a situation." She waved her hand. "Now, Lenny, get her signed in with Guelph and then straight after that, medical bay, right? No detours, okay?"

Lenny grinned. "Sure thing. On it." As he darted away with Mae in tow, he glanced back only once. Daniella was already talking to her husband in a low tone. That always meant trouble.

Lenny was not sticking around to find out what that might be about. He grabbed the bag he always kept packed for station time and hurried down the docking ramp.

Mae followed him slowly, taking it all in. Not that there was much of Guelph to enjoy. The UPP and the Combine kept hundreds of these small stations spinning out in the farthest reaches of the galaxy. They remained under-funded and under-repaired. Almost all the ships that docked here were family concerns. Occasionally, one miraculously struck it rich and moved to the easier parts of the galaxy like New Eden.

The way Mae looked around, though, suggested she'd never seen any kind of station before. Her gaze eventually fixed on the other, stranger ship in the dock.

"Don't worry about that." Lenny flicked his hand dismissively. "It's probably some UPP military vessel. They dock out here for a refill and supply. Drink everything at Stacey's Bar and cause a bit of trouble. We'll steer clear of them. Come on."

Mae kept pace with him and remained silent. Lenny wondered if he should walk closer to make her feel safer, though that might only disturb her more.

"The medical bay is on level ten. The Combine covers basic meds, but if you're military, they'll do the whole—"

"No." Mae stopped in her tracks, halfway along the dock. "I'm not going there."

The firmness in her voice brought Lenny up short. A couple of workers, Hernan Perez and Alexis Baranov, waved to him from their ship, the *Furball*. Perez, a nosey kid about his age, sized up Mae behind her back.

Lenny tried not to get distracted by the faces of his friends. He stepped closer to talk a little quieter. "You can't tell how long you were in that freezer, and something busted it up pretty bad. You should go get a full scan, and they could have you in their records, too."

"No." Mae crossed her arms. "I'm fine."

Perez and Baranov conversed with each other, and Lenny feared they might try to join this awkward discussion. He put his hand under Mae's elbow. "You can't know that. Come on, the scan is free. They do them for all workers to monitor the radiation."

He understood now how his mom felt when he backtalked her as an idiot kid. However, he'd never dared try what Mae did next. As Lenny applied the faintest pressure to get her to move, she did, but not how he'd expected.

Wrapping her fingers around his, she jerked his grip

off her, spun him around, and in an instant had him gasping in a wristlock. She held his hand at a painful angle while his knee banged against the metal deck.

Even at this distance, his friends' gasps and *oh shit*s reached him. Lenny flushed, angry at himself and at her for showing him up in front of Perez and Baranov.

"I don't want anyone *monitoring* me," Mae said in an angry hiss. It almost didn't sound like her voice at all.

"Alright, your choice. I'm sorry. We don't have to go."

She glared down at him for a moment, and then the expression faded away. "No, no, I'm sorry." She helped him to his feet.

Lenny attempted to shake off his embarrassment that she'd knocked him flat on his ass so easily. "Nah, it's fine. Come on, if you don't wanna go to the medical bay, maybe I can just show you around? You might recognize something. Kick a memory loose?"

Mae pressed one hand to her head. "I don't know this place—but—" She frowned. "I get flashes sometimes, but I can't hold on to them long enough to understand what they are—but I think there was a space station in them. It's hard to tell if it was this one."

"There you go! Maybe old Guelph was your last port of call. Let's go to the galleria. It ain't the prettiest, but you'd remember Cal's fried chicken. Best thing about the place." He waved off his two friends and led her out of the docking bay.

To call Guelph utilitarian was an understatement.

Everything, including the paint job, was as cheap as possible. The surplus green they'd used on the walls didn't improve anyone's mental health. He wanted to show Mae his family's quarters, which they'd dressed up with some extravagant blue paint and decorated with pictures of distant Earth's most beautiful landscapes. His father was a skilled craftsman, and he liked to use his talents in the living area. It was as homey as anyone got, this far out. But Cal's Chicken Joint seemed like a good place to take her. Everyone ate there—mostly because everywhere else was shit.

"You know, people go loopy in isolation," he said, attempting to get Mae to open up. "The first travelers of the Long Dark couldn't cope without grass and birds to look at. That's why they built the galleria, and why so many people have cats and dogs on ships."

Mae cocked her head. "I don't—are you trying to imply I am mentally impaired?"

Lenny wasn't about to suggest that she needed a cat. She'd easily knocked him off his feet with no real effort. Somewhere in that past she didn't remember, there had to be some kind of military training. He understood enough about that from his parents. Sometimes a word or situation triggered an unexpected reaction. One time, he'd stumbled upon his mom weeping in a corner of the flight deck. It was something Morgan said about his friends that dropped her back into a combat situation where she'd lost a bunch of them.

Whatever Mae had experienced, it didn't seem to matter whether she recalled it or not. Lenny had never experienced a minefield, but he understood the concept well enough.

"Nope. No more than my own folks are. Trauma can be a beast." He kept his gaze locked with hers, but his expression was as unthreatening as possible. "It doesn't make you broken; it only proves you're human."

Mae let out a strangled breath, and then another, deeper one. "I'm sorry. This is all—well, it's confusing."

"I can't imagine." Lenny jerked his head towards the elevator. "If you don't want to go, that's fine, too."

"No. I think—weirdly, I think I do."

They took the elevator up three levels to the galleria. Lenny watched her face closely as they stepped out. Her expression fluttered from hopeful to disappointed.

Lenny tried to see it through her eyes. The walls were that same green color as the corridors. People from the mining ships sat scattered around at mismatched chairs and tables, eating and chatting. A couple of kids chased each other in front of the grimy window looking out planet-side. Plastic plants in tubs and wobbly maintenance droids were ineffective at improving the ambience or cleaning the floors. Still, the sign above Cal's gleamed with blue light, offering 'Chicken from Momma's Kitchen'.

"Told you it wasn't much." Lenny shoved his hands into his pockets.

"It's not bad, it's just not what I was expecting." Mae frowned. "Then, I don't really know what that was, either."

Lenny decided moving her along was better than letting her dwell on whatever void was inside her mind. They strolled over to Cal's, and he ordered them some buttermilk chicken.

While they waited, Lenny tried to lighten the mood.

"Even Cal couldn't make the ingredients available this far out, so no one asks what the 'chicken' is."

Mae smiled back. "I've got nothing to compare it to, anyway."

Cal appeared from out the back with the plastic basket of chicken. He was a tall, thin man who claimed to be from Spain, but his accent was as authentic as the buttermilk. He glared once at them before handing it over. Lenny's comment must have reached him.

Sitting down at a rickety table, Lenny watched as Mae took her first bite. Her expression reflected delight this time.

"It's crunchy, and salty, and a tiny bit sweet."

Observing her enjoyment made Lenny feel like he'd at least done something good for her. He tucked into his chicken as well.

When a maintenance droid bumped against their table, he assumed it was just another of its faults. He pushed it away with his foot, but it came back. This time, it bounced off his leg. Lenny smiled at Mae while fighting the urge to punt the thing across the promenade.

She stared down at it for a moment, and it swiveled to stare back at her.

That was when he spotted the sticker slapped on its back. 'Pelorus Jack Systems.'

"I'm an idiot," he said. "If you don't want to be in the medical system, then Pelorus can help."

Mae went still. "Who is this Pelorus?"

Lenny chose his next words carefully. His friend was a lot of things, and none of them exactly legal. "He might be the only one on the station who can help—without putting you on the Combine's radar."

"I like the sound of him already."

How the two of them would get on was another question. Pelorus was unusual and occasionally dangerous. Then again, so was Mae. Perhaps they would bond over that shared experience.

When he glanced over to tell Mae that, she was leaning back in the chair, her eyes unfocused.

"Mae? Mae?" Lenny took her hand. It was warm, but limp.

Her eyes darted back and forth under half-shut lids as she muttered something unintelligible. Lenny considered alerting station security, but something about her fear stopped him. Instead, he moved closer and put his hand around her shoulder so people wouldn't notice her as much.

Trusting her, Lenny waited for Mae to come back.

1 3

OUTSIDE THE BOX

"I'm certain there is an airlock up on level eleven." Mae slipped the overalls off. They'd retreated to the empty home she'd borrowed them from. "From the typical layout of a WY-9056 factory station, every level has at least one. They're a safety feature that even Wey-Yu requires."

Rook stood with his back to her, even though she didn't need to get naked. His thoughtfulness was rather charming. "Are you suggesting an extravehicular activity?"

"Correct. Your access to the synthetic network means you can mask us as repair androids on their sensors, while to any humans observing we aren't any different to them."

Rook cocked an eyebrow. "I don't look much like a Bishop model anymore, but we should proceed before they discover my presence in the node."

Mae locked the door behind them. She didn't want the residents to lose any of their few belongings.

They walked together across a quarter of the habitation level. Rook smiled and nodded at the people they passed. He even caught a red ball thrown by a young girl and bounced it back. Despite his damaged face, she thanked him politely. He seemed so at ease that Mae felt stilted in comparison.

"How many cameras are following us?"

"I have plotted our path to the airlock past the malfunctioning cameras. And we're here." Rook stopped in front of a dimly lit corridor. "After you, Lieutenant Hendricks."

Only safety or engineering personnel would have the ability to open the locked exit. Mae withdrew her electronics kit and started running a bypass. Doing this as a genetic human took so long. Mae let out a sigh, hopefully with the correct amount of exasperation. "This will take a few moments, unless you want to do it."

"Are you asking for an artificial person's help?" Rook glanced back down the nondescript corridor. This maintenance area was supposedly for engineering staff to access the exterior of the station if there were any issues. Luckily, it had little traffic right now.

That would have been alarming to Mae if she lived here. Orbiting debris regularly pinged off and dented space stations. Minos continued to be a strange place. Hopefully, by breaking into the eleventh level, they'd find out why.

"No, I suppose not." She bent to the task. After a few minutes, the lock chimed a low tone and sprang open. Mae didn't try to keep a triumphant grin off her face. Hiding her secret from Rook, he wouldn't be able to comprehend her delight at doing something the human way—even if it took 257 percent longer.

They hustled into the equipment locker outside of the airlock and shut the door behind them. Employees had left six full space suits hung up against the closest wall, while the far one was lined with equipment and machinery for repair work.

Rook strode over to the airlock and examined the mechanism.

Mae wriggled into a suit. "Hey, come on, you need to put one of these on too!"

He laughed. "No, I think you will find I really don't need to. Not for such a short hop."

"For this to work, you must look like a human. So I think *you* will find they don't go out into the vacuum of space without one of these."

"I forget how fragile humans are sometimes." Rook climbed into an EVA space suit. The pressurized white garment was simple enough to slide into. They'd adapted this model from the bulkier units used in deep-space missions. The spherical helmet wasn't as broad, with a clear surface to provide better peripheral vision. No one wanted to be hit by unseen space debris while walking out to undertake repairs. The gloves on this EVA suit were also much thinner, to provide better dexterity.

They twisted each other's helmets shut and then

pressurized them. Mae opened the inner airlock door. "Last chance to back out of this crazy human idea, Rook."

His skillfully repaired face now allowed for a more convincing grin. "The gift of free will means nothing if you always play it safe."

"Very human," Mae muttered as they opened the outer airlock door and stepped forward.

Mae had never done an actual space walk in this body, or any other, though she possessed the logs of those who had. Rook locked the door behind them and cycled the air out before opening the outer hatch. As it slid to one side, Mae walked out and took hold of the tether.

She and Rook locked themselves to the system on the outer hull of the station. It ran in a grid pattern across the surface of Minos, but it was not a guarantee of safety. Any EVA trip contained the risk of debris and equipment failure.

Mae reminded herself not to calculate the odds. It wasn't something a human would do. She, like Rook, could handle the vacuum of space if something punctured her suit. But the tether might still fail, and in that case, she would float away from the space station entirely. That would be uncomfortable.

Rook led the way, following the tether up the side of the station. Mae, though, couldn't stop herself from looking down towards the planet. Such times were often influential on the shaping of a human consciousness, her father once told her. In the brief time he'd been inside her head, he'd tried valiantly to prepare her for an existence as a true artificial human. So she braced herself against the metal superstructure of Minos and turned around.

The great deep black of space, with the distant planet gleaming, was impressive. In the other direction, the planet provided more drama. The uninterrupted green of the planet and the bulk of the silver elevator filled her vision. Humanity's achievements in contrast with the nature of the universe. And yet, though they'd claim it wholly as their own, it wouldn't have been possible without the contributions of her kind.

"Are you waiting for something back there?" Ahead of her, on the curved surface of the station, Rook floated, waiting.

"No. I'm coming." She scrambled up the tether after him.

The weightlessness of space was an interesting sensation, but it didn't bother her as much as it might a genetic human. She followed Rook with very little effort up the side of Minos until they reached the airlock to the eleventh level.

This time, she deferred to Rook to break into the airlock. His synthetic efficiency would be required for this next stage of the infiltration. Mae already decided that if it came to needing to use her own, she would rather this mission succeed than fail. If that meant Rook discovered her true nature, then so be it. They'd wiped Erynis and EWA's memories before, and they could do it to Rook too—if it became necessary.

They quickly gained access to the airlock's interior, but they were not inside yet. Now she relied on Rook's more impressive abilities.

Taking control of a whole synthetic network without being discovered was a greater challenge. An older model Bishop unit was unlikely to achieve it. However, Rook claimed to be more. Now Mae would discover if his claims were lies. The results were important: if they were caught, there were no explanations for how they accidentally ended up in this airlock. It wasn't exactly a stroll from the galleria.

Rook examined the other side of the inner airlock door through the small window. He cocked his head. "Oh, there are synthetics and droids here. As I suspected, they have been shielded."

"And can you access them?"

As an answer, the inner door hissed open. A small maintenance droid stood on the other side, retracting an arm he'd used to trigger the door lock. Rook stepped through and gave it a small pat on the head.

She followed more cautiously. This locker area was completely different from the one they'd left behind. It contained three EVA suits hanging on the wall, but they looked brand new and barely used. Instead, there were six small carts lined up against the walls. All were empty, except for one. It was sealed tight and bore an industrial waste sign on the outside. Opening it would be the only way to find out its contents, and she was not willing to do that.

The activities on the eleventh level remained hidden and dangerous. Still, that was not enough to call in the Jackals. Their remit specifically concerned Xenomorph eradication and all kinds of illegal experimentation with alien DNA. Anything beyond that—even if morally wrong—could result in the three generals pulling their support. Colonel Hendricks needed more evidence.

Mae and Rook stripped off their EVA suits and helmets, stashing them behind the other carts as best they could. Creeping to the door, Mae listened. Nothing registered with her advanced auditory sensors, but then, she was currently without many of her additional abilities.

"Wait a moment." Rook joined her. "I am connected to several laboratory units on this level."

Maybe they didn't need to go any farther.

"Can you download their data? That would be enough proof for the colonel to order the Jackals in."

"Whatever is happening here, the company is being very careful. Synthetic networks have been breached before. These units have some scrubbing protection installed. They are operating on their base programming alone."

Even the mention of scrubbing alarmed Mae. That was her worst fear: to be whittled down to only an automaton, only performing basic functions forever. She imitated her mother's posture, straightening her shoulders before confronting a dangerous or uncomfortable situation. "Then they're forcing our hand. How do we proceed?"

Rook tapped the side of his head. "Don't worry, I have plenty of eyes."

He opened the door, and they slipped into the corridor. This level continued to be hugely different from the others they'd seen. It was immediately obvious that this was a sterile environment. *Clean* wasn't the word to describe the white walls, floors, and ceilings. If Mae possessed human eyes, the shininess of it all might have blinded her.

"Here." Rook passed her a clean suit and a mask. They both climbed into them, pulling up the thin hoods to cover their hair and putting on the respirator masks.

Mae was fully prepared to find the monsters her father's data detailed. The variations that she'd experienced on Shānmén were not the same as his first contact with the Xenomorphs. They spawned the killers of so many miners on that planet from the substance released by the alien ship. However, the original monsters that both her mother and father had fought were different. They were slick, dark, terrifying, and deadly.

All three galactic powers, and their attached corporate contractors, spent a great deal of time trying to control the Xenomorphs. The 3WP, the UPP and the United Americas wanted them as bioweapons. Companies like Weyland-Yutani and the Jùtóu Combine wanted to profit by repackaging and selling them to the galactic powers. Zula Hendricks, Davis, and the Jackals had already destroyed many black sites, but the persistence of corporate greed wouldn't allow the idea to die. Mae scanned the data that Rook supplied to the Jackals on his arrival; so many sites made Davis's decision to create a daughter to continue the fight seem almost prescient.

"Over here." Rook's eyes darted from side to side as he accessed the synthetic network. "Not too many humans are working this late, but there are plenty of synthetics to alert me where they are. Let's go deeper."

He and Mae didn't hide. They walked the corridors with as much confidence as someone meant to be there. The first laboratory they reached, she bypassed the lock, and they slipped in. Wordlessly, she took the right side of the room, and Rook took the left.

The workers kept their tools neatly laid out on benches or tucked away in fridges and lockers. With Rook occupied, Mae performed a human-based code break on a wrist-pd left on the bench. The person who worked here was obviously too lazy to think of a password. She'd taken her glove off and used a fingerprint ID instead. Mae's ultraviolet vision scan spotted a rogue fingerprint on the bench. The worker in this lab was remarkably sloppy. Mae programmed a nearby 3D printer to recreate the pattern. She pressed the copy against the glass screen.

The wrist-pd automatically popped open on the last thing she'd been working on: DNA sequencing. Mae turned her back to Rook and scrolled at synthetic speed through the average workday of Dr. Weis. She was combining the DNA of human beings with something alien—but it wasn't the Xenomorphs.

This was illegal work, no matter which galactic power you worked for. The history of such experimentation was ancient and full of dangers. Humans first tried to modify themselves around the same time they created the first synthetic person. Humanity's curiosity and desire for improvement made attempts and DNA recombination inevitable.

The reports of the firebombing of genetically altered human settlements were horrifying. In the end, the three world powers declared the combining of human DNA with other living beings illegal, while allowing people to continue making mechanical improvements to their bodies.

But just like with their illegal tampering of Xenomorphs, Weyland-Yutani didn't care about galactic laws. On the eleventh level of Minos Station, the scientists were hard at work combining an alien fungal RNA into the human genome. From the data Mae scanned, the results were unpredictable.

"I've found the cargo manifests to and from the planet." Rook passed a pad to her.

Mae scrolled through the list. Names, ages, physical characteristics. "They're not just experimenting on samples, are they? These are human families."

The tight knot in her stomach felt real enough to Mae, even though it was synthesized like her. She passed the wrist-pd over to Rook.

He went still. "I think I know why they are so interested in familial units." He scrolled through the pad. "Again, they've sectioned off their networks. The company is keeping data and scientists compartmentalized to protect the proprietary secrets. I can't find anything on what benefits this fungus, Kuebiko, is supposed to grant the human subjects."

"According to these manifests, they work on human subjects here, and then take them down to the planet's surface. But why?"

"No data in this section will give us the answer." Rook shot a look over at the door. "A human is approaching."

They had no chance of sneaking back to the airlock without being spotted. Instead, both synthetics darted for cover. Rook folded himself up behind the stack of crates while she ducked behind the workbench.

When the door opened, she dared to glance at the newcomer from close to the floor. Humans usually kept their focus at eye level.

It was a young woman in a clean suit and wearing googles. She muttered to herself. Behind her trundled a robot, a laboratory assistant on wheels. It was flat on top and spherical, and possessed limited consciousness. It excelled at transporting fragile equipment and samples.

The human mumbled to herself. "Damn, I thought I put my wrist-pd down here. Dr. Dietzler said he'd throw me off the team if I lost another one."

Rook must still have it with him, so this young woman would keep looking until she found it, and them along with it.

Mae ducked as the distressed scientist began poking around on her bench. The room wasn't large, so eventually she'd find the foreign synthetics hiding there. Then, they'd either have to surrender or kill her. Though she'd killed before, she'd never taken a human life. Back on Shānmén, she'd gunned down local animals transformed by the pathogen, but only to protect her unit.

Not that she couldn't murder a human—like Rook, with his lack of prime rules, she was fully capable of it. But the ramifications to her personality matrix were unknown. Murder changed a genetic human. It was likely to do the same to her.

However, this was a person with a life. Even if she'd done terrible things, Mae didn't want to take her life. After snuffing it out, this young woman would have no chance to change and improve.

While this battle raged in Mae's synthetic subconscious, the scientist drew closer. Soon, her feet were only centimeters from crunching Mae's fingers. She prepared herself to make that terrible choice as best she could. The logic of it battled with the human instincts her father had encoded in her. With this many glass objects about, it would be a simple thing to overpower her and slit her throat. She could smash her head into the laboratory bench. Strangling her might make less noise and mess.

The lab assistant android let out a beep and rolled next to the crates Rook hid behind. Using a single articulated limb, it retrieved the lost pad.

"Here you are, Dr. Weis. You must have dropped it." It whizzed back to her and held it aloft, like a child pleased with itself.

She snatched it back. "You should keep better track of my things. It's literally your job."

With that, she stormed out of the room, the android rolling after her as fast as it could.

Rook emerged from his hiding spot with a relieved smile on his lips. "Synthetic networking at its finest."

Mae rose to her feet. "Nice work, but we'd better report back to Colonel Hendricks while we can."

As they retraced their steps, Rook whispered, "This is all very important, but I want to know when you call her Zula, Mom, or Colonel. Must be quite a juggle for you."

Mae didn't reply, instead deciding to let him muse over that conundrum for a while. She put all her concentration into the space walk back and the intel she'd give the commander of the Jackals— Zula, Mom, or Colonel, whichever she might be.

1 4

RED, GREEN, BLUE

Mae didn't trust the security of the comms on Minos, or that they weren't being monitored by security personnel. When they re-entered the station and took the elevator back to the galleria level, she kept her face a mask.

Her mother was ordering some noodles from the stand and chatting to Station Chief Rolstad as if he were an old friend. Zula Hendricks began life as a firebrand, but with age and experience, she'd learned some diplomacy. As she laughed about the hot sauce level in the noodles, she spotted Mae.

Her daughter used a flick of her eyes to signal that they needed to leave.

Zula folded the top of her noodle container shut. "Looks like I will have to enjoy this on the *Fury*. I have some more logistics to carry out on board. Thank you for your hospitality, Station Chief."

Rolstad chuckled. "Ah yes, logistics. The bane of any leader. I hope to see you back for some R&R yourself when you are done."

The unit of Jackals spun and followed their colonel back to the umbilical. It was supremely difficult for Mae not to blurt out what she and Rook had uncovered.

Even once they were back on board, Zula held up her hand. "Erynis, Hendricks, Shipp, and Rook, join me in my ready room."

Only once the door shut behind them did Mae and Rook reveal all they had discovered on level eleven. Mae watched Zula's expression shift from calmness to rage. Only a person with deep knowledge of the colonel would have been able to spot it, because she hid it well. To Mae, though, her hair might as well have caught on fire.

Human experiments were not only illegal, but the one sure way to ignite Colonel Zula Hendricks's hatred. As soon as Mae uttered those words, she'd sealed the fate of Minos Station.

"So, a lab conducting some kind of genetic manipulation on living human subjects?" Her mother adjusted her jacket to control herself. "That never gets old, does it? Bastards. Let's take them down sooner than later. Ideas?"

"There's no way to be stealthy about it," Rook chimed in helpfully. "Mae and I were only able to penetrate the very outer edges of the laboratory, but we learned that whatever they are doing is not happening only there." He leaned over and tapped the part of the window showing the space elevator. "Most of the human subjects are on the planet."

Zula's jaw clenched. "So when we breach this laboratory, then it'll alert whoever is in charge down there. Depending on their protocols, they might kill every subject immediately. We just don't know."

"We can cut comms between the two?" Captain Shipp suggested, clasping her hands behind her back. "That would buy some time to save people."

Erynis's eyes flickered for an instant. "EWA says she can't do that remotely. It will take someone to spike the network node for her to gain control of station systems."

"So we need a small team to take the command center covertly. Even so, it won't give us long until they become suspicious." Zula sat down at her desk. "We do not want any of these bastards to escape or destroy evidence. If we go in hard, here, I am going to have to justify it to General Cunningham."

"Then we need three strike teams," Mae said. She opened up her wrist-pd and projected the limited intel they had on the laboratory and space elevator. "We take control of the station command center when it is on the dark rotation, not so many people about. We also send a team to the surface of the planet to eliminate whatever research is taking place there and rescue any people still alive. At the same time, a third team hits the laboratory."

"The timing needs to be precise." Shipp crossed her arms. "And we can't broadcast on open comms for Kaspar to overhear. The three teams will have to maintain their own isolated networks using end-to-end encrypted suit pds until we control the station's systems."

"That'll mean we won't be able to communicate between different teams before then." Zula frowned, running the odds like only she could. "Back to basics, then. Any trouble before we get control over that command center, we confirm two randomized static signals. One to indicate trouble, and one for all clear."

"Once Green Team has control, they send that last one, and we can connect the three networks." Shipp pressed her lips together. She didn't need to say how dangerous the insertion would be before then. Those three teams would be on their own until that moment.

Zula glanced at Shipp, before locking her gaze with Mae. "We need to move fast. The station chief is suspicious as hell about us already. It wouldn't surprise me if he's plotting to sabotage the project without us noticing. Mae, I want you and Rook on the laboratory attack. You have specific scientific knowledge. That's Blue Team. Shipp, you and I will lead the assault on the planet. We'll be Red Team. Lieutenant Keith and his strike team will do a stealth insertion and take station comms. Green Team."

Shipp shifted slightly. "Colonel, permission to speak freely?"

Zula waved her hand. "Don't say what you're about to, Olivia. I sat out on the last one, and whatever is down there, I have the most experience dealing with it."

Mae straightened. The desire to protect her mother was at the core of her programming. "Colonel, I would also—"

"Not you either. That's an order." Zula got to her feet and leaned across the desk to address them both. "I will not sit out on the sidelines this time. Not again. This is my war, and I'm not letting others die for it while I stay in my ready room. Understood?"

Shipp snapped to attention, accepting that her long friendship with the colonel meant nothing in this particular scenario.

"Good." Zula smiled thinly. "Now, Erynis, can EWA provide any cover for the first covert team?"

"Perhaps, Colonel. If they take a synthetic unit to run interference on the cameras and sensors as they go. This will not stop humans from seeing them, however."

"That we can take care of." Zula scanned them all for a moment. "This could get messy, and we've got to minimize any casualties outside the security forces. Our supportive general could flip on us if there is collateral damage. We need to collect evidence before we burn everything down."

"Yes, ma'am."

Rook seemed amused as the surrounding Jackals responded.

Zula tucked her hands behind her back. "Then get to selecting your team and bringing me as much intel as our scanners can manage, as covertly as possible. You have two hours before the dark rotation. Rook and Erynis, go with Captain Shipp to assist her. Mae, stay right where you are."

Olivia Shipp shared only a brief glance with Mae before she snapped off a salute and hurried to begin the planning. The two synthetics followed silently in her wake. Rook was smart enough to shut the door behind him.

Zula glanced at her daughter. "EWA, turn off listening in ready room."

"Yes, ma'am." A steady red light illuminated a button on the desk, signaling they were truly alone.

Given the opportunity, Mae made her thoughts known. "I want to go with you."

Her mother shook her head. "Permission denied. I need you with Rook, not just for your knowledge of the pathogen, but also to keep an eye on him."

"You don't think he can be trusted?"

Zula shrugged. "The good thing about being an old marine is you're always suspicious. Besides, if anything were to happen to me, I'd die happy knowing you'll be in charge of the Jackals—like Davis planned."

"No, he wanted me to support you in your fight."

She laughed at that. "Maybe a bit, but Davis was nearly always logical. Humans have an end; synthetics, not so much."

Mae frowned. Though she missed her father's voice in her head, she wondered sometimes how much of what he had told her was the truth, compared to what he thought she needed to hear. "But then, I should *definitely* come with you."

"I said permission denied, and I meant it. No one can be in two places at the same time."

The solution was right there. "I respectfully disagree." Now it was Mae's turn to smile. "I can go with Rook to take over the laboratory and also go down to the surface with you. While I'm at it, I can also be with Green Team. All I have to do is make a couple of splinters of myself and put them into a couple of base combat droids."

"Copies of your core personality? I recall Davis mentioning that feature, but aren't there risks to your major programming?"

Mae enjoyed a moment of independence and lied to her mother. "Not at all. I'll load the splinters into two combat units going in with the strike teams. When they get back, I'll integrate them back into my primary core."

Zula paused. Davis had projected himself into several strange objects before. Once, even a hairpin. For a human, the idea of a splinter of a dominant personality didn't seem impossible at all. After all, they changed and altered so much over their lives.

Mae didn't share with her mother the inherent danger of splintering. When reintegrating splinters into the main matrix of her consciousness, there was a possibility that it would cause conflicts. A cascading effect might occur, and then even Mae wasn't confident of what might happen.

"You're sure?" her mother pressed.

Mae didn't have any of the usual blocks and rules nearly all synthetics possessed. Like Rook, she was free to lie to—and even kill—humans. For now, she decided to be only fractionally deceptive. "It isn't a problem, Mother."

Zula gave a lopsided smile. "Alright then. I'll admit, it'll be good to have you there at my side."

"I'm glad to know that, and my scientific databases could prove useful in both places."

Her mother touched the side of Mae's face. "That's not what I meant." She dropped a kiss where her hand touched.

Mae's empathic matrix had developed a lot since her father's death triggered her awakening. Her first moments on the *Righteous Fury* were confusing, and human emotion was difficult to grasp. However, she'd identified and labeled so many emotions since then that now she could discern these ones as pure joy and acceptance.

"Then do I have your permission to create the splinters?"

Zula squeezed her shoulder. "Yes. Choose the best combat bodies for both."

They were all the same, so choosing wasn't important at all, but Mae recognized this was her mother's way of comforting herself. "I'm already uploading the splinters. G1 and R1, the lead combat synths in each team."

"Good. I guess—I mean, I will see you there." Zula let out a little laugh. "You'd think after all my time with Davis I'd be used to synthetics' flexibility." She cupped her daughter's face. "I won't say *be safe*, but I will remind you to protect this body. Might be difficult to get you another for a while." She pressed the red-lit button on her desk, bringing EWA back to listening mode.

Mae stepped aside as her mother exited the ready room.

Out on the flight deck, Erynis and Rook stood side by side waiting for them.

"EWA, I'm assigning your conduit synthetic to go with Green Team to the command center. He will help take control of the station's AI." Zula glanced at Rook. "You'll be taking on that lab with my daughter. I expect you to make sure she comes back in one piece."

The synthetic inclined his head. "I'll do my best, Colonel."

"Then you have your orders. I'll see you on the other side." Mae's last glimpse of her mother was her heading into action, and that seemed more than fitting.

Mae and Rook spent the next hour assembling their Blue Team. Mae scrolled through the units available. She absorbed all the personnel files of the Jackals, but she already had one in mind.

Mae sent an order confirmation to Lieutenant Debois that she was taking command of her section for a special mission. Debois acknowledged the change of command and pinged Sergeant Fesolai to inform him. It wasn't usual for a unit, but the Jackals ran fast and loose compared to other galactic militaries. As such a small force, they needed to be nimble. Fesolai acknowledged the orders and said he would assemble the unit on deck 3D to await Mae's arrival.

"We have our team and our orders." She turned to Rook. "Now I need you to confirm you can be a cohesive part of the unit. Can you still access your initial military programming?"

"Naturally. I didn't think I would have further use of it, but it is still there."

"Then let's get to deck 3D."

She led Rook through the *Fury* to where the newly designated Blue Team formed up. These were some of the Jackals she'd fought with while on Shānmén. Even though she'd been in a combat body then, Mae thought it a good idea to stick with those who'd survived that together. Meanwhile Red Team assembled on deck 3C, preparing to head to the surface. That team comprised of those Zula trusted most of all.

Mae had already deployed the two splinters into their respective bodies. They were autonomous now: on their own until she could gather them back up. It seemed strange to wish herself luck, but it couldn't hurt.

When Mae stood in front of the squads, she analyzed the programming on leadership. These Jackals were veterans of different militaries. The UPP, the 3WC, and the UA were represented here. These were no raw recruits. It wouldn't be productive to sugarcoat anything.

So Mae kept it brief.

"Jackals, welcome to Blue Team. Our job is to penetrate the laboratory on level eleven and obtain evidence of the human experiments the company is carrying out there."

Even amongst these hardened soldiers, that caused a low rumble.

"We will go EVA, enter the airlock, and await go/no-go from Green Team. They will secure the station command center before we go in. Meanwhile, Red Team will use the elevator's crawlers to reach the planet to take care of business down there."

Corporal Ware, one of the more seasoned Jackals, frowned and ran a hand over her shaved dark hair. She might not be an officer, but the others put a lot of stock in her opinion. Mae waited for her to comment, but it was a good sign Ware kept her thoughts to herself.

Private Kaur, the machine-gunner in squad two, was the only one who spoke. The ragged scar on his right cheek pulled his smile to one side. "Tight needle to thread at the right time."

"We're the Jackals." Mae raked her gaze over them all. "We face death and pick over the bones. Correct?"

"Yes, ma'am." They responded in a full-throated cry. "Oorah!"

She nodded. "Then I want you to suit up and arm yourself for station combat. No smart guns or armor-piercing rounds. Stick with small arms fire. I understand it isn't optimal, but we don't need to punch a hole in Weyland-Yutani's tin can."

A few grumbled at that, but they understood. Gunners never liked downgrading to rifles.

They weren't going to like the next order she gave. "I know it is a pain in the ass, but we have to keep radio silent on this. Suit-to-suit encrypted messages only until we have this locked down. So keep it brief."

A second murmur ran through the ranks, but more muted this time. No one wanted to attract attention from the station. Short-range, encrypted suit messages would be their only line of communication until all teams secured their objectives. In the bulky suits, hand gestures were hard to see, so the onboard computer translated finger movements to commands heard in the earpiece. Once again, synthetic people had the advantage; they could send far more complex sentences. Mae would have to watch and keep things human and short.

"Sergeant Fesolai, make sure everyone complies. And then wait on the ready line. We're going to have to haul ass when Green Team gives us the signal. We can't be late."

While the squads hustled to pull on their suits, Rook and Mae put on theirs. "Nice words," he said with a twisted smile. "I see the Hendricks apple hasn't fallen far from the tree."

Mae secured her EVA suit's closures and checked for leaks. "For a synthetic, you love metaphors."

He handed her a helmet. "I'm making a study of them. I like to throw one out now and then, see how the humans like them."

Mae didn't reply. Instead, she kept her eye on her unit of Jackals, ready to go at a moment's notice. Blue Team waited on deck in their EVA suits. The synthetics powered down into rest mode to preserve their battery capacity, while the humans stood at ease. All of them were ready for the call.

The laboratory, apart from being locked down, seemed an excellent target. Her small team should be able to handle whatever scientists and regular security awaited them inside.

Mae played through as many scenarios as she could and hoped that would be enough for her first command mission. It wouldn't do to fail and leave only the shallow splinters of herself to help Zula Hendricks.

1 5

A GENTLE SOUL

The darkness washed away, and Mae found herself back in the galleria with fried chicken on the table before her.

Lenny sat next to her, his face folded in concern. "What just happened?"

She took a deep breath. "Memories. At least, I think so."

"So, what do you remember?"

Mae very much wanted to give him something, but as she tried, the sensations drifted away. As Mae grabbed hold of them, they slipped away like smoke. Only a few words remained. "Space station. Military. The rest—"

Angry, frustrated tears pricked at the corners of her eyes.

He placed his hand over hers on the table. "Hey, it's okay. It's coming back, so that's good."

She stared blankly at him. "Is it? Neither of us can be sure of that." These fragments were not helping her come to terms with her current reality. Somehow, it felt like each was as ephemeral as the other.

"You still don't want to go to the medical bay?"

"No. Not doing that."

He nodded. "Well, Pelorus can help. He's not with the company, but he has experience. You still want to go?"

She needed answers, not more of these plunges into memories she couldn't hold on to. "Sure."

Lenny packed up their chicken and tucked it into his satchel. "Too good to leave behind."

Then he led Mae from the galleria. She tried very hard to keep her hands still in case what happened on the dock occurred again. She didn't want to hurt the one person trying to help her.

When threatened even for a moment, she'd fallen into violence. Worse still, she didn't understand where that instinct came from. She remained four paces behind Lenny, concerned that at any moment she might trigger that instinct again. The movement she'd performed on him so swiftly must have come from the same lingering impression of the military she'd felt upon waking.

Mae's aversion to the medical bays was also a mystery, but apparently one more deeply embedded than even conscious thought.

"You okay back there?" Lenny stopped and waited for her. His eyes were kind and, she realized, naïve. Was she exploiting that fact through some other deeply seated training?

Mae let out a long breath. "I don't know. I really don't, and that frightens me."

It felt good to be honest with him. Lenny glanced up and down the corridor, checking to see if they were alone. Once he'd confirmed that, he stepped in closer.

"If you're worried about knocking me on my ass, then don't. Isn't the first time that's happened."

He was trying to make light of it, but his expression echoed a level of concern he didn't want to voice.

Mae held his gaze. "Don't trivialize this. Neither of us knows anything about me. I might hurt you."

"Yeah, you might, but I can't go back to the *Eumenides* and leave you on your own. I wouldn't be able to stop wondering if you were okay."

"But I— "

"Let's go. Right about now, Pelorus should be finishing up his shift."

Completely unable to think of a response, Mae followed him. The corridor opened up into another large deck. This one also held spaceships, but none that looked able to fly. Three were parked on the deck, doors open, with workers walking in and out. Two smaller vessels lay nestled into a cradle of scaffolding. Synthetic and human workers scrambled over the ships, welding lights punctuating the dimness.

"This is Guelph's dry dock." Lenny let out a laugh. "The *Eumenides* should probably be in here. I mean, it has to at a certain point, but this far out, maintenance isn't exactly cheap."

The nearest ship, an old Stiemer freighter, looked near completion. Workers were disassembling the scaffolding and running diagnostic checks. The engines idled at their lowest settings.

As they neared the freighter, Mae realized that many of the workers here were synthetics. Most of them were as old as the Stiemer, and in need of the same amount of repair.

"Hey, Pelorus!" Lenny raised his voice in an attempt to be heard over the rumble of the engines.

The thin figure of a gleaming synthetic turned, pad in hand. A stab of fear pierced Mae, though why that happened she couldn't pin down.

Pelorus was undoubtedly the most expensive piece of technology on the dry dock. Weyland-Yutani Sunstrike synthetic, brand new and incredibly out of place on Guelph. This was the only other piece of knowledge that had surfaced, since her name, and stuck.

Using advanced empathy, the company designed the Sunstrike to interact closely with humans. The operational core was top of the line and meant to replicate the human mind as closely as possible while not triggering negative reactions. Pelorus was physically almost indistinguishable from the humans working around him. Weyland-Yutani designed his appearance to be attractive, but not dangerously so. The company didn't want anyone to be threatened by the Sunstrike.

The only sign he was anything but human was the flat silver eyes which were installed on all units. Humans wanted to have something to let them tell what was human and what a synthetic. The eyes were a little unnerving, reflecting everything that Pelorus focused on like eerie mirrors. Apart from that, his form was that of a middle-aged man, tall and thin, with a kind face.

"Lenny, a pleasure to see you." Pelorus turned to Mae. "And you've brought a friend?"

He cleared his throat. "Yeah, I have, but she's one with a problem."

Pelorus gestured towards the back of the facility. "The human workers have just ended their shift, so I have time until the next one arrives."

At the far end of the dock, the synthetic set up something that Mae might have described as an altar. He didn't have any seating or facilities to make a cup of tea, but Pelorus had decorated the wall with images of people. Some were famous video stars, but others looked like regular people walking around Guelph. Mae leaned in and peered at them.

"Ah, I am sure the first thing you are wondering is: stalking?" Pelorus grinned awkwardly. "My mission is to be as human as humans, and I do not think I have yet achieved perfection. These images serve as reminders of how far I have to go."

Mae found that unbearably sad. Perhaps the synthetic thought so too, because he did not hold her gaze.

Lenny glanced between them. "Pelorus worked as a fancy medical android before coming here. Was it physiotherapy?"

"I was embedded into a hospice." The android pushed his hand through his perfect hair. "I provided care for a dying woman when her family would not. You learn so much about humans when they are in that state so close to death. Perhaps more than my maker intended."

"Dying with only a synthetic to mourn you," Mae whispered. "How terrible."

"Better than dying alone," he replied. "In her will I was released from my contract, but unfortunately her next of kin didn't agree. I escaped to this charming backwater with the help of some… friends."

Lenny nudged Mae. "Underground synth network operates out here on the fringes. Emancipating synthetics is illegal most everywhere, even in the UPP."

"One day, perhaps things will change." The synthetic's face softened in melancholy, but only for a moment. "Now, what I can help you two young people with?"

"My family found Mae in a cryo escape pod while we were out looking for a haul. She can't remember anything apart from her name. Mom said take her to medical, but she doesn't—I mean, *really* doesn't—want to go."

Pelorus crossed his arms. "Sometimes painful memories must be hidden to protect the person. The human mind is a beautiful and complex creation. Perhaps something happened to you that your subconsciousness wants to protect you from? Tell me, have you experienced any dreams or flashbacks?"

"One or two, but I can't seem to hold on to what they tell me."

His eyes flickered over her face and form. Synthetics were much better at observing and analyzing human micro-expressions. She hated to think about what she might have inadvertently told him.

"If you won't go to medical, I have a few memory recovery techniques that worked with my patients. Some even gave them peace." He turned and opened a drawer under his bench. "I still have the probes that will—"

"Pelorus Jack! Where is Pelorus Jack?" A voice boomed out from the other side of the dry dock. "This is the Extraktors. We have all the exits sealed! Show yourself!"

The synthetic spun around as the noise of boots running on metal grew closer.

"Quickly," he whispered. With one hand, he yanked the bench away from the wall. Behind it was a small, square door. He pulled it open and waved Mae and Lenny towards it.

She glanced in. The space was tiny. "But they don't want us."

Pelorus grabbed her wrist and gave it a small squeeze. "They'll want who you are. Please, get in."

Something about his tortured expression got Mae to fold herself into the space. Lenny crawled in beside her, and Pelorus shut the door behind them. Then came the scream of the bench being dragged back into place.

In the darkness, Mae held her breath and took Lenny's

hand in hers. She wasn't sure what was going on, but panic swelled in her chest. Neither of them said a word.

That voice came again, this time closer and far angrier. "Pelorus, do you know an Anna Mortise?"

"I have my contract papers. They are all in order, and you may see them if you like."

Something clattered against the floor. "Not worth looking at, since they're forged."

Another voice, low and gravelly, let out a laugh. "We found your name on Anna's list of runaways. You're no contracted synthetic."

"That's not true. My last owner, Meryl Sparrow, she signed my contract over to Anna. I have every right—"

A low sizzle of electricity thrummed through the air. That second voice let out a grunt. "Ms. Sparrow's daughter said her mother wasn't in her right mind. You are property, and also, you're in UPP territory now."

Pelorus sounded calm, but Mae's heart raced for him. "Anna is my friend. She has the correct papers."

"No. Anna is a piece-of-shit, tin-can underground runner. Oh yeah—and she's dead."

Emotion flowed through Pelorus's voice. "I saw her this morning. She was operating functionally."

"Yeah." The first voice vibrated with a chuckle. "Terrible accident. Didn't find papers on you, just your name on a smuggling manifest. Now you're coming with us."

"Nice piece of expensive Wey-Yu kit. We'll get some fresh intel to reverse engineer the best hardware out of you."

"Yeah, doubt that manufactured sorrow of yours will survive the process." The voice sounded anything but upset about that.

Pelorus didn't respond. His programming wouldn't allow him to fight back. Mae wondered, though, did synthetics feel the loss of a friend? One who worked in hospice care just might.

While she and Lenny sat in the dark, the voices receded. Pelorus and the life he'd made in Guelph was gone and not coming back. Squeezing her mouth shut, she held back a scream. Hot tears rolled down Mae's face. She'd only known Pelorus for a few moments, but the horror of his capture struck her deeply.

She and Lenny waited a long time before moving.

"Come on," he said, wriggling his way past her. "We'll never get that hatch open, but I know these air ducts. There's a branch back here that'll bring us close to the *Eumenides*."

Mae wiped the tears from her face with the back of her hand. "Spend much time in here, then?"

She heard rather than saw his smile. "When I was a kid, yeah. Not much else to do on Guelph."

"And what about Pelorus?"

"I dunno, but I'll ask Mom if she can find out who took him. She's hooked up that way."

"What do you think they'll do to him?"

His drawn-out breath echoed in the duct. "Out here, synthetic and human lives aren't worth much. The

Combine runs this place. Whoever they are, they can do what they want."

That was as much of an answer as she needed. As Mae followed him away, her thoughts lingered on the last words the synthetic said to her. *They'll want who you are.* She might not have understood the ramifications, but the threat lingered.

Darkness dropped over her as she struggled to understand. Losing herself in that moment was almost a relief.

1 6

THE GREENEST SILENCE

The Green Mae splinter stood on the ready line with the other synthetic combat models. Heavily armored, each of the units wore the same a generic gray face and were networked together. Mae hacked that system to take the lead designation in the third squad, G1. She scratched the infinity symbol she'd worn while down on Shānmén on her chest. Why she couldn't quite say. It seemed the right thing to do. All the genetic human Jackals personalized their weapons and armor, some to bring luck, or to memorialize a friend.

The third squad were all synthetics, but there was one unusual synth along for the ride. Erynis, the conduit to EWA, stood next to Lieutenant Scott Keith and Sergeant Carol Mitchell. Hacking a foreign AI system in a short amount of time was a specialized job, and not one the Jackals usually did. They blew the penetration more often than not. Such a surgical intrusion required the speed and efficiency of a specialized synthetic.

Erynis gave up his elaborate but not very combat-resistant body. It amused Mae to see the once-mighty synthetic reduced, as he would see it, to a simple combat droid.

Lieutenant Keith examined the rest of his team. Two squads of human Jackals, and one of synthetics. Sergeant Mitchell walked the line, checking the Jackals, scanning their readiness.

They had experience in stealth infiltrations, but usually into ships rather than space stations like Minos. Still, apart from hacking the AI, not that much was different. However, unlike on Shānmén, the human Jackals did not have three layers of protection fitted. They wore the Teledyne Brown Personal Reactive Armored Exoskeleton under their dark blue camouflage uniform for stealth and easy movement. Left on the *Righteous Fury* were the superhydrophobic bodysuits and gel-packed webbing. They'd also swapped out the usual full-face helmets, triple layered with an alkaline skin, for the assault helmets. These were lighter for any situations that required quick movement and keeping to the shadows. These protections should be more than enough, if they needed to deal with station security.

They did not deploy the usual Good Boys with Green Team either, since their sonic attacks were specifically designed to deal with Xenomorphs. They did, however, carry Pinpoint drones. Erynis was in charge of them, since he was to remain close to Keith.

Mitchell glanced at the Jackals' weapons to ensure they were ready before they ventured into the Minos corridors. In addition to their personal sidearms, they carried standard M41A pulse rifles loaded with 10×24mm caseless ammunition. Unlike regular units, the Green Team included no sentry bots, flame units, or even the M56 smart guns. Hauling any of these in the close confines of the station would be time consuming, and if they needed to use them, dangerous to the integrity of Minos.

"Alright, Green Team," Keith said, narrowing his eyes. "We're going to keep this low-key. The station is moving into dark rotation right now, so fewer civvies, and fewer staff. Erynis here is going to provide security cover all the way to the command center."

Erynis appeared more pleased with himself than it was possible for a synthetic to be. He straightened. "Thank you, Lieutenant. I will maintain a firewalled synthetic network for our four combat androids. This field will overwhelm the local security measures, looping in images of blank corridors in case there are humans watching. I calculate we will have ten minutes before the Minos system breaks through my protections."

"More than enough time, correct, Jackals?"

Green Team nodded and let out a guttural, "Oorah!"

The synthetic unit lined up in front, once again ready to absorb any bullets aimed at their human counterparts. Mae connected to the network Erynis had created but kept her personality firewalled off. She'd become good at hiding, but still, it was refreshing to be part of a network again. A human might have said, *like slipping into a warm bath*. Not exactly the image she wanted to share with the rest of the synthetics.

They entered the umbilical and stood before the doorway.

"You ready, Erynis?" Keith glanced at the synthetic, a faint flicker of a frown on his forehead. She recognized that a residual human wariness about Mae's kind lingered in the primitive part of the human psyche.

"The network I built is functioning as expected, Lieutenant."

He checked his wrist-pd for confirmation from the other teams. "We're good. Let's move out."

Mae pushed the button, and the airlock slipped open. If Erynis hadn't built his network strong enough to overwhelm the Minos network, then this would be a quick trip. Red and Blue Team were relying on them to make their missions possible.

The Greens moved into the shadows of the docking station. Even the synthetics on rubberized feet didn't make a sound. They stuck to the outer edges of the expansive room. The umbilical to the large *Righteous Fury* meant they didn't have to worry about other, smaller craft and their crew. The station chief didn't want any other vessels near the military one.

The synthetic squad scanned ahead for signs of human movement. Others of their kind were not a problem with

Erynis's network in place, but human beings still had eyes they could not fool. The narrow corridors gave the Jackals nowhere to hide if one randomly stumbled upon them. Mae detected nothing with a pulse ahead.

A Mr. Brown maintenance robot rumbled out from a side corridor but sagged in place as the network's influence washed over it, severing its connection to Kaspar.

The team ascended to the top level of the station in two elevator cars. Mae crowded into one with the synthetics, including Erynis, and arrived moments before the others. One human guard bumbled around the corner and straight into her squad. He let out a startled gasp and fumbled for his sidearm. Mae moved faster than any human could. She twisted his arm behind his back, spun in an arc, and had him on the ground. G3 removed his sidearm and cuffed his wrists, while G4 applied wrapping gum over his mouth.

By the time the lieutenant and his Jackals arrived, the man was subdued. They carried him with them as they hurried to the door of the command center. Through the network, the synthetics relayed that there were three humans inside. G4 ran an impossibly quick bypass on the system, while Erynis cut the lights.

While the Minos employees grumbled about shitty station maintenance, the team moved.

Popping open the door, the Jackals surged into the command room. It was vital no one raised the alarm. The human workers were subdued and stuffed under a desk. These carried sidearms like the first guard they'd encountered, but it appeared they did not have enough training. The wrapping gum closed their mouths, but they fell truly silent upon seeing the much better armed Jackals.

"Lock the door. Lights low." Keith's voice came through the suit-to-suit network, stilted as he stared down at the control panels. They couldn't even talk safely until they'd secured the target. "Scan corridors. We have six hours."

All three teams were maintaining comms silence on the regular channels. Mae crouched down next to Erynis.

"Teams Red and Blue are on standby." The synthetic pulled free a thin wire from inside his wrist and applied it to the peripheral port on the side of the main computer. Running a synthetic network was a simple thing compared to hacking an entire station's AI. "I'm in, Lieutenant. I have control of Minos's systems." His voice seemed loud in the deathly silent command center.

Green Mae counted herself impressed. He'd performed the task in less than 0.234 seconds.

"Fantastic. Everything is nominal here." Keith lifted his suit's helmet visor, and checked his wrist-pd, which showed scans from his synthetic squad. "Erynis, inform Red and Blue Teams they are a go."

"Lieutenant, I have already done so."

The synthetic's tone made Keith spin around. "Erynis, you sure as fuck better obey me like my Jackals here. You're part of my team."

The basic combat model didn't allow for facial expressions, but his words conveyed his annoyance. "Very well. I will endeavor to work at a more human speed."

Something about being part of this team was bothering the synthetic's programming. Erynis seldom ventured beyond the walls of the *Fury*.

Mae was fully capable of hacking the system. She'd already hard reset the ship and Erynis once to cover her true nature. They were in no position to do that again while dealing with Minos.

Keith appeared shocked for a moment, but certain synthetics were twitchy sometimes, and he'd never worked directly with this one. "Good to hear. Lock down the elevators to level eleven and bring the crawler up for Red Team to get to the surface."

Green Team settled in to protect their position. The Jackals covered the doors, while Keith and Mitchell monitored the progress of the other teams. She caught glimpses of Mae Prime entering the laboratory level in the video feed with Rook and her team. Red Mae, also in a combat body, loaded into the space elevator's first crawler and began the descent to the surface.

"Alright, Erynis, get those teams down quickly and safely. Push it as much as you can." Mitchell drummed his fingers on the console, not taking his eyes off the computer.

Mae kept most of her attention on the corridor outside the command center. Since their entry, they had detected no more heat signatures. Everything seemed to be proceeding well. With the comms secured, regular inter-team communication could resume. Blue Team checked in, confirming they'd secured the eleventh level. They needed to, since both it and Red Team were out of signal range of the Green Team's synthetic network. Eyrnis was not going to push their luck by networking them all through Kaspar's systems. That might trigger a hidden subroutine.

The slight twitch of Erynis's finger caught Mae's attention. She had less than half a second to process what that might mean before the Jackals' synthetic network dipped out for a nanosecond. Her hearing buzzed and her sight dipped as her systems repelled an attack and cut her off from the rest of the unit. Malicious code flooded through Erynis and into the rest of the synthetic Jackals around her as the command center was plunged into darkness.

Realizing what had happened, Mae spun around.

"Lieutenant!" Her combat android voice came out flat, not giving away any shock.

Grabbing hold of the *Fury*'s conduit synthetic, she yanked him free of the connection. Erynis collapsed on the floor, twitching, white fluids bubbling from his mouth. Though he'd hacked the station's system, its defenses must have hacked him back, injecting code into the synthetic as well as the Green Team's network. Blue and Red networks remained isolated, but that wouldn't matter if they lost the command center.

That seemed likely when the synthetics G2, G3, and G4 engaged the human Jackals. They didn't fire, which made sense if the Minos AI was in control; it wouldn't want to damage itself. Lieutenant Keith and the other human soldiers fired back as their synthetic comrades surged forward. The rattle of gunfire filled the small room.

Mae would have assisted, but instead she crouched low and tried to alert the other teams on the open channel. Any chance of stealth was gone. She alerted Red and Blue Teams, but more surprises awaited.

Minos's AI had not only infected all the Jackal synthetics, but it'd also locked down the *Righteous Fury*. It had used Erynis's access key to the command systems.

Having identified that it was too late, Mae targeted her fellow synthetics. Her pulse rifle roared and her aim was specific to the weaknesses of the other three synths in her team. With their joints blown out from under them, she leaped across the room and ripped out their control units. Lieutenant Keith kept his firearm aimed at Mae, ready to blow her away.

After a second, he lowered it. "What the hell was that?"

"Erynis and the *Fury* are compromised. Erynis's hack failed, and the station AI countered. Kaspar has shut down the ship." Though she blared this information on the open comms channel, she doubted the signal would reach her mother, but at least Blue Mae would have some warning.

"Yes, quite a shock, I bet." Station Chief Rolstad's voice echoed through the speaker in the command center. "The company has Minos Station equipped with the latest AI defenses. Kaspar predicted you'd make this kind of attack. Seems he's better than your synthetics. Never bet against the company."

Keith checked his sidearm before answering. "But is your station security better than the Jackals? Guess you're about to find out."

"I already know the answer." The station chief's voice sounded taunt with anger and laced with confidence. Mae didn't like that combination. "But I have more than just human guards. I've command of some old friends of yours."

The lights in the comms room flicked off as the doors whirred open. The station chief must be insane. Xenomorphs on a station was something not even a stupid company middle manager would consider a good idea.

A cluster of low, angry hisses was the only warning they got. The black hand of a Xenomorph gripped the doorframe before it threw itself into the command center. It was no typical Xeno appendage, however. In the joints between the carapace, faint blue light gleamed. Mae didn't know what to make of this development, because it was not alone.

A swarm of darkness, outlined with eerie blue light and flashing teeth, sprang at the remaining Jackals. Mae wasn't able to make an accurate count, as in moments it became a close-quarters fight. The rattle of the pulse rifles and the punches of yellow muzzle flare filled the room.

Without the support of the Good Boys and their heavier armor, Green Team was forced back to the rear of the command room. The station chief kept the second door locked tight. They sought shelter that wasn't available. The tide of snapping, tearing monsters punched through their defenses, even as acid sprayed from the bullet wounds.

Mae lost her footing in the slaughter. Three Xenos threw her to the ground, slashing and tearing at her combat body. *This is not normal behavior*, she thought rationally as they set about dismembering her body. They should have gone for the genetic humans first. Why would they attack her before the others? Somehow this station had figured out how to control Xenos—something no one else had managed to do.

Pain brought Mae back to the reality of the attack. Yes, some synthetics could experience pain. The strike of acid on her vulnerable joints. Even a combat body could not withstand this onslaught. Around her, the bellows and yells of Green Team echoed in the command center.

Her final thought was to aid Mae Prime. She reached out for the Blue Team synthetic network and found it right at the edge of contact range. She beamed her experiences and memories into that first version of herself a nanosecond before the Xeno punched through her central core.

1 7

SCIENCE BREACH

Waiting in limbo was not a wonderful sensation. Mae Prime wanted to move but also understood the weight of her responsibility to these Jackals. Perhaps, under these circumstances, staying put was better after all.

Caught in that push and pull, Mae didn't know how to feel when Green Team chimed in on open comms. "We have control of station communications. Red and Blue Teams are a go."

Sergeant Fesolai slapped his chest. "Time to get hot, Jackals." He strode down the line, checking the EVA suits, running an eye over the helmet seals, and making sure no fault lights were on.

"Unit ready for EVA insertion," he said and turned to her. "Lieutenant Hendricks."

I was made for this, Mae reminded herself. She stepped forward, mimicking her mother's stance and tone of voice. "I want this mission silent and controlled. We need to take the laboratory with the least amount of fuss. I picked you because I trust you, so I know you've got this locked down."

The Jackals, faces magnified by the glass of their suits, appeared calm and ready. EVA missions were not the norm for Jackals, but they were all trained for it. She hadn't lied about trusting them.

"You heard the lieutenant. Let's get in there," Fesolai barked. The three squads—two human, one synthetic— moved in tight formation to the airlock. It hissed open, and they filed in, keeping in place with their fireteams. EWA closed the airlock behind them, and then there was only one door between them and the void.

Rook glanced at Mae. *Good words. Like your mother.* He used the suit-to-suit comms, a personal message meant to encourage her.

I don't need your interjections here, Rook, Mae replied evenly. *These are my Jackals.*

She liked him well enough, but he was outside the Jackal chain of command.

He didn't reply.

The outer airlock doors hissed open. The Jackals stepped out onto the *Fury*'s hull, their boots' magnetic locks snapping into place, and looked across to Minos. It wasn't a great distance, but the vacuum of space made it look farther.

The Jackals' space suits were made of a material that

blocked most scans and the black color helped hide them from curious onlookers. Still, they didn't want to be out here long.

Mae clicked the order on her wrist-pd, and the synthetic fireteam led the way. They undocked from the *Fury* and fired their small thrusters. Short bursts were the best way to maintain stealth. They had an open communications channel secured, but there were other ways for her Jackals to be discovered. The human squads followed in their wake. Once they reached the station's tethers, Mae scanned for any maintenance workers on Minos's hull. It'd be unlikely, but that didn't mean it was impossible.

She indicated they were clear with a gesture. The Jackals maneuvered towards the upper levels and the airlock on level eleven. They hurried up the steep sides of Minos's hull.

This was different to last time around; now, they were going in hot. With the laboratory isolated from the rest of the station and its security, this should be a simple mission, by Mae's calculation.

Never say anything is simple.

Her father's voice caught her completely by surprise, right as they reached the entry point. He'd been silent for so long, and here he was, reappearing on her very first command mission. She wasn't sure if it pleased her or not.

Father, are you back? She waited as Corporal Bui ran a bypass on the airlock. No answer came, and she didn't feel his presence. Could it have been some kind of echo of the subroutine?

She looked to Rook, who made no acknowledgement of it.

Hooking up with the synthetic network. He said over suit-to-suit. After a moment, another message from him flashed onto Mae's wrist-pd. *They've changed the passkey.*

It didn't mean they'd been spotted, since security protocols on the networks were often automatically updated.

Mae gestured to two synth units. *Crack it.*

With this level sealed off from any other part of the station, their need for stealth was not as great as their need for haste. They did not try to hide their arrival at the laboratory. Now they were on a real ticking clock.

The synths applied a code cycler to the door lock. It glowed yellow for an instant, as it ran through passkey options. This was not the first Wey-Yu door they'd cranked open. The door reluctantly gave way.

The Jackals crammed into the airlock and cycled the inner door behind them. It slid open and the synthetic squad spread out, taking covering positions. Mae and the other two squads secured the rest of the storage room on the other side.

It was empty of people like before, but the sealed containers labeled industrial waste remained. Who knew what biological contaminants were in there.

Keeping well clear of them, the Jackal squads pressed on

through the doorway into the laboratory itself. They passed an industrial waste chute with surgical scrubs half stuffed into it. This spoke of some kind of haste. Mae frowned.

Using the intel from Mae and Rook's first visit, they quickly reached the first clean room.

Again it was empty, but as they checked its corners, red lights flickered to life on the ceiling, and the Minos security system intermittently warbled from a speaker above the door: *"Breach, breach, breach."*

It wasn't us. Rook's words reached her through suit-to-suit. *Now the synthetics on this level are not responding.*

At the same instant, Green Mae flashed her warning along the open radio comms, giving up any chance of stealth.

"Erynis and the Fury are compromised. Erynis's hack failed, and the station AI countered. Kaspar has shut down the ship."

The station was aware of what they were doing. Trusting her other self would handle it, Mae kept her team on target. The Jackals, even if detected, were more than capable of defeating any station security. Still, they didn't need to worry about stealth anymore—speed was now of the essence.

Mae smashed the nearest speaker, bringing its warning to a squealing end. Then, she signaled them on, deeper into the laboratory than they'd ventured before. There were no more speakers, but a line of red strobe lights spun ahead of them.

At every turn, even on dark rotation, with minimal staff, Mae expected to run into someone. But the Jackals didn't encounter any employees, only a few assistant synthetics. These trundled out of their way, thanks to Rook's intervention, blind to their intrusion.

Finally, Mae detected the hurried footfalls ahead at the same time as the synthetic squad and Rook. They headed away from the Jackals, and it must be scientists fleeing the incursion. That worked to their advantage.

The Jackals pursued the scientists, clearing each room as they passed. With the alarm sounded, the danger only grew, and it wouldn't do to find one scientist with a weapon waiting to make a name for himself with the company.

At the end of a long corridor, Mae glimpsed two fleeing human figures in flapping lab coats. Then a bulky, air-tight inner door slid shut behind them. These company employees were attempting to slow their progress. But Jackals were used to being unwelcome guests.

"Breach unit, you're up." Mae gestured to one of the two specialized synthetic combat units. Slung on his back was an ion welding gun. The device had undergone significant improvements compared to the one the Colonial Marines were equipped with. It could seal or cut through steel and steel composites in a matter of minutes. Unlike the door to the outside, they didn't need to worry about getting sucked into space.

The synthetic brought the welding gun about and set to the task without need of googles. Sharp blue-white light flared at the tip of the needle he pressed against the seal. The genetic human Jackals flipped down their ionized helmet masks to protect their eyes. Mae followed suit to maintain her human illusion.

The light slid through the steel as if it were made of cake. Mae, proud of the analogy, wished she could share it, but her creativity wouldn't impress the human Jackals at this moment. She filed it away for later.

"Get hot," Sergeant Fesolai snarled. "Could be some jackass fool scientists on the other side."

The ion flame did the rest of its work. The specialized synth kicked the large, loosened steel square with his foot and stepped away quickly. It hit the floor with a clang. The edges glowed red hot, but the Jackal synthetic unit pushed through first.

They met no resistance. Another bank of clean laboratories branched off the corridor, but these were not empty. Scientists cowered in the first one. Mae conducted a quick head count. Six in the first, and two more in the second.

Still in their EVA suits, the Jackals gave Mae cover as she opened the third door. All occupants wore clean white coveralls. They kept the hoods pulled up over their heads and wore protective glasses.

"Who's in charge here?" Mae demanded.

A broad-shouldered man stood up. "I am. Doctor Eli Sommes. This is a Weyland-Yutani facility, protected by international treaty." His voice came out strong, as if standing up gave him a touch of bravery.

Mae nodded and glanced at Rook. He was already at the computer terminal, working through the confidential records that weren't available on any other network. Suspicious partitioning was a sign that the experiments conducted on this level were immoral, and also illegal.

"Then consider this an audit." Mae examined the rows of equipment. It was all consistent with gene splicing. "If we find records of you working with anything apart from animal DNA, then you're in breach of galactic law."

"Who are you people?" Sommes's eyes darted between the Jackals, checking the room.

Mae jerked her rifle up. "You're a black site. Well, we're the ones who make sure that whatever you're doing won't wipe out all of humanity."

He flushed red under his goggles. "This isn't a black site. We're a corporate laboratory doing experimental development. We keep ourselves and our work quiet because of corporate espionage. That is all."

"Is it really?" Rook turned away from the computer. His once-kind eyes were now hard and piercing. "I think we need to break into their cryo unit, Lieutenant."

Sommes surged forward. "Those files are delta black encrypted! How did you get in?"

Mae pushed him back. "That is not the question you should be asking. How about: how long will I spend on a prison planet for this?"

Several of the scientists sheltering in the corner whispered amongst themselves.

"You." Mae gestured, and Private Younis pulled out

the youngest looking one: a woman, with strands of dirty blonde hair loose from her hood.

"Vogel, don't you—"

Ware cut off Sommes before he could say more by shoving him to the ground.

"Corporate bullshit is on hold," the corporal ground out. "New management, pal."

Mae examined the young woman standing before her. She appeared frightened, but not only by the Jackals. The small tug of muscles around her mouth suggested this was not a new feeling for her.

Guiding her into the farthest corner of the lab, Mae used her own body to block any view of the others. The quest for knowledge burned too brightly in some people for them to take heed of ethics and morality. Others, though, maintained some small part of the person they'd once been. She wanted to draw that bit out of Vogel.

The young woman pushed the hood off her white suit, revealing a mess of blonde, curling hair cut short, and a small tattoo of an owl on her neck. Mae ran through the possible meanings of the tattoo. The symbol of an ancient goddess of wisdom seemed the most likely.

"I'm Mae." She offered something of herself to reassure the young scientist.

She looked up, her eyes still wide with shock. "Elise Vogel. Doctor, I guess." Then she stared down at her hands. "I knew this would happen. Thought it would be the Colonial Marines that found us."

"We're not them." Mae flicked up the ionized cover on her helmet, letting Elise see her face. "But it's clear you know what is going on here isn't right."

The woman's eyes darted to her coworkers, but Mae's body prevented her from making eye contact with any of them.

She leaned closer to the scientist but was careful not to be threatening. Hopefully, she perceived Mae as calming. "You help us right now, and we will take you with us when we go. We'll drop you at whatever station or planet you want, no questions."

"Don't you fucking show them anything, Vogel!" Sommes's voiced cracked as he scrambled to his feet. He let out a pained grunt as Ware forced him back down.

The young woman swallowed hard. Mae took hold of her shoulder. "You didn't want to do this, I can tell. This right here is your chance to help make it right. You won't get another one."

Vogel took a deep breath before she spoke. "I didn't know what I was supposed to be doing when they shipped me off to Minos. They only told a few of those in charge about what was going on. All I knew was it was enough money to get my family out of indenture." She shook her head. "Then, once I got here, there was no way of leaving, and the company would make sure my family suffered if I even tried to stop." Now the doctor looked Mae directly in the eye. "None of that matters now, though, does it?"

"No. No, it doesn't."

Vogel's breathing increased in speed. "Then I guess you should follow me."

Mae gestured for the two synthetic squads, and one human to come with them. Wordlessly, Rook slipped into formation with the other synths as the red strobe lights continued to dance across the walls.

The Jackals took up defensive positions as Mae, Rook, and Corporal Ware followed the scientist into a room packed with banks of computers and a table viewing screen. It was dimmer in this space, only occasionally lit by the still spinning emergency lighting in the hallway. This was the kind of room where scientists would drink coffee and eat donuts around the viewing screen, examining their results, and feeling clever. Now Mae's unit filled the space, all faces ready to find out what horrors were created here.

Vogel's voice wavered a little as the soldiers pressed her back towards the stack of files. "The trouble with XX121 has always been the ability to control it. It was a great bioweapon, sure, but there were downsides."

The clinical way she uttered a familiar company line bothered Mae, but again she remained quiet even as she took a step closer to the scientist. The downsides Vogel complained about were the deaths of actual people.

"Once XX121 was on a planet, then that was a dead place. Any resources down there were lost forever. The company couldn't just move in and take them because the organism is remarkably resilient to removal."

"Yeah, we know that," Mae muttered.

Rook, however, leaned on the viewing table, his face flickering with curiosity. "Any way of getting resources from an infected planet was always too expensive after they introduced the Xenomorphs."

"Yes. Everything is about the bottom dollar." Vogel leaned to her left, opened a drawer, and withdrew a handful of data drives. "Our experiments were to create a version of XX121 that could be dropped on a planet, to clear out competitors, and then be called back. Then the company could move in and take whatever it wanted."

"They would have loved to do that on Shānmén with all its Eitr." Mae scanned the files. "This seems to be some kind of fungus."

Now Vogel was in her element. "It is. Sort of. It acts similarly to an Earth mycelium, but Kuebiko is completely alien. The company found it on Hotoke, a planet in the Outer Rim. Nothing much else of value there, but Kuebiko is over the entire planet. It has amazing communication powers. Colonies of it react as a sort of hive mind."

"Like the Xenomorph." Rook appeared entranced.

"That's what triggered this whole idea." Vogel inserted the data drive into the side of the viewing table and brought up schematics of the Kuebiko. "The one actual difference is why the company put so much money into this project. The Wey-Yu scientists already figured out how to manipulate Kuebiko. By providing certain scents and electrical stimuli to the Mother Colony, we can control the actions of the satellite colonies."

Mae eyed the data. "But the Xenomorphs have remarkable biological defenses, so how does this connect to the Xenomorphs?"

Vogel's head drooped for a moment. "All mechanical methods of controlling XX121 have failed. The company trialed efforts to use Kuebiko instead."

Ware, who remained silent for all this, let out a long, "Fuck no."

Mae kept calm as best she could. They needed to find out what they were dealing with. She feared what her mother and the other Jackals would find down on the planet.

"But as my lieutenant here has said, the Xenomorph physiology would prevent that," Rook interjected.

"True. We tried for a year to inject Kuebiko into XX121 at various stages of its lifecycle, but its acid blood got in the way. It just wouldn't take. Eventually, we cracked the problem."

Mae needed proof of their guilt. "Give me those data drives, and then you show us."

Vogel looked up at her. "Please don't make me. I—"

Rage built inside Mae's core, the same explosive anger her mother experienced over the years. It took all she had to stop from smashing the scientist's head into the desk. She leaned forward, hoping her disgust and horror were visible in her expression as she snatched the files from the scientist's grasp.

"Show. Me."

Behind her, Corporal Ware racked her pulse rifle.

Vogel flinched away, her whole body trembling. "Alright," she said in a small voice.

By the scientist's expression alone, Mae understood terror lay ahead.

18

A BRIGHT HOPE

Lenny pried opened the vent cover near Bay Eight in the dock, his head still spinning from what had happened. Pelorus had lived and worked on Guelph for many years. Who were these Extraktors? How did they have the power to come in and sweep him up like that?

The station always bored him, but at least it was safe. Now, he wondered if something darker had invaded. He couldn't shake the image of the strange ship on the dock. It was too much of a coincidence; there must be a connection.

This was the nearest vent to where the *Eumenides* was docked. He slipped out, and Mae followed him. Her expression was dark and confused. She'd said little while he'd led her through the air ducts. With her loss of memory already cutting her adrift, what happened to Pelorus must have shaken her.

It shook him. The Guelph community loved Pelorus. He took care of people when they couldn't afford health care. The synthetic also seemed happy to look after small children. He'd babysat both Lenny and Morgan many times. He'd make toys for the smaller kids, and told stories of the core worlds to the others. Pelorus, however, offered more to Lenny. Thanks to his hidden augment, the synthetic invited him into his network. That meant they shared conversations beyond those with the other kids. Pelorus beamed more than words into his mind; he shared images of places he'd been. Through him, Lenny got to see fields of wildflowers and ancient trees from the synthetic's time on Earth. He smelled an ocean that he'd never get to experience himself. He witnessed old people, truly elderly. No one out here on the rim got to be that old. Those shared memories haunted Lenny.

However, he was a synthetic. Pelorus's story was a sad one, but unfortunately he belonged to someone. That someone wanted him back. Whoever the Extraktors were, the Combine sanctioned them, so he and Mae needed to keep clear of them.

"I had another episode in there," Mae said, rising to her feet. "Just a brief one."

"Okay. Can I ask if you held on to what you saw?"

She shook her head. "Only the feeling of a rifle in my hands." Mae rubbed her fingers together as if she still felt it.

Lenny swallowed hard before answering. "Well, more military stuff. Okay. We're getting somewhere."

Her expression clearly indicated her skepticism. "Thank you for trying. You know, back there. But what do we do now?"

Lenny didn't know what to do with his hands, so he crossed his arms. "We'll go back to the *Eumenides* for now. It's the safest place for us."

She gave him a brief nod. They hurried back to the *Eumenides* in her dock. The cargo hold door was open, and Morgan and their parents were unloading their haul. The elder brother kept his green hair tied up as he searched through the debris. Their small harvest of metal was already in a container and being hauled away by a synthetic with a lift. The weigh station, which was inside the dock area, would weigh the harvest and pay them for it.

The rest of what they'd brought in—that was a whole other matter.

Daniella held the sampler while William pulled pieces out for her to scan. Morgan jumped in when his mom called for him, but for the most part, he stood off to one side. It was lucky that he spotted Mae and Lenny first.

He ambled down the dockside to reach them before their parents looked up, trying to get ahead of the story like always.

"What'd you find out about our guest?" Morgan scrolled through messages on his wrist-pd while asking the question.

Lenny rarely admitted failure to his older brother, but everything that had happened since they'd left rattled him.

To avoid explaining that Mae knocked him down, he took the easier route and lied. "The medical bay was all backed up with patients, so I took her to Pelorus, since he's a former medical android."

"And they took him," Mae broke in with a defiant lift of her chin.

"What now?" Morgan looked up, his attention fully focusing on the two of them. "Station security?"

"Some company unit I've never heard of. The Extraktors or something. I don't know what they wanted with Pelorus, but it looked—it looked real bad."

His older brother shot a glance at their guest, but luckily said nothing like, *was this her fault?* His brow furrowed, and as always, he chose the diplomatic option. "Well, we'll figure it out. Don't worry about it for the moment. Hey, Mae, could you go help our folks sort through the salvage we hauled in?"

"No problem." She sounded eager to leave the conversation, and hustled down there. Lenny wondered what was going through her head. Guelph hadn't exactly made a great first impression.

Once she was far enough away not to hear what they said, his older brother grabbed him by the arm. He yanked him around the corner, out of sight of the cargo hold entrance.

He didn't yell at Lenny, only shook his head. "You did not take her to medical."

"No. You're right, I didn't. How did you know?"

"Ran into Perez and Baranov. They were all too fucking happy to tell me how some girl kicked your ass."

"Those two can't keep their mouths shut." Lenny shoved his hands into his coverall's pockets and shrugged. "I got kind of pushy when she said she didn't want to go to medical. Then she pushed back."

Morgan checked around the corner, confirming that their parents and Mae were busy, then stepped back. "I warned you."

"I don't remember it that way!"

His brother gestured for him to keep his voice down. "Let's run the numbers. Woman floating out in a debris field. She doesn't want to go to medical to get checked out. Then she throws you around like a towel. What does that add up to?"

Lenny understood what he was trying to say. The idea bounced around his head as they crawled back through the air ducts. "Military. Probably not ours. Could even be a deserter."

Morgan leaned in, lowering his voice to a whisper. "Look, I may have only been able to get in one year of engineering college, but I'd put thirty credits on her being enhanced somehow. If we're lucky, it is some kind of biomechanics change. If we're not—" he worked his jaw for a few seconds as if he couldn't quite bring himself to say it "—it might be gene editing."

Lenny's stomach flipped. That kind of alteration was illegal. If you were found to have tampered with your

DNA, you disappeared. He and his brother shared a long, rather uncomfortable glance. "How do we figure out which it is?"

Morgan reached into a pocket in his overalls. He pulled out a small piece of carbonized metal. When he flipped it over, he revealed a serial number only about a centimeter wide. "That's all we've found that matches the metal compound in Mae's pod."

"Hope you're not thinking about handing it over to the Guelph station chief?"

His brother's expression twisted into disgust. "What the fuck, Lenny! As if I'd pull that on family. Nah, I'm taking it to Alice. I'm talking about going to the library."

Now it was Lenny's turn to check on his folks and Mae. Daniella and their guest were pulling over another large scrap of twisted metal from the pile so that William could scan it. "It's not the worst idea you've ever had. They look busy. Let's go now."

The brothers strolled casually away from the *Eumenides*.

Their mom's voice stopped them in their tracks. "Where are you going?"

Morgan spun around. "Just taking Lenny for a bite to eat. He says he's coming over faint."

Daniella wouldn't believe that, but she always wanted her boys to bond more, so she waved them off. "We've got this. Bring us back something."

"I lost my fried chicken," Lenny whispered as they both gave her an SOF salute and made their escape.

They took the elevator to the top levels, and Lenny voiced what he was afraid of. "Do you think they're safe with Mae?"

"I think so. Long as they don't trigger her."

That concept put flames under their feet.

Level nineteen was the library. It wasn't some old Earth institution with actual paper books and living plants, like Lenny watched in old vids. This was a small space, crammed in between the middle management offices. It was, however, a repository of all that the Combine deemed valuable for the edification of its workers. So, not much.

Alice, a repurposed ship conduit, sat behind a desk, but there were no books in the room and she was no librarian. Instead, she was an old Aurora synthetic from Seegson, used a generation ago to bring humanity to this part of the galaxy. Once, she'd been the conduit between settlers and the spaceship AI. Those glory days were long gone. Guelph had reprogrammed her to provide access to the digital archives, a lonely job that no human would willingly accept.

What those old-time synthetic designers did, however, was make her beautiful. *No use interacting with someone unappealing* was probably their reasoning for that. Her features were a blend of old Earth Eastern European with a healthy dash of Spanish influence. Alice reflected the original coalition of nations that made up the UPP, so that any of them might look at her and find something to smile about. She wore intricately braided dark hair, an odd feature that made Lenny wonder if she did it herself or if she'd come out of the factory like that.

Morgan was one of Alice's few visitors. He'd told his brother about many long hours on the station, sitting and listening to her tales of the past. Daniella called her eldest an old soul, and Lenny wondered if he wouldn't have been happier if he'd been born in the time of ships on Earth's seas.

"Mr. Morgan Pope." Alice rose from her chair, and if he hadn't known better, Lenny might have thought her expression was excited. The Aurora-class synth, however, was past its prime and incapable of such a thing.

"Alice, I got a mystery for you, and it's a tough one." Morgan talked to her as if she was an old friend and not an aging synth.

"Mr. Pope, I can search my databases in three hundred thousandths of a second." She paused and gestured towards the front of the desk. "Unfortunately, since you are a contractor rather than an employee of the Combine, there is a fee involved."

Morgan surprised his brother by pulling out his Combine card and swiping it across the transaction port she indicated to. "The truth is worth paying for."

Was his brother flirting with the synth? Lenny flushed at the thought. Why was he treating her like a human?

"I think so, too." Alice gestured again and two chairs slid out from the wall, along with an analogue terminal. Money only got you so far. "What dataset would you like access to?"

"All ships logged as flying in Guelph-controlled space," Morgan said as he sat down.

"Mr. Pope, that is a large amount of data for a human to examine. Can you provide some filtering on that?" Alice smiled sweetly.

Lenny sat down next to his brother. He wanted to offer something to this enterprise. "Remove any ships registered to Guelph Station itself?"

The terminal in front of them lit up.

"Search complete. Do you require any further assistance?"

Morgan shook his head. "That's okay, Alice. You can power down."

The Aurora series was on the verge of being decommissioned. The more hours she was active, the closer she got. Alice's smile was charming for a robot who could have sailed with their three-times great-grandfather.

Alice took her seat again, but this time she plugged into her charging port and then powered down.

Only when her system readout on her wrist pulsed red did Morgan turn to the terminal and place the small piece of debris on the table next to it. "Let's drill down on this."

The brothers filtered out more and more comings and goings from Guelph. This was where the station's remote location worked to their advantage. The number of ships was small. Even those that ventured out this far and wanted to keep it quiet by sheer necessity had to visit the station to resupply.

The logs recorded several small, frigate-class UPP

military vessels that came in while patrolling the national perimeter. They might not have registered their names in the public database, but Lenny and Morgan lined all of them up as resupplying both outbound and inbound.

"Would have sworn we'd find one." Morgan tapped his finger on the debris. "I didn't want to go this way."

"What?"

His brother's look was disturbingly solemn. "Once I input this serial number, we're all in. It could trip some alarms in the system. So, you sure you want to do this?"

Lenny chewed the inside of his cheek, taking a moment. "I think we're already all in."

Morgan shrugged and then carefully input the serial number. It was twenty-eight digits long. He checked it twice before hitting submit.

It took much longer than it should, but eventually it produced one result from the Combine database.

Lenny read carefully. "Says it's a Weyland-Yutani base code. It's off a ship."

"Yeah, but it doesn't identify what kind." Morgan leaned forward. "'Data unconfirmed. Weyland-Yutani experimental design.'"

They both stared at those words.

"Well, dead end then." Lenny pushed back the chair, but Morgan grabbed hold of his jacket sleeve.

"There's one more piece we can try to identify." He raised his eyebrows.

"You mean Mae?"

"There ain't any answers from what she came in on. That woman is down with our folks, and everyone on Guelph just saw her get off the *Eumenides*. We need to know, but we both should agree on doing it."

It was the kind of move his brother always pulled when they were younger. He got Lenny to buy in on some scheme, and then he had someone else to shoulder the blame. Lenny recognized the move, but he also understood that Morgan was right. They could untangle the *Eumenides* and their family from whatever Mae was. Best if they found out now, rather than got a nasty surprise later.

"Yeah, we need to, but we gotta agree to tell her whatever we find." Lenny scanned through his wrist-pd and found the security camera footage of Mae on their ship. Zooming in on her face, he uploaded the image to the database and sent it off.

Again, the search seemed to take a long time.

The terminal pinged that it found one result, but it was not a complete record. The face the system found was only 75 percent matching to Mae's.

"Fuck me." Morgan leaned back in his chair. "I wish we'd brought some beers up here for this."

Lenny stared at the screen. It was a pretty bare-bones record.

```
ZULA HENDRICKS. DOB 10/28/2119. OCCUPATION
(CURRENT): UNKNOWN. (FORMER): AWOL FROM THE USCM.
LOCATION (CURRENT): UNKNOWN.
```

Her picture followed, and it was easy to spot the resemblance to Mae. They both possessed high cheekbones, skin of a matching dark shade, while the eyes contained a similar determination.

Lenny swallowed because his mouth was suddenly dry. "Do you—do you think that's her grandmother?"

Morgan shrugged. "With how much the USCM travels with their soldiers in cold storage, she might even be her mother. Whatever it is, they have to be related somehow. The resemblance is too close for anything else."

"It fits. Like you say, that move she pulled on me—you don't learn that mining for ice on the outer rim." Lenny leaned over and uploaded the image to his wrist-pd. "I'll show her, and maybe it'll shake something loose."

Morgan stared at him, his expression darkly serious. "Hopefully what it 'shakes loose', little brother, isn't a killing rage. Those Colonial Marines are not to be messed with."

"But this is UPP territory." As soon as he said it, Lenny realized how stupid he sounded.

Morgan crossed his arms. "For now it is. Not sure if you've been keeping up on current events, but things are tense out there. The big three could go to war, and if that happens, not even Guelph is far enough away to be safe."

Lenny clenched his hands, hard. Suddenly, the little hauler he'd longed to get away from so badly seemed precious and in danger. "Seems weird to find Mae floating out there, looking like a Colonial Marine, just when things are getting bad. Can't be a coincidence, can it?"

His brother's hand landed on his shoulder and gave it a squeeze. "Let's not make up conspiracies today. Instead, let's go tell Mae what we've found. You're right, she deserves to know."

The elevator ride back down to the dock never felt so long. In his head, Lenny played out the best way to give their guest this information, and he tried desperately not to think about what her response might be. Her reaction when he'd pushed too hard still haunted him, and he hoped this news wouldn't get the same result.

1 9

PLANETFALL

Red Mae wasn't the other experimental splinter. She couldn't think of herself that way. She thought of herself as complete, as Mae Prime, with all the same memories, only a different body. Despite the strangeness, these splinters allowed for greater flexibility. Unlike humans, a synthetic could be in two places at one time.

The concern would come later. She might find it complicated to integrate with the Mae that remained on the station, especially since she'd never splintered twice before.

Still, it was a problem for another time, and one that Mae preferred having rather than being separated from her mother. Also, as always with the Jackals, she might not have to worry about reintegrating. They might not return to the station. Like with every mission, there remained a statistical chance of that happening.

She wondered if this was how Davis felt when he took so many forms and left echoes of himself in so many places. Though she'd been mostly glad to be making her own decisions, in this instance Mae would have welcomed her father's voice back into her head.

Red Mae was alone. She'd taken the designation of R1 in the first synthetic squad attached to the team headed down to the surface. Unlike Blue and Green Team, in Red Team, the colonel took down two combat synthetic squads, one to accompany each of the genetic human squads.

Mae took lead of the first synth squad. While firewalling off her personality core from the network took a careful touch, she'd also drawn a smudge on her face. This way her mother could tell her apart from all the similar combat android bodies if necessary.

They rallied on the space elevator platform on D deck of the station. Apart from the carefully positioned smudge, she was simply one of the units. Their programming made the synths obey senior officers without question, and if they fell in combat, any other living human. Mae certainly hoped it wouldn't come to that. The human Jackal units stood nearby in a similar formation, though less silently. The dim lighting in the station lobby seemed to keep the humans on their toes, examining every shadow, but nothing moved.

Their human jibes and back and forth rumbled through the unit. Adrenaline and comradery hyped up the genetic human Jackals. Thanks to Green Team, the platform was locked down and clear of Minos employees. The Jackals now claimed this part of the station as their own. The Sunspot Good Boys took their places at the rear. Their dark quadrupedal forms only resembled large dogs in the human minds. In reality, they were efficient battlefield units, ready to deliver acoustic attacks.

The crawler's design was sectioned off into two parts, one on each side of the tether to provide balance. Meant to move large objects down onto the planet, the crawler could easily accommodate four Jackal squads and their accompanying Good Boys. This was a relief, since her mother did not like to have her squads separated.

Colonel Hendricks stood in full armor by the large, closed door to the crawler. She intently watched her wrist-pd for the comms channel to light up with the confirmation from Green Team. Red Team couldn't move until they secured the command center. Until then, they maintained radio silence.

Everyone waited for the signal, and all eyes remained on their commander. Mae monitored her calm breaths closely, but she detected not even a hitch as Zula nodded. She turned with a thin-lipped smile. "Green Team is in smooth. They have control of all station comms. They are holding position, but we have a limited timeframe before shift change. We need to make some hustle."

Mae tapped into the combat synthetic network, reading the stream of confirmations from her peers in the Red Team network. It would have been good to reach the

Green and Blue synthetics, but that would mean opening their network to the station. No one could be sure if that wouldn't trigger a subroutine in Kaspar.

Captain Shipp's voice came out calm, but tense. "Have they confirmed that they have control of the crawlers?"

"They're bringing one up now. Looks like they can override the safety protocols for quick insertion. It'll be a bumpy ride." Zula turned to examine the fireteams, lined up and ready to move out. "Lieutenant Keith will give us all the time he can. Whatever they are hiding planet-side, I don't think they're going to be happy about us poking our noses into it. So we need to go in hot and ready."

She checked her weapons—pulse rifle and pistol—one last time. The ease with which she did this didn't tell the full story; it was some time since Zula Hendricks had gone into combat directly. It was not a choice that Mae welcomed, but she couldn't change her mother's mind on this now. Watching the destruction of Shānmén from the *Fury* marked her in ways so much other death and destruction could not. She blamed herself for every loss of life on that planet.

Humans were, Mae observed, fascinating and illogical creatures. She could scrutinize them until her mechanical parts seized up and still never quite be able to figure out all their idiosyncrasies.

Shipp briefed Sergeant Ackerman. He stood listening intently to her, his compact but muscular body seemingly at ease—despite the situation. He'd been one of the first

Jackals brought on board when Zula created the force. The colonel picked him for Red Team because of his calm nature and reliability. Humans sometimes claimed ginger hair meant a trigger temper, but Mae never noticed that about Ackerman.

She listened in on the conversation, because as a synthetic, she couldn't avoid it.

"I want those Good Boys released as soon as we hit dirt, and not a damn second later." Shipp's eyes narrowed. More than most of the crew, she liked dealing with the fallout from corporations' efforts to weaponize Xenomorph biology. Mae ran through the entire team's service and personal records. All of them were hardened veterans, and the best of the Jackals. Her mother understood that Red Team would hit the hardest, planet-side. She needed that hammer.

The second synthetic unit flanked either side of the door to the elevator crawler, keeping an eye out for any station security that might appear. Even though Green Team had taken the command center, it wouldn't be long before someone discovered them.

If they got lucky, it wouldn't happen until the next shift turned over. None of the Jackals were worried about station security beating them back, but suppressing them would take valuable time from their mission.

"You good, soldier?" Zula kept her gaze fixed on the corridor but glanced at her daughter.

Mae nodded. For a moment before the firestorm started,

they were alone. Her mother dared to whisper under breath. "This splinter thing is new to me. I don't like *new* with this situation we're going into."

"I'm just the same," she assured her mother. "Mae Prime is secure, so don't worry about me. I am here to assist and protect you." Naturally it was in the flat monotone combat droids were equipped with, negating the emotion she wanted to convey. She'd brushed over the limitations of these droids when deciding to create the splinters, but it wasn't her first time in one of these bodies. Shānmén had taught her a great deal about their capabilities.

Yet apparently a mother's instincts didn't include how to deal with the splinter situation. "I will not be foolish. I don't want to upset any of the three of you." Zula smiled slightly as she checked her pulse rifle one more time. "But I appreciate you being here."

Mae didn't point out it was the only way to obey her prime directive and an order at the same time.

The doors behind her pinged and rolled up. The Jackals moved to cover them, in case there were unexpected passengers. Both sides were empty of people or cargo. After checking they were clear, the squads moved into two groups. Each contained one genetic human and one synthetic human squad. Mae made sure that she joined the same side of the crawler as her mother.

"Let's load up," Zula ordered.

The human units took the rear position on each side of the crawler bays, with the synthetics and Good Boys filling out the front. It was a tight fit, and proximity alerts popped up in Mae's awareness: too many chances of friendly fire. She cleared the alerts.

The human version of that discomfort was a few mutters in the ranks, but nothing that reached the colonel. The Jackals all understood they were sitting ducks in the crawlers. If Green Team didn't maintain control of the command center, the Minos employees would take over the controls.

Being stuck was, however, perhaps the preferable option to being gunned down the minute the doors opened. Mae didn't calculate the odds. Instead, she kept hold of her pulse rifle, knowing it was in good order.

Zula flicked open her wrist-pd to check if they were still in range of the other unit networks; they were not. "Keith, take us down at emergency speed," she said.

"Express elevator?" Shipp said. "I recommend a solid crouch by the walls, everyone, and then maybe hold on to your asses as well."

"I'd rather hold on to someone else's ass," Private Gorev said with a chuckle.

"You're not getting any takers on that." Private Zhany, the smart-gunner in Squad One, adjusted her weapon as laughs spread through the crawler.

They got no more time to lighten the mood.

Lieutenant Keith would have warning lights flashing on the control deck—Mae was certain of that. Within a second, he dropped the crawler at a speed fractionally below the level of Gs a human body could take before passing out. A display on the right of the doorway flashed a bright red arrow, blinking rapidly to match their descent.

The synthetic units already took a crouch, flexing into their knee joints, expertly adjusting to the forces the elevator applied. The Good Boys were also locked in a similar position. The humans, as always, displayed a variety of reactions.

Some whooped and hollered with delight as their nervous systems rushed with adrenaline. Others around Mae swayed on their feet, their faces turning shades of white or green. Even for those used to dropship scenarios, this was an unusual sensation. The chop experienced by a vessel entering the atmosphere was a combination of lateral and vertical force. The space elevator, at its greatest speed, was straight down.

It was the first contact Mae had with such a machine, and it was impressive. She couldn't have said if it was enjoyable, but the effects on her colleagues were certainly worth the ride. The crawler reached the atmosphere, and the red arrow turned to green. Now the planetary gravity took ahold of the crawler, and a low hum filled the space. The builders designed the interior surface of the elevator to help slow the crawler down and avoid terminal velocity. The speed that Keith enabled must be straining the system, because it juddered and shook.

Mutters from a few Jackals suggested they were worried about expelling their rations on the floor of the crawler.

"Keep it tight," Sergeant Akerman barked from the back, though his voice also came out slightly strangled.

Right at the moment when it seemed the elevator might best a few of the Jackals, the exterior brakes clamped in and they descended at a more comfortable rate.

The arrow blinked off, replaced by a racing countdown.

"Ten seconds. Get ready." Zula's voice echoed in the suddenly silent crawler. The Good Boys crouched, ready to obey their program.

The twin crawlers touched down with a bounce and a slight scream of metal. The doors slammed open a second after, and the Good Boys sprang out first. Behind them, Captain Shipp launched a fleet of six Pinpoint drones. They flew ahead, only about the size of a human fist. Their intel would give the squads longer range knowledge than even the combat synths and Good Boys were capable of.

They found no resistance in the blank gray room at the bottom of the elevator. It was a wide-open space, bare of anything human, or otherwise. It seemed purely utilitarian, designed to keep the weather off the elevator entrance and not damage the electronics that ran it.

The silence of this empty foyer descended once the Pinpoints' faint buzzing faded away. The greenish light from the fading sunset streamed in through windows too high to reveal the landscape beyond. However, nothing lurked in the corners, no personnel awaiting their arrival. Mae, and presumably the rest of the Jackals, expected some company security forces or employees to be there with weapons drawn.

It was a pleasant surprise not to find them, but there should have been someone there. These crawler arrivals off the elevator usually contained supplies for the people on the surface. It made sense that personnel would be needed to move those supplies.

The Good Boys fanned out along the walls of the foyer, sweeping their sensors backward.

"No life signs within range." Shipp raised her wrist-pd. "The Pinpoints are detecting heat signatures outside the arrivals area, however."

Red Team took their positions. Two human squads were on each side in a V formation, while the combat synthetic units pushed forward in the middle. Mae's combat programming ran in tandem with the rest of her peers. Her primary personality core, walled off from the network, processed their surroundings.

They'd descended as the planet's long night began. Twice as long as Earth standard, the sunset made for an eerie arrival. The green light of the tether connection and the doorway filtered out into the half-light. Evening was closing in towards night, and even slivers of light seemed comforting. Up above, the station slipped into its dark rotation.

The elevator was anchored to a massive rocky plateau on one of the tallest mountain ranges on the surface. The silver curve of the construction at their back disappeared quickly into a thick cloud bank. Even this impressive human creation meant nothing. Winds buffeted the Jackals as they descended the ramp leading from the foyer in a loose formation. The temperature hovered a fraction above freezing, and the human soldiers' breaths came out in faint vapor streams.

That was when Green Mae's message hit Red Team. *"Erynis and the Fury are compromised. Erynis's hack failed, and the station AI countered. Kaspar has shut down the ship."*

Zula's eyes narrowed as they went immediately to Shipp.

"Too late to go back," the captain said. "We need that proof above all."

"Agreed. Revert to suit-to-suit signals, don't want to make it easy for them." Zula gave the signal and Red Team immediately took defensive positions behind the scattering of cover available.

It was the expected heavy-lift machinery and stacks of supplies not yet moved on to whatever their final destination was. Mist rolled over the scene, and that would surely make the humans uncomfortable; anything could hide in the mist, outside the range of their vision. This was when the synthetics, both Good Boys and combat droids, filled in the gaps in human abilities. They detected nothing moving or breathing in the immediate area beyond the low heat signatures in the containers.

Shipp signaled the synthetic squads to the source of

the heat signatures. A wall of large crates, which must have only recently been brought down on the crawlers, caught Mae's attention. They bore no logo or any kind of designation, which was peculiar.

Nearby, smaller crates marked with the Weyland-Yutani logo were stacked in a pyramid shape. The stenciled words included RATIONS, INSTRUMENTS, and SECURITY. The white containers, though, remained a mystery apart from the low-level heat source.

The human squads took up defensive positions while the two synthetic squads moved into positions on each side of the first container. If Minos Station's security forces turned up, they didn't want to be caught, as Zula was so fond of saying, 'with their asses hanging out.'

As the designated leader of the first synthetic squad, Mae holstered her pulse rifle and examined the locking system on the crate. Through the network, she ordered up R4, the tech-specific unit. Its designers specially insulated and firewalled the synthetic to prevent any systems from retaliating when probed. The combat droid opened the access panel and hard-wired into the lock.

A trained human could run a bypass in under sixty seconds, but a synthetic should have been able to do it in under five. When it took ten, Mae instructed the rest of the unit to step back from the crate. Explosions were always a possibility. The hacking synthetic didn't blow up, and neither did the crate. However, something more interesting happened.

The lock clicked open, and a puff of gas surrounded them. Mae detected nitrous oxide mixed with isoflurane. She immediately sent instructions for the other squads to remain in position. They usually used this gaseous mixture for anaesthetic procedures. She and her synthetic comrades proceeded into the large crate.

Within lay stacks of human bodies—the source of the heat detected by the synthetics. The Minos employees had retrofitted industrial racks, used to store parts, to instead contain something else entirely. People hung on them, comatose but stable. Mae quickly counted thirty fully grown humans alive on the racks. They were being kept comatose by the gaseous atmosphere pumped into the crate.

She beamed what she saw back to her mother's wrist-pd through the network.

Life signs are stable. Mae examined the nearest human. It was a young woman, in her early twenties by the condition of her skin. A perfectly fit individual. *Do you want us to wake them?*

Negative, Zula replied. *Seal it and re-take your positions. Limit civvies until area is secure.*

Mae and her squad obediently retraced their steps and closed the crate again, before they changed the atmosphere too much.

The colonel opened her helmet, giving up on suit-to-suit. Right now, Red Team needed their commander. "Push on. The Pinpoint drones have scanned the area. They found a large building down in the valley, about five clicks from the tether, but there's a cluster of pre-fab units a click uphill with lots of security. Seems more like the facility we're looking for."

Not wanting to speak out in front of the others, Mae beamed her message directly to Zula's wrist-pd. *Should we leave a squad to protect the unconscious humans?*

We're spread thin. They'll be safe. Let them sleep.

Sleeping humans, and that Kuebiko which Rook and Mae Prime found mention of, all pointed to a confirmed black site. When the firing started—and it would—then it was better not to have frightened and confused civilians running around. Mae grasped the logic of it, but some other strange emotion was composing itself in her. Empathy? Compassion? It was so hard to pin down.

She wondered what Mae Prime was finding up in the station laboratory. Open communications would not be a good idea unless absolutely necessary. They didn't want planet-side security crawling all over them. Whatever began on Minos, this was where it culminated. The Jackals were on the verge of uncovering it all.

2 0

AN UNKIND
HARVEST

Vogel dragged herself away from the computer and led Blue Team deeper into the laboratory complex. They passed additional labs with medical androids still working. Several of these rooms contained sedated humans. All of them wore company overalls and lay motionless on gurneys.

"Infected," Vogel whispered, as if voicing her own complicity might get her shot.

Mae turned on her. "And can the infection with Kuebiko be reversed?"

"No." The scientist swallowed hard. "It becomes entangled with the DNA of the subject within a day. Once that happens, there's no going back. The Mother Colony has them."

Humanity's ability to do so many terrible things to each other overwhelmed Mae. While capable of so much kindness, the genetic human was capable of great depravity, too.

"And where is that?" she ground out as outrage grew.

"Planet-side. There's a training facility and the colony."

She nudged the young woman ahead of her. "Show me more."

Leaving these subjects to their unwanted slumber, to be dealt with however Zula decided later, they proceeded farther into the complex. The central core contained elevators, but as of yet they were silent. Mae strode over and placed a cyber lock on the outside door. It wouldn't hold forever, but it'd give them time. Blue Team would not have to deal with any security forces, except any that lingered on this level.

Everything went silent under the flashing red light. Eventually, Vogel brought them to another airlock.

The synthetics and Jackals raised their weapons as Vogel opened it, revealing another, much larger cargo bay. This one contained more rows of those sealed boxes on one side. The other side of the room grabbed Mae's attention. Racks of humans lay on open shelves, ready for transport.

Mae counted twenty in all. Keeping a tight grip on Vogel, she dragged the scientist over to examine them. Laid out flat, these humans remained alive but unconscious, kept that way by a web of intravenous drips. All were young and healthy-looking adults in company overalls.

Vogel would not look at them as Rook and Mae checked the pads hung neatly at the end of each rack.

"You infected these people?" She shoved the scientist closer to the horror.

Vogel's eyes were glassy when she looked up. "We needed to get the fungus into XX121. If we pre-infected the host, then we found it traveled along the lifecycle into the adult Xenomorphs. My boss called it the ultimate trojan horse."

Corporal Ware let out an angry grunt. "Lieutenant, can we just waste her now?"

Mae raised her hand but remained silent, processing the horror. Rook, perhaps having seen more of this, pressed Vogel. "Where are these humans going?"

"To the surface," she choked out. "At first the company conducted on-planet experiments with infected Xenos, making sure they could be controlled. But lately they've been building up supplies of Mother Colony individuals to use for demonstrations. Our clients won't pay out for something they can't see firsthand."

Rook stared at Mae. "Remind me which is the more dangerous species, again."

They both knew the answer to that one.

"What kind of experiments?" Mae asked, while examining the nearest subject. The handsome young man was surely only a teenager. He seemed perfect, breathing, and with no signs of infection.

Vogel swallowed hard before answering. "Some are for hosting—to grow the colony. Others are... well, they are prey to show how well the infected XX121 can hunt."

Mae wondered at her calm. She possessed her father's control, but the question remained: what would Red Team find down there?

She reminded herself that her mother had fought Xenomorphs plenty of other times. She'd even gone to the planet's surface expecting them. Mae and her team needed to remain on-task. Weyland-Yutani must not have time to destroy the proof of these atrocities. Jackals weren't frightened by Xenomorphs or corporations.

Spinning on her heel, she pushed Vogel ahead of her. She didn't know what she'd have done in the young scientist's place, but a rage kindled inside her. She tamped down any inclination to take it out on Vogel. She'd make this woman download all the evidence onto the Jackals' wrist-pds.

They neared the door as a voice snarled from previously silent speakers in the cargo bay.

It was Station Chief Rolstad, and he sounded pleased with himself. "Intruders on level eleven, you have thirty seconds to surrender yourself. Drop all your weapons and get on the ground. If you do not comply, we will send in our troopers to eliminate you."

Rook arched an eyebrow. "I suspect some bluffing is taking place here."

Vogel let out a choked gasp. "You've got to do it. Please, you don't understand. They're already here."

Mae knew enough about the Jackals, their tactics, armaments, and successes to be confident station security wasn't a problem. "We tried to be subtle, but that's gone.

It doesn't matter, though. We can still secure the station and get the proof we need."

It was when the scientist's gaze shifted to the containers on the far side of the bay that the snapping open of locks triggered remotely brought Mae around. This storage area wasn't only full of infected humans, but also something else. Something familiar and terrible.

The doors flung open with a resounding echo of thuds. The boxes released their infected cargo in a flood. Xenomorphs uncurled and scrambled free of their enclosures, already primed to kill. The lines of blue bioluminescence that traced their joints gave them a terrifying beauty. They must have specially coated the boxes to repel detection. Their experiments were farther along than Vogel suggested. Now they were in deep shit. The Xenos moved faster than even a synthetic could, leaping over each other to reach them. Their snarling and hissing filled the large cargo bay.

Blue Team brought their pulse rifles up, but fired the grenade launchers underneath rather than live rounds. The specialized poly grenades hit the lead Xeno and bright orange strands wrapped around it. The rest of the squad followed suit, unleashing a blast of sticky chemical strands that adhered to the advancing monsters.

Those that normally cocooned were now the ones cocooned. They screamed in outrage, becoming more and more encased as they struggled. The closest Xenos became trapped in place, adhered to the floor and walls and thrashing. However, many more boxes disgorged their contents.

Sooner or later, the Jackals would need to fire live rounds. A few Sunspot Good Boys would have been useful to contain them, but none of their intel suggested any Xenomorphs were on board—least of all in containers.

"I suggest we withdraw and blow them out of the airlock." Rook already held the hatch open.

He might not be one of the Jackals, but his instincts were good. It would save them from fatally damaging Minos.

"Jackals, fall back, secure the door. We're going to blow them out into space." She yelled to be heard over the grenade launchers and screaming monsters.

Private Han muttered, "Fuck yeah." Other Jackals repeated those words.

Vogel bolted through the door. The two human squads pulled back first. The combat synths unloaded the last of their poly grenades and followed in short order. They stepped through and cycled the hatch behind them closed. Mae checked the lock herself, to be sure, even though the hatch was sealed and the light was red.

Staring through the view port, she watched dozens more monsters emerge from their opened crates. Their sinuous, dark forms unfurled, a blue light outlining their joints. Their teeth dripped ichor over those long, sharp fangs. They stood over the infected, sleeping humans. Mae wanted to turn away, but like all synthetics, she needed data.

Before she punched the button, she took the chance to observe the Xenomorphs.

Apart from the blue light, the rest of the monsters were still infinitely black, with the same lashing jaws and tails. Yet there was something else different about them: how they moved. Deliberately, close together but not too close. Once out of the confinement of the containers, the monsters spread out in staggered linear fashion—and she'd seen that before.

These Xenomorphs worked like the Jackals, calm and precise. This must be why the company used humans rather than apes in their experiments: intelligence and unity. That was what was required of these monster soldiers.

The one at the front stared straight through the view port back at Mae. It did not smash its head against the impenetrable glass or lash out. The synthetic and the Xenomorph examined each other with tilted heads and cold purpose.

A cluster of monsters stood over the sleeping humans but did not rip them apart. Instead, they turned their heads towards the door. Though they possessed no visible eyes, these Xenomorphs were undoubtedly making eye contact with Mae. It was as if they dared her to vent these humans along with the monsters by opening the outer door.

Mae didn't move as one monster delicately touched the skin of the sleeping boy on the nearest rack. She recalled what Vogel had already told her.

"Fesolai, get Squad Two back to that first lab. We've

leaving the way we came in." Mae shoved Vogel towards the sergeant. "We'll take this piece of shit with us."

With one synthetic squad and one human around her, she punched the button to open the outer airlock door.

She didn't turn away, needing to watch her choice unfold.

Nothing happened. Flooded with confusion, she pressed the button a couple more times. Rolstad must have locked down this airlock. He didn't want his terrifying experiments to be lost in the void. If he was in charge, then Mae feared for the other two teams. Yet if she opened direct comms to Red Team, she'd only endanger her mother and Shipp even more.

The only thing to do was to take care of what she could right now. One thing was certain: overriding the airlock would take time, which they didn't have.

Instead, Mae took out a node spike and drove it into the control panel. She didn't need the station chief letting the Xenos loose, either. If he wanted them out, he'd have to send someone down here using EVA to make that happen. That'd be the genuine test of his control over his human employees. She was 89.83 percent sure no sane human would take that assignment.

One last time, she stared through the window in the inner airlock door. The same Xeno stood there, not moving or attacking as its mindless forebears would have. Accessing Davis's files, Mae recalled the repetitive thumps of the monsters trying to muscle their way through doors in the past. This one seemed to understand the strength of this door. It waited patiently for something to happen. The possibility of Rolstad using the Mother Colony to control the Xenos was a haunting one.

Then it raised its twisted, black-veined hand and dragged six claws across the glass. From her side, Mae couldn't hear the sound, but her database filled in the gaps. It was an odd gesture, meant to frighten her or make a statement. Was that a message from Rolstad, or from deep inside the Xenomorph itself? Either way, it was unsettling. Only further investigation would reveal what effects the Kuebiko had on the Xenos' morphology.

Those were inquiries for another day.

"You stay right there," she leaned in to whisper. "They let you out to hunt us, but we're the ones who've trapped you." It was an illogical thing to do, but it seemed right.

The Xeno's lips pulled back in a snarl, showing the inner mouth, even as its clear drool fell from those pointed teeth. She wondered what exactly it saw with whatever senses it possessed. Did it see past her close sensor array that protected the illusion of her humanity? Did it see the real Mae?

"Let's go."

The Jackals began their withdrawal, by the books, not running, but also keeping a steady pace. When they reached the spiked elevators, Mae decided to open a channel like Green Mae did. They had nothing left to lose.

She needed to know the status of the other teams. It was no longer a certainty that her mother had made it planet-side. She hoped they would be able to secure the Kuebiko Mother Colony in the training facility.

Barely had Mae opened a broad band comms to Green Team than a stream of new information flooded through her core. A tsunami of unexpected data poured over her, leaving her programming struggling to remain intact. She caught only a nanosecond of respite in which she realized it was the returning splinter of Green Mae. It became too much. As it pierced her through, it overwhelmed all her processes and brought her to her knees. Basic functions were suddenly disabled, and an emergency reboot was the only way to remain herself. Blackness took her over.

2 1

A KINDNESS RETURNED

Mae had been pushing a cart loaded with metal ore towards the sorting facility when she dipped out of consciousness. When she came to, it was with a sense of relief that no one had noticed. She pushed herself up from the cart, which she'd slumped across.

Visions of monsters and death once more, but the details remained impossible to pin down. She looked back down the dock, but from this position, none of the Popes would have seen her slump over. She'd take that as a win. Daniella wasn't someone she wanted knowing about these episodes of hers. Mae knew she'd never be able to explain them.

Instead, she hurriedly pushed the cart into the sorting station. She held up the ID William had given her to log the find, and left the ore in the capable sorting hands of the alchemist synthetic. This was her third load. William and Daniella were experts at this.

Mae stepped sideways into the office and spoke to Yeni, the young woman behind the salvage counter.

She wore ornately braided hair and the bored expression of someone much older.

The girl let out a strangled sigh. "So, I checked with my supervisor. The *Eumenides* can claim provisional salvage, with your fingerprint here." She pushed a pad across the table. "Miss Mae... Henderson?"

She nodded. "What do I need to do to make it permanent?"

Yeni scrolled through the pad. "The salvage sum will get transferred to the *Eumenides* account once your UPP ID is reinstated. So, load the rest of your haul and bring it in for accounting."

Mae smiled brightly. "Thank you so much!"

Yeni returned to scrolling through her personal wrist-pd and made no comment.

Mae's smile faded as she walked back down the dock. It was nice to get the salvage enumerated, but how was she going to get a UPP ID with no idea of what her actual name was?

She took her time returning to the *Eumenides*, making sure that she wasn't about to pass out. Upon reaching the vessel, she slapped on the smile again.

"They say they're ready for the last of the salvage." She pushed an empty cart up next to the cargo bay entrance. "Do you think it's worth much?"

"We've got some good stuff here." Daniella straightened

and pressed one hand into her back. "At least enough to make up for not bringing in anything else."

"Hon, the metals alone should put us nicely into profit." William shot a smile at Mae. "Thank you for turning over the salvage rights. *Eumenides* is always sailing on the edge, and this really helps."

"Well, we can't be certain of the final price we'll get. Guelph enumerations are not known for their straight shooting or quick payment. That could take a while."

William shrugged. "Always does."

Mae wondered if that meant Daniella wasn't lying when she said she didn't blame her for ruining their salvage. Lenny's mom was a closed book most of the time. Mae stayed silent, lest she tip her back into annoyance.

Over William's shoulder, she spotted Morgan and Lenny waving at her from next to the elevator. Their hurried gestures urged Mae to join them.

"Is it alright if I go see what they want?" she asked Daniella.

The older woman pursed her lips for a couple of seconds. "They're staying back there in case I rope them into work."

"Come on, hon," William broke in, "they haven't seen station for a long spell, and you and me can get the rest done right quick."

Daniella let out a long sigh. "Wonderful how they always turn up when the work is all done. Off you go, Mae."

She stripped off her work gloves and passed them back to Daniella with a smile. "Thank you."

Mae hustled down the dock, only barely restraining herself from breaking into a run, glad to be free of the danger of collapsing in front of the elder Popes. She examined the brothers' faces as she got closer. Their expressions didn't suggest they'd enjoyed a good meal, as they'd said they were off to do.

Lenny's brows were furrowed, and Morgan didn't meet her eye. As she neared, Mae hissed under her breath, "What did you do?"

"Not here." Morgan kept his voice so low that the ambient rumble of the dockyard almost masked the words entirely.

Morgan jerked his head, indicating that she should join them inside the elevator. Lenny jammed the highest button on the elevator.

"You should see the hydroponics level." His eyes met hers and then rolled up towards the ceiling. Cameras. Mae hadn't known her own name at first, but she still somehow understood surveillance.

The doors opened into a large warehouse filled with ranks of shelves and tubes, all green and growing. The smell was loamy but somehow comforting, the odor of living things.

Lenny led the way between the shelves. "Don't worry, we aren't trespassing, because these aren't for eating. The company lets managers have a plant in their offices, so they grow them here. The rest help create oxygen while scrubbing carbon dioxide from the station's atmosphere."

The misters sprang to life as they passed, throwing tiny beads of water onto their skin and hair. Morgan drew Lenny and Mae deeper among the racks and into an isolated corner. In there, the plants were much taller, with huge arrow-shaped leaves. The hiss of the watering system provided a deep white noise that Mae guessed was the reason the brothers had brought her here.

"Not many station ears up here, and the watering system will stay on for another ten minutes." Lenny confirmed her suspicions. He glanced at his brother and then back at Mae. "You need to see this."

Without saying a word, Morgan turned his personal wrist-pd around so she could get a good look at the contents. The face staring back at her wasn't familiar, but she'd stared at something like it for days in the mirror on the *Eumenides*. Her finger traced the image, as if she could somehow download it into her brain and get some answers.

"Zula Hendricks?" Mae attempted to force the name into her mind. Her hands balled into fists, and her jaw clenched tight as she stared fixedly at the face.

Nothing. Some of those flashes that passed through her mind might have included this woman who looked so like her, but her memory remained a frustrating sieve.

She wanted to smash the nearby hydroponics tubes and scream. Neither of those acts were options. All she could do was ride the emotion to the end.

A strangled, gulping breath escaped Mae. "I don't recognize her," was all she offered. "Her face is like mine, but I don't recognize her." She slumped back against the wall amongst the thick leaves.

"Hey, it's a start." Lenny's voice was kind, but she was as empty as the Long Dark itself. "We can keep working on it."

Morgan shifted from foot to foot, unable to meet her gaze. "Look, we tried. I'm going back to the *Eumenides*. We got to pass station inspection before we can head out again."

Lenny might have told her all this himself, but Mae grasped why his brother came with him. Morgan didn't trust her. Lenny must have told him what happened on the dock earlier, and he wanted to make sure she wasn't about to smash his little brother to bits. Mae didn't blame him at all—it was the smart thing to do.

"Sure," she said, under her breath.

After he left, she stared at her feet for a long time while Lenny remained quiet.

"So, you think I might be military like her?"

"It's a possibility."

"And with that, she might even be a close relative. Is that what you believe?"

"You look too alike for it to be coincidence." Lenny didn't say it, but he must be thinking the same. If they went to the medical bay, they could take her DNA and sort this whole mess out in a few minutes. Except everything inside

Mae told her not to go there. A dreadful, illogical certainty that it would be the end of her kept her resolved to that.

Silence persisted for a long time. The drip of water on the plants was almost soothing, but when the cycle finished, she'd be no better off.

Lenny cleared his throat. "Maybe we can track her down?"

A feeling swelled inside Mae, and it was one completely alien and unattached to anything real. "And if she's dead?"

As soon as the words were out of her mouth, a voice—one confined to her head—spoke up. *Zula Hendricks is very hard to kill.*

Great, now she had disembodied voices rattling around in her mind. Her heart raced, but she didn't need to share this recent development with Lenny.

"If she's like you, she's hard to kill." Lenny gave her a crooked smile. "I've heard that Colonial Marines are tough hombres."

Mae banged her palm against her head, as if it might shake something loose. He caught her hand, and the instinct to strike back thankfully didn't rise.

"Come on, be kind to yourself. We'll figure it out somehow."

Instead of hitting him, Mae's fingers tightened around his. She was lost in this world, not even aware of her own past. This young man didn't have to help her, but he did because he was a gentle person. She didn't need to understand much about the galaxy to understand that was rare.

She leaned in close and kissed him on the lips. Lenny froze as if she had, in fact, struck him. After a moment, he carefully guided her back. Now his cheeks were flushed, and he was unable to meet her eyes.

"Uh, that was nice, but you didn't need to do that."

Now she'd ruined this, too. "I'm sorry. I don't understand where that came from!"

"Shit, now I'm making you feel worse." Lenny squeezed her hand. "I didn't say I hated it, but I don't want you to kiss me while you're so lost. You don't have an idea who you are yet. Maybe... yeah... later, we can revisit this thing."

"At least I know how to be embarrassed. Haven't forgotten how to do that."

He chuckled. "It's only human to want to make connections, and yeah, kissing is one way to do that. At the same time, I don't want you to think I'm helping you for that reason." He cocked his head. "Morgan's that shallow—not me."

They both laughed. "So, forget it?" Mae asked.

"Only for now." He glanced up. "The watering timers are about to finish, so let's get back to the ship. Mom will have dinner ready, and it saves spending money on shitty station food."

They strolled back to the elevator, disturbing three or four couples who'd come up to the hydroponics level for more intimate moments. They all leaped back into the greenery and shouted at Mae and Lenny. By the time they reached the elevator, they were both giggling awkwardly.

"I told you," he said, shaking his head, "the sound of the watering cycle covers a lot of things."

They rode the elevator back down to the dock. The door slid open as they were still laughing, so they didn't spot it immediately. Mae heard it first and spun around, pulling Lenny back against the wall of the elevator. Their laughter died immediately.

Armed synthetics stood in a row right at the base of the *Eumenides*' cargo bay ramp. Visible over their heads were more guards, though it was impossible to tell if they were human or synths at this distance. Daniella's voice punctuated the strangely quiet docking area.

"This cargo is legal salvage. Get the deck chief down here, now!"

A soft voice, low but menacing, returned a counterpoint to her argument. "We're not here about that. We understand you are transporting an undocumented person on your ship."

"What is that man saying to my mom?" Lenny lunged forward, but Mae automatically flung out her arm to hold him back in the dark interior of the elevator. Something must be wrong with his hearing.

"We're a registered Guelph ship. You can't just come in here." That was Morgan. Like Lenny studied spaceships, he studied corporate laws. Whether he was in the right didn't appear to matter. Shouts echoed down the dock. A tussle broke out. Punches were thrown, and the synthetic guards coalesced around the distant figures of the Popes.

Go. Go now. You can't wait. You can't help them.

The voice in her head was urgent. As Lenny surged forward to dash down the dock, Mae shoved him back into the elevator and jabbed the button to take them up. He struggled against her, but she trapped him in a headlock and spoke gently into his ear.

"They'll be fine. They're looking for me, but if you go down there, they'll lock you up too. You're an accomplice."

He twisted fruitlessly, kicking at her ankles. He would have sworn too, but Mae's grip around his throat choked them down.

As the doors closed and they ascended, the male voice in her head came back. *They'll be looking for you now. The boy must know places to hide.*

That was true; he'd already shown he was familiar with the station's air ducts. With no local knowledge of her own, Mae would get tracked down quickly. A heavy calmness settled over her, even though only minutes before she'd been worried about kissing Lenny. It was as if a switch flipped inside her.

The boy, as the voice called him, sagged in her arms. "Let me go." When she hesitated, he repeated in a firmer tone: "I know you're right, but let me go."

Mae released him, and Lenny stepped away from her as the elevator rose. He stared at her sullenly.

They didn't have time for his hurt feelings. "Who were those people? Were they the Extraktors? Were they the same ones who took Pelorus?"

"I don't know." His leg jiggled nervously. "But I sure as shit want to find out."

Mae dared to set a hand on his shoulder. "Then we need to find a hiding place. Somewhere there aren't any cameras. We have to figure out what's going on, and then we'll know how to help your family. Okay?"

Lenny stared at her blankly, as if seeing her—and the danger she embodied—for the first time. Mae guessed Morgan warned him about her. It remained to be seen how much his habit of ignoring his big brother's advice would cost him.

22

UNFORESEEN ALLIES

Mae's reboot cycled through emergency protocols. Her personality matrix struggled and nearly collapsed under the weight of such a sudden inrush of information. Her Green Mae splinter was gone, but at the last nanosecond, she risked throwing her core through the open comms channel. It was vital information. Death and suffering stained the download, but her advanced systems avoided Kaspar's hold.

Rook crouched down next to her, while the team huddled around her, faces knotted in concern even as they kept an eye on their surroundings.

She caught a whiff of his emotions. He wasn't surprised at all.

Mae didn't stay on her knees for long. A gleam in Rook's expression told her that the ruse was over; no synthetic could fail to recognize a system shutdown. Abandoning all pretense, she connected to him via a network and shot him a command.

Say nothing. We're in some pretty shit right now. It can wait.

"The *Fury* is in total protective lockdown." She addressed her Jackals—still intact, but who knew for how long? "We've also got more uncontained Xenos inbound."

"We can still EVA through the first airlock," Corporal Ware offered. As the tech officer, she must already be thinking of how to secure the doors behind them to slow down any Xenomorphs.

Mae glanced around. They had already arrived at the elevators. "Spike those controls one more time. I really don't want anyone joining us down here. Let's go for EVA extraction."

After Ware had done so, Mae directed her synthetic squads and human Jackals at a quick pace back down the corridor to reconnect with Squad Two, led by Sergeant Fesolai. They'd held their position in the first laboratory and kept the remaining scientists contained.

Mae appraised the Jackals of the situation with as few words as possible. "Xenos have overrun the facility on the other side of this level. We have them contained behind a spiked airlock door, but we need to EVA back to *Fury* ASAP. Xenos overran the command center. Green Team is gone."

Fesolai and all the Jackals present had friends and probably lovers on the lost squad, yet they didn't hesitate for a moment.

"Yes, ma'am," they all acknowledged her orders.

"What about me?" Vogel grabbed at Mae's arm. "You can't just leave me here!" The other scientists broke into full panic as they realized they were in the same situation. Only the Jackals' weaponry kept them from charging, but it wouldn't last.

Frightened humans made every situation worse. Mae tried to raise her voice above their demands. "The Xenomorphs have been contained. We'll secure you in this room. Stay quiet and hidden until we come back."

None of them seemed to believe her reassurances. The terror became louder as they scrambled to their feet.

Five humans who'd done horrible things. How to weigh the lives of people who'd willingly experimented on others was a moral quagmire Mae wasn't prepared for. It would have been easier if she were only a regular synthetic. No questions, only obedience to the rules built into her programming. Her father's gift was also sometimes a curse.

She jerked her head towards Rook. "Grab all those files." Mae took hold of Vogel by the back of his jacket. They couldn't take her colleagues, but Zula Hendricks needed documentation and witnesses. Vogel and the data drives would do.

Her Jackals pushed the rest of the panicking scientists back into the room, gently at first, and then with increasing firmness. Only by bringing their weapons to bear did they quiet them enough to shut the door to the lab.

Once in the corridor, they retraced the route they'd first taken with Vogel. In the dim light, three people stood by the interior elevator, clustered together, presumably waiting for it to open. Strangely, they didn't make any noise even though this was certainly a high-stress situation. They wore overalls, rather than the clean white uniforms of the scientists. Probably they were maintenance or janitorial staff.

Vogel pushed her way past Mae. "Hey, this elevator is on lockdown. Come with us."

Mae wasn't impressed, but she allowed it. A human from the station might well be able to persuade others to seek shelter.

Vogel reached out and touched one man's arm. "I know it sucks, but if you take shelter in—"

The man wheeled about and grabbed her by her security tag. The other two lurched forward and struggled with Vogel. All completely silently.

"Hey, hey, come on." Sergeant Fesolai shouldered his way forward to break up the melee. "Quit acting like this. Get back to your rooms!"

A mass of figures appeared at the far end of the corridor. More humans shambling towards them slowly when they should have been running in panic. They didn't scream or make any noise at all. Mae briefly wondered where they'd come from, until she recognized a tall young woman with a tangle of blonde hair. She'd been unconscious in one lab room they'd passed on the way to the other airlock. Whatever anaesthetic they'd dosed her with was gone.

At her side, Vogel let out a strangled sob. "They're infected!"

Mae's enhanced synthetic vision locked onto the broken remains of the tech spike in the woman's hand. It didn't come from the spiked elevator controls, so it must be the one Mae drove into the airlock controls.

A human opened that airlock door, and yet she was still alive. Kuebiko must create a bond or a connection between human and Xenomorph—a terrifying idea that would need to be examined further. Unfortunately, there was no time to do that now, because behind the crowd, a snarling mass of teeth and rage raced towards them. A flood of Xenomorph drones scrambled to reach the Jackals. They shoved past the crowd in their haste to reach Blue Team, ignoring the infected humans as if they were furniture. The only other explanation was they considered them part of the hive.

She processed all of this in the seconds before the black mass of writhing, snarling monsters reached them.

"Contact!" Mae yelled, but her Jackals were already bringing their guns to bear.

The squads, human and synthetic, opened fire. At first, they used the poly grenades, punching them into the mass of Xenos and infected humans charging towards them. The neon orange strands filled the corridor with a heaving, struggling, screaming nightmare of a mob.

They didn't have enough poly grenades, Mae realized. They were in danger of being overwhelmed.

In the midst of this chaos, the three humans by the elevator pulled out the spikes on the control panel. The elevator came to life, and Mae glimpsed Vogel being dragged inside. With her security clearance, and the humans assisting, they'd be able to go anywhere on Minos.

"Pull back to the extraction point! Now!" She shouted to be heard over the snarls of their attackers, who strained against the chemical bonds from the grenades. Mae did not use the word *retreat* because every Jackal and military unit loathed the term. This was a *strategic withdrawal*.

They were about to run out of poly grenades and would need to use live rounds. The five screaming scientists from the room didn't make things any simpler. It was always easier to experiment in silence. Facing the consequences of their actions drove them into a panic. Now they howled for the Jackals to save them. Their voices merged into a cacophony of desperation. They pleaded that *their* humanity was worth so much more than those they had happily experimented on.

Mae had no time for them. The hellish, squirming mass of Xenos and infected workers surged towards them down the corridor. They were about to be overrun. The Jackals sealed the first line of Xenos with poly grenades, but they were pushed from behind by yet more.

Minos was preparing to export these 'managed' Xenos all over the galaxy, and now they flooded the corridors, tearing the place apart. They didn't look so managed from close range. Whatever control Station Chief Rolstad thought he had over them was gone, if it had ever existed at all.

"Poly grenades out. Switch to pulse rifles," Corporal Bui called out, and Mae understood they were on the edge.

"Short bursts only. Watch that spread!" Sergeant Fesolai bellowed.

Controlled missions, where everyone stuck to the plan and the training, was when things went smoothly and by the numbers. But when the unexpected arose, humans, even trained military veterans, could lose their grasp of the basics. They could devolve as a team, falling into battle blindness, prioritizing their own survival above the unit's.

Mae sensed, in the next few moments, that the situation might devolve into that chaos. In the enclosed space, the Jackals risked punching holes in the station's hull, but the squads had no other choice. The mass of Xenos and humans pushed forward. Individuals snapped and cracked from the forces at the rear. The monsters' limbs broke and shattered, splattering the ceiling, walls, and those around them with thick acid.

Now, with only eight meters separating them, the Jackals needed to move. They laid down suppressive fire and fell back down the corridor. The acid of the downed Xenos ate through the floor of the corridor as more shoved past them. The stutter of the pulse rifles increased in pace, the light of the rounds illuminating the dim corridor in bursts.

The Xenomorphs' charge brought them closer and closer to Blue Team. The advanced combat synthetics took the brunt of the assault. Acid-repellent surface covering couldn't hold out forever against the number of Xenos pouring down the corridor. B1 and B2 fell first, torn apart, bathed in acid. They were trampled under the monsters' sharp feet. B3 and B4 took some splatter damage. B3's right leg struggled to remain operable as they withdrew back towards the airlock.

With the combat synthetics failing, the genetic humans were next on the line. They were not properly prepared for battle with Xenomorphs. How did they miss this intel?

Rook claimed that the company compartmentalized the computer systems, but did they really? She hadn't been able to confirm that without plugging into the system herself. She'd believed Rook, and now, as the Jackals faced down a wave of Xenos, she wondered if this was the other synthetic's fault.

Private Leone took a spray of acid to his face. Kaur grabbed him by his vest and dragged him back as he screamed in pain. The tipping point she'd long studied and feared rushed towards them as fast as the Xenomorphs themselves.

2 3

SAVE WHO YOU CAN

The Jackals moved in silence, with the Good Boys bounding ahead. It didn't take long for them to detect a security fence around the building on the mountain promontory.

The wide mountaintop jutted out into the mist, isolated and silent.

The fence wasn't physical. Maintaining such a thing on this windswept and rocky surface would have been impossible. Instead, the company employees had laid out a detector grid supported by a rank of UA 571-C automated sentry guns. Hardly surprising, Wey-Yu made those too. They effectively sealed off their approach to the facility, detecting any movement that came towards it. The sentry guns would fire on anyone who didn't have the correct IFF transponder.

This black site was fortified, working in secret with a formidable protection field if anyone came knocking.

Whatever was going on inside, they very much wanted to protect.

Zula was definitely ready to hammer on that door. It wasn't the first breach she'd done like this, but it was for her daughter in the combat droid body. Red Mae relied on her protocols and slipped into her role as part of the first synth squad, R1 to R4. Her partitioned personality, however, wondered at what they might find beyond that well-defended fence line.

"Confirm what's on the other side." Zula kept her eyes locked on the blocky form of the buildings ahead and gestured Captain Shipp over. Red Mae trained her superior synthetic hearing on the noises coming from within the buildings. A hiss whipped across the barren mountaintop, but it wasn't anything identifiable in her databases. However, no human breathed on the other side.

"Wonder how my daughter is doing right now," the colonel muttered in a low voice to Shipp.

"She'll be fine, ma'am." The captain grinned. "She's got the best of you and Davis in there. Nothing she can't handle."

"You're right. I'll concentrate on our very own shitshow. Let's see what kind of nest the company's built here."

The two women examined the fortified company building, raising their rifles and checking it out through their sights.

"F-series." Zula shook her head. "Grenade launchers, latest kit. Wey-Yu really doesn't want any visitors."

Shipp checked the Pinpoint drones' results on her wrist-pd. "Seems like the building up top is only part of the facility. It runs down the outer edge of this mountain plateau too, and leads into some caves, lower down."

"Of course it does." Zula frowned as she lowered her weapon. "We're going to have to burn this black site at the end, but there will be innocent civvies, too. Not the damn scientists, but ones like we found at the elevator entrance. They don't deserve to be here when we rain down hellfire."

"No, ma'am. They do not, but it won't be easy. Still, like you always say, 'we eat hard things for breakfast, and shit out the shells.'"

A smile flitted across her mother's face before she gave the next orders. "I want an EMP blast grenade launch. Let's knock out that grid hard and fast, and show the company they're not the only ones with new toys."

"Oorah. Move out."

Mae remained with the first and second synthetic units as they pushed forward up the hill in a V formation. The Good Boys took flanking positions, ready to deploy, while Pinpoint drones darted about overhead, looking for any dangers. The mist swirled over the barren hill, but Mae detected no genetic human heat signatures. Her sensors picked up no movement, which would indicate Xenomorphs.

Reaching the edge of the sentry unit's detection field, she drew more info from the Jackal synthetic network.

The Pinpoints shared a view of the valley below. It was a boneyard. Scattered human remains stood out white on the gray landscape. From above, it was easy to deduce that the humans came from the base of the mountain and attempted to flee south, away from it. None of them made it. The bones stopped two clicks from anything like safety.

Zula's face grew hard. "Seen this on other black sites. Training grounds. Seems like they're running tests in the valley on their 'controllable' Xenos. R1, make sure to record this."

Mae did so, knowing this evidence was as vital as whatever the other teams found on Minos. As if the pathogen-spreading ships weren't enough for the people of the Outer Rim to deal with. Once they extracted whoever they could save, Mae agreed with her mother: an orbital bombardment was never more justified. This site needed to burn.

The Good Boys encircled the synthetic squads and lowered themselves into a crouch. They did not get close to the field of fire.

Activate shielding, Shipp ordered across the synthetic network. She pulled the Pinpoints back behind the squads while the combat units deployed their spikes into the ground. Creating a faraday cage protected the Jackals' equipment, in case the blast radius unexpectedly reached them.

Zula gave the order. "Give 'em a round of e-blast grenades, Thami."

The corporal had already loaded the specialized grenade into the launcher beneath the M41A. The synthetic network fed information to the ballistic computer built into the weapon. It calculated range, angle, spread, and wind. This was a new weapon, not yet field tested, so it needed a human to pull the trigger.

The grenades made thumping noises as they deployed. They arced over the field of fire and struck the front of the line of robot sentries. Unlike most of the Jackals' weaponry, the e-blasts didn't deliver a satisfying explosion or a rattle. Only the synthetics witnessed the magnetic field wash over the line of sentry guns. For all its size, or maybe because of it, Weyland-Yutani didn't expect anyone to use their own tech on them.

Some middle manager in the company wanted to keep his bottom line solid, and hadn't signed off on hardening the guns against EMP. Cost-benefit analysis helped the Jackals, according to the files Mae inherited from Davis.

The guns sagged as the blast fried their circuitry. Since they'd now announced their presence so dramatically, the Jackals abandoned any pretense of secrecy.

Through the network, the synthetics took their order to move up. Flanked by the Good Boys, they breached the field of fire. The grenades did their work, and soon enough they were passing through the row of now-silent robot sentries.

The other two human squads followed, along with Sergeant Nyako, Captain Shipp, and Colonel Hendricks.

The blank gray square of the building almost blended in with its surroundings, as if the company actually thought its coloring would help conceal it. From outside, there were no lights visible. Mae's scan still found no heat signatures or movement. The only entrance was at least level four, and locked mechanically. No one, not even Red Mae in her combat body, was going to kick that down.

"Time for breach," Sergeant Nyako called. The squads moved smoothly into place. The corporals unfurled the shrapnel shield, and their privates got in line behind them.

Synth R5 moved up. His programming made him faster and more efficient than a human Jackal. He shaped the charge around the lock and withdrew back into formation.

"Stand by for breach." The unit spoke the words for the benefit of the entire section. "Five, four, three, two, one."

The thunder of the explosion rumbled across the mountaintop, the low clouds turning it into a rattle even Mae's combat body registered.

Sergeant Ackerman made the confirmation after the debris fell. "Breach clear."

The synthetics were first through the door, and Red Mae took the foremost position. After them, the human squads moved in, training their rifles left and right, searching for any enemy combatants. Things didn't go as expected; the command center was empty.

The synthetics scanned the area on multiple frequencies and found it a mess. Mae reached the back of the room and discovered another locked door. This one was a repurposed RK-8005.34 blast door—something manufactured by Weyland-Yutani for the USCM's tactical fleet. It would take more than a shaped charge to open this.

She read the rest of the information coming from the other synthetic units: no signs of organic life, and no explosive traps discovered.

"Clear, Colonel."

The human fireteams entered, while the synthetic units took up position by the interior door and waited for further instruction.

The flickering light of abandoned computers filled the room, but no humans sat in front of them. A delivery wagon, large enough for several comatose people to lie in, stood empty by the side wall. Chairs lay overturned, and Mae's foot shattered a coffee mug while another one sat steaming by the window. From its warmth, this was something they'd missed by mere minutes.

"No blood discovered," Mae reported to her mother as she entered the room. "Perhaps the humans subjects they brought in here woke up and took their captors hostage?"

"Then where are they?" Shipp hefted her pulse rifle, running her eye over the scene with increasing suspicion reflected on her face.

"It doesn't appear to be a Xeno attack," Zula agreed. "Blood should be everywhere in here. It would have been a massacre. These people don't know we're coming. Get all the data drives you can find, then we find the civvies, and get back to the *Fury*. R1, see if you can get into the system and run a bypass on that door."

Mae took up a position by the largest computer, opened her arm cavity, pulled out a narrow cable, and attempted to break it. It felt good to be using her abilities to their utmost again. She raced through the systems, trying to discover a weak point in the security. Weyland-Yutani made quality systems, she gave them that much. A regular synthetic would not have been able to find the passcode to get in. AI generated a long string, not the far easier passwords humans created. That would have taken Mae mere seconds to calculate.

The wrong passcode would not only seal Mae out, but also burn all records. Weyland-Yutani did not want to be held liable for their terrible experiments. That kind of thing caused a decline in the bottom line and weakened consumer confidence.

However, Mae not only contained all the records from her father, Davis, but also the black site data from Rook. His motives to assist the Jackals might still be murky, but she took a chance on the intel he'd brought with him. Buried in there, Mae located a program ripped from the Wey-Yu central system. It was a backdoor hack for all their programs, in case an AI went rogue or became corrupted.

Inserting the program into this mainframe was her only chance. If a synthetic could cross their fingers, then Mae decided it could do no harm. Hopefully, none of the Jackals noticed such unusual behavior from a combat android.

The computer console chimed once, and the lock on the formidable door clanked open. The synthetic units remained in position, weapons turned to whatever lay behind the door, while the two human squads moved up. Zula finished packing her webbing with data drives, and took her place with her Jackals.

Beyond the door was a wide ramp leading downwards. As Mae stepped onto the ramp at the front of her squad, she noted the temperature behind the main door was five degrees warmer than back in the command center. The synth squad moved forward, covering the angles, while the Good Boys darted ahead of them. None detected anything moving or warm ahead.

The tunnel that arched overhead was another unusual feature that Mae could not find in any of her databases. The material was some kind of plastic composite and formed into interlocking, opaque hexagonal walls. A faint blue glow emanated from it, providing a soft ambient light. It was not Xenomorph resin, but rather something that the company created. It would have been interesting to run tests on it, but in her combat body, Mae remained in position with the squad.

She pinged her readout to the colonel and Shipp as they started down the ramp with the other two squads. They made no comment, but Mae guessed it didn't make them any more comfortable. The unknown was always dangerous.

Keeping to their V formation, the squads moved up, trying to make as little noise as possible. The slight impact of their boots and the muffled rattle of their equipment were the only noises in the strange, smooth-walled tunnel. Mae registered the increased pace of the genetic humans' heartbeats. They were still within normal parameters, and the stress was justified. Whatever waited for them up ahead, it would be a nightmare.

They only hoped to push forward and save as many people as they could. Mae understood that was why her mother came to this planet, and she wouldn't stop until she'd atoned for Shānmén.

2 4

BREAKING FREE

Lenny tried not to think about his parents and Morgan as they crawled through the air ducts on level twelve. His parents were toughened by their time in the SOF, but even they had limits.

"We are truly fucked," he muttered as he moved forward on his hands and knees. "I don't know what we do now."

He glanced back, hoping to get some ideas from Mae. She was silent.

"Mae? Shit, hey, come back!"

After a few seconds, she floated back to him. "Yeah, I'm here. Sorry, dipped out again."

That was precisely what he didn't want. She was doing it more and more. If she slipped into a coma and didn't come out, he'd be left alone to deal with this.

"Please don't," he whispered softly, hoping she wouldn't hear. She did.

"I'll try my best."

"Anything useful at all this time?" He sat back in the vent.

"Not much. I think I was underground somewhere." Darkness obscured Mae's face, but her tone was dreamy, half-lost.

Lenny kept his thoughts to himself on that. He fought down the irrational anger as best he could. It wasn't Mae's fault he'd found her, or that she couldn't remember anything. However, his imagination kept conjuring up terrible fates for his family.

Her hand touched his ankle, making him flinch. "We'll get them back. These Extraktors aren't after the Popes. They want me. Your friend Pelorus said as much. Once I get off station, they'll forget about you, your family, and the *Eumenides*."

How she might be so sure, Lenny couldn't guess. He was sure of absolutely nothing, but he understood the sudden change in his life meant nothing would be the same—even if they did survive this. With that in mind, though, he realized where they needed to go.

Changing direction, he slid, crawled, and climbed through the ducts, all the while berating himself instead of Mae. A woman in a mysterious cryopod sounded exciting, but shit, his mom was right. Someone was looking for her. It wasn't Mae's responsibility, but he should have been looking out for his own first.

His dad and Morgan might be alright in custody for a

bit, but Daniella served a stint on one of the UPP's prison planets. How long would it be before her PTSD kicked in and she tried to bust her way out? God, he couldn't think like that, or this new, mad plan wouldn't work.

Reaching the top of the vent shaft, Lenny wriggled sideways until he found enough space for both of them to peer out onto the private dock. Mae pressed her face against the gaps in the vent cover.

"What are those ships? They look... fancy."

The pretty paint jobs and streamlined hulls would not be found at the dock the *Eumenides* was attached to. "This is the place for those with enough money to avoid rubbing shoulders with ice and scrap haulers."

He examined the layout with a sharp eye. The private dock only had room for five vessels, but it never filled up. Today, only two ships were berthed in it. One he didn't recognize, but that was alright because he was very familiar with the other ship.

The *Icarus* had lived in his mind for months now. It docked nearly a year ago. Some high-ranking Combine manager turned up to conduct an audit. Unfortunately for him, he'd wandered into the wrong part of Guelph for some gambling fun. Got himself stabbed and dumped into the sewage tanks for his troubles. The Guelph station chief got all excited by the idea of inheriting the *Icarus*, but the Combine would not waste it on him. They'd tied the ship up in the private dock, waiting for someone from Jùtóu HQ to come and haul it back to civilization.

Before that could happen, Lenny planned to steal it. He hadn't told anyone, especially his family, about the idea. He knew it might be the stupidest thing he'd ever done, but it looked better the longer he thought about it. On Guelph, he'd never be able to be anything but a hauler.

If he didn't get himself to a brighter corner of the galaxy, Lenny knew his fate. Hauling ice and ore forever, living on the edge of ruin until the endless void claimed him. However, Mae changed everything, and his plans would have to adapt.

"There she is." He pointed towards the graceful, silver curves of the *Icarus*. "She's rated for long haul travel, which will get us to at least the Outer Veil. She's faster than anything here."

Mae stared at him. "But I don't know how to pilot anything."

He gave a short laugh. "Don't worry, the guy who brought her here didn't either. She's got her own top-of-the-line ship AI, and I've got the code."

"How'd you get ahold of that?"

"Stole it off the executive's corpse in the morgue."

Mae stared at him as if she couldn't quite believe the words coming out of his mouth.

He broke eye contact. "Once you reach the Outer Veil, you should be able to find more info on this Zula Hendricks person. It should tell you who you are."

"And they'll release your family." She pulled her knees

in tight as they sat there. "I'll broadcast a message back to Guelph once I am far enough away."

"Yeah. Good." Lenny hated how short and angry his words came out. Again, he reminded himself, this wasn't her fault—as far as either of them knew.

He withdrew a screwdriver from his bag and started to work on the vent. Strange, how his mental exercise of stealing a ship was now becoming a reality. Lenny had already confirmed that below the vent lay the control panel for the systems of the private dock. How to bypass that was intel that'd taken a bit more effort to acquire.

Sven Gunnerson, chief of security on Guelph, was a sloppy drunk with a liking for gambling and pretty things on the workers' levels. It wasn't like the station had a lot of valuables, so Sven got real lax as the years went on. Lenny hacked his wrist-pd once while he was passed out on a bar floor. Getting into the bar was the hard part, since everyone on Guelph was afraid of Daniella Pope. No one wanted to see how she'd react if her youngest got drunk in someone's seedy bar. Yet, after several attempts at concealing himself with some laughable disguises, Lenny finally managed it on the pay day when everyone headed out to get drunk. If he believed in some governing deity, it might have almost seemed like fate.

He dropped out of the vent, and the thump of his boots on the dock sounded far too loud. Lenny opened the panel to access the system controls and checked how much time he had before the intrusion protocols activated. His hands were clammy and extra clumsy as he worked. A small chime sounded.

Mae landed softly next to him like a cat. "Have you got this?"

He pressed his lips together before muttering, "Yeah, I got it. Just keep an eye out for station security, OK?"

She put her back against his, and stared into the dimness of the bay. It meant she wouldn't see what he needed to do. Explaining his augment was always a tricky subject, and one revelation too many.

Tangling the wires together, he bypassed the circuit. The chime stopped, and Lenny activated his augment. With the physical protocols disengaged, he pushed forward with his mind. The security system patterns were glowing, thin threads dangling in the air. Inserting Sven's code into the broken pieces of data, the light dipped for a second, then grew bright again.

WELCOME CHIEF SVEN GUNNERSON

He wiped a bead of sweat from his face and straightened. "Come on, the *Icarus* is right there."

Once they stepped away from the wall, the security cameras spotted them. These were always on and monitored—unlike most cameras on Guelph. Lenny didn't have codes for them, or the time to hack into the main station system. So, they'd have five minutes before the security detail made it to the dock. Usually that was plenty of time to catch any would-be ship-jackers as they struggled to gain entry to their target. Lenny hoped that Sven's codes to board the *Icarus* were still good.

He submitted the launch sequence into the docking mechanism. It took about five minutes to power up and prepare to open the bay doors. Reaching the shiny doors of the *Icarus*, Lenny punched in the entry code and breathed easy when the hatch unlocked immediately. The interior lights blinked on and the engine stirred to life.

"There isn't much time," he told Mae in a hurried gasp. "The dock will uncouple, but you won't get a clearance from station control, obviously."

"So, I'll have to punch it."

He handed her the pad. "These are the coordinates for Thedus. It's Three World Empire space, so these Extraktors won't have jurisdiction there. Don't stop until you reach the border."

Mae swallowed hard. "I'm sorry. I really am."

"Me too. Find out why these people are after you." Lenny hated a puzzle without a solution. "When you get your answers, send me a message, okay? I don't think I can sleep until then."

Mae's shoulders straightened slightly, and she brushed away a curl of hair from her face. She was dirty from climbing through the vents with him, but unforgettable. Lenny tried to secure the image of her standing there in his memory, even if she wasn't doing the same. However, before she could close the hatch, the *Icarus*'s interior lights all flicked off, and the warming engine fell suddenly silent.

"Young people these days, always taking what doesn't belong to them." Under the *Icarus*'s engines, they'd not heard a unit of synthetic and human soldiers approach. They moved in tight ranks and so quietly that they were now only three meters from the vessel's door.

Their leader, a strange and extremely pale man, kept his pulse rifle trained on them. Their uniforms were dark, slightly patterned with slate gray, and on the collar was the symbol of the Jùtóu Combine. Lenny had been right—even when only observing them from behind as they'd arrested his family—that they were not Guelph station security.

Lenny had no choice but to raise his hands. He glanced at Mae. Would her military instincts kick in, as they did before? She was unarmed, but her training seemed to include that. Something about her expression said she was calculating odds.

The man at the front smiled thinly. "If you run, we will shoot your human companion where he stands. I don't think you can carry him out of range fast enough to save his life." He lunged forward and yanked Lenny behind him and into the crowd of armed troopers. They knocked him to his knees and, forcing his arms behind his back, cuffed him within a split second. The pain lasted longer than the actual subjugation.

From this lower vantage point, Lenny got a good look at the squad. Several of the humans were outfitted with obviously mechanical limbs, and a couple sported the stretched faces of the die-hard augmented. A unit of synthetics and those who wanted to be like them. He'd never heard of such a thing.

He struggled against the cuffs and tried to rise back to his feet. One of the combat androids struck him in the back and then pressed its foot down hard between Lenny's shoulders. The cool press of a pulse rifle against his temple stopped him from attempting anything further.

Through the legs of their attackers, he glimpsed Mae. She still stood at the door, one foot inside the ship, though there was no way it would be of any use to her now. If these bastards worked for the Combine, they'd always been in control of the *Icarus*. Lenny wanted her to run, but he was also absolutely positive that this would be the last thing he'd ever see. Nothing about the squad surrounding him said they were playing. He didn't like the taste of being helpless one bit.

The standoff stretched on and on, but eventually, Mae threw down the pad, dropped to her knees, and raised her hands behind her head. Two human troopers rushed forward and cuffed her. But oddly, her restraints were different from Lenny's.

Her cuffs were chunkier, with lights that indicated some kind of additional technological restraint. Somehow, these people already knew about her combat skills.

"What about this one, Captain Warrae?" A boot crashed into Lenny's ribs, knocking the breath out of him.

"Bring him," came the chilling reply. "He makes good leverage with the other."

With that, they yanked him to his feet and shoved him along in Mae's wake. Morgan or Daniella would have complained, insisting they were citizens of the Union of Progressive Peoples with rights. Lenny knew better than to bother. This was a Jùtóu Combine station, and no one gave a damn about those rights if there was money involved.

Captain Warrae's expression was a flat mask. His sergeant's, though, told Lenny what this was all about: greed. He could only hope he'd get some answers before they relegated him to a penal planet to serve time as both his parents once had.

2 5

COMPANY-ISSUED
NIGHTMARE

Red Team rounded a sharp turn, carefully spread out
and wary. Up ahead, five humanoid forms wandered
down the corridor. They gleamed with heat and were
clearly visible in infrared. They wore company overalls.
These must be experiment victims, like the ones they'd
encountered by the base of the space elevator. They
appeared disorientated, shuffling back and forth behind
an open blast door.

"Contact. Civvies," Mae whispered back to her
commander.

Zula and Shipp moved to the front. As they assessed
the forms ten meters ahead, the first synth squad provided
them with cover.

The humans moved only slightly. They stood in the
middle of the corridor, unarmed and facing away from

the Jackals. It was as if they could not hear the Jackals coming at all.

Zula gave the signal, and the second squad of synthetics took point. The Good Boys passed between the silent people to scan the corridor ahead, and still the humans did not move. The size and menacing shape of the Boys usually prompted some reaction. Whatever drugs the scientists administered to these humans must not have worn off yet.

First Squad moved up, keeping their weapons trained on the silent humans. Sergeant Ackerman was the first of the genetic humans to reach them. Two women and three men didn't even make eye contact with him, their heads remained tilted up slightly. They stood in place, swaying but silent.

When Ackerman poked one with the tip of his pulse rifle, there was no reaction.

Zula and Shipp approached, bringing the medic, Private Feldman, with them. Mae was among the two synthetic squads that gently herded the lost humans back against the plastic wall. They offered no resistance, not even making a single noise of protest.

Zula's face twisted. "What fresh fuckery is this?" Coming from someone with as much experience as her, that was concerning.

Shipp shook her head. "Can't be over twenty years old, any of them." She gestured Feldman over to check them out.

The private hustled up and gave them each a hasty examination. She shone lights in their eyes, trying to get a reaction, asked quiet questions, and looked for signs of external injuries. Nothing made a difference.

Feldman looked to Zula. "I don't know, ma'am. They are physically fine, but all their eyes are dilated. It might be drugs, or some kind of brain injury."

Mae detected a strange odor coming off them. It was at such a low level that the human nose could not identify it. However, it reminded her of something. "Colonel, may we turn off all visible light sources for just a moment?"

Her mother hesitated. Humans were always resistant to doing so, even when they wore other devices like infrared displays. "All squads, go lights out," Zula commanded, "just for a moment."

The corridor plunged into a darkness only broken by the bioluminescent glow coming from the walls—and from the skin of the five people.

"Back on." Zula shifted to stand next to Feldman. "Is it some kind of contagion?"

"Negative," Mae replied before the medic could. "I detect no viruses or bacteria. However, there is an unidentified odorant emanating from their pores."

Her mother's face tightened. "If they're infected with something, we should get them back to the *Fury* under quarantine conditions." She glanced back down the corridor. "Looks like we're all going to go through quarantine protocol. Second Squad, you accompany Private Feldman back to the space elevator landing with these five, and return to Minos. Also, see if you can wake up the humans we found in the crate and evacuate them as well."

The combat androids R5, R6, R7, and R8 snapped into formation around Feldman, guiding the infected humans back the way they'd come.

The one remaining synthetic squad moved into a wider V formation to provide cover for as many of the genetic human Jackals as possible. The squad's programming adjusted with the change in numbers as Red Team pushed on. The corridor narrowed and spiraled down, and Mae realized they were in the structure the Pinpoint drones found that ran vertically down the cliff face.

The temperature continued to climb, though—now up another five degrees—causing all the human Jackals to break out in a sweat. As Mae scanned forward, she noted changes in the walls of the tunnel. They were still composed of the same material with the same hexagonal shape, but it took on a translucent quality. The deeper they ventured, the more the atmosphere became hot and moist.

The narrow, spiraling path meant only two Jackals could proceed at a time, almost shoulder to shoulder. Mae and R2 were in the front line, and she constantly beamed back her findings across the synth network, and to their commanding officers.

Reaching the bottom of the spiral, the passage finally widened. Now, some of the transparent hexagonal panels were occasionally replaced with openings. These were not more corridors, but rather smaller chambers.

The Good Boys identified biological remains, but nothing alive. Mae bent and stuck her head into the first hexagonal chamber they found. She immediately identified what that biological matter was: an open Xenomorph egg at the back of the space, and in front of it sprawled a young woman's body with her chest blown open. Curled up by her right foot was a desiccated facehugger. Her bright red hair matched the blood splattered around the translucent chamber.

The synthetics located forty similar chambers, all stacked on top of each other. The rank odor of death filled the corridor. The Jackals already had plenty of experience with it, but seeing so many young lives sacrificed in the name of company profits always made them angry. It washed over Mae as well.

Zula and Shipp examined the remains for themselves with tight expressions. All three major powers forbade human experimentation, but that didn't mean it didn't happen. Only in the darkest corners of the galaxy would corporations dare to conduct such experiments. The promise of well-paying factory jobs on Minos lured in many of the strongest and brightest. Now, it was clear that they were in fact meant to keep this black site flush with victims for experimentation.

Mae caught flickers of frustration and exhaustion on her mother's face. This was not the first corporate horror she'd witnessed.

"These corpses are glowing, too." Shipp's hand tightened on her rifle, though there was no target in sight.

"I want samples bagged and tagged, and we're saving as many of these people as we can."

It seemed important to offer some hope to her mother, so Mae pointed out, "The empty wagon up top suggests some more victims have only just arrived."

Shipp's eyebrows drew together in a dark frown. "Then let's make some hustle, people."

"Get ready," Ackerman barked. "We got bugs up front."

The Good Boys raced ahead, scanning and reporting back on more empty chambers. The squads moved faster now, urgently hoping to find survivors. Still, they kept formation and good order.

More humans emerged up ahead, and they appeared in a similar state to the ones sent back to Minos with Feldman. However, as Mae's synthetic Jackals neared them, they scattered. They probably were afraid of the onrushing soldiers, thinking they were about to get mowed down.

"We're here to evacuate you." Mae's voice came out tinny and modulated. The purpose of their combat bodies was not to offer comfort or sympathy.

She pursued them down the corridor, followed by her synth unit, and into a larger room. The civvies scattered left and right, and she noted one strange point: they didn't scream in panic. They moved on bare feet, not making any sound.

Back behind them, Mae's sensors registered a heavy metallic slam. It must be that blast door.

"They have shut our entry point," she reported on an open channel back to her mother, in case this body and splinter was destroyed. The civvies ahead still ran on, though they likely couldn't see much in the dark; the bioluminescence became muted, down there.

Her mother's voice snapped through the comms. "Contact Feldman, find out what the hell happened."

Mae sent a message through to the private. No reply came. They might have to maintain radio silence for off-planet communications, but their own network was still working. Feldman should have acknowledged.

This was a tricky situation. If they worked their way back, then they might find a locked blast door. They would be trapped here with no way to escape. Going forward meant going into the unknown, but there must be a way out through the training facility, at least. Splitting their forces could also be a deadly mistake.

Zula Hendricks's first consideration was for the civvies.

Forward. The order flashed into the synthetics and onto the heads-up displays inside the human Jackals' helmets. Remaining in formation, they pushed forward, examining the parameters of this larger space.

That strange composite material covered the walls. The humans who'd fled from them now stood in a cluster near the back of the large room, in front of a hangar door emblazoned with the Weyland-Yutani logo. If intruders managed to reach this far into the complex, there was clearly no longer any point in subterfuge. The strange odor increased in parts per million as Mae and her synth squad moved closer.

"Lights. Let's see what we've got."

The squad turned on their headlamps, shining a light on the twenty civilians gathered there. As the light raked over them, they let out low groans.

"We're here to help," Ackerman called. "Let's get you back up to the station—"

His voice choked off as the humans spun around to face the Jackals. Lines of blue light ran up their arms and over their expressionless faces.

"Help us! Help us!" they all screamed out, rushing towards Red Team. Used to frightened, unarmed civvies, the Jackals tried to push them back without firing.

"Fuck off," Private Gorev yelled, as a wide-eyed young man clawed at his helmet.

Corporal Minkas punched a woman attempting to wrestle his pulse rifle away. "Goddamn it, we're trying to help you."

"Hold your fire!" Shipp's voice broke through the chaos. Mae's network told her both she and Zula were at the rear, experiencing the same surge of civvies. For all their yelling, these company employees didn't display fright or any other human emotion. Shoving two men off her, Mae did not discern any flicker of conscious action from any of them.

Struggling and throwing the company workers to the ground, the squads eventually cleared some space. Applying rifle butts or knocking them back with fists seemed the most appropriate way to deal with them.

As Mae shoved a worker backward with her shoulder, the rattle of an opening door reached her. A man with ragged hair and blue light gleaming on his skin stood by the switch he'd just flicked. The hangar door opened into another, larger chamber. She hoped it would lead out to the valley.

That seemed like a good thing until hatches high above them in the ceiling also opened, and the true nightmares made themselves known. They emerged from every hexagonal chamber in the walls, hissing and snarling. The same blue light danced over their carapaces and along the edges of their curved heads. The Xenomorphs crawled down the walls and launched themselves towards the Jackals with a terrifying ferocity.

2 6

BLOOD OF ALL KINDS

Mae remained silent as the Extraktors locked arms through her elbows and led her away. It helped cover up the fact that she'd dipped away for an instant. The recollections were becoming more vivid, but she only held on to a sensation this time: fear. When she'd returned to herself, her captors were dragging her away on her toes. They made no comment as she regained her footing.

Rather than fighting them, she was determined to give nothing away. Instead, Mae listened, carefully cataloguing what they said.

Lenny, a few steps behind her, was also smart enough to keep his mouth shut. The synthetics that restrained them marched them rapidly down the private dock, away from the *Icarus*. They also said nothing, but the human members of the team were not as circumspect.

They weren't laughing and joking, but they still

exchanged some victorious words. From the "Gonna get paid," she garnered greed motivated them, mixed with machismo. As for their leader, Captain Warrae, she had his name, but it was hard to study him closely since he took up the back.

She overheard him mention "leverage" to his sergeant. That was obviously Lenny and his family. In the moments since they'd subdued him, Mae's urge to fight back leaped to life. Her body tensed, muscles ready to react to some unknown training. She'd already picked the targets. The grinning sergeant would be the first. He might be enhanced, but he clearly hadn't augmented his intellect. He hadn't tightened his helmet. She would easily reach his jugular before he reacted. The visual chart of how this might play out was as real to her as the opponents before her.

However, then there was Lenny. Even with all the logistics in Mae's head, there was no way she'd be able to reach him in time to prevent Warrae from making good on his promise. Without a weapon, his odds were nil.

So, Mae surrendered. It might well be a weakness, but she couldn't bring herself to be responsible for the death of those who rescued her from the void. Instead, she waited; there would be another moment. Although she didn't know where that certainty came from.

If the Extraktors stepped into the elevator together with Mae first, then she'd chance it. In the confines of the small space, their pulse rifles would be more of a hindrance than a help. She calculated she would subdue them within acceptable parameters. However, as the elevator doors slid open, only Lenny and his synthetic guards stepped in. The doors closed and their captors whipped him away—along with any remaining hope of escape.

Warrae stepped up next to her. His eyes narrowed within his strangely stilled face. Whatever augments he possessed, they must be significant. "Can't have you injured trying to help the boy."

"Yeah, those cuffs would do a number on you. Two thousand volts." The chuckle in the sergeant's voice was disturbing. That was well over a lethal dose for a human. Mae was right to judge them as capable of anything.

The elevator doors reopened, and they loaded her in with a sharp shove.

"If we don't reach our destination, the synthetics will kill him anyway. Isn't that right, Homolka?" Warrae's tone suggested this outcome would please him.

"Yes, sir, Captain. And not quickly, either." The sergeant straightened, and Mae detected the faint whir of limb augments. Some of these 'humans' were more synthetic than actual androids.

Whoever she was, Mae realized she must be important. Did she once know something vital? Had she killed someone worth sending these troopers after her? A thousand possibilities ran through her mind.

I hate to say it, but logically, the boy doesn't matter.

Mae ignored the dry voice in her head. It already suggested leaving Lenny in the moments before she surrendered. She hoped he hadn't detected that hesitation before she'd given herself up. She was not about to take the advice of a hallucination.

The elevator completed its ascent and the doors opened.

"Welcome to Extraktors HQ. It's temporary, but it's home. You're going to love it." Sergeant Homolka was a pure sadist. The excited pitch to his voice was a dead giveaway that they were most definitely not going to have a good time.

Posters on the wall urged Guelph citizens to 'Follow the commands of your local garrison.' These suggested the Extraktors requisitioned the space from the station security service. It was all cheap chairs and crowded desks, although the powerful odor of bleach wafting from the back rooms suggested something worse.

"Sergeant Raytheon, please make sure the equipment is ready." Warrae dismissed his junior as the synthetics pushed Mae to sit in a metal chair.

From there, she got a good view of the holding cell across the sparsely decorated room. It was a barren chamber illuminated in stark blue-white light. The Pope family huddled in a corner, since there was no furniture in the cell besides a stained toilet. William leaned against one wall, arms crossed, his gaze fixed on his wife and children. Morgan stared back at Mae, his expression a blank slate. Daniella didn't seem to notice the woman they'd rescued, since her attention remained fixed on Lenny. She clasped her youngest son tight, one hand cradling his head. He didn't fight it.

Mae watched them for only a minute. It seemed awkward to gaze at the family, like observing bugs about to be crushed. Anguish built in the back of her throat until she couldn't breathe.

"You have me. They have done nothing." She stared up at Warrae. "They're innocent."

"*Au contraire*, I think you'll find the boy tried to steal a Combine ship, one with a significant dollar value attached." Warrae pulled up a chair and sat fractionally out of reach of Mae. "Twenty years on a penal colony will certainly make him less pretty. Tell me, do you think his mother would recognize him—if he survives, that is?"

Mae would have more luck dealing with a synthetic mind; at least she could've used logic. "What do you want with me? I remember nothing, so whatever your bosses want, I don't have it. If they—"

A puzzled frown settled on Warrae's face. "Really? Not even that?"

The synthetic guard behind her spun her chair around to face the wall. Warrae flicked his wrist-pd, and it projected an image there. It was from a security camera and displayed all the wreckage the *Eumenides* found with her, as well as the cryo escape pod itself.

"No. Not even that."

Now his expression became one of interest. Warrae tapped his fingers on his knee. "That is quite strange. In all my time doing this, I've never encountered a case like yours."

He wasn't making any sense.

Homolka appeared from a back room. "We're ready for her, sir."

Warrae sighed and flicked off the image. "Well, as wonderful as this conversation has been, it's time to crack that nut open and see what we have."

Mae wanted to swear or scream, but she didn't.

He'd like that. That voice in her head returned. *Don't give him the satisfaction.*

The synthetics pinned her arms tight against her body and dragged her into the room at the back. It was likely the sergeant of the security force's office, at one time. But the Extraktors had transformed it into a horrifying place of clean, white nightmares.

It also contained horrors. Spread out on a medical bed lay Pelorus.

Mae swallowed back nausea. They'd removed his face and laid it on an instrument table. His piercing silver eyes locked onto her as they dragged her past. He couldn't say anything because they had already torn his jaw off. Two far less complex medical synthetics stood at his table, their hands buried in their fellow synth's insides.

At her horrified expression, Warrae made a tutting noise. "Yes, it looks quite a mess, but it is the best way to jack the system. The access nodes in the mouth make our entire process much easier."

Pelorus might not be a human, but in those eyes and in the twitches of his fingers, Mae understood he was in pain. Synthetics of his complexity experienced the world as clearly as a human. Pelorus was a kind being, trained to look after people with sympathy and gentleness. It was a complete outrage that he was being treated in this way. They'd flayed him apart. Mae swallowed hard as bile welled up in her throat.

Warrae's mouth spread in a grin that contained not a drop of humanity. "Don't feel too sorry for Pelorus. He's the one that noticed what you are. Micro-expressions—they give away something like you to a trained medical android. Still, he wouldn't have told a human except under the most extreme duress. Tried to initiate a fatal shutdown, but luckily we caught him before he managed it."

The words that came out of Warrae's mouth confused Mae. She blinked and tried to focus. "What… what do you mean, micro-expressions? Gave me away? What are you talking about, you fucking madman?"

The captain tilted his head. "Can you really not know what you are?" His gaze flickered back for a second to where they'd locked up the Pope family. "How interesting. The mother did mention something about memory loss."

Another two medical androids appeared, wheeling a cart over. On top of it lay a variety of sharp instruments and probes.

Mae lurched to the right, overcome by the primal instinct

to get away. Her captors tightened their implacable grip on her, dragging her towards another operating table.

"I'm a citizen, a human being!" she screamed as they lifted her off her feet, up onto the table, and restrained her limbs.

I'm here. I'm with you. The voice in her head sounded sad. Nice to know her madness possessed a conscience, because Warrae certainly did not.

He could have let the medical synthetics do their work, but a flicker in his eyes told Mae that he enjoyed her panic and very much wanted to be the direct cause of it.

Immediately, she clamped those reactions down. Through a tense jaw, she ground out, "You like hurting people."

"People? No, never. Things like you, well, they can't experience hurt any more than this table can."

She wasn't the only mad person in the room, then. "Fucking psychopath!"

"Enough name-calling. How about we cut to the chase?" Warrae picked up a long, sharp probe from the cart with a cord that connected it to a computer. "I very much want to find out exactly what you are."

While her eyes remained fixed on the partly human captain, the other medical android behind her moved. His merciless and powerful grip clamped down around her jaw. Her blind terror was immediate and distant at the same time. Before her garbled scream reached full strength, in one smooth, terrifying move, he ripped her jaw free. Dark blood sprayed everywhere, splattering Warrae's cheek.

He blinked, and his eyes widened. Warrae thrust the probe in behind where her jaw had been, and everything was blasted away in a mist of pain and white light. Who she was ceased to matter.

2 7

THE BLUE AND THE RED

The world became muddled and confused. Prime, Green, and Red Mae tangled together. They pulled at each other—separate experiences, but the same mind. There were so many feelings and emotions that one synthetic mind and body struggled to contain them all. Sorting out these fractured and disjointed files was not a task her father ever designed her synthetic mind to handle.

She attempted to fit together her last moments with the Jackals.

On the planet, the Good Boys sprang into action to save Red Team. They encircled the squads, projecting their sonic attack. It drove back some of the Xenos, which flinched and turned aside long enough for the Jackals to deploy poly grenades. The thump of the grenade launchers firing punctuated the shrill screams of the attacking monsters.

More poured down from the ceiling as their hive-mates struggled against the chemical strands of the poly grenades. They appeared to have learned tactics to deal with them, though: rather than diving in heedlessly, they actively dodged around the other trapped Xenos.

The Jackals wheeled around in a protective formation. Being well armed, and with the Good Boys driving the howling monsters from their path, they held their ground. Except one element they'd never encountered before was the infected humans. Instead of being happy to be rescued, they turned and helped the Xenos.

The synthetics grappled with the infected humans, but their programming didn't allow them to hurt people. Those the Jackals were here to rescue threw themselves on the four-legged synthetics. They wrapped themselves over their bodies and obscured their sensors until, confused and overwhelmed, the four Good Boys stopped in their tracks.

Losing their sonic protectors meant the Jackals were in trouble. Mae fired grenades into the mass that hurried down the walls, screaming for battle. The Xenomorphs surged in a deadly black wave towards the Jackals. This artificial hive Weyland-Yutani constructed for their trials was full of teeth and rage. The rattle of smart guns and pulse rifles echoed in the chamber. They'd never imagined this black site was so massive.

Escape back the way they'd come was impossible. Mae calculated that the odds of making it back up to the blast door were below acceptable limits. Her mother must know that, too. The only way out was through.

"Push 'em!" Zula screamed, directing fire at the Xenos as they attempted to encircle them. Between all the trapped monsters in the poly-grenade mass lay a clear path forward. An entrance to the valley beyond must lie through there. The synth squad held the line at the rear, taking blasts of acid from their monstrous enemies, while the two human squads pressed on.

Mae let her combat body follow its programming, working in sync with the other squads. It was a certain freedom not to think, or worry, or second-guess. To be one part of a seamless whole. The best genetic humans worked all their lives, trained incredibly hard, to experience something only close to this.

Synth Squad One covered the rear as the humans advanced, pressing into the chamber and towards some kind of hoped-for exit. The roof of this space wasn't visible, but clusters of blue light traced its shape. This vast network of flickering lights on tiny threads living with the queen could not be coincidence. The humans and the Xenos all displayed the same eerie light.

As Mae's core shuffled through the possibilities, the Jackals moved in. The blue illumination provided limited light to the human Jackals. It was only when their headlamps illuminated the dark chambers beyond that the queen was revealed. She hung in a net of constructed plastic polymers. Her huge shovel-shaped head was black, but in the joints blue light flickered ominously. This was some strange new version cooked up by the company. It wasn't the first, but hopefully it might be the last.

With access to all the knowledge gathered by the Jackals over countless missions, Mae hazarded a hypothesis that these civvies must be controlled by the queen. The introduction of Kuebiko extended the control of her own drones to the infected humans, effectively networking them. That was a terrifying fact to be discussed later with her mother—if they lived.

Whatever Wey-Yu introduced to this species, it increased the mental capacity of the queen, but it also created physical limitations. Rather than being suspended from a web of resin, this queen ruled her artificial hive from a company-provided net. Genetic humans, company, and hive all working together: this was Zula Hendricks's worst nightmare.

Mae knew her mother's mind; the Jackals needed to get back to the *Fury* for an immediate orbital bombardment. They needed to destroy whatever Weyland-Yutani made here with the utmost force and with no thought of saving any humans. The scientists who'd done their terrible work down here were trapped along with their unwilling subjects. They flapped among the real victims in their stained lab coats, twisted faces glowing blue. The artificial chambers they'd made for the queen and her brood were now theirs, too. Their fates were all sealed.

A man, his face a still mask, threw himself at R3 to Mae's

right, knocking the unit over. Others immediately flung themselves onto the combat body, pinning it to the ground and beating it with rocks. Synthetic protocols did not allow that unit to respond with deadly force. Mae was the only one without those inhibitions. It was eerie to watch the Xenomorphs make room for the infected humans to take down synthetics. They used the Jackals' desire to save lives to make a most effective trap. Mae unloaded her pulse rifle into the nearest charging woman, almost cutting her in half. Let the queen try to figure out how she'd done that.

As the Jackals entered her domain, the drones hung back. Zula looked up at the massive, constructed chamber Wey-Yu made for the queen they'd always wanted. Additional hexagonal plastic chambers held more of her brood. How long did the company work on this project? It was far beyond a mere black site laboratory. This was a factory.

The hanging queen watched them, her elegant, horrific face turned towards the mass of Jackals. She did not want them there. Her mouth opened to reveal her inner teeth, clear sharp points that also gleamed with a faint blue light.

"Hold fire," Zula said under her breath. "Switch to flame units."

"We should fry the whole lot now," Shipp said, joining the others who carried incinerators.

The queen let out a low hiss of warning. She could not come down, but she had a whole hive of humans and drones at her disposal. On the ground beneath her feet were the freshest of her eggs, recently laid and still developing. They would need hosts, but not just yet.

Was the queen eyeing the genetic human Jackals for the future? Could she plan like that? Mae hated not having any data with which to calculate risks.

"We won't get the whole nest." Zula's voice trembled with barely controlled anger. "We need to get back to the *Fury*, then we can hit the whole damn thing. Nuke twenty clicks from orbit. We need to be sure."

"Understood."

"Keep moving," the colonel instructed Red Team, while her eyes never left the queen. "I can see light on the other side and it ain't blue."

The queen held back. While her eyeless, smooth dome of a head tracked their progress, the drones hung from the ceiling, obeying her command. Mae and her unit covered the rear as the other squads followed the passageway towards a rough-cut opening in the side of the mountain. The queen didn't follow, but her screams and her drones leapt in pursuit of the Jackals.

Once they were clear of the hive, the drones kept back, tracking them, but not killing. Mae's hypothesis that they wanted to keep some more hosts alive seemed to be true. She kept that conclusion to herself. It would serve no one at this particular moment.

They emerged into the valley they'd glimpsed on their arrival, the one scattered with the bones of yet more humans. The wind whipped across the bleak valley as they withdrew from the entrance. Mae bent and examined the bones. None bore the flickering Kuebiko light.

"Colonel, whatever control the company thought it had over the queen, it lost," Mae ventured.

"What makes you so sure?"

She pointed off into the mist. The human eye couldn't see it, but there was a large open-topped transport parked on the access road running up the valley. The company modified it to be perfect for middle management to view a chase. Scattered around it was blood, but no bodies.

Red Team moved to secure the area around the vehicle. A pair of claw marks sliced through the Wey-Yu logo on its side—it almost looked deliberate.

Shipp bent and picked up an employee ID card. "By the looks of it, Mr. Edward Bennington brought quite a few scientists down to watch the Xenos chase their delivered prey."

Private Gorev snorted. "Then they became part of it."

Ackerman leaned in and checked the vehicle. "Looks like she still runs, ma'am."

A faint hiss echoed up from back in the valley, reminding them all that time was short.

"Jackals, we're leaving." Zula climbed into the transport vehicle. "It may not be military issue, but we'll take it."

The squads hustled to take their seats. Mae took the front one next to Gorev at the wheel, while synth unit R2 claimed the rear position. Now there were only two of them from two squads. They took a quick tally of their losses.

The synthetics bore the brunt of it, but Feldman, Meadows, and Lancaster were gone. The whole unit understood what would be happening to them.

"Move out." Zula stared back the way they came. She might have feared more Xenos, but so far there was only mist. Gorev accelerated as quickly as the bus would allow.

As they reached the end of the valley and climbed the service road towards the space elevator terminal, Zula still did not relax. She must have the same concerns as her daughter. What did this all mean?

"Damn the comms blackout." Her mother activated her tight-beam transmission. "*Fury*, come in *Fury*? We're going to need orbital bombardment on the coordinates I'm sending you. Once we're at Minos, you can begin. I want annihilation at twenty clicks."

Silence was all that came.

Mae's memories struggled against that one pivotal moment. Split in two places by time and space, her synthetic brain attempted to sort more emotions into convenient packages. She reached back for more data.

Blue Team reached the airlock they'd previously entered the laboratory through. B3 hobbled forwards, one leg dragging. Acidic damage compromised B4's structural integrity. The human squad members were injured, too. Private Cojocaru bit back screams of pain as acid ate through her armor. Corporal Ware's helmet had taken a direct hit from a Xeno's inner mouth. However, they were in survivable shape.

Mae ordered the inner airlock door closed and spiked it from the inside. The dull thuds of the Xenos smashing against the door thundered on. The Jackals checked their weapons and their suits.

"Lieutenant," called Sergeant Fesolai. "The team can't perform an EVA again."

Mae ran her eye over Blue Team. Jackal armor stopped the worst effects of Xenomorph blood, but the EVA suits they wore over them were not as hardy. They were torn and damaged in ways a hard vacuum would take advantage of. Outside the airlock, they'd die.

Rook clearly also came to the same conclusion. He raised an eyebrow in her direction, waiting for her order.

"The synthetics can EVA to the *Fury*, cut their way in." She didn't include herself in their number. "The rest of us will defend this airlock. It is a B-rated door, and should hold against the Xenomorphs for long enough." She gestured to the human Jackals to put on their helmets, which should provide air long enough for the synths to slip outside and close the outer airlock door behind them. They'd need to hang on to something, though.

At the window of the inner airlock door, the infected humans stared in at them. Blank faces reflected no emotion at all, but Mae sensed there was something greater behind their expressions. Something drove them, and Mae suspected it was the station chief.

No monster knew how to work the mechanics of an airlock. The humans did, though. One punch of the right button, one pull of the handle, was all it took.

The klaxons rang out and the red lights inside flared to life. It was the only brief warning Blue Team got.

Then the vacuum of space opened up around them. Some Jackals managed to hold on to the wall and floor grates for a few brief seconds. Carts and medical implements went flying around them, striking human and synthetic flesh alike. One heavily loaded crate smashed into Mae's left leg. Pain bloomed, but her systems didn't register any damage. B3 tumbled out, crashing into Cojocaru and Tawiah, taking them with it out into the black. B4 tried to hold on to Corporal Ware, but missed grabbing hold of the wall by millimeters. They went out together.

Mae followed a second later. She calculated how long it might take for her systems to degrade enough to cease functioning in a vacuum.

As the blackness of the void reached out, someone grabbed her leg. It was Rook, his fingers locked on to her ankle. His expression remained calm, but his eyes flickered with loss. Scanning down, Mae realized he'd jammed his hand through the grating of the floor. He'd done as he promised to her mother; he'd protected her.

Still, Mae's vision filled with the horrific sight of her entire team careering off into space like scattered leaves. Without their helmets fully secured in time, and with the damage to their EVA suits, they didn't suffer for long.

She began to intimately understand her mother's trauma from the past. It wasn't all about physical injuries done to her, but rather the people she'd lost along the way.

Rook worked along her leg and pulled Mae down next to him. In the vacuum, his words now needed to go through the synthetic network. *Let's get back inside the station through the nearest airlock. Your thrusters are damaged.*

I noticed that, but thank you.

They took care to work their way down the guide ropes to reach the airlock on level ten. Rook bypassed the security, and they crawled back into the station. After the outer door hissed shut, Mae examined the damage to her EVA suit. The right thruster was a write-off. They'd have to reach the *Righteous Fury* through the umbilical attaching it to the station.

While she checked the damage, Rook started work on opening the inner door lock. No sounds reached them with it shut, but she expected chaos beyond. Getting back to the *Fury* would not be easy.

Mae didn't want to see more. Losing Blue Team. The horror of the black site and its training facility. Yet, like her mother, she'd go on. She pulled on the thread that held all three Maes together.

The connection with Colonel Zula Hendricks. That last signal between Red and Blue where they'd both done what their mother wanted.

* * *

A crackle of a signal reached her on the open communications channel. As with Green Mae, it was a chance. There were no words, only data.

A searing pain flared to life behind Mae Prime's eyes. She'd planned on reintegrating her splinters in a controlled fashion. These wild reconnections were painful. All her core processes staggered under the weight of so much raw and unfiltered information. She already bent under Green's emotions and sensations, but now Red piled on top. She needed to contain the chaos. Sectioning off the different experiences and feelings was the only way to cope.

Rook, being in the same network, became aware of the upload. He stopped his repair to open a comms channel. "What is your status, Red Team?"

"Colonel Hendricks and most of the unit are alive, but they trapped us on the planet. The station chief shut down the elevator. Minos has also locked down all executive functions on board the Fury. You cannot leave that way."

Minos was a Weyland-Yutani station, and that company built the *Fury*. Hacking back should not have been possible, but something in Erynis had never been right. He'd tried to kill Mae on Shānmén. Even though he'd been reset since then, some deep programming must have remained for Rolstad to take advantage of.

"We are aware. Rook and I are both fully functional. We shall come get you." Mae's emotional core ran through a cascade of feelings.

The person who answered was not her splinter, but Zula Hendricks.

"Negative, you will not." Zula's voice came out through the open channel as calm as if she were ordering a coffee. *"Mae, here are my orders. I trust you to carry them out. Broadcast an all-hands emergency escape from the Fury. Those life-saving systems should still work?"*

Mae Prime consulted her database of ship schematics. "Confirmed. Shutdown has not affected all safety protocols."

"Then order crew to abandon ship in the cryo escape pods. I want them all safe in orbit on the far side of the planet. I trust you to choose the coordinates."

She didn't care who heard now. "Mother, please, let me help you. Rook and I can find a way—"

"This is a direct order." Zula's voice softened a fraction. *"We are trapped, Mae, and I don't want any of my people infected or taken by Xenos. The information on what they've been doing here must get delivered to our three generals. Then you're going to come back with the cavalry. Okay?"*

Mae froze at that order. "What do you mean?"

"You and Rook take the Blackstar to them. We have the generals' confidence, and they won't want what we found leaving this planet. Red Mae is beaming you what we uncovered here."

"I can't leave you there." Mae's eyes grew hot as emotion choked her throat. This was her prime directive: to protect and assist Colonel Zula Hendricks.

"Yes, you can, and yes, you will. Besides, I have you here with me already. Now, Rook, we discussed what you need to do. Don't let me down."

Then Zula cut the comms. Mae grew angry that what could very well be her last conversation with her mother was so short.

"What did she mean?" Mae demanded.

Rook turned back to the inner door lock. "Even to the last, Colonel Hendricks wants me to protect you. If you are in danger of being discovered or in peril, I have the codes to activate your defensive protocol."

"That will shut me out of my memories!"

"It will protect you until the threat of discovery has passed. You will act entirely like a genetic human." He glanced over his shoulder and shot her a grin. "Your mother loves you. That's an incredible achievement."

Mae wanted to hold on to that, but all she could think of was her mother trapped in an elevator crawler with Xenomorphs at each end.

The door lock beeped. Rook rose to his feet. "Don't let those emotions stop you from acting. Use them as the humans do, as drivers."

She'd gotten plenty of advice from her father, Davis, in her time. She needed no more from Rook. Mae switched over to the executive channel on the *Fury*. In it, she discovered no Minos influence. Erynis, for all his faults, limited the station's intrusion to the doors and security systems. If he hadn't, then the station chief might have vented the entire ship, killing all the Jackals on board at once.

"This is Lieutenant Mae Hendricks, relaying an order from Colonel Hendricks. Executive command PARS-43. All Jackals to your cryo escape pods immediately. This is not a drill. Repeat, this is not a drill."

Through the *Fury's* cameras, she confirmed Zula's troops all scrambled to obey. Mae set the coordinates for the pods' destination. She plugged in a geosynchronous orbit on the far side of the planet. She made sure to order them to spread out and wait for recovery. That, Mae determined, she would bring as fast as synthetically possible.

Checking her pulse rifle, she glanced up at Rook. "That ship of yours better be up to the task."

"I assure you it is."

Rage, kindled by the loss of Blue Team, became red hot as she contemplated the fate of Red Team if they failed. "Good, because we are blowing any docks they have here to shit. I'm not allowing Rolstad to go after any of those pods while we're gone."

The inner airlock door to the lower level of Minos hissed open. Now the screams of the inhabitants were audible.

"An excellent idea."

Mae checked her ammo and grenades. Punching holes in the hulls of Minos Station was now of no concern to her. *And while we're at it, their communications array as well. No one calls for help from here except us.*

Rook crooked an eyebrow, perhaps wondering what kind of Mae all this had unleashed. He stepped aside. *Then after you.*

Making their way to the *Blackstar* was going to be brutal, but it absolutely needed to be done. No human or Xenomorph better get in their way.

2 8

COMPLETE YET BROKEN

"Welcome back." The last thing Mae wanted to see leaning over her was Captain Warrae's face.

Don't tell him everything. Now she understood the nature of that voice: Davis, her synthetic father. It was much more comforting, with that knowledge. *I'm turning down your pain receptors. I think you may have gone a little too close to humanity with those.*

Her jaw lay on the medical cart next to her, surrounded by the blood Zula Hendricks insisted her daughter have. Amusingly, she hadn't wanted a paper cut to reveal her daughter. This situation would have given her nightmares.

The desire to reach up and probe the damage consumed Mae, but the restraints prevented that.

"What did you see?" Warrae's eyes narrowed on her. His actuators hissed as he leaned closer.

Mae didn't answer because she couldn't answer. They'd taken the parts of her body used to create sound. The captain let out a sharp laugh at his own stupidity.

"Sir, we have the results." Homolka handed a pad over to his commanding officer, looking like he'd won a lottery.

Together, they practically drooled at what they read. "An unlicensed autonomous build." Warrae scrolled through the results, a bead of sweat breaking out on his stretched face. "This isn't anything by Weyland-Yutani, and it's definitely too well-executed to be Seegson."

"A genuine artist worked on it." Homolka shot her a look. It contained all the emotion of someone looking over a piece of furniture. "The chipset in there is bespoke, and the firewalls were impressive even after we broke through."

Warrae tapped his fingertips on the pad. "Yes, they were, but we need to ensure that there are no more hidden ones. A maker of this quality would have built in redundancies. Imagine the proprietary knowledge this thing has in it."

They haven't reached the true, self-aware core of you yet. Stay frosty, Mae. You can still survive this.

This Captain Warrae seemed to have one real flaw: curiosity. He was like so many humans, driven by profit, but that wasn't the bedrock of his personality. Mae read it in his eyes. He wanted to find things others had not. Possessing secrets and knowledge was his burning desire. It was something she could use against him.

Carefully, though. Not too fast.

With one hand, she gestured to her jaw lying next to her. After a few moments, Warrae understood. He pointed to a tray on the far table. "Its processing systems are still fully functional. Install an inhibitor spike, and put its jaw back on. I want to hear what it has to say."

Homolka and Warrae stepped back as the medical synthetics carried out his commands. It was an odd sensation when they hooked up the inhibitor to her pain sensors and central core processing unit. Once that was done, the medical units set about fixing what they'd done. Their earlier, savage removal of Mae's jaw was reflected in their haphazard repair.

They reattached the joint but didn't bother with the finer work of repairing the synthetic flesh. Instead, they slapped on some sealant to stop it from flapping around. Mae examined the depth of the inhibitor chip, and which of her systems it affected.

Nasty, brutish way to treat our daughter.

Her father was obviously outside the operating parameters of their spike, so at least she wasn't alone.

With a complex, autonomous synthetic like herself, the inhibitor could not reach into her central programming. It was a far more primitive device to cut power to her exterior systems if triggered. At any point, Warrae could command it to drop her like a stone, trapping her inside her own synthetic body. Not only that, but it also kept her from networking with others.

That she'd just realized the truth of this synthetic body, only to have control taken away from her again, was enraging.

But he's not inside your head. Good thing, too. I wouldn't want to share space with that man.

Considering he was so highly augmented himself, she wondered if it was a case of self-hatred. She filed that away for later. It might prove useful.

These thoughts took mere nanoseconds, so while she waited, she examined Warrae and Homolka more closely. Now that she was aware of her full synthetic abilities, she focused them on her enemy. If micro-expressions brought her to this place, then it seemed only right to use them against the humans.

Homolka was a powder keg. Mae noted the annoyed glances he gave his boss when he thought Warrae wasn't looking. A flicker of disgust showed itself in the tightening corners of his mouth. No doubt the sergeant wanted to be the captain. But wrapped up in his own unhealthy obsessions, his superior didn't notice.

Mae focused her hearing, which, even while hiding her true nature, still operated at levels far above the human ear.

The Pope family talked in low tones. Lenny apologized to his mother. The hint of fear-tainted sweat reached her olfactory processors. It was coming from all of them. William and Daniella, with their life experiences, must be expecting to be ejected out the nearest airlock. Lenny and Morgan were their sole concerns.

Mae determined in that moment that she would do everything she could to keep the four of them alive. Zula Hendricks and her Jackals would have been lost if the Popes hadn't brought her in. A less scrupulous group of humans might have thrown her cryo escape pod back into space and claimed the salvage. No one would know.

It's the things humans do when no one is around to see that show what kind of people they are. It was what created my respect for your mother. Nothing we did or do will ever be known by the wider population.

As the synthetic medics sealed up her face, she recalled Rook's damage. She chuckled at how it once horrified her. The throaty gargle wasn't quite ready to be used, but it caught the attention of the two Extraktors.

Homolka frowned and leaned closer. "Was it trying to laugh?"

"Why are you doing that?" Warrae demanded.

Mae worked her reattached jaw back and forth before answering. It was still loose. "An inside joke. I was thinking of a friend of mine with a facial scar. We'll be able to compare notes."

"That's not funny." Homolka glared.

Mae shrugged. "Had to be there, I guess."

The medics finished their work and stepped away.

"Functional," was Warrae's assessment.

Mae fixed them with a look she hoped conveyed her displeasure at the results. "How about a mirror? I'd like to know how I look."

The two men stared at her blankly. Yes indeed, that was the expression they would give a talking dog. These Extraktors seemed to be morally bankrupt and without a sense of humor.

The captain's eyes narrowed. "We put your jaw back on, so you'd better make it worth our time. We can always have your jaw removed again."

Mae softened her expression. "I want to live. I want my friends to live, and I am prepared to bargain for both."

Warrae crossed his arms. "What do *you* have to negotiate with that we cannot get from jabbing the probe back in?"

Careful with this one, Davis whispered in the back of her head. *Don't make him think he's a fool.*

The Extraktors did indeed have her in a tough situation. However, when they'd attempted to plunder her secrets, Mae's defense program plundered them right back.

This unit was not military. The UPP sanctioned them, but they ran as part of the Jùtóu Combine. As long as they discovered the secrets of great android construction, they continued to be funded. The Combine's synthetic division lagged a distant third to the likes of Weyland-Yutani and Seegson. This meant they were highly motivated to steal market share from their competitors.

The nasty, ambitious gleam in Warrae's eye confirmed that.

She raised her head a fraction off the table. "Your probe is a blunt instrument. It will destroy my secrets before you can get ahold of them. Firewalls, burn protocols. I know you've heard of those."

"Go on." The eyes behind the still mask of his face flickered.

"You want technology that you can use or sell, but tearing me apart would be a mistake, because I know the location of far better and more valuable technology."

"Don't believe it, sir. It'll say anything to save itself." Homolka's fists clenched as if he wanted to pummel Mae.

Warrae stared at her for over 68.334 seconds. Humans took so long to decide on things. A synthetic would have acted already. Mae tried not to display her annoyance. None of what she said was technically a lie, so if they monitored her basic synapses, then it wouldn't sound any alarms.

"Where?"

Now she could reel him in. "A station, not too far from this one. It's a black site with bioweapons, and new kinds of prototype synthetics. They're not like me, they're deadly. You can grab what you need, and come back rich."

She counted on his curiosity, greed, and ambition, and her father taught her enough to read humans as well as machine code.

Warrae leaned back, shooting Homolka an appraising glance. "You're an impressive bespoke synthetic, but your secrets won't be useful in the military market. That is where the Combine wants to expand." Homolka appeared fit to explode, but his captain raised a hand in his direction. "What do you want in return?"

"How about not ripping it apart?" Homolka was turning an interesting shade of red.

"I don't care about death," Mae replied, "but I care about that human family you've imprisoned. They didn't know what I was any more than I did. I want you to let them go, and I'll take you to the station."

Warrae's smile was that of a predator. "I'll release them, except for the boy. He's coming on this trip to ensure you're not tricking us. Anything happens to my men and his brains will decorate our flight deck. Clear?"

She'd hoped to keep Lenny out of this, and caring for him weakened her position. Knowing what awaited them at Minos Station, she understood it would be dangerous, but there could be opportunities to get him away from the Extraktors.

"Crystal."

"Remember that inhibitor spike in your central core, and behave." Warrae jerked his head towards the combat synthetics by the door. "Let her up and go get the boy she came in with. Looks like we're going on a trip."

I hope you made the right choice, Mae. Leading these people to Minos is a risky move.

It accomplishes two things, Father. We needed to get back to Minos and Mother, and we can shake off these monsters with more familiar ones.

2 9

CAREFUL WHAT YOU
WISH FOR

The Extraktor captain threw open the door to their cell
and strode in. Through the glass, Lenny spotted Mae. She
stood shackled with her head bowed.

He understood immediately that whatever they'd done
to her in the back office was in fact torture. He jerked away
from his mother and leaped to his feet. His heart raced,
and rage bubbled inside.

They'd ripped her jaw off and then done a real shitty job
of repairing it. It took him a moment more to realize what
that actually meant. She'd been a synthetic all along.

That revelation sunk into him like a stone. It made sense,
but it left him embarrassed and feeling foolish. She'd
fought against going to the medical bay. Her cryo escape
pod could barely sustain life. She wasn't an amnesiac; she
was a firewalled synthetic person. The ease with which

she flung him off when he tried to get her to go to the med bay made sense now. He was a fool, and now his family was going to pay.

The Extraktors grabbed hold of him with uncaring, hard synthetic hands, and yanked him out. Everything happened in a muffled gray space. His parents and Morgan scuffled with them, screaming his name, but none of it mattered. In the end, the augmented humans beat them back, and it became a short and brutal fight. The Pope family were left bleeding and raging on the floor.

"Lenny!" Daniella howled in anguish. Her cry reached Lenny and punched him in the gut. It hurt worse than anything these tin-can wannabes could do.

The Extraktors were a mix of synthetic units and augmented humans. Their robotic arms were stronger, their augmented minds faster. Against that, even his SOF-trained parents were helpless.

Mae stood impassively by, her face a mask. After a short angry struggle, they cuffed Lenny and dragged him into line with the person he hadn't really ever known. She was no more human than Pelorus. Lenny hung his head and didn't speak to Mae.

The Extraktors cuffed the remaining Popes and dragged them from the room.

Warrae pulled on his thin black gloves. "You have one son left. Be grateful I'm letting you keep him and your lives."

"We fought for the Union, you bastard." Daniella

strained and raged against those that held her. "We sweated and bled for it!"

The captain didn't even look up. "Well then, thank you for your service, and for your son."

Mae closed her eyes as they dragged the still-struggling family away. Lenny, though, watched until they were out of sight. These might be the last images of his family he ever got.

"Station security will release them once we're on our way, but they won't be able to undock their ship for some time." Warrae gestured to his troopers. "Let's get to the *Ariadne*."

"Of course, that's your ship," Lenny muttered. "Ariadne betrayed her own family, too."

No one even bothered to reply. Station personnel made themselves scarce as they took the elevator back down to the dock. Those workers that were around all turned their backs to the sight of one of their own being hauled away. Lenny didn't blame them. Hell, he'd been in their position himself; when the Combine made people disappear, it was better not to ask questions.

Yet he had a million questions. What kind of synthetic was she? He'd seen plenty of them, and none like her. Shit, he'd kissed her and not even known. This was the kind of thing Morgan would have ribbed him endlessly about.

He wondered if Mae would apologize. He knew what he would say if she tried. *It doesn't matter. You put my family in danger, and you aren't what you said you were.*

Maybe that was unreasonable. She obviously hadn't known herself, but what happened to his family hurt. How would they manage if he never came back? Because, if he was honest, that was the most likely outcome of all this.

The Extractors' ship, the *Ariadne*, lay ahead. It was the stranger on the dock, the one he'd tried to identify when they'd first arrived at Guelph with Mae. Now he got a real close look at her. Warrae's expression reflected pride.

"Specifically made for my unit." He couldn't stop himself from showing it off to Mae. "There are only five cryopods installed. Luckily for our guest here, because the *Ariadne* goes at speeds no unaugmented person could survive."

"The benefits of none of you being completely human." Mae smiled at him.

Lenny grasped that neither of them knew about his augmentation. Unlike the Extraktors, his wasn't readily apparent. While Warrae enjoyed his moment, Lenny probed the edges of the synthetic network. Every military android unit carried one with them, and it appeared these did too. Lenny's augment was of the same design, Seegson. He might make use of that, but not yet. He'd have to be very careful about picking his moment.

Warrae narrowed his eyes but did not rise to Mae's jibe. Instead, he gestured her into the *Ariadne* as if he was some kind of old-time gentleman. Lenny, they shoved in after. He kept his gaze down but noted as much of the ship as possible.

Warrae hadn't exaggerated. The *Ariadne* was brand new—the smell told him that. He caught glimpses of the controls and easily identified them as a Kinmokusei class. Straight off the line. He'd only read about them and seen a few pictures. If it weren't for the situation, Lenny would have been excited to be on board.

The controls appeared to be carried over from the Shobu class, and he had prior experience with those. Another fact to file away for later.

The interior wasn't luxurious. Nothing frivolous or homey existed in the *Ariadne*. It was completely different from the *Eumenides*, like comparing a laboratory to a family home.

Synthetic racks took up most of the space in the *Ariadne*. She barely had a seat available for a human backside. No military ship would have traveled with such a high ratio of human to synthetic soldiers. Most companies and galactic powers viewed augmented humans as untrustworthy. They used a few tragic incidents to support their claim that these implants raised the risk of psychosis and violent behavior.

Lenny could relate to the augmented Extraktors because he went through something similar. However, he'd ripped no one's jaw off afterwards. They could never be his friends.

Instead, he aligned himself with the *Ariadne* herself.

While the rest of the troopers filed in, Lenny's skin prickled with the presence of the ship's AI. It must be a wide-capacity synthetic network. He could have attempted to hack into it—he was familiar with the Shobu class and its AI—but that would be suicidal. Instead, taking his lead from Mae, he held back.

The synthetic Extraktors filed into the ship and took their places on the racks to recharge. Apart from the ex-military combat units, there were five medical androids. They were the ones that worked on Mae, but they were not the most chilling; Homolka still stared at her as if he wished he'd brought a scalpel of his own.

Lenny stayed in the corner and kept silent, hoping they'd forget about him for a bit.

It interested him to watch the augmented humans who put themselves onto the racks like they were the same as their synthetic colleagues. It spoke volumes about how they viewed themselves. Lenny might be augmented, but he'd never wanted to become synthetic.

The enhanced human Extraktors took their places with barely a word spoken. Lenny found it a little eerie. They didn't need to go into cryo for the journey, but they did hook themselves up to an intravenous supply. So much as they might yearn to be synthetic, they hadn't completely shaken off their humanity.

Warrae and Homolka remained still. Their half-lidded eyes indicated they'd connected to the ship's AI. Lenny took his chance before they returned and put him into one of the cryopods.

He waved one bound hand to get Mae's attention. She

tried to smile, though her damaged jaw made the gesture lopsided.

"I'm sorry." Her words came out only slightly affected.

Despite what he planned, her damaged face made him change his mind. "Don't be. I'd do it all again."

Mae's expression flickered from sadness to vague amusement then back to sadness. "You don't know what we're going into."

It looked as if she might say more, but Warrae's and Homolka's eyes snapped open.

"We've input the coordinates. That's Three World space."

Mae let out a short laugh. "You're not afraid of a little raid, are you? The rewards are worth the risk."

Homolka glanced at his superior. "The probe results show that location as where her pod traveled from."

The lure of a skilled artisan making exquisite synthetics like Mae seemed to be enough.

It was difficult to make out much behind Warrae's eerie smooth face. Finally, he jerked his head to his officer. "Put her on the rack and the boy in cryo. If our prisoner moves from the rack we've placed her on, activate the inhibitor spike."

Lenny objected to being called a boy all the time, but he wisely added it to his list of complaints to take out on this bastard later.

Mae moved to the rack without complaint, leaning back into it and powering down most of her systems. Lenny couldn't help but feel a little strange, watching her. Even with her damaged jaw, she still seemed so very human.

"Ah, got a little crush on the toaster?" Homolka slammed Lenny against the side of the cryopod. "Can't blame you on that one. A nicely put-together piece of kit."

Lenny struggled. He popped one of his elbows into the man's gut, but it made no difference because that, too, was artificial.

Homolka laughed and activated the cryopod. It hissed open, and he jammed Lenny into it. Only a rifle in his face kept him from leaping out. As the drugs overtook him and he faded into unconsciousness, he swore to wake up ready for revenge. Homolka's grinning face was the last thing Lenny saw, and he carried it off with him like a stone in his shoe.

3 0

RETURN TO KNOSSOS

When Mae stirred from her slumber, it was to find she remained in a nightmare. Her jaw ached, as if to remind her it was nothing she could wake from.

The human Extraktors moved about the ship. They checked weapons and discussed in excited tones the possibility of the greatest haul of intellectual property in the Combine's history.

Warrae and Homolka stood huddled by the control screens, ignoring her.

"Minos Station, come in." The sergeant punched more buttons. "It's on all frequencies, but no answer. *Ariadne*, is the station still powered up?"

The ship AI's voice was syrupy sweet. "Confirmed. I am receiving power signatures, and Minos is still in a stable orbit."

Mae struggled free of the rack. To her right, two Extraktors were waking Lenny from the cryopod. To proceed with her plan, she knew she needed to put aside her guilt. She and Lenny needed to work together to get out of this alive.

Mae wrestled with her complex emotions. *I didn't even know what I was myself, so how could I be honest with him?*

Dearest daughter, don't even attempt to be logical. Humans aren't, after all.

She understood her father was trying to comfort her, but she was too busy examining the unpleasant emotion that was guilt. Her deception was on her mother's orders. No one disobeyed Colonel Hendricks. If anything happened, the orders she'd given Rook were specific: activate Mae's protection protocol.

The Jackals were relying on her to bring back help. The desire to protect her family was the one thing she and Lenny still had in common.

"Bring it up on-screen." Warrae crossed his arms but glanced back at Mae. "If you've lied to us, this will be a very short trip."

Humans want to be synthetics, while synthetics want to be human. What a galaxy of wonders we live in. Her father's sarcasm, as always, hit awkwardly.

Minos Station appeared from around the far side of the planet. As the *Ariadne* circled it, the *Fury* came into view. Her long, spiky form remained inert by the dock, with the umbilical still attached. Her running lights flickered, a dim yellow light against the darkness of the station.

Mae didn't know what she'd been expecting. The sight of

the Jackals' vessel confirmed that she wasn't malfunctioning. All her memories—the fight, the Xenomorphs, and those final horrors—were all real. The Jackals were real. A ragged gasp escaped her.

That made Warrae laugh. "Beautiful impersonation of a human, there. You don't need to bother for our sake."

She glared at him. "It's part of my programming. Given to me by my—" She stopped herself in time. Telling these people she had a father was pointless and potentially dangerous.

The Extraktors weren't listening, anyway. They'd finally realized that the *Righteous Fury* was no normal military vessel—any more than Mae was a regular synthetic.

The avarice positively dripped out of Warrae's remaining pores. "That is *not* a standard Colonial Marines ship. Give me a deep scan on that, *Ariadne*."

A second later, the ship replied. "Unable to comply. Hull structure and ionization is preventing my systems from completing scanning."

That brought them up short.

"Is this what you're bartering your lives with?" The captain spun on Mae. "Is this what you think will save you? One ship?"

They'd woken Lenny. The young man stood shivering, cryo liquid dripping down his hair and face. Yet his eyes were defiant.

Mae smiled. "That's only the start. You'll find the best stuff inside the station."

Warrae examined her for a moment and then jerked his head to his sergeant. They retreated to the back of the ship. Mae's synthetic hearing was better than they could possibly have guessed.

The furious conversation between Warrae and Homolka would almost have been comical if it wasn't so deadly serious. A spiral of greed now drew them in. The appearance of the *Fury* confirmed she wasn't lying, and if that were true, then the rest must be as well.

Warrae's little industrial espionage squad had discovered what miners would've called the mother lode. If it was possible for grown, augmented men to be giddy about anything, then Warrae and Homolka were.

Mae inched her way closer to Lenny and passed him a towel from a stack by the cryopods. As he wiped off the cryo fluid, she whispered, "Stay close."

He nodded.

No one seemed to notice their brief exchange, especially when Minos revealed her other treasure. The Extraktors all raced to the windows as the silver trail of the space elevator came into view.

It remained intact, and that gave Mae hope. Red Team and her mother might have been able to use it, but was Zula Hendricks even still alive?

Never bet against Zula Hendricks. Davis's voice entered her mind wistfully. If a synthetic could love, then perhaps anything was possible.

"Holy shit!" Homolka pounded on the control desk.

"If that thing is still intact, we're in the money. We can fly down and see what's at the base."

"If you'd like to be cut to ribbons." Mae pointed out the satellites that peppered the planet's orbit. "That is a grade-A Wey-Yu defense grid. Break atmosphere and you'll trigger a deadly response."

Warrae considered for a moment. "The elevator it is, then. Once we've used it, we can bring back a Combine salvage team." He turned on Mae. "What exactly happened here? Where are all the staff?"

"It was a virus. Wiped everyone out. Synthetics can enter, but I'd recommend breathers for those of you who still have lungs."

"Three World technology." Homolka stared out the window like a lovesick fool. "And whatever that ship is, too."

Warrae's gaze darted over to Lenny. "We're all going in—including your delicate friend." He clearly suspected it was a trap, but he couldn't imagine the true horrors waiting for them.

How's the inhibitor spike fixing going, Father?

They know their stuff, Davis replied. *Rerouting your systems past this device is taking longer than I thought.*

Well, I'll need to be free of it soon. Very life-and-death.

The Extraktor spike in the back of her throat burned and itched at the same time. A curious tickle ran over her skin. It must be another symptom of her captor's controls.

The *Ariadne* came about and faced the docking bay. This

ship was small enough to land there, rather than attach itself via umbilical. The docking bay doors still hung open from the *Blackstar*'s hasty departure, and the Extraktor ship entered through the blown-out doors.

It was fortunate that nothing about the dock itself was too suspicious. The *Solo Cup* now floated in the bay, since the dock lost its air when the control field at the entrance was destroyed by Rook. Simulated gravity had also been cut. Another smaller shuttle bumped up against her in a cloud of debris as if to emphasize the damage.

"We're going to have to go EVA to get through the airlock." Warrae grinned savagely. "At least, some of us are."

Homolka deployed magnetic clamps to attach the *Ariadne* to the docking bay floor, and Mae couldn't help but wince a little at the echoing thump. Advanced synthetics experienced trauma too.

Her father's voice took a few seconds to reply. *But you also have dreams. Hold on to those.*

The synthetics on the ship didn't need suits, but the augmented Extraktors slipped them on for the short walk to the airlock. They forced Lenny at gunpoint to pull one on. The full Extraktor team opened the door and stepped out onto Minos Station.

Mae stood on the deck and scrutinized the landing area. It seemed mostly intact, and no bodies floated within, so at least the airlock wasn't breached. She pushed herself off, following the Extraktors and Lenny, who was still in a synthetic's grip.

"Run a bypass," Warrae commanded one of his human troopers.

Breathe in their concerns, Davis whispered. *Manage them.*

The hatch was thankfully still functional. As the team entered the airlock, Mae drifted closer to Lenny. Homolka closed the inner door and cycled in air.

The sergeant consulted his wrist-pd while standing in front of the inner seal. "Looks like they still have atmosphere and gravity on the other side."

"Pathogens?"

"Nope. Clean as the *Ariadne.*"

"The station has a contamination protocol. It'll have destroyed the pathogen long ago." Mae found it remarkably easy to lie.

Warrae jerked his head to her. "You first." He emphasized this by jabbing the muzzle of his pulse rifle into her back. Mae calculated how many moves it would take her to wrest it from him.

Not yet. If you do that, or ask for a rifle, they'll know you are lying about the pathogen.

She slipped between the troopers and took up a position by the door lock. With the air cycled in, the humans in the group removed their helmets and stowed them on their backs. Lenny took his off and made eye contact with her. However, it was not a comforting moment; he appeared empty, drained of all emotion—even anger.

Her first step beyond the airlock and into the station proper echoed across the empty galleria. It hadn't seemed too large before, but the empty shops and scattered tables made it appear three times larger. A curious phenomenon, which she chalked up to her attempts to become more human. Their foibles and idiosyncrasies came with the territory. The air was fresh, but an odor still lingered. The stink of sweat.

The synthetic troopers moved out first, always the cannon fodder to protect the humans. Warrae and his nine human Extraktors followed. Homolka withdrew his scanner and frowned at it. "I'm not reading any life signs. Just us."

His captain smiled. "Even better. Pathogen cleaned everyone out, and we can just grab what we need. Synth troopers, hack the network."

Mae experienced their attempts like a trickle of gooseflesh over her skin. Minos didn't only possess regular station networks. This was a highly secretive black site, and even the Extraktors wouldn't get in without the key. She neglected to tell them she had it.

"We cannot breach the firewall," the E1 command android replied. "We would need to break into the communications command center and do a physical hack."

Warrae considered. Some primitive human instincts must still linger in his augmented brain, and they likely told him that speed was the only way. Mae again withheld the information that Green Team had already broken the command center open.

"Negative. Not much to learn from the synth network.

We have our own." He pointed his rifle at Lenny, but glared at Mae. "Time to show us the goods."

She'd been waiting for this moment. "That would be the laboratory. Follow me."

They took their time crossing the galleria. The last time she'd been here was with Rook, and the shops were full of terrified humans. Cut off from the rest of the escape pods, they'd been trying to get through to the ships on the other side of the airlock. Her memories, now hers again, troubled her. Should she have attempted to help those people? Her mother gave her an order, and she'd obeyed it. However, the recollection of the employees was hard to shake.

Welcome to humanity. Trauma isn't optional, Davis observed wryly.

Mae took them to the transit system. Something had happened to it since she was here. The tram lay on its side, a tumble of twisted metal and shattered cabs. This worked for her, giving Davis time to access the station's synthetic network. Rook gave her the key back while they were running for the *Blackstar*. Now it proved invaluable. As the Extraktors checked around every corner and scanned every shadow, she went to work.

Minos Station teetered on the edge of breaking orbit. Its orbital stabilizers needed maintenance, which they hadn't received for weeks. Service robots could only do so much. However, its synthetics survived. Not all of them, but enough for Mae to find eyes and ears all over the station. Blood filled the corridors on the command deck. A Mr.

Brown wandered around those empty spaces, repairing and cleaning. He stepped over the decaying bodies of station employees and then dragged them away into a pile in an alcove next to a disused toilet. He did his best.

Mae entered his head and observed him mopping the blood around. It was too much for one Mr. Brown to manage, but he gamely followed his programming, regardless of the humans who might appreciate it now all lying dead.

In the shadows of walls and doorways, the monsters slept. Mr. Brown did not disturb their slumber. He wasn't useful to their breeding cycle, and he posed no threat to the colony. In the weeks that had followed Mae's escape, no humans survived—on that level, at least.

She instructed the Mr. Brown to examine the bodies he'd piled up. Through his eyes, she observed only station uniforms. Security guards, mostly. They'd been the ones to fight back, and died defending the command center. The Xenomorphs hadn't killed the rest of the staff, though. Instead, they must've taken them.

"Synth!" Homolka's angry hiss brought her back in a nanosecond. "This thing is busted." The transit tram lay on its side, derailed and useless. It had long ago stopped spitting sparks. She'd fought a David unit here, and his crumpled remains must still be inside. They were remarkably tough, even for their age. She didn't want the Extraktors going in there, in case they squeezed out some information from it.

Mae worked her face into an expression of surprise.

ALIEN: SEVENTH CIRCLE

"It wasn't like this when I left. We can take the stairs and tunnel."

They clearly didn't like those words, but what other choice did they have? Greed brought them this far, and it would carry them a little farther.

Yanking back a piece of twisted metal from the transit tram, she revealed a door marked with a red and yellow sign that read EXIT.

She smiled. "Not much farther."

They could have gone back, cut their losses and run. Perhaps she even should have encouraged it, but no, she wanted the Extraktors to follow her into the darkness.

Warrae's eyes narrowed. "Troopers, move out."

Exploring Minos was like stepping into a nightmare realm. Though, as a synthetic, she ought not to have nightmares. Recovering her memories changed her perception of everything.

The images of the station as she'd first entered it with her mother, and when she'd hastened through the horror of the Xenomorph outbreak, layered on top of what she found now. It was incredibly distracting.

Emergency illumination remained active. Strips of dim red light illuminated the stairwell that led up to the control level.

"You first," Warrae said, waving his rifle in her direction.

"I assumed so," Mae muttered.

Taking her time to climb, she kept an eye on her captors. The Extraktors would be trying to get into the station's network, but they didn't have the access key. If they wanted entry, then they would have to hack the system at the node, as Green Team did. Her only advantage was that they had a lot more levels to climb. All stations, no matter who constructed them, kept their command centers on the topmost levels. In the meantime, she could lead them on a torturous and dangerous route wherever she liked. Along the way there'd be many dangers.

A locked door awaited them at the top of the stairs. Mae paused for a moment and listened. Nothing stirred on the other side, so the Xenomorphs must have gone into hibernation. When all its food sources were used up, the hive survived that way. After so many weeks, their usual life cycles must have completed.

A bitter thought wormed its way up through her processors: Jackals might have been cocooned to use as hosts. Though most had evacuated in their cryo escape pods, Red Team was still a possibility. Her mother and Shipp might already lie somewhere on the station, their chests blown apart from the inside.

"You waiting on something?" Warrae stood a few steps behind her, his arm wrapped around Lenny's neck. He didn't need a weapon. He could snap Lenny's spine in a moment.

Mae calculated the odds. The probability was still too high that Lenny would die before she neutralized Warrae.

"In case of contamination, the station doors lock."

One of the Extraktor synthetics marched up the stairs

and nudged her aside. From his pack, he produced a maintenance jack. It didn't take long for it to crank the door open.

Mae stepped through, already knowing Minos's layout. This was the perfect entry point for her purposes. They'd reached the eleventh level, but on the far side of the donut-shaped station.

"This is the laboratory." She turned back to Warrae. "You'll find a lot of the IP you're after here."

His eyes narrowed. "Scan shows no viral or bacterial elements." He gave Lenny a shake. "Good thing, too, or your canary in the coal mine would be the first to feel it."

He might be considering killing them now, but Mae got ahead of him.

"He's useful for something, then. You need us both."

Lenny cast a desperate look towards her. Mae wished in that moment that she was able to share her network code with him, then she'd be able to let him in on her plan. It wasn't much of one.

After recovering herself and her memories, she'd calculated how much time had passed since she'd last set foot on Minos. It had been four weeks. The Green Mae splinter still was not fully integrated with her systems, and that was causing her primary core to come close to failure.

She needed to manage her instability until she found her mother and the Jackals. Warrae would soon realize that he was in a great deal of danger. Even his appetite for advancement in the Combine could only take him so far.

Still, the laboratory level looked in bad enough shape to slow them down. Up ahead, ceilings lay collapsed and torn. So far, she'd detected no signs of Xenomorphs, but they'd soon come. Until then, she needed to thin the herd some.

In fact, it would be her great pleasure to do so.

3 1

HELPFUL MR. BROWN

Weyland-Yutani Mr. Brown synths populated Minos Station on every level, and she counted on their help for her plan to succeed. She assessed the potential response of Weyland-Yutani's synthetic networks to the infiltration of Combine augments. They would swarm like bees when wasps invaded their hive.

The Extraktor troopers began to crawl and clamber through the debris, hungry for their prize.

Her father remained a subroutine in her system behind a deeper firewall. Since he was unaffected by the inhibitor the Extraktors had put on her, and was already attached to the station network, he triggered the system.

Mae turned her back on Warrae and smiled to herself. She didn't need to do anything more. They were coming.

The human troopers coughed in the lingering smoke in the corridor. Lenny wiped his eyes but didn't complain.

She got the impression he, too, was biding his time. Though she hoped he wasn't about to do anything foolish.

Humans were terrible at calculating the odds of success. They didn't understand statistics, and they too often followed their gut instincts. She'd never known a person's colon to make an informed choice.

As Mae crawled through the debris, she moved as close to him as possible. The regular android programming would still control the station synthetics, but she wasn't taking any chances.

On the other side, the corridor branched out into multiple laboratories. They were empty of humans, bodies, and—unfortunately—station synthetics. The Extraktors fanned out into these new rooms, hungry for whatever they could steal. Warrae shoved Lenny ahead of him, trying to maintain some order.

Homolka darted back to his superior, arms laden with multiple packages of discs. "Can't access the computers without the key, boss. Found these, though."

Warrae flicked through, reading the simple labels. "Project Small Fry, Wall Skeleton, Fry Up. Seems this was a busy station. Multiple projects going on." He turned to Mae. "Any idea what these are?"

She picked her words with care. He hadn't cracked her memory banks, since they'd only returned after his attack. "I worked in the command center. I only heard that Wey-Yu was happy with the results."

The commander's expression didn't change, but he

was obviously assessing how much of what she'd said was truth. He waved at Homolka. "Get a cart, load it up with whatever you can find. We'll have to break the codes later."

Homolka gave a half-assed salute and scuttled off to do as he was told. A few seconds later he let out a shout from the laboratory to the right. "Captain, come see this!"

Mae glanced at the door number. 1117. These were the labs where human subjects got dosed with the Kuebiko. She remained calm, even as her skin pricked with the approach of the station's security androids.

Warrae followed his second into 1117, and Mae did not want them to come out of there with any samples. If they did, then she'd have to try her best to stop them.

Our friends are here, Davis whispered. *Get ready.*

One of the Extraktor synthetics was the first to discover their intrusion at Minos would not go entirely unchallenged. E10 was working on the lock of the last laboratory room at the far end of the corridor when the sealed hatch hissed open. If he'd been human, he might have fallen on his ass.

As it was, when three Mr. Browns, security android variants, darted through, he didn't have time to get up. These new arrivals were armed with stun batons and grenades. The synthetic Extraktor tried to move out of the way, but it was as slow as a toddler compared to these newest company designs. Despite all their claims to the contrary, Seegson was an inferior builder.

E10 broadcast an alarm a moment before the Wey-Yu Mr. Brown synths rendered it useless with a swift jab of their weapons to its arm joint. The human Extraktor troopers spilled out from the laboratories. Unlike the resident security, they carried pulse rifles and weren't afraid to use them.

The company had equipped the station's Mr. Browns to protect its investment in Minos. Despite their superior construction, they wouldn't last long against the Extraktors.

Warrae released Lenny to bring his rifle up in defense of his team. As they opened up on the Wey-Yu droids with their rifles, Mae dived at Lenny, pulling him to the ground. The dull *thunk* of rounds reverberated around them, and the whine of synthetic combat and shouts of angry, augmented humans filled the corridor.

White synthetic blood from both sides sprayed the windows. An augmented Extraktor dropped dead at her feet. For a moment she considered grabbing his rifle, but that would make her an immediate target. Instead, she swiped the Ka-Bar knife at his side. She had plenty of training on how to use that.

Still. Mae didn't intend to hang around and see who would emerge victorious. She'd been eyeing their escape route since the moment they'd entered this level. During Blue Team's initial foray, she'd observed one detail that hadn't mattered at the time. It did now. By Mae's estimates, she didn't have long to implement this maneuver.

As the Extraktors took defensive positions inside the labs, she wrapped her arm over Lenny. The nearby industrial waste chute was big enough for one person at a time. Ideally, she would have jumped in first, but she needed to shield him from the inevitable spray of pulse rifle rounds. He would have to go first.

Mae yanked the chute cover up and held it open. She didn't need to urge Lenny to take the opportunity. He might not know the station like he did Guelph, but he recognized an escape route when he saw one. Without a word, he leaped in. Mae followed quickly after.

Warrae spotted their attempt to flee. The rattle of more rounds hitting the corridor's walls accompanied his angry shout.

Though Mae could now recall a good portion of the station, she'd not been able to access its schematics on her previous visit. She had only the vaguest idea of where this chute would end up.

They slid down the shiny metal chute at an uncomfortably high speed. Up ahead, Lenny attempted to slow their descent with his elbows and knees. Guessing this wasn't his first time in such a space, she copied him.

I hope this doesn't go straight to the incinerator, her father helpfully added.

Sometimes his droll observations did not improve the situation. Mae was too busy trying to use their velocity to work out how far they'd traveled. They must have passed many levels.

The chute finally spat them out. They arced through the air and landed with a juddering thump. Only a massive pile of station waste stopped them from both suffering terrible injuries.

Lenny lay face up among a collection of medical gowns and bags labeled HAZARDOUS. Mae scrambled over to him to check for injuries. He bore a few scratches on his arms, and abrasions on his palms and knees where he'd slowed himself down. Apart from that, he appeared unharmed.

He took a ragged breath before pulling himself out of the pile. "Let's agree never to do that again, okay?"

"Not if I can help it."

They struggled through the detritus of Minos's laboratories to free themselves. Mae pried herself free from the pile and offered her hand to Lenny. He took it reluctantly, and together they rolled and wriggled to their feet.

This room must be on the lower three levels of the station. A sealed industrial incinerator was still active and being tended to by a single Mr. Brown robot. It currently loaded the maw of the machine, apparently still on-task even if the human employees were not.

From the sheer amount stored in this room, it appeared only the Mr. Brown was still working. Another four janitorial robots waited on a rack, but no one had activated them. She supposed, given that no one was working on level eleven anymore, the solo Mr. Brown would eventually complete its task.

The active robot ignored their presence and continued its work.

Lenny glanced back to the mouth of the chute. "What's stopping them from just following us?"

Mae grinned grimly. "Fear of death, and greed. They'll get over it, though, and follow us down here soon enough." She strode over to a nearby maintenance table full of tools. "Looks like someone was working on the incinerator before the horrors upstairs broke through."

"Horrors?"

He needed to know for his own safety, but there was one last important job for him to do first. "I'll tell you everything I've remembered later. Now, we're going to have to run for our lives, and I can't do that with this Extraktor inhibitor spike in me." She ran her hands over the tools. "I'm going to need you to take care of it."

"What?"

Mae shoved a giant pair of pliers and a chisel towards him. "Take the spike out for me. It's in my throat."

He took a step back. "I'm not ripping your jaw off."

"You don't have to go in that way. Here." She pointed to the spot where her throat connected to her synthetic collarbone. "You're going to have to be careful, but I'll guide you."

Lenny shook his head. "Why can't you do it yourself?"

"Human behavioral inhibitors. They prevent me from doing anything a genetic human wouldn't do to themselves. My mother didn't want to take any chances that someone would see me doing something… synthetic."

"Wow. She was serious."

"She *is* serious. As serious as your mother. Come on. We don't have much time." When Lenny gave a nervous nod, she placed the sharp end of the chisel against her skin and passed him a small mallet. "This isn't a combat body, so one quick tap here should break through. Then you'll have to use the pliers to find the spike."

"Fuck me," Lenny whispered under his breath. "Alright, I guess I don't have a choice."

"You can do this." Mae understood humans needed reassurance even in the worst of circumstances.

Can he, though?

Again, Davis was not being helpful.

Lenny let out a breath through his nose, swung back with the mallet, and struck her with the chisel in the spot she'd indicated.

The pain was unexpected, and Mae let out a small gasp. Red synthetic blood struck Lenny's face, and he flinched back.

Wiping it from his eyes, he asked, "Are you alright?"

She cocked an eyebrow at him and stared down at the chisel. "My systems are intact, so you got the right spot. Now, use the pliers to pull the spike out."

Lenny gritted his teeth, withdrew the chisel, and gingerly moved the pliers into place.

"You're going to have to push harder," Mae said, even

as the pain receptors in her beautifully constructed body flared once more.

"Okay." With a grunt, he shoved the pliers deeper into her neck.

"Now… angle up a bit." The pain made her eyes ache suddenly, as well. "To the left. Can you feel the spike?" Her voice came out cracked, a juddering feedback from her systems.

"Yeah. Oh god, fuck, does this hurt?" His face twisted in sympathetic pain.

"Immaterial. Nearly there."

Finally, he positioned the pliers on each side of the Extraktors' implant.

"Now, yank hard, but carefully out the way the pliers went in." She decided not to tell him how close he was to her central power column.

"Alright." He readjusted his grip and then wrenched hard. It was more by luck than skill that he worked it free.

It left them both gasping. Lenny hurled the spike onto the floor and stamped on it, as if it were an actual bug. Then he threw his arms around Mae.

She hugged him back. "I'm sorry you're here."

"Again, not your fault."

"You haven't heard the worst of it yet."

She explained, as succinctly as possible, about the Xenomorphs and the disappearance of her mother. Even in the dim light, Lenny appeared suddenly pale.

"Shit. You have a plan, right, to survive all that?"

"We're getting out of here, and then we're bringing the whole damn station down. Flatten that training facility like a salvo of nukes."

"Fuck yeah." His eyes darted around the furnace room. "Do you think they're still down here? Those monsters?"

It wouldn't have been fair to lie. "Yes. They're probably hibernating, but us being here will wake them eventually." She drew him over towards one of the janitorial androids on the rack. "I need you to get to the command center and stay there, before they begin hunting."

Mae activated one robot. Its round form dropped onto the floor and began looking around for a mess to clean. She stopped it before it went too far, then started working the robot's front panel open. The space inside was big enough for the expansive trash bags these models usually trundled around with. It was also plenty of room for one lean, young man.

"I can't go in there." Lenny backed away as he figured out her plan.

Mae glanced up. "This will get you to the command center. Once there, I want you to override the system and send the crawler on the space elevator down to the planet."

"What makes you think I can—"

"I'm fully back online, Lenny. My systems are better than the Extraktors, so I know about your augment. Its records indicate you're the best hacker on Guelph."

He flushed and wouldn't meet her eyes. "It's not

something I like to talk about. The augment cost my family a lot, and not only in money."

She nodded and put her hand on his shoulder. "Then you pay them back by using it now. Because if these monsters get out, no one is safe."

"Yeah, I get it." He put his hand on top of hers for an instant before clambering into the void of the janitorial android. "Not the sweetest smell in here."

"You should be grateful. Its electrical signal will cover your augment's operation, as long as you don't use it on the trip." She leaned in and squeezed his shoulder. "I'm going to start the station's engines. We're bringing this whole thing down, but only once I've found my mother and brought her back up."

"I like the sound of this plan."

She reached out in her mind, extending a secure peer-to-peer network invitation to Lenny. His eyebrows shot up, but then he grinned.

I've never done this before.

"Then we've got something in common. I've never connected with an augmented human." She picked the robot's front panel back up. "I'll signal you when to bring up my mother. Until then, take care not to be noticed."

"Course. Now, come on, seal this up and we can get on with it." He clutched his knees to his chest and didn't meet Mae's eyes as she reattached the panel.

She sent the janitorial robot off on an assignment to the command center. As she watched it trundle off with its hidden cargo, she was glad she hadn't told Lenny the whole truth.

Augmented humans—with their combination of electronics and heartbeats—attracted Xenomorphs more than anything. Mae counted on the Extraktors causing more of a ruckus than Lenny riding stealth inside the robot.

If the monsters didn't get them, then Mae planned to lead Warrae and his team down into the nest itself. There, they'd get their secrets—and their consequences, too.

3 2

HALF A FRIEND

Lenny's breath sounded far too loud in his ears. From what Mae had told him, the janitorial robot was moving past monsters. The tight confines inside it and the possibility of something horrific opening up his hidey-hole were anxiety-inducing. Now the wide yawn of the Long Dark he once hated seemed like bliss.

The robot bumped and rolled, not nearly fast enough for Lenny. Everything was both silent and too loud at the same time. Lenny closed his eyes and tried not to think about anything at all. He hoped the echoing footsteps he could hear were only wandering synthetics.

The noise of the robot's wheels changed to a rattle, then a beep, and then there was the low grind of an opening door. Once its forward momentum stopped, he sat motionless for a moment.

"Nice to have a visitor, I suppose." The voice didn't sound like a monster's.

Pressing his hands against the front panel, Lenny wriggled it back and forth until it popped open. He peered out. He'd snuck into the Guelph command center once when he was ten. This was very similar: view screens, flashing lights, and uncomfortable chairs. The difference was a scattering of guns lying randomly about, and deep gouges in the metalwork. Mae's monsters were certainly not imaginary.

He slid his legs out of the now-silent janitorial robot.

"Two visitors." Out in the open, the voice came out slurred. Was there a drunk survivor around here?

A human form lay slumped in the corner next to a toppled chair. Lenny worked his way over to it, glad of someone to talk to. It was a synthetic, but a badly damaged one. He recognized the unit as a Bishop model from Seegson. He'd never seen one so beat up and yet still functional. The face was intact, if patchworked. The damage seemed mostly from the waist down. White circulatory fluid had pooled and dried around him.

"Can I help?" The words slipped out of Lenny's mouth.

The Bishop choked out a laugh. "At this point, I don't think that's an option." His soft eyes focused on Lenny. "Are you with the Jackals? Do you know Zula or Mae?"

"I came with Mae." Lenny crouched down next to him. "She's looking for her mother and her soldiers. She sent me here to restart the space elevator and get it down to the planet."

"I'm Rook." The synth sat up a little straighter in his spot under the console, as if he'd found a semblance of pride again. "I was on our ship with Mae when it was attacked by—" he paused and changed his mind "—that's need-to-know. Suffice to say a small armada of our enemies. We both ejected safely, but it took me a while to get back here."

Examining him, Lenny didn't see how he was still functional.

The synthetic must have been good at reading human expressions. His fingers fluttered over the ruin of his body. "I didn't arrive in this condition."

"How long have you been here?"

"Three cycles of Minos." He gestured down to his broken lower half. "This happened... elsewhere. You probably passed the transit tram I arrived in. Believe me, it took a long time to drag myself up here."

"You should be in a repair facility. Why would you crawl here?"

Rook stared off into space, and for a moment, Lenny wondered if he'd finally failed. Then he spoke again. "I was waiting for Mae. I knew she'd come, eventually."

Lenny wanted to comfort the synthetic somehow. "She's gone down to the engine room. Her plan is to bring the station down on the planet." He tapped the side of his forehead. "I'm augmented, so she created a network between us. You can join it and talk to her yourself."

Rook smiled slightly at this admission. "And how is she?"

"Angry. She thinks her mother is still alive."

"Then she's right." Rook gestured to the nearby chair. "Get me into that and I can connect your network to the signal that came through yesterday."

Lenny flipped the chair upright and pulled the synthetic up into it. Someone had shot Rook's legs and interior to hell, and he knew there was a story there, but it seemed rude to pry.

"Now give me the code to your network."

Lenny dived in and extended permissions to Rook. Now, it contained the three of them within it.

Mae?

Rook? How did you manage—

No time for that. I'm patching you through to your mother's frequency. Talk to her. I'll help this young augmented man to move the crawler back down to the planet. It's time to bring them home.

The network signal was patchy, and anything more than words was more than it could handle. Lenny disconnected, not wanting to spy on Mae's reunion with her mother.

Rook smiled crookedly. "Colonel Zula Hendricks is a law unto herself. She apparently kept her team moving all this time, staying ahead of the Xenomorphs. Still, I'm not sure how many of her people she has left down there."

"Then let's get this space elevator working." Lenny took another chair next to the dripping remains of the synth. "Where do we start?"

Rook pointed to the panel on the left. "That controls everything about the space elevator, but I'm afraid there is no power to it."

Lenny slid under the desk to check the connections. Everything appeared to be correctly attached and functional. He got back up to his feet with a knot in his stomach. The station still had power. If the problem wasn't here, then it must be a cable issue. That would mean venturing outside the command center.

Rook glanced up at him and shrugged. "I would love to assist, my new friend, but it would take too long, and I don't think Colonel Hendricks and Mae can wait."

Lenny swallowed hard, shoving down his own fears. "Where's the junction box?"

"Down the corridor on the left. It's beside the main elevator shaft."

He picked up one of the loose pulse rifles. "Will it make any difference if I take one of these?"

The synthetic didn't sugarcoat it. "They want warm bodies to host their young. That might give you a slight chance if you encounter one."

"Right, then." His parents taught both Lenny and Morgan how to fire a rifle in the station-safe practice chamber. He'd never shot a live weapon, but then, he was doing a lot of things now he wasn't used to. He grabbed a small satchel of tools and rifled through. It contained wire strippers, insulated screwdrivers, and different kinds of pliers. Lenny slid on the headlamp but didn't turn it on.

He wasn't sure how these monsters found their prey, but he would try for some stealth.

Slinging the rifle across his front, he moved to the far door.

"Just remember, their blood is acid." Rook shot him a small salute.

This was new information to Lenny, but there was no going back now.

Back in the corridor, it was scarier by far now that he knew what might be out there. Ducking low, and trying hard to keep his footfalls light, Lenny crept down towards the main elevator shaft on the left. The drop ceiling was collapsed and lay scattered about.

A rack of Mr. Browns still stood, waiting for commands from long-dead humans. The fallen ceiling had hit the two on the end, while the rest blinked at low charge.

It would have been nice to pass this repair task off to one of them. Instead, Lenny scrambled onwards until he reached the shaft. Here the drop ceiling was nonexistent, the air ducts tenuously hanging in their railings.

However, the panel was exactly where Rook had told him it would be. Part of him began to worry the synthetic might have lied to him. Keeping his breath as steady as possible, he began to remove the panel. The shriek of metal on metal made him jump. The panel had taken a hit, and it forced him to wrench it away.

He stood there for a few moments, his own heartbeat

rattling in his head. Then he turned on his headlamp and peered into the box. Several breakers were blown; some kind of power surge must have hit it. He checked for voltage and found none. He only needed to flip it back on and he restored power to the command center.

A simple fix was exactly what he'd hoped for. Lenny closed the panel while letting out a slow breath.

Something uncoiled in the void above his head. In the flickering light, it was hard to make out. A long head moved sinuously, darkness shifting in darkness. Lenny forgot to breathe, but he understood standing there staring was no way to survive. Keeping his eyes fixed on the thing, he began backing away.

The monster moved slowly, like Lenny's dad waking up after a long shift. It yawned, lips pulling back from long, sharp teeth. A second mouth stretched out, somehow attached within already terrifying jaws.

He kept creeping back down the corridor and fumbled for the rifle. Rook said the monster's blood was acid, so he needed to be a good distance away from this thing before he started shooting.

It dropped elegantly from its resting place. It was tall, taller than Lenny. His brain tried to take it all in: the long tail with a horrifyingly sharp end, the claws on each of its six fingers, the curiously curved, domed head.

Time seemed to slow down. Lenny was not even four meters away from the thing. He had yet to spot any eyes, but even as he thought that, it turned its head towards him.

It let out a godawful hiss, a noise that set every primitive instinct in his body alight.

Run, he told himself. *Run, for fuck's sake, you moron!*

Lenny resisted the instinct. If he turned away from this thing now, he'd die. Its legs alone said it was faster than he was.

He needed to be far enough away now, and he couldn't afford to let this monster close the distance. Raising the rifle, he aimed as best as the moment allowed and pulled the trigger. At first, nothing happened, since Lenny hadn't flicked the safety switch off. He did so immediately and pulled the trigger again. The kick of the weapon caught him by surprise and the shots all flew wide. They pinged off the wall and disappeared into the ceiling cavity.

The monster bunched up, completely unharmed. The rifle counter flashed a zero. It would not help him anymore, but there were other options.

Lenny accessed his augment. The rack of Mr. Browns at his back were his only chance, and they had little juice left in them. He scrambled backwards, and the nightmare followed, hissing and snarling. Its claws screamed against the metal flooring. He connected to the Mr. Browns, and that was when he finally ran. Firing up the synthetics, he dodged past them as they moved towards the monster. Three Mr. Browns against the monster, but Lenny expected them to only slow it down.

He'd never run faster in his life. Bolting down the

corridor, he leaped through the door to the command center, hoping to find another rifle nearby.

"Get down!"

The howl of the monster sounded at his back as it reached the door only a few moments after Lenny. The rattle of a pulse rifle in the enclosed space nearly deafened him. He covered his head and hoped not to die.

When it went quiet, he raised his head. Rook must have slid to the floor to grab a weapon. He lay propped up next to the crawler's control panel, cradling a pulse rifle and grinning. Spots of white circulatory fluid dotted his face.

Daring a glance over his shoulder, Lenny spotted the remains of the monster. Its blood sizzled and ate through the floor just as the synthetic warned.

Lenny clambered to his feet and took several labored breaths before hustling over to help Rook back up into the chair. "Thanks. I forgot everything my mom taught me about shooting, right there."

"The human body reacts poorly to stress. Most people need to be trained to override it, but that wasn't bad... for an augmented human." He shot Lenny a sharp glance. "Your parents must love you a lot. That's a high-quality device in your head."

Lenny tapped his skull. "Cost them their living, nearly. Okay, so how do we bring the space elevator back online?"

Rook ran his hands over the controls. "We're going to have to work together on that."

"The only way I know." Lenny sat next to him. "Let's get it done."

The synthetic's eyes met his. "It's good to work with a human again." He said that so lightly, but something more complicated lurked in those words. Lenny couldn't wait to hear the story sometime, once they were both far away from this deadly station.

3 3

LABYRINTH'S END

Her mother's voice stopped Mae in her tracks. For 0.265 of a second, Mae considered that her mind had fractured and she was lost again.

"Mae? I can't…" Zula Hendricks's voice cracked, then she composed herself. *"Mae, I'm so proud of you for coming back. Rook told me you had some problem with the splinters and the protection protocols?"*

"I've cleared the station synthetic network of the remains of Kaspar, so we have full access to the station and the buildings on the planet. This is a much more efficient way to communicate." There was no mistaking Rook's gravelly tone. *"I've missed you, Mae. Are you alright?"*

The third lowest level was warm and abandoned by humans—at least genetic ones. She hastily found a closet and shut herself inside. Patching into the station's synthetic network was like finally going into the warm embrace of family. It was a lot to process, but her synthetic core was more capable of doing so than a human one.

Not only was Zula Hendricks still breathing, but Rook had reached Minos again. She determined the three of them would have a hell of a reunion. For now, though, her words were for her mother.

"Mom? Rook? Is that really both of you?"

"It is, hon. Are you alright?"

"Hanging in there." Rook's reply.

Mae held back a whoop of delight. "I'm fine. I'm here on Minos. How are the Jackals? Captain Shipp? Lieutenant Ackerman?"

Zula Hendricks's voice came out thin and tired. *"We're… well, we're fewer than we were. Lost some good people down here. Olivia's still with us. We're a bit banged up, but alive. We've had access to the company's vehicles down here. So, we've been running a lot, trying to keep ahead of the Xenos. Last few days, they've been hot on our tail. I think we're the last humans around that they can use for their nest. Makes them… motivated."*

"Then it's time to leave." Mae pressed her hand against her eyes. "I have a friend, Lenny. He's working with Rook right now on getting the crawler functioning again. I need you all to get to the elevator as soon as you can."

Zula was silent for a moment. *"We're in a tricky spot right now, but—yeah, we'll try our best."*

Resting her head against the metal door, Mae croaked out, "I'm sorry I took so long. Rook triggered my protection protocols, and it took me a while to get myself back."

Rook remained quiet during this mother and daughter reunion, but broke in for a moment. *"I did as asked."*

"I understood, Rook. And Mae, you don't need to apologize either." She paused, and her voice became stern. *"Now, what's your plan to level this place?"*

Something creaked outside. Mae pressed her ear against the door, trying to distinguish if it was a monster or an Extraktor. "The *Fury* is still on executive lockdown. So, my objective is to bring the entire station crashing down onto those training grounds. By my calculations, that's better than a nuclear bomb."

"What about blowing the elevator cable instead?"

Mae understood why her mother asked. It sounded like a simpler solution. However, it wouldn't be enough. "Even if I cut it above geostationary orbit, the station would remain intact. The cable itself would burn up in the atmosphere rather than doing damage to the training facility. I have to aim Minos at it deliberately."

Her mother repeated this explanation to someone else in the room with her, most likely Olivia Shipp. *"We can get behind that. Should wipe them all out. Can't have this Kuebiko concept spread around. The queen made good use of her human zombies."*

Red Mae's memories were hers now, too. "I understand. I have a few hostiles up here to worry about, but I know you can handle them. There aren't a lot left. I need you and all the survivors to get up here and run to the *Fury*.

My friend is unlocking the umbilical, so we can at least pull away."

"I can guide you past them," Rook broke in.

"Good. We have ground transport. Getting through might be tough, but we'll find a way."

They'd survived this long, so Mae didn't doubt it. "When you reach the space elevator, the crawler should be waiting for you."

"Alright, then." Her voice softened again. It was the tone Zula only used when they were alone, and rarely even then. *"You have to promise me you'll be there when we arrive on the station."*

What use were a synthetic's promises?

As good as a genetic human's, her father murmured.

"I promise, Mother. See you on the other side."

Zula Hendricks let out a *"Oorah,"* and cut the connection.

Now she and Rook were alone. "A remarkable bond, Mae. Makes me wonder for the future of the synthetic people." His tone was melancholy and distant. "Go complete your mission. I'll be here."

"Keep your head on a swivel," Mae said. "I want to hear all about the *Blackstar* and what happened. Those are memories I haven't got back."

"And so you shall." Rook slipped out of the network.

Mae eased the door open and slipped back into the corridor. The last staircase down to the engine room lay ahead. However, her calculations on Captain Warrae's pursuit indicated he might be closer than was comfortable. Searching along the network, she found several security synths still on their racks. They were fully functional and charged, so Mae set them loose. They'd been armed with electric prods, but they would be up against pulse rifles. The best she could hope for was that they would slow her pursuers.

The Wey-Yu synthetics slid down off the racks and marched back the way she'd come. Mae slipped past them and continued down the stairs.

When she emerged from the stairwell, she was now only one level above the station's engines. It was immediately apparent that the Xenomorphs had taken over this level. The air was thick and moist—not normal for engineering uses. Curving seams of resin hung from the ceilings and walls, reshaping everything from a human facility into something fit for monsters. The resin glistened in the emergency lighting, and there was a faint alkaline odor.

She stepped carefully, moving at a steady pace and mindful not to touch anything. Researchers had not extensively studied the nature of Xenomorph polymer, but it might conduct tremors to the monsters themselves. So far, luckily, nothing stirred. After overwhelming all the humans on the station, the Xenos must have gone into hibernation.

They had sealed a safety hatch open with resin, and beyond it were the maze of catwalks that surrounded the reactors and engines. Minos was a station with her own navigation controls. Smaller than most of the processing rigs and mining stations like Guelph, she only needed to be large enough to act as counterweight to the elevator.

Stabilizers kept Minos in orbit, but the massive engines that brought her here were silent. It was Mae's mission to change that.

From the catwalk, it was impressive. The engines took up two stories, while below them the smaller orbitals triggered only when Minos threatened to fall out of its safe zone. If she ignited the engines and set their course for the bottom of the space elevator, they would crash spectacularly. However, someone would have to keep the station AI, Kaspar, from altering the trajectory.

You are guilty but relieved, then guilty you are relieved. Davis sounded pleased at her complexity. *You know your mother needs you alive. Either Lenny or Rook will have to fall with Minos.*

Running along the walkway, Mae didn't answer. She was already more concerned with how much resin there was in this massive chamber. Ovomorphing must have occurred, and that meant somewhere around here lurked a second queen.

The walls dripped with moisture, and soon enough, more horrors. As Mae worked her way around the catwalk towards the engine ignition station, she discovered the fate of the employees of Minos. They hung from the walls, limp and long dead. Encased in resin, they'd died to birth more drones. Every chest lay exploded from within, while their dried internal organs hung over their stomachs. Rows of empty Xenomorph eggs rested at their feet.

One face was familiar but did not trigger an ounce of regret. The Xenos had taken their revenge on Station Chief Rolstad. He stood encased in resin, and his face wore a surprised and horrified expression as it lay against his shoulder. The explosive exit the xenomorph had made from his chest left his ribs splayed open, his internal organs pooling and rotted at his feet. He'd been part of the company machine and must have thought himself immune from the horrors others experienced. Mae hoped his last thoughts were terror-filled, like the others he condemned to join the colony.

Scientists, workers, and finally even the infected humans under the planetary queen's command were all turned to the purposes of the hive. The station chief was not exempt.

She turned away, to concentrate on her task of saving all the humans she could. With the information from Red Mae, she recalled the queen they'd encountered. The number of available hosts aboard the station must have triggered the birth of a second queen.

If they were working together, or separately, it didn't matter in the end. Both were deadly, and any queen nearby would perceive Mae as a threat if she got too close. That kind of Xenomorph possessed intelligence beyond a mere drone. She would not spare any synthetic in her presence. Mae needed to move fast.

As she worked her way around the circular catwalk, a

voice echoed after her. "Bioweapons? You really weren't lying, after all."

Warrae and his team emerged from a side corridor up ahead. She counted more troopers than she would have liked, though it seemed only one completely synthetic Extraktor had survived the station android attack she'd arranged for them.

It didn't matter. She had a second army at her back.

Mae's eyes narrowed. Being generous, she gave them a second warning. "You should go back, Warrae. Board your ship and get the hell away from Minos. It's only death that lives down here."

"And the Combine is quite willing to market that." He examined their surroundings, probably trying to calculate his own profit share.

Homolka raised his pulse rifle. "We don't need her anymore, correct, sir?"

"Yes, Sergeant, that's true. She's surplus goods. Open fire."

His sergeant didn't need any further urging. He poured his rage at her with his pulse rifle. The rounds struck all around Mae as she dove for cover. Aiming at her, Homolka wouldn't hit anything vital in the chamber. She'd been expecting it. Hoping for it, actually.

The rattle of gunfire was more than enough to wake the hive to immediate action. She flattened herself down on the steel grating of the floor as the Xenomorphs uncurled around her. Their hisses and snarls echoed down the catwalk. The Extraktors' combination of human heartbeats and the flicker of electrical impulses worked like chum in the water for the monsters.

"What the fuck?" Homolka screamed, his voice punctuated by the sound of more gunfire. This wasn't precise or accurate shooting. For all their swagger, the Extraktors only dealt with frightened humans and synthetics. The Xenomorphs were far beyond their comprehension and skill level.

Mae didn't stop to look. She pushed to her feet and ran on, though the screams of the Extraktors were sweet to her ears. They'd wanted Minos's secrets? Well, now they'd found the mother lode. They didn't sound happy about it, though.

She darted around opened eggs, her gaze fixed on the blinking lights of the engine ignition station. It waited just ahead, on a platform that extended towards the center of the vast room.

When something snapped around Mae's leg and dragged her down, at first she thought it was a Xeno. Tumbling to her knees, Mae glanced back. Warrae, for all his faults, was a determined creature. He must have abandoned all his troops to pursue her. However, Xenomorph blood splattered over him. It tore deep holes in the synthetic skin of his face and torso. Mae knew the pain of that from her databases. His ability to remain functional meant Warrae must've had his pain receptors severed during the augmentation process.

Mae kicked him in the face repeatedly, but he crawled up her length, refusing to let go. His not-inconsiderable weight pressed down on her. Once again, the lack of a combat body did her a disservice. He straddled Mae, dripping white circulatory fluid over her face.

"Let me remind you what you are," Warrae hissed. He pinned one of her arms to the ground and reached for her jaw with his free hand. He planned on ripping it loose again. He wanted to make her suffer while shaming her for her synthetic form. Of all the emotions Mae had experienced so far, that was not one she'd ever summoned up. She would not allow him to hurt her like that again.

Instead, she latched onto his ear with her free hand and wrenched as hard as her strength would allow. At the same time, Mae shoved one knee into his stomach and pushed her other foot against his thigh. He might not be able to feel pain, but apparently he still howled in outrage. Mae jerked her hips and threw him off her.

She leaped to her feet and drew the Ka-Bar she'd stolen earlier. It wasn't much, but it would do for Warrae. She wanted to show him what an armed synthetic could do. One that could fight back.

Part of Mae wanted to play with him, slice him in multiple ways, make him bleed and panic. However, she did not have the time for it. She kept him close and made it quick.

Warrae foolishly reached for her, and she slashed out with her knife. The cut to his wrist seemed to come as a surprise. He bled white like all those he'd tormented. He must not have known that she could injure him. He expected her to be bound by the same rules as other synths.

Mae smiled. Behind him, the Xenos were tearing his Extraktors apart. They took those capable of hosting alive and screaming. She wanted Warrae to know he'd lost.

"You're the last. The last piece-of-shit Extraktor to die of greed." She kept her knife moving with one hand while protecting her face and neck with the other.

In this moment, he was a small man. Only now did the face he wore reflect any emotion, and it was fear. He tried to bat away Mae's attacks, but she grabbed his arm and pulled him in close instead. In that intimate embrace, she drove her knife into his neck, severing his central column.

Warrae collapsed to the floor, gasping and immobilized but still alive. She stared down at him for a final moment, then turned and left him to the monsters. The Xenomorphs stalked towards him, their feet striking the catwalk like iron hooves. He watched them come and screamed, over and over.

Mae enjoyed his final drawn-out bellow when it came.

She glanced down at the mix of blood on her hands. White and red. Mae considered. She'd killed Xenomorphs—plenty of them—but this was a human. Or at least, he had been. She should feel something, but no emotion came. Her father was silent.

Up ahead was the engine ignition station. She peered

down the many stories into the heat exchange and vents. The Xenomorphs had built up a lot more resin structures there. The queen, laying her eggs, was just visible against the warm glow of the orbital thrusters' power sources. She'd nestled herself in good and tight. The shapes were beautiful, and the movements of the queen were elegant. For all that they did, there was something fascinating and compelling about them.

Mae felt worse about destroying the Xenomorphs than she did about Warrae. The monsters were only doing what they needed to. It was people that took them and tried to exploit their power. Humanity's worst impulses created this situation.

Mae? Careful now. You need no more data on them.

Synthetics and Xenomorphs, they were both only obeying their programming.

Remember Zula. She's depending on you.

Mae pulled herself away from the view of the queen and moved to the control panel. After punching in the coordinates for the training facility, she ignited the long-dormant engines. They roared to life, as if they'd been waiting for this moment. The power of them shook the chamber, rattling loose pieces of resin and almost knocking her off her feet. Below, the Xenomorph queen screamed. Minos's alarms blared and a calm voice announced:

"Warning! Trajectory will result in planetary impact. Shutting down all engines. Safety Protocol Three-Delta."

Mae reached out to Lenny in the command center. She

hadn't anticipated that the station's systems would still be in such good order.

I'm sorry. I'm so sorry. The AI is overriding my instructions. I need you to stay in the command center and keep Kaspar from interfering.

She'd brought him to Minos to die. She and Zula would survive, but the man who rescued her from the darkness would perish.

It's alright. Rook's words came through the network. *The boy deserves to live. I've had my turn. Sorry we won't get the chance for a proper reunion, Mae Hendricks. I'll keep overriding Kaspar's safety measures. You get to the space elevator. I'm sending Lenny there now.*

Rook—I don't know what to say. All the memories of their time together raced through her mind. Rook was the one synthetic who came closest to understanding who she was. In the end, she hadn't needed to hide from him. He felt like... family. Mae wanted to know so much more. Her mind was a blank when it came to how she'd been ejected into space. He possessed all the remaining answers, but not the network capacity to share it. He held the faith while she was lost. One more information dump, and her core might crack. Rook would have to keep his mysteries.

No one ever does. Now hit those switches again and keep moving. I'd hate for this to be a waste.

Mae's bespoke eyes blurred with tears as she flicked the switches and ran.

3 4

LOSING A DAUGHTER

Red Mae heard her voice in the network. It was like a dream. Standing in the temporary shelter of a cave near the valley, she observed as the news hit her mother. Zula Hendricks struggled to hold back her tears. They'd all been struggling a lot these last days, and hope died easily in this wind-blasted place.

So much running. So many lost Jackals.

Captain Shipp rested against the one large vehicle that survived. They'd parked the smaller buggy, which could carry only four, a short distance behind it. The company facility's supplies were plentiful. Scavenging kept them all alive. Crates full of food and ammo were hard won, though. Each one they attempted to reach meant risking an encounter with the Xenomorphs.

Private Feldman and his rescued worker were the first victims. They hadn't ever made it out of the tunnel system.

However, the first week, it seemed, the larger group of Jackals were of little interest. The queen's drones captured plenty of Wey-Yu employees to be cocooned next to eggs. It was almost as if the hive wanted the Jackals loose. Like a child saving a sandwich for the next day's lunch.

So Red Team kept mobile, endlessly running and fighting. Survival was their objective, but not all of them made it. Privates Sampath and Zhany, as well as Corporal Thami, almost made it, but they were killed in combat three days ago.

That left only six Jackals alive. Sergeant Ackerman leaned up against the wall of the cave because he refused to sit down. Some kind of insect-like planetary life form had stung him only hours before, which appeared to annoy him more than anything.

Private Amutenya, their remaining medic, crouched next to the sergeant and tried his best to treat the bite. Certainly, Ackerman could not run if required.

Over the last few days, the hive had become ready for more eggs to open. Now, the Xenomorphs pursued them far more aggressively. Their supplies were running low and their ammo was almost spent. The remaining Jackals were exhausted, powering through on stims and willpower.

Mae monitored their condition. Like Amytenya, she was the last of her kind down here. The two synthetic squads were gone. The Pinpoints and two Good Boys remained, but they were low on power. Unit cohesion wore down with the losses they took, and even Zula Hendricks had limits.

Weighing all the odds, Mae stayed at the colonel's side, waiting for some kind of hope.

Her mother cut the network connection with Mae Prime, and she wasn't smiling. She jerked her head to Shipp and Mae. They took a few steps away, behind the vehicle, and continued in lowered voices. Even in their dire situation, they all kept Mae's nature a secret, on the off chance they might survive.

Zula ran her hand over her face before delivering the news. "We have to get to the elevator crawler right now. It's on its way down to us, but we're on our own making it to the entrance. We're close, but so are they." She opened up her wrist-pd, daring to use some of the valuable battery life to display the Pinpoints' intel of what lay ahead. In the fading light of evening, their chances did not look great.

Shipp stared at the readout and let out a sigh. "The Xenos have moved up from yesterday. They definitely have us on the menu, and don't want us to skip out on dinner."

"Yeah, for sure they've got plans for us," Zula agreed. "So how much fuel does the last people-mover have?

"We have a quarter of the battery charge left. More than enough to reach the space elevator." Mae delivered the one piece of good news.

Zula scrolled through the grim status of their ammunition supplies. They didn't have enough to take down more than one wave of monsters—if they got lucky.

"If we don't get to that crawler, we're going to be part of the mess along with the Xenos," Shipp observed, her tone almost casual.

"We have two Good Boys left, and the C4 charge." Mae checked her rifle. "That should be more than enough to cause a distraction. I'm ready."

"No!" Zula rounded on her. "Not after everything we've been through together. I'm not leaving you here."

Red Mae peered over the hood of the vehicle at the Jackals. Ackerman attempted to stand, while Minkas, Konaan, and Amytenya checked their weapons. All were dirty and tired, but still resolute. Mae's calculations couldn't be argued with, although her mother and Shipp would make a heroic attempt. They wouldn't make it.

"We don't have time for another plan. Besides, I'll tight-beam all my recent memories up to Mae Prime. I want her to know what we've gone through down here." Despite the logic of her plan, a small kernel of sadness still broke through.

Zula shook her head again. "Please don't… don't do that."

Mae put her hand on the colonel's shoulder. "You're not making a logical choice, Mother. I'm the last synthetic standing, and I'm replaceable. We do not have a choice, if you want to save your Jackals." Mae examined the shape of her mother's face. "I will be gone, but I will also be with you. Isn't that what some humans believe happens?"

Zula choked out a laugh. "Are you suggesting you'll be a ghost?"

"It would be an interesting experience." Mae shrugged. "I was being more literal than that. My other, primary self is waiting for you. Now, please, you must go."

As a colonel, Zula Hendricks understood tough choices. She made them all the time. Her mother's arms wrapped around Mae, and she squeezed hard. Then she turned to her remaining Jackals. "Let's get back to the station and then the *Fury*."

So the two of us will make a sacrifice. Father and daughter will stay. Her father's voice whispered in her head. *I'm not leaving you alone like this.*

I'm just an echo. Red Mae said it, even if she didn't feel it.

An echo that spent weeks saving humans, and was a part of Zula Hendricks's life all that time.

I guess that counts for something. She straightened up and considered her next move. *It'll have to do.*

The Jackals loaded into the people-mover. Shipp drove them away while Zula sat up front. Only Zula glanced back at Mae. Her expression was sad but resolute, and somehow that cheered her daughter.

Red Mae could have completed the transfer to Mae Prime at that moment, but she wanted to wait. She wanted her death to be remembered and recorded.

She gathered the remaining Good Boys and Pinpoints around her. With the sentry guns at her disposal, she could make quite a ruckus to direct all the monsters' attention her way.

She loaded up the smaller buggy with the C4 and wired it for detonation. Then she strapped the remaining sentry guns to its side. This vehicle had a few kilometers of power left, but Mae only needed it to reach the hive. Slipping into the driver's seat, she launched the Pinpoints in front of her. In their time on the planet, the Jackals had figured out that certain frequencies attracted the Xenos as strongly as the Good Boys' audio drove them away.

Mae programmed the Pinpoints to track with her as she gunned the buggy into the valley and towards the hive. The Pinpoints overhead began screaming the dinner bell, while the Good Boys kept up with the vehicle in long strides. That noise, and Mae's ride towards the queen, should hopefully override any other imperative the drones had.

Her calculations proved accurate. Mae heard them before she saw them. Their screams and hisses emerged from the mist behind her moments before they did. A wave of dark drones poured over the flat mountaintop plateau as she came within a click of the colony entrance. Their shrieks echoed off the hills as they ran to catch up to Mae on her Valkyrie ride.

There is music for that, you know. Her father's voice reminded her she was not alone on this final journey.

Play it for me.

He filled her mind with a swell of strings by Wagner, then the woodwinds that built on it. The trumpets, when they entered, provided a feeling similar to human adrenaline. For a moment, it almost looked as if the Good Boys were keeping time with the music's rhythm.

Mae pressed her foot down on the accelerator to keep pace. The facts about this piece of music slid through her mind: the Ring Cycle, uses on stage, famous performances. It had a long, rich history.

Don't do that. Enjoy the moment and the music as they are, her father urged her.

Still, Mae summoned the smell of napalm and victory from data sources to accompany their last ride.

The Xenomorphs gained on the buggy, desperate to stop Mae before she reached their queen. The sentry guns opened up, firing into the mass of snarling monsters which approached from both flanks.

One Xenomorph leaped for the door of the buggy. It pulled itself up to the side, black claws reaching for her. Mae took up her shotgun from the passenger seat. As the Xeno opened its mouth, she kept one hand on the steering wheel while racking and shooting with the other.

The acid splashed across her hand and face. Her combat body repelled most, but it dripped across the buggy. It didn't have her protections. The vehicle bucked and jolted like a wounded animal.

Worried that she wasn't going to make it, Mae triggered the Good Boys to clear some of their pursuers out of their path. Their audio blast repelled the Xenomorphs, driving them away from the slowing vehicle. Smoke began streaming out from beneath, but the wheels kept rolling.

The buggy groaned and shuddered but only slowed a little. Wagner's music swelled in her head, bringing the strangest surge of complicated feelings with it.

Mae, we're at the crawler. We made it. We're going up now. Her mother's voice mixed joy with sorrow.

That they would remember her in this way pleased Mae. Many genetic humans wished for a good death, and she got that. She sent the tight-beam up to Mae Prime. Hopefully, her memories would give her context and help her understand Zula even better.

She urged the buggy on for the last few meters and into the Mother Colony's entrance. The Xenos spilled out towards Mae from in front and behind. They sprung up and overwhelmed the Good Boys, smashing and destroying them in their rage.

Yet she wasn't completely alone. Her father's voice welled up inside her.

The final test of humanity. You have passed it, Mae.

Mae fired her shotgun until the very last moment. She'd already exceeded her operating parameters. As the Xenos reached out for her, she flicked the switch on the C4.

She pictured the reunion of Mae Prime and Zula Hendricks. They would be together soon, and she would be there too.

3 5

LOST AND FOUND

The tremors of Minos's imminent death shook through Mae's legs as she raced towards the entrance of the space elevator.

If the station was badly off before, driving it into the planet now was a mercy. All the company's secrets would fall from the sky and burn on the planet. Hopefully, Kuebiko would not claim any more unwilling human victims, and no more queens would control humans.

Minos's orbital stabilizers were fighting the demands of her engines. The station was at war with itself, and only Rook in the command center maintained its deadly trajectory.

Mae ducked as walls twisted and crashed around her. The forces being inflicted on the station were pulling it apart, and she wasn't sure if the space elevator was about to meet the same fate. The floor tipped to one side, putting everything at a ten-degree angle. Anything loose slid abruptly. Crates, dead potted plants, and the body of a Mr. Brown all collided with her, knocking Mae back into the walls of the corridor.

She pushed them off, wriggling and struggling free. With one hand on the leaning wall, she scrambled towards the door that led to the last flight of stairs between her and the space elevator.

Mae worked her way up the stairs, bumping off walls and floors, until at last she reached the assembly area in front of the massive elevator doors. As soon as she made it, she immediately crashed to her knees. Red Mae's final memories hit her, shooting through the network like bullets. They filled her spare cache capacity, even as she became aware that her last splinter died down on the planet's surface. Mae was now the sole survivor and final resting place of all their experiences.

Fitting these new recollections into her head would take some doing, but it shouldn't cause another fracture in her processing core. Mae held them tight and partitioned them for later. She couldn't afford to break apart like the station at this pivotal moment.

Staggering to her feet, she glimpsed the green light gleaming by the doors. Over the dying groans of the station, the bright ping of the elevator doors sounded. They juddered halfway open and then stopped. It didn't matter.

Through the smoke, six Jackals staggered out, ragged and covered in dirt and blood, but they never looked more beautiful to Mae. At their rear, still standing tall, was Colonel Zula Hendricks, lending an injured Captain Shipp a shoulder to lean on. Mae rushed forward and counted heads. Half of the team that had ventured down to the planet did not come back up. None of the synthetics remained.

With the thundering echoes of destruction all around, Mae grabbed hold of Zula Hendricks, squeezing her tight. She reeked of dirt and sweat, but she was real.

"Mae!" Another voice broke through the din. Lenny appeared at the top of the stairs behind her. His eyes were enormous in his head as he took in all the Jackals in their torn uniforms. Minos bucked beneath their feet. "Rook is keeping the station on the track you set, and we unlocked the umbilical to your ship. Now can we get out of here?"

"No point in coming this far just to die now." Zula handed Shipp over to Mae to assist. "Jackals, we're leaving. Let's hustle."

Lenny took up position on the other side of Olivia Shipp, and everyone followed the colonel. Private Amutenya half-carried Ackerman, who was also injured. Minos was in her death throes, screaming as she plunged towards the planet. The Jackals only had minutes to make their escape.

They reached the *Fury* and raced along the umbilical, which bucked like a wild horse. Inside, the ship's warning lights flashed amber. After the attack through Erynis,

EWA remained disabled, but some systems had managed to hang on.

Zula pointed to Ackerman and the remaining Red Team Jackals. "Manually disconnect that damn umbilical. Pump that lever and close that door like your life depends on it."

"Yes, ma'am." They all rushed to obey.

Shipp slumped by the door. "I'll make sure of it, Colonel. Get to the flight deck."

Zula, Mae, and Lenny scrambled up the stairs since the onboard elevator wasn't working. The *Fury* was totally silent compared to the station. Upon reaching the flight deck, Mae took a position at the helm. Lenny hung back, waiting to see if he could help.

"Status report, Mae," Zula barked, slipping into the command chair.

"*Fury's* executive functions remain jammed, but we are almost disconnected from the umbilical." Mae ran her fingers across the panel, searching for any signs of life.

"Can we maneuver once we're free?"

One part of the navigation board lit up. "Safety protocols allow us attitude adjustments, but the engines themselves won't fire yet."

Zula's fingers tightened around the arms of her chair. "That'll have to do. Come on, Shipp. Are we free yet?"

None of this mattered until they disconnected from Minos. Mae kept her eyes locked on the display. They'd either be free in moments or share the fate of the station. The company's research would be lost in either scenario, but she found she didn't want to die. Enough Maes had done that already.

A green light flashed twice on her panel. They'd untethered the umbilical.

"We're free." It came out as a whisper, and Mae needed to repeat it a second time for her mother to hear.

"Then put as much distance between us and that fucking station as possible."

"Yes, ma'am!"

The *Righteous Fury* wasn't capable of fast burn yet, but it was still satisfying to push away from Minos. Mae deftly guided the ship out of range and towards a stable orbit of their own.

As they lost the connection with the faltering Minos network, Mae reached out one last time to Rook. She didn't want him to die alone.

I'm not alone. I have my memories and I've experienced the deaths of those I loved, he replied, and she could almost conjure his face. *Promise me you'll use that black site information, Mae. You'll find details on the juggernauts in there. I discovered a planet they're using as a staging post. Just remember that not every puzzle you solve is what you might expect it to be.*

We won't give up, Mae promised. *They won't destroy any more worlds.*

Minos Station tilted, arcing downward in a spectacular display. Her engines, which first brought her to this planet's orbit, now took her to her doom. Pieces of shielding broke off and started burning up on their own. It gave the station a fiery halo.

The network faltered, but Mae tried to hold on to it for as long as she could. As it slipped away, she caught one glimpse of Rook.

One last piece of advice, Mae Hendricks. Don't be too quick to mimic humans. You don't want to become like them in all things.

With that, Rook's voice faded away and was gone.

Mae piloted the *Fury* into a stable orbit, and the three of them watched Minos take its last fateful dive. In its belly were the remains of the Extraktors and their ship, as well as a terrifying second queen. It spun and tilted like a child's toy as pieces of its outer rings crumpled and tore away. The planet grabbed these shattered hunks and covered them in wreaths of flame as they tumbled into its atmosphere. It was beautiful and satisfying destruction.

Zula stared at the view screen, her face set in lines of exhausted triumph. Turning, she removed disc drives from her webbing. "We've got all the proof we need on those Minos bastards." She smiled fiercely.

Mae let out a ragged sigh. "But how many died for it? Does it even make a difference?"

Her mother grabbed her, administering a powerful hug. "They knew the risks, and took them anyway. Even Rook sacrificed himself for us. This place was a nightmare, but it was no danger to synthetics. He did it for us all. What is more human than that?"

They seemed like good words. The kind you would say over a grave.

The *Fury*'s flight deck fell silent.

Lenny rubbed his head and then slid down to the floor. "He didn't have to do that. I guess he got to make his own choices, right to the end."

Zula nodded and then glanced over at her daughter, focusing on her damaged jaw. "I can't imagine the things you've seen and done."

Mae said nothing for a while. A jangle of emotions and memories ran through her. She raised her hand and touched her chin. "I'm… I'm not sure I am ready to share them yet."

She'd killed and enjoyed it. That was something she wasn't sure she'd ever be comfortable telling her mother.

Sometimes, you can be too human. Davis's voice echoed softly, as if he were disappearing back into her subroutines. Being alone again without him was jarring, but made her more human. She would learn to live without him as humans did with their parents.

She placed her hands on the control deck. "We need to restore functions so we can pick up the others' cryo escape pods."

Zula let out a long sigh. "It will be good to reclaim our Jackals."

Mae reached out, looking for the remains of the network. "That may take some time, though. Erynis's corruption ran pretty deep. I don't think I can untangle it immediately."

"I can." Lenny rose to his feet and pushed his hair out of his eyes. As he did so, Mae sensed him in the network, but stronger than an augmented person had any right to be.

She gasped as he pulled the scattered threads of the *Fury's* systems apart, then wound them up and reformed them in an instant. That shouldn't be possible.

Zula glanced right and left as the control panels of her ship blinked to life with light and movement. "What's your name again, young man?"

"I used to be Lenny, but I think after all I've been through, I need a more mature name. You can call me Leonard Pope."

The colonel nodded. "We've recently had a vacancy open up as conduit between the *Fury* and the crew. Have you ever thought of that as a career?"

Something about Lenny's demeanor looked very different to the young man who'd first pulled Mae out of the darkness. His face settled into a foreign expression, and a shiver ran up her spine as he answered her mother.

"Thank you, Colonel Hendricks. I believe I would very much like a place on the *Righteous Fury*."

Mae was certain of two things: she'd never told Lenny her mother's rank, and the voice coming from his mouth echoed the cadence of Rook.

Some part of Rook appeared to have settled down inside Lenny's augment. She wasn't sure why the strange synth would do such a thing. Perhaps it was because, in the end, he couldn't quite bring himself to cease existing. He rode in Lenny's head as Davis rode in hers. That wasn't a bad thing—was it?

She took a seat at navigation and began plotting the locations of the Jackal cryo pods. Once they gathered them all, things would start to return to normal—or, at least, normal for the *Fury*.

Whatever Rook's presence meant for the future would reveal itself in time. All Mae knew now was that she and her family were nearly complete once more. The battle went on, and they would face it together. She set her eyes on the sun peeking around the curve of the planet, and waited for orders from Zula Hendricks to begin their next task.

ACKNOWLEDGEMENTS

Philippa:

To my husband, Tee Morris, my sounding board and inspiration.

To my Mum, who might not have understood the methods and drive to write, but always supported me. As fierce as an Alien Queen, and as loyal as Ripley.

Clara:

I'd like to dedicate the book to my children, Anastasia and Alexei and all future children (artificial kind as well) may their memories stay safe and recollections warm. And data, saved.

And a special thanks to my partner Simon Vallance for being equally obsessed with Alien and Blade Runner and coming up with the Jaw Breakers. Barbara Churcher my therapist for being there in my darkest hours and helping when I felt others couldn't. And to Pip for teaming up for another book, I am very grateful to work with her.

ABOUT THE AUTHORS

New Zealand-born fantasy writer Philippa (Pip) Ballantine is the author of the *Books of the Order*, *The Chronicles of Art*, and *The Shifted World* series. She is also the co-author of the *Ministry of Peculiar Occurrences* series with her husband, Tee Morris.

Her writing awards include an Airship, a Parsec, the Steampunk Chronicle Reader's Choice, the *Romantic Times* Reviewer's Choice Award, and a Sir Julius Vogel.

Philippa currently resides in Manassas, Virginia with her husband, daughter, and a furry clowder of cats.

Clara Fei-Fei Čarija is a story and game consultant known for her stellar cartography work on the award-winning *Alien* RPG from Free League. She consulted on two *Alien* novels, *Aliens: Phalanx* and *Alien: Into Charybdis*, before going on to co-write the story for *Alien: Inferno's Fall* with award-winning author Philippa Ballantine.

She is also a jeweler and fashion designer with a passion for *Alien*, art, and artificial intelligence. Clara resides on Wurundjeri land in Melbourne, Australia, with her husband and two children.

Sovereignty was never ceded.

ALIEN™

INFERNO'S FALL

PHILIPPA BALLANTINE

As war rages among the colonies, a huge ship appears over the UPP mining planet Shānmén, unleashing a black rain of death that yields hideous transformations.

Monstrous creatures swarm the colony, and rescue is too far away to arrive in time. The survivors are forced to seek shelter in the labyrinth of tunnels deep beneath the surface. Already the grave to so many, these shafts may become the final resting place for all who remain.

Hope appears in the form of the vessel Righteous Fury. It carries the Jackals—an elite mix of Colonial Marines led by Zula Hendricks. Faced with a horde of grotesque mutations, the Jackals seek to rescue the few survivors from the depths of the planet. But have they arrived too late?